A Killer Among Us

Books by Lynette Eason

WOMEN OF JUSTICE • BOOK THREE

A KILLER AMONG US

A NOVEL

LYNETTE EASON

Revell

a division of Baker Publishing Group
Grand Rapids, Michigan

© 2011 by Lynette Eason

Published by Revell
a division of Baker Publishing Group
P.O. Box 6287, Grand Rapids, MI 49516-6287

Printed in the United States of America

ISBN-13: 978-1-61129-669-3

This book is a work of fiction. Names, characters, places, and incidents are the product of the author's imagination or are used fictitiously. Any resemblance to actual events, locales, or persons, living or dead, is coincidental.

Published in association with Tamela Hancock Murray of the Hartline Literary Agency, LLC.

To the One who lets me write.
I love you, Jesus!

MONDAY

1

"You don't want to do this." Detective Kit Kenyon stared past the barrel of the gun and fixed her eyes on the man before her.

The forty-four-year-old blinked against the sweat dripping into his hazy green eyes. A thick tongue swept out against dry lips, and his gaze darted from her to the door to his wife, who sat on the floor under the window weeping softly.

Melanie, his twelve-year-old daughter, winced at the harsh hand ensnaring her long brown ponytail and never took her terrified gaze from Kit.

"Virgil?" Kit pushed gently. "Right now you haven't hurt anyone. In fact, you've cooperated nicely." Except for the part where she'd asked him to end this peacefully.

But they were getting there.

"I've got a clean shot." The voice whispered in her earpiece.

She tapped her fingers once against her leg. A signal that said, "Not yet." She didn't want anyone dying today if they didn't have to. Virgil Mann's eyes were clear. No drugs in his system. And he was listening to her.

She'd been talking to him for over three hours, and it had to be at least a hundred-plus degrees in the cramped single-wide trailer. Breakfast was six hours ago and her stomach growled.

Kit ignored it and the humid heat and focused on Virgil. She'd maneuvered the man into such a position where the sniper could see the two of them.

Definite progress.

Much talk along with a lot of give-and-take had resulted in the release of the two youngest children: two-year-old Jessie and four-year-old Nathan. Now she just had to get him to let Melanie and his wife, Anne, walk out of the musty-smelling, breath-stealing metal box.

"She told me she was leaving me." The words came out on a sob. Two fat tears trickled down his grizzled cheeks, and Kit felt an unwanted pang of compassion. He looked like a mad four-year-old who didn't get his way. The gun in his hand squelched the sympathy.

Shock blanched Melanie's tearstained features as she processed her father's words and she cut her gaze to her mother.

Finally. For three hours, he'd ranted, raved, listed everything he'd done for his unappreciative family, but hadn't said a word about what sparked his rage. Now they were getting to the heart of the matter. "Aw, Virgil, I'm sorry. You don't deserve that, do you?"

Of course he did. Kit was glad the woman had gotten up the courage to do something. She just wished she'd left first and talked later.

The gun wavered. "No, I don't. I do my best to provide for this family. She told me I needed professional help. Wanted to go to some marriage counselor. Stupid woman trying to tell *me* what to do. Thinks she knows best." His lip curled in disgust.

At this, Melanie's eyes glittered with anger. The girl opened her mouth to say something and Kit quickly intervened. "She shouldn't have treated you like that. She's the one who needs help, right?"

"You got it." Another swipe of the tongue. His grip loosened on Melanie's hair and the girl shifted away from him a fraction.

"What if we got her the help she needs, Virgil?"

He blinked. "What do you mean?"

"Just what I said. What if you and I get her some help? You'd be doing what any good husband would do. You'd be the man she fell in love with once again."

Virgil blinked the sweat from his eyes and squinted. Kit looked at Melanie. The girl shifted again, her anger dissipated, weeping softly now. Then her father brought the gun back down to aim it at his wife, fury returning once more. "What if I just shoot her and be done with it? Always trying to tell me what to do."

Melanie whimpered. Kit took a deep breath. Tapped her fingers again—this time with two quick snaps against her chin. *Shoot on my signal.* If she curled her hand into a fist—and she would if Virgil's finger even twitched on the trigger—her guy would place a bullet between Virgil's eyes.

In her ear, Chad, her second, fed her information. "Virgil's sister is here. Said her brother has the need to be in control. Hates authority or anyone feeling they're better than he is."

Yeah, she'd already figured that out.

Chad continued, "Said his wife and kids have been going to the little church up the street. Ever since they started going, she's been getting 'uppity,' pushing him for marriage counseling, telling him they needed to get right with God."

"Hey Virgil." She had his attention back on her although the gun stayed on his wife. "Hey, you make the decisions around here, right?"

His breath stuttered out and he looked confused at the change in subject. "You bet I do. I have the final say-so in this family."

Kit nodded, making sure her outward appearance said she was thinking about his words. Inside, she weighed her options. Every word she said counted, might mean the difference between life and death. His death, his wife's. Hers. But she was good at reading people and she was 99.9 percent sure how to handle this man. Unfortunately, it went against negotiation protocol. Rule number something: Never remind the shooter he wants to shoot. Did she dare chance it? Did she dare not? Still keeping her body relaxed, her posture nonthreatening, she asked, "So, you want to shoot her? Okay, let's say you do it."

Surprise rocketed his eyebrows and his jaw sagged. "What?"

A harsh breath whistled in her ear. "Kit . . ."

But she had Virgil's number now. She urged, "You say you want to shoot her. Or you think you do, but have you thought out your future after the bullet does its job?"

More lip licking. "Wha-what do you mean?"

"Just think about it for a minute. Do you love your children?"

"Course I do." He looked outraged at her question.

"So what's going to happen to them after Anne's dead and you're in jail?"

Or dead. "Because if you kill her, there's no turning back after that. No second chances. No way to right that wrong." She paused and looked at Melanie. "And your little girl will hate you forever. So just think about those facts for a few minutes before you decide what to do."

His Adam's apple bobbed, his eyes flickered to his daughter whom he still had in his hard grip. Her gaze sought his. Her brief moment of anger had faded back into fear. "Daddy, please don't kill my mama."

While the plea wrenched at Kit's heart, bringing unwanted memories to the surface, she could see it also had the desired effect on Melanie's father. The man's countenance softened for a heartbeat.

Kit pressed it. "Come on, Virgil, you still have a way out. You can still be the husband your wife needs, the daddy your children need. And they do need you. They look up to you to show them the way to go in life, to make sure they're safe at night. Who's going to do that if it's not you?"

The gun lowered. She had him.

Quiet weeping from the corner echoed in the small room. Virgil shifted and sighed. "If I give in, though, I'm going to jail, aren't I?"

What to say? Lie or tell the truth? His eyes probed hers. She hedged. "Possibly. But you've never done anything like this before, right?"

"No."

"Then maybe you'll just get a slap on the wrist and probation."

"That's a big maybe." He looked skeptical.

"True." No way was she telling him he'd serve time. But she wasn't going to outright lie to him, either. He was thinking. He knew he'd have consequences. If she said he wouldn't, she'd lose him immediately.

Watching the indecision cross his face, she waited, forcing herself not to push him any further. Briefly, she allowed herself to think about Noah, her partner of three weeks. Three weeks to get to know a man and be willing to put her life on the line for him.

He was a good cop with good instincts, and she wished he could have come with her. She could use someone else watching the big picture outside while she dealt with everything else from the inside.

Unfortunately, she didn't expect him anytime soon. As she'd hurried into the situation in which she now found herself, she'd left him in the middle of a messy murder scene.

Noah Lambert looked down at the life cut short and felt his anger burn. Just as he did every time he came across injustice, unfairness, and things that were just plain wrong. *God, I know you're in control, but it sure seems like the devil gets the upper hand most of the time.*

God wouldn't hold the observation against him. Noah had a running dialogue with the Almighty when it came to his life—especially his job. And he knew God understood where he was coming from.

He knelt beside the body. A young man, Walter Davis, shot in the back of the head.

Serena Hopkins, the medical examiner, took a sample of blood and bagged it.

Noah asked, "How long has he been dead?"

"I would say since about eight o'clock this morning. He was found around 8:30, right?"

"Yeah, we got here around 8:45, took a look around while waiting on you, then Kit got called to a domestic violence hostage situation and had to take off."

Serena breathed a sigh and reached up to swipe the sweat from her forehead with the back of her wrist. "Sorry it took me so long to get here. I was in the middle of an autopsy with two staff out sick when I got the call."

"No problem. Unfortunately, he wasn't going anywhere."

"Is this how he was found?"

Walter Davis lay facedown on the floor.

Noah nodded. "Just like that. I'm guessing he's missing an eye." In disgust, he pointed to the opaque orb staring from its resting place on the desk. "The killer positioned it so that it was looking at the body."

"Think that means anything?"

"Yeah. I just don't have a clue what. No one's touched anything except the surrounding area. We left the body for you."

"Aw, a cop after my own heart." Her furrowed brow and down-turned lips betrayed her attempt to lighten the mood.

Joking on the job might seem terribly crass and disrespectful to some. However, for those who worked in the field, it was a defense mechanism, a coping strategy. A way of dealing with the sick things humans were capable of doing to one another.

Serena turned the body over onto his back. More flashes as the photographer took pictures of the new position. "One eye blown out by the bullet, one extracted by a sharp instrument." She gave a sigh, a weary breath blown out between pursed lips. She looked up at Noah. "So, how do you like Kit as a partner?"

Noah didn't hesitate. "She's a good cop—that was obvious

right from the start. We've only known each other a few weeks, but I felt like she'd have my back from the get-go, you know?"

"That's great." Serena's gloved fingers tugged something from the victim's empty eye socket. "Looks like our killer left a message for you."

Interest quickened his pulse. "What does it say?"

She unfolded the bloodied piece of paper, and Noah read over her shoulder, " 'Life's a laugh. How does the death penalty feel? An eye for an eye . . .' "

Noah looked at her. "Weird."

Bagging the letter, she shook her head. "Definitely. I'll be interested to hear what it means when you figure it out."

Noah looked up at the still weeping coed who'd found Walter. Heather Younts. Poor girl. He'd questioned her through her tears and had gotten that she'd come to the dorm to walk to class with her boyfriend. Approximately thirty minutes before her arrival, she'd texted Walter and received an answering text from Walter saying he was waiting for her. When he didn't answer her knocks or the phone, she'd gotten security to check it out.

This is what they'd found when security had opened the door.

Noah looked at his watch for the third time in an hour. He still hadn't heard from Kit. Was that good or bad? He wasn't sure yet. This was his first time with a partner who was also assigned to work with SERT, the Special Emergency Response Team. And this was the first time she'd been called out in the few short weeks they'd been together, even though they both knew it could happen at any time. She'd been with the department a little over six months now. Originally, she was partnered with a veteran detective who retired about six weeks ago. Then Noah and Kit were paired up, and they were both learning—and adjusting to—each other. So far, so good . . . after a rocky start.

The call from SERT came just as they had gotten to the murder scene, and he'd waved her to go. He could handle the murder scene by himself. Been there done that before. But he had to admit, the itchy feeling of not knowing what was going on with his partner distracted him. He found he didn't like being out of the loop, unable to back her up if she needed it.

Of course, she would have capable officers on the scene with her if she needed something, but still . . .

Noah pushed that problem aside. He canvassed the murder scene once more, going over each detail in his mind. He'd already taken copious notes, knowing he'd have to fill Kit in. What was he missing? Anything?

"We'll need the laptop for the computer forensic officer."

Serena grunted. "Too bad Sam's not working with you guys anymore."

"So I hear. I came after she decided to stay home with her baby."

"Hey, Noah."

"Yeah?" He turned to see Jake walk back into the dorm room. Jake Hollister, thirty-five years old with gray-streaked blond hair, was the lead crime scene unit investigator. He had an object packaged in a crime scene bag.

"Found this stuffed in a bucket of bleach in the janitor's closet."

"What is it?"

"A Tyvek jumpsuit. Your garden variety kind. You can buy them online."

"Soaked in bleach. Great."

"We got to it in time. It did test positive for blood spatter. Look at the arms. There's more blood on the right one. I'm guessing our killer is right-handed."

"I'd go with that. Any brand on them? Do you know where they came from?"

"Nope. If there was, it's been cut out. I still might be able to figure out where it came from once we get it back to the lab."

"Thanks, Jake."

"I'll let you know if we find anything else."

"I've got something," Amy, another CSU member, called.

"What is it?"

She looked up from the closet. "He was in here. I've got a bloody footprint."

"What size?"

"A nine and a half."

Noah thought about it for a few seconds. To the room and no one in particular, he said, "So, thirty minutes before the girlfriend arrives, she gets a text from Walter, telling her he's waiting for her."

Serena stood, fluid grace in the movement. "Right."

"Okay, so did he know the person he let in? Or did he open the door at the knock, thinking it was the girlfriend, and get a surprise when it wasn't?"

"No sign of forced entry?"

"None." He walked to the room window and looked down. From the second floor, he could see the crowd of college students behind the yellow crime scene tape, most silent and watchful. Others whispered behind their hands. Some had left to go to class, only to be replaced by newcomers. Was the killer in the crowd even now?

Officers mingled, asking questions, taking notes. Noah narrowed his eyes. Did anyone stand out? For a minute more, he stood there, studying the group. Nothing—and no one—drew his attention.

"He was handcuffed," Serena observed. "Or tied. Looks like some kind of friction around his wrists."

Noah looked and saw what she was talking about. They weren't raw, but were definitely bruised. Walter had struggled.

"So he was forced into the chair and cuffed."

"Our killer knocked him across the mouth too. Knocked out a tooth."

"In the chair, cuffed. Yelling? Why didn't anyone hear him?"

Jake spoke up. "I asked the security guard about that. It's quiet up here this time of day. Most everyone has classes. Very few people around."

"This sock might explain his silence." Amy held it up for them to see.

Blood saturated it.

"The killer stuffed it in his mouth to keep him quiet."

"After he knocked out the tooth."

"Then he walked behind Walter," Noah stepped to the back of the chair, "and shot him in the head."

"Why would he go in the closet?" Serena was playing along with him—if he couldn't have Kit, she was the next best thing.

"Because Heather arrived."

"If she'd had a key . . ."

"Right, but she didn't."

"So she left to get help."

"And our killer stripped down and walked out, stuffing his bloody evidence in the bucket of bleach that he planted ahead of time in the janitor's closet."

Turning back to her, he watched her pull off her gloves and stash them in a red hazardous materials bag. She motioned for the two men from the coroner that she was finished with Walter's body.

Then she looked at Noah. "All of those are good observations that raise a lot of questions. Sorry I can't help much. I can tell you this," she reached behind him and handed him a plastic bag, "I found this as soon as I walked in. It was lying beside his body."

Noah held the object and turned it from side to side. "A gavel?"

"Yep. That's what it looks like to me."

"Do you think he meant to leave it?"

Serena shot him a look. "I haven't taken up mind reading yet."

"Cute." He pursed his lips. "All right. So our victim is a law student. We find a miniature gavel on the floor next to him. Is it his? Or the killer's?"

"Good questions."

"The lab can run it for prints and see what we come up with. What else do you have?"

She blew out a sigh. "From the size of the wound, I can tell you that Walter was killed with a small-caliber handgun. Probably easy to hide, easy to use. Single gunshot wound to the back of the head at close range."

"Why did Walter let him inside in the first place?" Noah answered his own question. "He trusted whoever it was."

"That's my guess."

Noah blew out a sigh. "So we just track down everyone he knows on campus, ask each one where they were between 8:00 and 9:00 this morning, check each story, and find out who's lying. Should take, what?" he mused, "two or three months to go through all that?"

Serena clucked her sympathy.

Tossing the sarcasm aside, he said, "All right, I'm done here." He wished Kit could have walked the scene with him, but she'd have the photographs. Noah had requested more than usual—pictures from every conceivable angle so she would have the scene in detail.

He watched the men roll Walter's body toward the door and something clicked. "Wait a minute." The men stopped and Noah pulled the white sheet back to examine Walter's wrist.

Serena paused. "What is it?"

"Does it look like he's missing a watch he wears regularly?"

"That's some pretty white skin in the midst of a developing tan. If you discount the marks made by whatever he was restrained with."

"Either he didn't have time to put the watch on before he was killed—"

"—or the killer took it," Serena finished for him.

"Yeah." He looked at Jake, who was in the midst of packing up his gear. "Hey, Jake, did you guys find a watch anywhere?"

Jake thought for a moment, then shook his head. "Nope, no watch. I'm positive, but I can check the contents of what we recovered if you want. But there wasn't any watch."

"Okay, thanks." Noah exchanged a look with Serena. "Interesting. Wonder what that means?"

"You have any other murder cases matching this MO?"

"Not that I can think of offhand. I'll pass it on to Captain Caruthers. He'll be familiar with any cases where the murderer takes an item off his victim."

"All right. I've got to get back to the lab."

"And I've got a partner to check on."

Worry ate at him. They'd been partners for a little over three weeks; he'd barely had a chance to argue with his superior about the fact that he wasn't ready for another partner yet when he'd been informed of his pairing with Kit.

And he'd specifically not been ready for a female partner. His heart still ached for the last one—not in a romantic sense, but just for the loss. She'd never known it, but her husband had come to him and placed a heavy burden on his shoulders. "Watch out for her, Noah. I don't know what I'd do without her."

And he'd failed. She died.

Did this one have a husband or significant other who would expect him to babysit her?

Not wanting to find out, he'd protested, been voted down, and Kit had knocked on his door two hours later. The instant zing of attraction he felt when he saw her standing there had simply fueled his ire.

Resigned to the possibility of babysitting her on the job, he snapped at her to get her tail in gear. She merely blinked at him and arched a brow.

Then meandered over close enough for him to smell her perfume. He liked it. She leaned in, standing in his space, making him a tad uncomfortable. But his feet would rot before he'd back away from her.

Very softly, she spoke. "Let's get one thing straight right now, *partner*." She nearly growled the word. "You treat me with respect, I'll return the favor. If you can't do that, we're going to have some very serious issues. And frankly, I don't need issues with someone I'm going to have to trust my life with. Are we clear?"

He crossed his arms, jutted his chin. "Trust is earned, lady."

"Yes." Finally she moved back a step. "It is. But so is disgust. I don't know who did a number on you, but it wasn't me. I don't deserve it and won't accept it."

Guilt hit him and he silently admitted she was right. Out loud, he said, "Then let's get started."

They managed a truce of sorts over the next two weeks while he showed her the outstanding cases and brought her up to date on everything they'd be working on.

Now, as Noah pulled into the trailer park, he had to admit it hadn't taken her long to earn his respect. He climbed out of the unmarked car. The heat sucker punched him as beads of sweat immediately put in an appearance on his forehead and upper lip. How he hated summer. And technically summer hadn't even arrived. It was only the second day of May.

The air breathed tension as he crossed the dusty gravel drive to duck into the air-conditioned SERT van. He sucked in a breath of cool air and looked at Charlie Dunn, who worked at the computer. "How's she doing?"

"Hanging in there. I think she's actually going to talk him down."

"She have on a vest?"

Charlie sighed and rubbed his chin. "She did when she went in. Don't know how she'd keep it on in there without passing out, though. Bet you ten she took it off."

"I'm not a betting man. So, what's up with her? She can't stay out of the line of fire and talk him down? By going in there, she's just given this guy another hostage!"

Agitated, he slipped on an earpiece to listen.

2

The Judge rubbed his eyes, weary with all of the thinking he'd had to do lately. Searching for the perfect family, seeking ways to administer justice. And when it was all said and done, he'd go home and rub his old man's face in it.

Over and over and over again. He giggled at his repetition. Threes always made him feel better.

Feel better, feel better, he echoed in his mind.

Then frowned. They'd have no choice but to admire him, to praise him for his brilliant mind and methods.

Especially those who'd laughed at him.

Those who'd mocked him, humiliated him.

Like Walter.

Poor Walter.

The Judge stretched out on the couch across from his father, who was seated—as usual—in his special armchair. He was awfully quiet this morning. "Nothing to say, old man?"

Silence.

The Judge grimaced. No matter. He wouldn't let that spoil the moment.

He closed his eyes to bask in his brilliant accomplishment. It was still alive in his mind, so recent and so real that he could feel the adrenaline's residual effects.

Ah, yes, Walter had been surprised to see him outside his door so early.

"Oh . . . What are you doing here?" Walter had said as he pulled open the door. "I thought you were Heather."

At first, finding out that Heather was on her way had frustrated him, but he decided he could make the necessary adjustments. In fact, that had made the process even more interesting. He shortened the trial, pounded the gavel, and pronounced judgment, all before Heather had come knocking.

Really, he was grateful Heather didn't have a key. He didn't want to put Heather on trial and sentence her today. Besides, he wanted to enjoy this singular victory.

A snicker escaped him. Then another girlish giggle.

Walter wouldn't be rolling his eyes at him again.

Twenty-five-year-old Bonnie Gray watched her mother swallow the heart medication, then took the glass from her shaky fingers. Only fifty-seven years old and already, it was like she was ninety. Grief splintered Bonnie's heart and she bit her lip to hide the tremble.

Tucking the covers snugly around the frail woman, she leaned over to press a kiss against the soft forehead.

Her mother patted her cheek. "You're a good daughter, Bonnie. What would I do without you?"

Bonnie smiled, love for her mother surrounding her, briefly pushing the grief aside. "You've taken care of me forever. I don't mind helping you out. Now get some rest. We'll talk when I get back."

Her mother glanced at the clock and rolled her eyes. "A nap in the middle of the day. Ridiculous."

At least she hadn't lost her spunk. Her heart was just wearing out too fast. The medication helped, but she tired so easily these days, Bonnie feared she might lose her before they found a donor.

Shoving those thoughts away, she said, "Mary is here. She'll check in on you in a little while. I've got to get to class, all right?"

"That's fine, dear." Another pat on the cheek. "I'm so proud of you. Graduation is coming up. Pretty soon, you'll be practicing law with your daddy. You'll make partner in record time, I just know it." She shot her a shrewd look. "And not just because of who your dad is. You'll do it because you're smart and deserve it."

Bonnie smiled again, gave a little laugh to hide her aching heart. If she could, she would have given her own heart to her mother. "That's the plan, Mom." She kept her tone upbeat and light. "I'm young and naïve enough to believe I'm going to change the world."

Her mother sighed and closed her eyes. "You will, Bonnie. You'll do something wonderful with your life." Then her eyes popped back open. "But don't forget I want to be a grandmother one day."

A pang hit her. "I know."

"I haven't seen Justin around lately. Is everything all right?"

"Everything's fine." She nearly gagged on the lie, but didn't have the time to share all of the recent changes in her love life. Not that she wanted to share them all. Some things were better off left unsaid.

Bonnie squirmed under the woman's scrutiny. She needed to work up the courage to tell her about everything, ask her advice—beg her forgiveness. Instead, she just leaned over, gave her one more kiss, then stood. "I'll be back later tonight. We'll have supper together."

"Goodbye." The word was a whisper. Already her mother was slipping into sleep.

Bonnie hurried to her room and grabbed her things, her car keys, and her purse. As she did, she saw the picture on her nightstand. Justin's laughing blue eyes stared back at her. Why did she still have it? In a fit of anger, she slapped it facedown. She'd dispose of it later. Keeping the picture was too much like she was holding out hope that they would one day get back together.

But that wasn't possible. She didn't even need him now anyway. She'd found someone else. Someone who was crazy about her. Someone she never would have thought had the kind of feelings he did until the night she'd shown up on his doorstep crying, unsure where else to go . . .

But Justin . . .

She drew in a deep breath and admitted he'd been her first real love. The only man who'd ever made her even think about marriage.

And his memory still hurt.

They'd made a trip to the beach and had had so much fun. Grief twisted through her. She'd found the drugs two hours before they were supposed to drive home. She'd been crushed, devastated.

"Are you crazy? Do you know what would happen if these were found on you and I was with you?" she screamed as she threw the bags at him.

And he tried to explain. "I just need a little help dealing with the pressure of school. I'm not a junkie, I swear. Look." He went to the suitcase, grabbed the bag of white powder, another bag of pills, and flushed them down the toilet. "I won't touch anything ever again."

But it didn't matter. Once was enough. And the fact that she'd been with him when he had them on him. What if they'd been stopped? "I can't deal with this right now. I need to get away from you."

She stormed out with his curses and pleas ringing in her ears, hailed a taxi to the airport, and snagged a rental car. She alternated between crying and beating the steering wheel all the way home.

It was a wonder she made it in one piece.

That night she sobbed on her best friend Chelsea Bennett's shoulder and avoided Justin's calls.

When she refused to answer the door and threatened to call the police if he didn't leave her alone, he finally complied and her heart had shattered into a million tiny pieces.

Until her "friend" had picked it up and begun the process of putting it back together.

She picked up the picture frame she'd slapped down and opened the back of it. Removing the picture she'd hidden, she stared down at the man who'd let her cry on his shoulder that night. She hadn't even been aware of driving to his house, what she'd been searching for, but this man had been there. He'd opened his arms and she stepped in. Cried out her grief at the death of her relationship.

And he held her and then kissed her.

And she responded. Desperately needing someone to help her forget, if only for a few hours.

Even if it was the wrong thing to do.

The guilt in his eyes nearly killed her. So she'd leaned over and reassured him that he had nothing to feel guilty about.

From the safety of his car, he watched Bonnie leave the house. Little miss Bonnie. So rich, so snotty, with her nose stuck up in the air every time she looked at him.

Well, he'd soon fix that. He tapped the miniature gavel against his palm. Flipping his left wrist, he glanced at his watch and swore. He didn't have much time.

He had to get back before he was missed. His fingers itched to place the pistol to the back of her head and pull the trigger. But not until she'd had a fair trial. You couldn't get the death penalty until you were found guilty.

He had no doubt the verdict the jury would reach in the trial of Bonnie Gray.

After all, there was only one juror, one judge—

And one executioner.

3

"Ask 'em."

"What?" Kit cocked her head in a listening way. Sweat trickled down the middle of her back. She'd slipped the vest off after an hour. If she'd left it on, she'd have passed out from heatstroke by now.

"Ask them what they'll do for me."

"Sure, I can do that. Who do you want me to ask?"

"The . . . the DA. Yeah. Get the DA here. I wanna talk to him."

Kit pulled out her phone, then paused. "I'll do this, Virgil, but you know they're going to want something from you first."

"What? What do they want?"

He reached back to take a swig from the water bottle behind him. The case of water had bought the freedom of little two-year-old Jessie. Kit refused to drink more than a sip every so often. No bathroom breaks allowed on this job.

Kit motioned toward Melanie. "Let her go."

For a fraction of a second, she thought he might refuse. She even saw his lips begin to form the word. Then Anne stood, her long blonde hair stringing down her face, sticking to the dried tears on her cheeks.

"Let her go, Virgil. You're right. I shouldn't have said I'd leave you."

Not caring where the woman's backbone finally came from, just glad it had appeared, Kit nodded. As long as the woman said the right thing, she'd let her talk.

Anne stepped forward. "Let Melanie go outside and the three of us will talk. We'll straighten this out and I'll tell them it was all just a misunderstanding, okay?"

Virgil shifted, his eyes darting back and forth between his wife and Kit. Kit kept an encouraging expression on her face and an eye on the gun. He still held it steady even as he studied Anne's face. Melanie gently pulled away from her father. Virgil didn't let her go completely, but he no longer looked like he was pulling the girl's hair out by the roots.

Anne held out a hand. "Come on, Virg, let her go. She's not a part of this. I'm to blame, not her."

In one frantic move, Virgil shoved Melanie into Kit's arms and grabbed his wife's wrist to pull her to him. "Get her out. I never wanted to hurt the kids in the first place."

Kit took Melanie by the hand and picked up the cell phone. Virgil didn't know about the piece in her ear and she preferred to keep it that way for now. She pressed the number for her boss. He picked it up before the first ring ended. "You got a hostage coming out?"

"Word travels fast. Virgil has agreed to let Melanie go."

"Tell her to run as soon as she hits the porch. We'll have someone meet her."

Kit opened the door and sunlight streamed in through the crack. She took a deep breath of the fresh humid air and felt fortified. Melanie hesitated on the doorstep and took one last look back at her parents. Her father held her mother in the same position he once held Melanie, his hand tangled in the woman's long hair. Anne blinked back tears of pain but said nothing.

Melanie met her father's eyes and opened her mouth for one last plea. "Please, Daddy," she whispered.

"Get out of here, girl."

Kit pushed her on out the door. Keeping one eye on Virgil, she watched Melanie race down the steps of the porch and across the gravel drive. One of the SWAT members grabbed her and hauled her behind a protective barricade. They would make sure she was physically unharmed, then pump her for any information she could give about her father. Kit's second would send the information into her ear.

Kit turned back to Virgil and Anne. Now, it was time to get serious.

"You think she's going to be able to talk him down?" Noah asked.

Chad reached around Charlie to grab his water bottle. "She's got a good track record. One of the best I've seen. If anyone can do it, she can." He studied the conversation being typed out by Charlie.

Noah lifted a brow at that. "Really?"

"Yeah, hadn't you heard?"

"No, I missed that tidbit."

"Talked a guy into letting his wife and son go her second day on the job as a rookie street cop."

"What? Where was the negotiator?"

"On his way. Kit got there first on the domestic disturbance call—realized the guy was escalating and took charge. When the negotiator finally got there, the hostage taker wouldn't talk to anyone but Kit. She handled it like a pro and it all ended peacefully."

Noah pondered this as he listened to the silence coming from the house. What was she doing now?

The cell phone next to the computer rang. Chad pressed a button and Kit's voice filled the van. "I need the DA on the phone."

"What?"

"The district attorney, folks. Get me the DA, please." A pause. Virgil mumbled something, but Noah missed it. Then Kit. "Virgil's ready to cut a deal, but he wants some answers."

Noah's lip curled. "Just what kind of answers does this guy think he's going to get?"

Chad ignored him as he dialed the number that would put him through to the district attorney's office. Within two minutes, he had District Attorney Stephen Wells on the other line. Chad's rapid-fire explanation brought the man up-to-date on the situation.

His voice filled the van as he promised to be there within ten minutes. "Although, we can't make a habit out of this. I can't start showing up and cutting deals for everyone who decides to take a hostage."

"Yes sir, we realize that. Nobody's ever asked for you before. But, I'll just warn you that the media is here covering this, so if you'd rather not . . ."

A pause.

"No, I'll come."

Chad hung up and connected back to Kit. Noah marveled at the man's proficiency. A professional through and through. A man Noah wouldn't mind calling partner.

Not bothering to dwell on what he couldn't change, he listened to Kit soothe the still agitated man. Watched her on the large screen in the corner. Someone had managed to slide a camera through a vent for video feed. Her blonde curls looked dark and were plastered to her head. Sweat stood out across her forehead. He watched her rub her cheek on a shoulder as Virgil hauled his wife by the hair to the kitchen.

Kit stayed put, talking softly.

A knock on the door brought Chad's attention around even as Charlie's fingers flew over the keyboard, recording everything said between Kit and Virgil.

Stephen Wells stepped inside followed by a young man in his early to midtwenties. A clean-cut fellow, his eyes took in the van and the occupants.

The DA was a smooth-looking man, who no doubt would end up in Congress before too long. From what Noah knew, Stephen also seemed to genuinely care about the little people, the underdog.

"All right," he said, "tell me what to do."

Noah offered a hand. "Hey Stephen, thanks for coming out."

Stephen shook it. "No problem." He gestured toward the other man. "This is Edward Richmond, my intern." Noah shook Edward's hand and the young man gave him a slight smile. "A brilliant kid who gets to follow me all over for the next few weeks. Now, let's get those women out of there and Virgil behind bars."

Noah looked Stephen in the eye. "Are you prepared to say what it takes to make that happen?"

"You bet."

Edward slipped to the side. "I'll just hang out over here out of the way."

Noah nodded his appreciation.

Chad went to work, filling the DA in on every detail he considered important while his fingers flew expertly over the gadgets in front of him. After about a minute, he said, "Okay, I'm putting you through now. I've got you hooked up. Our guy with the gun will only be able to hear you. I'll be right here coaching you in what to say if you need it. Offer him respect, understanding, compassion—even if you don't feel it. Can you do that?"

"Yes." A short nod accompanied the word.

"And you feel comfortable using the information I just shared? You remember everything?"

"Yes." The man drew in a deep breath and looked as though he were mentally preparing for battle.

"If you have a question about a name or something, lift your right finger and I'll switch screens and bring it up for you to read."

"I've got it." A hint of impatience.

"Great. Now, this is the line you'll use to communicate with Virgil. Can you hear me?"

"Loud and clear."

"All right, you're through."

Stephen cleared his throat, then said, "This is District Attorney Stephen Wells, Mr. Mann. How can I help you, sir?"

Chad looked at Noah and gave a thumbs-up for the DA. Respect all the way.

Noah's stomach curled at the DA's conciliatory tone, and he suppressed the desire to rush the house and take care of it his way. Beating the guy to a pulp would be so satisfying. But like always, he called on years of self-control and forced himself to be still, to listen.

Forty-five minutes later, with assurances of the best deal he could do for the man, Virgil's wife burst from the door. A SWAT member grabbed her in the same manner he'd done the daughter and pulled her to safety.

The family was out.

Now it was just the man with the gun—and Kit.

Noah prayed she was as good as Chad and Charlie seemed to think she was.

Kit stared at Virgil. Feeling a little light-headed from the heat, she blinked hard. Sweat poured from Virgil's brow and he gulped heaving gasps of air. The gun wavered.

"Clear shot, Kit," came the voice in her ear.

A tap on her leg told the shooter "No."

"All ready, Virgil?" she asked. *Please be ready,* she pleaded silently.

"You sure you trust that DA dude?"

"I'm sure. You fulfilled your part of the deal, he'll keep his, I promise. Now, lay the gun down."

Virgil's eyes twitched, his hand trembled. He was tired. "I . . . I don't know. I don't know if I can go to jail again."

Kit's stomach twisted. "Virgil, we had a deal. Have I broken any promises I've made to you today?"

"No. No, you haven't. But not all cops are like you. What if they lied?"

"Nobody lied to you, Virgil. Now put the gun on the floor, okay?"

"I can't. I don't . . . What if . . ." Again his Adam's apple bobbed, but the gun lowered. Sweat dripped into his eye and he lifted his gun hand.

Bright red blossomed from the center of his forehead.

As though in slow motion, Kit watched his eyes flutter in surprise, swore she saw a flash of wounded betrayal, then they blanked as he dropped to the floor.

4

The door to the trailer ruptured open as Kit flew out. "Brian!"

Noah exited the van to intercept her. "Kit."

She ignored him. The fury on her face sent chills through him.

Her eyes roved until they lit upon the SWAT member stretched out on top of the van. She raced for the ladder and grasped each rung with a slap that brought her to the top in a flash. "Are you crazy?" she screamed. "Why did you shoot? I signaled for you to stand down!"

Noah hastened up the ladder, not so much worried about Kit as the damage she might do to Brian.

And the fact that the dead man's daughter had broken away from her mother to race to the now silent trailer.

Torn between wanting to go after the girl and rescue Brian, Noah motioned for one of the other SWAT members to go after her. Then Noah turned to watch the action before him.

"He raised his gun, he was going for you!" Brian yelled back.

"He was not! I'd talked him down. He was going to *place* the gun on the floor." Fists clenched by her sides, she glared daggers at the man.

"Kit . . ."

She whirled. "Stay out of this, Noah."

He held up his hands in the gesture of surrender. Back to Brian, she hissed, "You didn't have to shoot."

Then she did a one-eighty, shoved past Noah, and made her way back down the ladder. He saw the subtle tremble in the fingers that gripped the rail.

He shot a look at Brian. The man stared down at Kit, his fury almost matching hers. Then he brought his gaze back up to Noah. "I couldn't let him shoot her."

"Yeah. I know."

Something else flickered in his gaze and he looked away.

Noah stared at Brian. "You care about her as more than a professional, don't you?"

Guilt flashed for a nanosecond, then the man shoved his rifle into the case. "He was raising his gun, man, not lowering it. My feelings don't matter."

Noah hesitated, then shook his head. "Yeah. Just tell it like you saw it."

"He raised it, I swear."

"I wasn't there, I don't know. Like I said, just tell it straight in the debrief and everything will be fine."

Brian blew out a sigh and scrubbed a hand down the side of his face. "Right."

Noah climbed down and went to find Kit, trying to make up his mind whether to wait and let her cool off or approach her while she was still all emotional. With his last partner, he knew how to handle her. At least for the most part.

With Kit . . . not so much.

"Why did he shoot him?"

The tearful question came from his left. He spun and saw Melanie. Blood covered her hands. Grief twisted her young features and Noah felt his compassion level register off the charts. She hadn't deserved any of this.

Before he could answer, Melanie's mother pulled the girl into her arms and led her away.

Which left him to deal with Kit.

He pictured putting his arms around her and letting her have a good cry on his shoulder. Slamming the brakes on that line of thought, he stepped back into the van where he found her talking to the DA and his intern.

"You did a great job, Kit," Stephen offered.

"Fat lot of good that did Virgil." Suppressed fury made her words tight, forced out between stiff lips.

"That's a shame, Detective. Your shooter should have trusted you." This came from the intern.

Kit shot him a grateful look and swallowed. "Finally, someone with some common sense. Too bad you weren't there to help Brian do his job right."

The intern flushed. A small smile played around the corners of his lips before he raised his fingers to cover it.

"Kit . . ." Noah placed a hand on her arm, and she dropped her chin to her chest as she sucked in a deep breath. Noah's fingers tingled at the feel of her bare skin under his and he gave a slight jerk in surprise.

A curse sounded from behind him and they all turned as one to see Brian standing there, listening in on the conversation.

Regret sliced across her face. "Brian, I'm—" Noah watched her face harden as she cut herself off. He knew what she was thinking. She wouldn't say she was sorry. She believed Brian was wrong. He'd killed a man against her orders.

With a defeated sigh and one last look at Brian that was a cross between a glare and an apology, Kit opened the door and left. Once again, Noah followed, wondering if this was going to be a pattern. He took a deep breath and hoped Kit cooled off fast. They had a case to discuss.

Three hours later, Kit slammed her locker. The debrief had gone the way she thought it might. Everyone agreed Brian had done what he needed to do to keep her safe.

Everyone except her, that is. A knock on the door made her jump. "Yeah?"

His voice came through the cracked door. "Kit, you decent? Ready to discuss this case?"

Noah. She pulled her tank top over her head and walked over to the door. Swinging it open the rest of the way, she looked up into her partner's tired eyes and wondered if hers reflected the same fatigue. "Hey." A glance at her watch nearly made her groan, but she nodded. "Sure."

"Come on, let's grab a bite to eat while we discuss."

Relief flooded her. She was starved. "Great. Let me just grab my purse."

She snatched it from the bench and met Noah just outside the glass doors. "I snapped at you today. I'm sorry." Surprise shot his brows north and Kit flushed. "What, you didn't think I knew I needed to apologize?"

"Oh, I knew you knew, I just didn't know if you would do anything about it."

His snappy comeback had her sputtering. Then laughing. He grinned and she shook a finger at him. "Okay, you got me." Then she sobered. "But Brian didn't need to kill that man and I'll never be convinced otherwise."

"I'm sorry."

She shrugged. "I suppose I need to apologize to him too. Not for biting his head off about shooting Virgil, but just . . . in general maybe. I don't know." Noah stayed quiet and she grimaced. "He thought he was doing the right thing . . . at least I hope so. We all make mistakes, I guess." She ground her molars, then sighed. "I've just got to put it behind me. It's the only way to move on."

"Been there."

His soft look of understanding made her stomach jump in surprise—and her toes curl with attraction. Hello? She mentally smacked herself. What was she doing? Feeling?

Not *that*.

Attraction between partners didn't mix. But this was the first time they'd laughed together and it felt good.

Too good. "Yeah, I'm sure you have." She swallowed hard and changed the subject. "So, what's to eat around here?"

Noah led the way down the hall. "We've got some good choices. The hospital cafeteria is within walking distance. And so is Flannigan's. It's just around the corner."

"I've heard about Flannigan's. Let's go there." Her sisters, Jamie and Samantha, had mentioned the restaurant, but Kit had yet to eat there.

"Flannigan's it is then." Noah pushed open the double glass doors and they stepped out onto the sidewalk.

Kit gasped as the heat sucked the air from her lungs. "I'll never get used to this heat. I mean, it got hot in Raleigh, but somehow, it just feels hotter here."

"How did you stand it in that trailer earlier?"

Kit thought about that. "I don't know. I was hot and sweating like crazy, but I guess it didn't register. I didn't think about it. All of my senses were focused on Virgil and his family. Everything else just kind of wasn't important."

Sadness flickered through her at the reminder.

Then they were there. Noah opened the door and she slipped ahead of him into the restaurant's blessedly cool interior.

Once seated, Kit ordered a double cheeseburger, large fries, and a milkshake.

Noah stared at her.

"What? Why are you looking at me like that?"

"I just realized we haven't eaten many meals together. I figured you for a salad and smoothie kind of girl."

Kit laughed. "I like those too, but after my day I need something a little more fortifying. I want grease, fat, and carbs—and a lot of 'em."

He shook his head. "Looks like I've got a lot to learn about you."

She let the smile slide south. "Oh, there's not so much to learn."

Shrewd eyes narrowed. "Hm. Somehow I doubt that."

Once again, she felt a flush rising to the surface and counteracted it by asking, "Okay, I have a question I haven't asked yet, but I think now's the time."

"Shoot."

"What do you have against female cops?"

Noah sputtered, nearly choking on the sip of tea he'd just taken. Grabbing a napkin, he wiped his mouth and looked into knowing brown eyes. "Excuse me?"

"You didn't like me from the get-go. I thought now might be a good time to find out why."

Observant and pretty. Great. "Uh, yeah. I mean, no."

A tilt to her head brought her blonde ponytail swinging around. Her eyes stayed glued on his, nailing him for an honest answer.

With a sigh, Noah leaned back and looked out the window, then back at her. "Look, it's not you. I had a female partner once. It didn't work out so well."

"What happened?"

"She was killed."

Kit's brows slammed together. "How?"

"On a case."

No judgment on her face. "Okay. So, what happened?"

"She made a dumb decision and paid for it."

"Where were you?"

He scanned her expression for any condemnation. None yet. "I was there."

"Doing what?"

Noah wanted to groan. "You're like a dog with a bone, aren't you?"

"Yeah, a pit bull. So, what were you doing?"

Surrendering to the inevitable, he propped his elbows on the table and rubbed his eyes, buying time, trying to think. Finally, he said, "There'd been a kidnapping. A five-year-old kid. We'd gotten a tip saying the child was being held in an old abandoned house on Spring Street. My partner and I were the closest ones available, so we headed over there immediately to check it out. Backup was on the way, but we got there pretty quick."

Kit's brow furrowed. "Seems like I heard something about this. Your partner ran in without waiting on backup?"

He nodded. "She said the kid's life was on the line and she was going in." A sick look crossed his face. "I had a bad feeling about the tip. It just . . ." He shrugged. "I don't know what triggered my internal alarm, still don't know, but I knew if we went in that building . . . anyway, I told her we needed to wait on backup."

"And she ignored you."

"Yeah. She took off and I hesitated, trying to decide whether to go after her or hang back and see if I could figure out why I was so spooked. After about three seconds, I decided I couldn't leave my partner on her own, so I started after her. As soon as she pushed the door open, the whole place exploded."

The waitress appeared with their food. Kit stared at it, then back at Noah. "I'm so sorry."

His heart thudded at her soft words. "Yeah. I am too."

Not wanting to make her uncomfortable, but not wanting to stray from his sincere desire to say grace, Noah folded his hands, rested his forehead against them, and closed his eyes.

Lord, thank you for this food—and thank you for sparing Kit today.

"Hey." She reached out and touched his hand. "Are you all right?"

He looked up and smiled. "Just thanking God for the food." He paused. "And that you're alive to enjoy it."

He saw her gape, then snap her mouth shut. "Really?" Clearing her throat, she squeezed ketchup on her hamburger. Then paused. "Thank you. That's really touching and I appreciate it."

He studied her expression. The comment was sincere, and a warmth he hadn't expected hit him in the vicinity of his heart.

Then she looked uncomfortable, fidgeting with her napkin,

then taking a sip of her drink. He wasn't surprised when she changed the subject. "The explosion. Is that where you got that scar?"

The blemish ran from the bottom of his ear to curve under his jaw and disappear into his shirt collar. Absently he traced it, still not used to the feel of it, wondering what she thought about it—then wondered why he cared. "Yep."

"How long ago did this happen?"

"Three months."

She snitched a fry and popped it in her mouth, concern pulling her brows toward the bridge of her nose. "And the kid?"

"We found him. Alive, thank God. His dad had him stashed away and called in the tip, trying to throw us off the trail and shake us up a bit. He's now in jail for murder along with various other charges."

"And you feel responsible somehow for your partner's death?"

"I should have stopped her."

"Have you had any other partners besides her?"

He shrugged. "Sure."

"And have any of them ever made a dumb decision while on the job?"

Noah sighed. "Yeah. And I see where you're going with this, but—"

"But nothing. I'm sorry for your loss and I'm sorry that she did that, but you weren't any more responsible for her decisions than you are for mine. She was a professional, she made a mistake. Unfortunately it's a mistake no one can undo, but it's certainly not your fault." She paused to take a bite of a french fry, but he could see her mind wasn't on the food.

"Just like you're not responsible for Brian pulling that trigger today?"

She froze, then closed her eyes. "Yeah, just like that."

Noah stabbed a bite of lettuce with his fork. "Maybe we'll both be able to convince ourselves of that one day." As he chewed, he studied her. Fair skin that glowed with good health, brown eyes with faint circles underneath that indicated she wasn't sleeping well. He wondered why. She had her blonde curls pulled up in her standard ponytail, and he found himself picturing what they would look like down around her shoulders.

Blinking, he cleared his throat. "Let's make a pact."

"What kind of pact?"

He raised his glass of sweet tea. "To no dumb decisions."

A faint smile lifted her lips, deepening the dimple in her cheek as she lifted her water bottle. "To smart decisions, staying alive—and catching the bad guys."

He pulled out the file to fill her in on the murder she'd been called away from and did his best to ignore the thumping of his heart.

A loud clanging that said getting to know Kit might be the best thing he never wanted.

TUESDAY

5

After another restless night, Kit rose earlier than she'd planned and decided to get her run out of the way. Before she changed into her jogging stuff, she texted Jamie, one of the sisters she'd moved to Spartanburg to get to know: "If ur up, going 4 a run. Want 2 come?"

Almost immediately, Kit received a response. "Be right there. Wait on me!"

As she took her time getting dressed, she thought about her sisters.

Samantha Cash Wolfe, who was a former FBI computer forensics expert, now a stay-at-home mom to her almost six-month-old little boy.

And Jamie Cash Richards, a contract forensic anthropologist for the Spartanburg County police department.

Two sisters she'd only known for about ten months because their birth mother had given her up for adoption. Sisters who'd been drawn into law enforcement because of extreme personal experiences.

Just the same as she.

How ironic.

"Aw, Dad, you sure threw a monkey wrench into my life when you told me I was adopted."

On his deathbed, he'd confessed that Kit wasn't his biological daughter. Stunned, she'd stared at him. With tears running down his face, he said, "You have the right to know. Your mother never wanted to tell you, but you should know."

Shoving aside those memories and the emotions they invoked, she thought about her sisters' husbands. Dedicated men, one also a detective and the other an FBI agent. Admirable men who worked hard to make this world a better place for their family and friends.

Like her partner, Noah Lambert. Her "very good-looking in a rugged macho sort of way" partner with his reddish blond hair and perceptive green eyes, broad shoulders, and . . .

Get off that track, Kit. That train's not going anywhere. She was to meet with the subject of her thoughts in an hour to go over Walter Davis's murder. She needed to have a clear head, which meant she needed coffee. And lots of it.

Only it would have to wait until after her run.

Rats.

The doorbell rang and she grabbed her cell phone to clip it on the side of her shorts. She opened the door and looked into a mirror. Curly blonde ponytail in a black scrunchy, slight freckles, and chocolate brown eyes.

Kit blinked and Jamie laughed. "I know. It freaks me out every time too."

Shaking her head, Kit joined in the laughter. "I'll get used to it one day. You ready?"

"Ready."

Jamie tugged at the sleeves on her long-sleeved T-shirt.

"You don't have to be self-conscious about your scars with me." Kit dared to speak the words she'd been thinking for months now.

Her sister froze, then gave a half laugh. "I'm not so self-conscious anymore. I think I simply do a lot of things out of habit now."

And yet she still wore her long sleeves no matter the season or temperature.

Jamie had shared her horrific story of abduction and torture at the hands of a psychopathic killer, one that had Kit sick for Jamie's sake. But one that piled blocks of respect one on top of the other for the woman.

"All right then," she smiled, "let's go."

Jamie set the pace. She'd only started jogging after Kit had asked her to go along. Now she was as much an addict as Kit. "So, how are things going with the new partner?"

Kit felt the flush start. Glad she was jogging as she needed an excuse for the heat in her face, she gave a nonchalant shrug. "He's a good detective. Probably one of the best that I've worked with. I like him."

"Uh-huh. I hear he's not too hard to look at either." Jamie smirked.

"You know, you're not going fast enough if you can jog and talk at the same time."

Jamie shot her a teasing look and picked up the pace a bit. "I'm just kidding with you, but word also has it that not only is he a great detective, he's a super nice guy."

"Who's your source?"

"Dakota and Connor."

"Of course," Kit muttered.

"I heard about the hostage thing yesterday."

Not a subject she really wanted to talk about. "Hmm."

"Don't blame yourself, Kit. You're good at your job and already well-respected in the department."

Kit shot her a look and raised a brow.

"And that came straight from the captain. I overheard him talking to the mayor."

"Eavesdropping, Jamie? You should be ashamed."

Jamie shot her an innocent look and pursed her lips. "Hey, if people want to discuss stuff like that while I'm working on a body, it's not my fault." Jamie worked in the morgue and did contract work for the police department.

Kit shook her head, even as grateful appreciation slid through her. She *was* good at her job, and she couldn't deny the pat on the back felt good.

Her cell phone rang and she pulled to a stop. Jamie jogged in place beside her. She glanced at the ID.

Noah.

She couldn't stop the little flutter in the pit of her stomach. And why did her knees feel shaky all of a sudden? She blamed her breathlessness on the run. "Kit here."

"Morning. You up?"

"Yep. On a run with my sister." She loved using that word in relation to herself.

"When you get here, will you want some coffee?"

"You'll be my new BFF."

That produced a laugh. "I'll be at the office in thirty. See you there." He hung up.

Thirty minutes? Did the man never sleep? Determined to beat him there, she grinned at Jamie. "Think I can get to the office in thirty minutes?"

"If you've suddenly developed the ability to move faster than light speed."

"It's worth a try. Come on."

All conversation ceased as the jog turned into a full-out run. By the time they arrived back on Kit's front porch, they were both breathless and laughing. Kit raced through her shower, yanked her hair back into its customary ponytail, and snapped her sunglasses on top of her head.

"I'll lock up." Jamie grinned at her.

"Thanks, it was fun. See you later!"

She flew out the door.

"Hey Kit!"

She paused, hand on the handle of her car, and looked over her shoulder. The twentysomething young woman who lived in the other side of the duplex stood on the porch, her fingers wrapped around the end of a leash.

"Good morning, Alena. How are you?"

"I'm great. Roscoe's ready for his early morning run before I have to get to class. I was getting ready to knock on your door to see if you were interested in joining us."

Kit smiled. She and Alena, a student at Wofford Law College, often jogged in the mornings when Jamie wasn't able to make it. Roscoe, Alena's German shepherd, usually accompanied them. "I've already been this morning. Let's try for tomorrow. Deal?"

"Sure thing."

Kit hopped in her car and headed for the office, her mind on Alena. She wondered if her neighbor knew Walter Davis. Walter had been on the verge of graduating law school. Alena had just started. With a mental note to ask the next time she saw Alena, Kit pulled into her parking spot in front of the police department.

Noah's car was already in his spot.

Rats. She'd had too many delays this morning. Oh well, there was always tomorrow.

Hurrying up the steps, she wound her way around the roomful of desks to find hers. Noah was seated at his. His desk was crammed right next to hers, their ends nearly touching. File cabinets lined the area behind them, and the copy machine made getting to her desk a tight squeeze.

She made it in just under thirty minutes. Barely. When she plopped into her chair, the light breeze she stirred blew several papers from Noah's desk to the floor next to her chair.

She threw her purse into her bottom drawer, grabbed the steaming cup of coffee from the pile of files, and took a greedy sip.

She gasped as the liquid burned her tongue on its way down her throat, then sighed as the caffeine hit her system.

He smirked. "That was fast."

Kit took another scalding sip, then set the cup back down. Bending to retrieve the scattered papers, she said over her shoulder, "You said you had coffee and would be in the office in thirty minutes." Papers in one hand, she reached for the cup again. She took another sip and deadpanned, "I hate cold coffee."

He grinned and it was all she could do not to blink at how his face crinkled into attractive lines and crevices. Clearing her throat, she said, "I appreciate it. That was really thoughtful."

His smile faded. "I'm not always the jerk I appeared to be the first day we met."

"Hmm. That's good to know." Inwardly she admitted she'd already figured that out. She took another sip of the coffee and handed him the papers. As he took them, his fingers brushed hers and she jerked. An envelope fell to the desk. While she fought the flush she could feel creeping up into her cheeks, she looked at the envelope.

"What's this?"

He leaned over. "Oh, that's from the boys' home across town."

"Boys' home? How are you involved there?"

"I send them some money occasionally and play big brother to a few of the kids every once in a while."

Studying him, she saw he was a little embarrassed, but her admiration for the man just went up a few notches. "That's really cool, Noah."

One side of his mouth lifted in a lopsided grin. "Thanks."

"What made you get into that?"

After a brief hesitation, Noah shrugged and said, "The director goes to my church and he asked me if I would be interested in giving back. I said sure."

For some reason, she had a feeling he was leaving out pertinent information. Instead of pushing him for more details, she switched gears. "So, tell me about our homicide."

"All right." He read from his notes. "Walter Davis, age twenty-six. Lived on campus in one of the graduate apartment complexes. Was getting ready to graduate with honors from the law school, going to be a defense attorney."

"We need a list of acquaintances. Friends, co-workers, family, et cetera."

Noah waved his notebook. "Got that covered. He was dating a girl named Heather." He filled her in on the text message Walter had sent telling her he was waiting for her.

"Could the killer have known about this text message, knew Walter was alone, and beat Heather there?"

Noah shrugged. "Could have, I guess. If she sent it in his presence and he asked who she was texting."

"Or Walter knew his killer and told him Heather was on her way over."

"Or that," he agreed.

"Did we get a printout of all of the text messages between his phone and hers?"

"Right here." He handed her the sheet.

She scanned through it. "Nothing much here."

"That's what I thought too. If Walter knew his killer, he didn't text him. At least not in a way that's obvious. And there are no threats on here. We'll still need to question everybody he had contact with over the last few days because, if you ask me, this doesn't look like a random killing."

He told her about the miniature gavel. "I don't know if it belonged to Walter or the killer. It could have been just something he had on the desk that got knocked off in a struggle—only there wasn't any sign that Walter struggled. Honestly, it looked like he let his killer in, sat down in the chair, and waited to die." A pause. "If you discount the bruises around his wrists where it looks like he was restrained in some way."

Kit blew out a sigh. "Any video from the security cameras?"

"Not really. We requested the video from the time of Walter's text up until thirty minutes after the security guard called it in. The only thing on it is students coming and going. No one stands out. No one looks suspicious. A lot of students, a lot of baseball caps. You can see some faces, others are hidden. There's nothing to work with on that end."

She leaned back in her chair and crossed her arms. She'd studied each picture. "And it's going to take forever to get any

DNA report back." She paused as her eyes focused on each detail in the picture. "You said the watch is missing."

"Right, it wasn't found in his room. His girlfriend, Heather, said he never took it off, so we're thinking the killer took it."

"What did his family have to say?"

He snorted. "They were a dead end. Apparently they weren't close, hadn't spoken to Walter since the beginning of the semester."

Kit slapped the paper down on the desk. "All right, who do you want to question first?"

Heather Younts, Walter Davis's girlfriend and fellow law student, still seemed to be stuck in the shock phase of grief. Noah felt for her, but he needed answers. She'd agreed to meet them if they came to her apartment. She didn't feel like going out.

Seated on the couch in the tastefully decorated living area, Noah and Kit worked to probe Heather's mind. Kit leaned forward, forearms on her thighs. Noah tried not to wonder if the nose ring Heather wore was painful. He tried to picture her standing in front of a judge looking professional. He couldn't do it.

Focusing on Kit's words, he ignored the body jewelry. She was saying, "Heather, this is really important. Walter would want you to think clearly and help put his murderer in jail."

Tears leaked down the girl's face, but she made no sound. Then, "How do you know what Walter would want?" The question came out low, angry. Her eyes flashed.

Kit paused, shot a look at Noah. "Because we've questioned quite a few of his friends and know that more than anything he was all about justice. Justice for those who didn't have the ability to get it themselves."

Heather flinched. "Yeah, you're right."

Her brief spurt of anger faded as fast as it had appeared. She took a deep breath and blew it out. "Um . . . okay. The problem is, I don't know what I can tell you that will help. Walter was a great guy. He didn't have any enemies, didn't do drugs, hated alcohol because of what it did to his older brother . . ." She shrugged and spread her hands. "I just don't know!"

"That's fine, Heather," Kit soothed. "What about the day before Walter died? The week before? What was he doing?"

"What we were all doing. Preparing to graduate, participating in the mock trial, registering for the bar exam, just stuff you do before you graduate, you know?"

"And you can't think of anyone he may have made mad?"

"No!"

"What about someone jealous of your relationship with Walter?"

At this question, Heather paused, then shook her head. "No, no one."

"You hesitated. Did something cross your mind?"

"Oh, not really. I mean, there's this girl that's graduating with Walter. She's always had a crush on him, but he's never shown her any interest."

"What's her name?"

"Stacy. Stacy Hall."

Noah wrote the girl's name down and pulled out his iPhone. He sent a message requesting the schedule and address of Stacy Hall. He looked back at Heather. "Do you know if Walter had a little miniature gavel that he kept in his room?"

"A minia—" She broke off and frowned. "No. I've never seen one there before. Why?"

"Just wondering."

"All right." Kit stood and shook Heather's hand. "Thank you for your time. And once again, we're so sorry for your loss."

The girl nodded. "Thank you. I'm really sorry I'm not much help. Please, please find who did this to Walter." The last word came out on a suppressed sob.

This time Kit placed a hand on Heather's arm and gave her a reassuring squeeze. "We will."

Noah patted her back as he passed her, then stopped. "Do you have a church family?"

Surprise lifted her brow. "No. Not really. I'm not from around here."

"It might help." He pulled out a card and handed it to her. "That's my pastor's card. He'd be glad to talk to you if you feel like it would help."

Her fingers curled around the small piece of paper and she gave a small smile. "Thank you."

"Anytime."

Noah hated to see the pain she was going through and felt it was his responsibility to offer comfort where he could. Having God on your side would go a long way toward making things better.

They left her staring at the card, tears making silent tracks down her cheeks.

Kit climbed in the car and Noah felt her studying him. "What are you thinking?"

"That was nice."

"What?"

"Offering your pastor's number to her."

"Oh." He couldn't control the flush he knew was creeping up the back of his neck. "Yeah. She looked like she might need someone to talk to."

Kit was silent for a minute, then asked, "What church do you go to?"

"The community church that your family goes to."

"Hm."

"You're welcome to come sometime, you know."

"I know. I've been asked."

"Ah." Silence descended once more. Noah took a deep breath and debated. Should he ask her? She said she'd already been asked.

But not by him. He cleared his throat. "Wanna come this weekend? If we have time, I mean."

She looked at him. "Maybe."

Noah thought he saw a small smile playing around her lips. "Good. All right. Shall we find this Stacy Hall person and ask her a few questions?"

"Let's do it."

6

Six hours later, Kit let herself into her house, kicked off her shoes, and hung her keys on the hook just inside the door. Stacy Hall had been a bust. They'd finally tracked her down and found her in the hospital. She admitted to having a crush on Walter, but knew he had a girlfriend. Plus she had an alibi for his murder. She'd been undergoing an emergency appendectomy when Walter was murdered.

A knock on her door pulled her back into the foyer. A glance out the side window made her smile. She opened the door. "Hi, Alena."

Her duplex-mate smiled. "Hey, the mailman put some of your mail in my box." She handed over the envelopes.

"Oh, thanks. You want to come in?"

"No, I'm meeting some friends at the movies, but thanks anyway."

"Sure. Let me know when you want to go running. I need it."

Alena laughed. "I will. See you later."

She watched the girl jog down the walkway and jump into her car. So full of life. So eager for what the next day would bring. Kit shook her head. Had she ever been that young?

Yes, once upon a time. Before her father had dropped his bombshell on her.

Her stomach growled, distracting her. She headed for the kitchen for an apple and gave a disgusted grunt when she realized she'd eaten the last one this morning.

"Great." She was starving. An apple wasn't going to do it anyway.

When the phone rang, she seriously considered ignoring it.

But it might be her mother. Her adoptive mother. Even though the woman had said she wasn't going to call and beg Kit to come home.

Or it could be work.

Grabbing the handset from the base, she looked at the caller ID and felt a lift in her spirits. She clicked it on and said, "Hey Jamie, what's up?"

"Hey there. Dakota and I are babysitting tonight. Want to join us for supper?"

Phone in Chinese takeout or have a home-cooked meal with her sister, brother-in-law, and nephew for company?

A no-brainer.

"I'll be there in ten minutes."

The sound of Jamie laughing rang in her ears and she felt the weariness of the day slide from her shoulders. Grabbing her keys, she practically ran for the car.

Eight minutes later, she pulled into Jamie's driveway. Dakota had moved in with her after they'd married, and now the little two-bedroom, two-bathroom cottage-style house was up for sale, but so far there'd been no takers.

Kit rapped on the door and Jamie opened it with Andy in her arms. Red-faced with tear tracks on his cheeks, he opened his mouth mid-squall and stared at the newcomer. Kit looked at Jamie. "Having a hard time?"

"I need a negotiator. I'm willing to give him anything he wants, but he's not talking."

Kit grinned and held out her arms.

Andy studied her for a brief moment, then fell into them, snuggling his head under her chin. Stunned, Jamie turned to look at Dakota, who just shrugged.

Andy leaned back in Kit's arms and stared at the sky, his temper tantrum forgotten. She crooned into his ear, "You like the stars, little man?"

He seemed fascinated by the shining lights so far above him. She looked at Jamie, who still stood in the doorway watching them. "All you've got to do is figure out how to capture his attention."

"Then talk some sense into him?"

Kit grinned and nuzzled the now quiet baby who'd jammed a fist into his mouth. Slobber rolled past his pinkie knuckle to land on Kit's thumb. She laughed and dried it on his bib. "You are just the perfect little baby, Andrew Wolfe." He babbled something back and Kit smiled. "I totally agree."

The hair on her neck spiked and Kit jerked her head to the right. Nothing.

Then why did she feel like she was being watched? Like she had a great big target on her back?

"Okay, you two, get in here." Jamie shook her head. "Honestly, I feel like a terrible aunt."

Shoving aside her sudden paranoia, Kit slid past Jamie and carried the baby into the den and sat in the rocker. A gentle push with her toe set the chair in motion, and within minutes little Andy was asleep.

"Unbelievable," Jamie whispered under her breath. "How'd you do that?"

Kit stood. "Just part of my charming personality. Where do you want him?"

Jamie led the way into the guest bedroom. "Just lay him on the bed. I've already put the rails up." She spread pillows at the foot of the bed. "That should do it. I'll check on him every few minutes, but he should be fine with the monitor right here." She turned on the monitor and the sisters headed into the kitchen.

Kit asked, "Where's my food? I'm starved."

Laughing, Dakota made her a plate and the three tucked into the spaghetti, talking about nothing of any great importance, just enjoying each other's company.

When Kit finally left, she realized more than her stomach was satisfied. Her heart felt full too. She was grateful for the time with her family. The evening just reinforced that she'd done the right thing in seeking them out.

And yet she felt sad. An inexplicable sadness. Really, her emotions didn't seem to make sense these days.

With exasperation, she wondered how it was possible to feel happy and sad at the same time. Happy to have found her biological parents. Happy she had two sisters and brothers-in-law, and a sweet little nephew. And yet, sad. Because she was hurting the woman who had raised her. And no matter how mad she was about her adoptive parents keeping her birth a secret, she truly had no real desire to hurt her mother. Not really.

As she walked up the steps to her home, she pulled out her cell phone, sat on her porch, and began to dial the number she knew by heart. The number she'd grown up with as a child, then a teen, then an adult. Her mother's number. Only, the woman wasn't really her mother.

And yet . . . she was. Kit sighed and rubbed her forehead. She hung up. Then mad at herself for her indecision, she started punching the numbers again.

Mid-dial, she stopped. Looked up and frowned. Once again, the hair on the back of her neck tingled and she felt a shiver dance up her spine.

Her fingers crept to her weapon as she scanned the darkness. The familiar feel of the gun in the holster offered little comfort. She unsnapped the strap that held it in place.

Was someone there? Watching her?

She felt exposed and backed up to her door, eyes still probing the night, the house across the street, the cars that appeared vacant and still. A dog barked from behind Alena's door. Roscoe. Barking at her or something else?

As her eyes continued to scan her surroundings, her fingers fumbled for the latch, got the storm door open. The doorknob refused to turn. Locked. And her key was in her pocket.

The door beside her burst open and she gasped. Roscoe ran into the street barking, Alena stumbling after him. "Roscoe!"

Heart thumping, Kit pressed a hand to her chest. "Alena, what's wrong?"

Her neighbor slapped a hand against the wooden railing and stared after her dog, who'd disappeared. "I don't know. I hurried home from the movies because I knew my mom would be coming in and didn't want to make her wait on me. About five minutes after I got here, I let Mom in, then Roscoe started going nuts, whining, scratching the door. He was more agitated than I've seen him in a long time."

"Will he come back?"

"Yes. Eventually."

"What do you think he's going after?"

The girl shrugged. "I don't have a clue. I wonder if someone was sneaking around out here."

Kit frowned. "I didn't see anyone when I drove up."

"Maybe around back?" Alena looked nervous now.

Pulling her weapon, she told the girl, "Go back inside. I'll check it out."

A woman appeared in the doorway. An older version of Alena. "My word, what's going on out here?"

Ignoring the woman's question, Alena backed toward the door. "Should I call 911?"

"Not yet. Let me just walk the perimeter. If there was someone here, it's most likely he's long gone by now. Especially with Roscoe chasing after him."

Alena nodded and took the woman by the hand, saying, "It's all right, Mom, Kit's a police officer. She'll handle it." The women disappeared back into the house.

Gun held steady, Kit rounded the corner of the house. The floodlights illuminated the small backyard.

Nothing moved.

She crossed the yard, following it onto the neighbor's property directly across from her little duplex. Everything was still. Quiet.

Then a low whine reached her ears.

She trotted to the left, across more grass, and finally she reached the road where she found Roscoe sniffing the asphalt.

"Roscoe, come here, boy."

He looked up, then back down, paced a few steps down the street, then came back. Kit reached down and scratched his silky ears.

"Roscoe, was someone here? Huh? Did they get in a car?"

He licked her fingers and turned to head toward home.

Giving the road one last look, Kit followed the dog, staying watchful and alert just in case someone was still out there. Someone who was invisible to her. Someone who might be watching her as she moved. She shuddered and picked up the pace.

Back on her porch, she rapped on Alena's door. "It's me. Kit."

The door opened instantly. Roscoe darted inside and Alena's worried gaze met hers. "Did you find anything? Anyone?"

"No. False alarm, I guess."

"I'm so sorry."

Kit waved off her concern. "Let me know if you need anything during the night." Because while she hadn't found anything suspicious in the midst of the night shadows, she doubted she'd rest easy.

And she'd forgotten to ask Alena if she knew Walter Davis.

Excitement thrummed through the Judge. Could it be? Could he have found her, the one he'd been looking for? He'd watched her from afar, watched her carefully. So far, it looked as though she fit the criteria. The perfect woman, the perfect wife—and the perfect mother. All three.

He'd keep watch for a while longer, but he couldn't help the kernel of hope that sprung to life. He might have to move sooner than he'd anticipated. But that was all right. He already had the perfect home—or it would be as soon as he got rid of his father. He just needed the perfect people to fill it. And as soon as the opportunity presented itself, he would.

WEDNESDAY

7

She was right. Once again a restful sleep eluded her. Tossing and turning all night didn't make the hours pass any faster, and she finally crawled out of bed at 5:30. As soon as the sun started to peek over the horizon, she took her morning run without Jamie or Alena and Roscoe, her tennis shoes slapping the asphalt with a regular rhythm. Obviously, Alena's mother was visiting, so Kit didn't want to disturb them this early.

She'd almost texted Jamie about running, but she really needed time alone to think. If someone had been watching the house last night, the big question was, why?

This morning she felt the need to keep looking over her shoulder, her mind replaying the events of last night—then jumping to the case she still needed to solve.

Footsteps sounded behind her and she whirled, hand reaching for her gun in her shoulder holster.

The one that wasn't there.

She'd put on the ankle holster instead this morning.

She had just rounded a curve, so she crossed the street and knelt as though to tie her shoe, keeping her eyes peeled for whoever was behind her.

Her hand hovered above the gun.

More fast-paced footsteps.

"Kit!"

The figure came into sight and Kit let out the breath she'd been holding. Standing, she exclaimed, "Jamie! What are you doing, you crazy girl?"

Jamie caught up with her, holding a hand to her side. "Do you run like that all the time when you're not with me?" She gulped air. "I really hold you back, don't I?"

Kit smiled. "Not at all. Why didn't you text or call me if you wanted to meet this morning?"

"I did."

Kit's smile turned into a frown. She snatched her phone from her side and read, "Wanna jog this a.m.?" She looked at Jamie. "I'm sorry, I didn't see it. I thought I checked it before I left."

"It's all right. I figured I'd go ahead and come on just in case. I like this route. It feels safe."

"Yeah, well, I'm not so sure about that," she muttered. Her eyes flicked from one end of the street to the other. Across the street was the park, where a man walking his dog had just emerged from a wooded trail.

"What do you mean?"

Kit forced a smile. "Nothing."

Jamie shot her a ferocious look. "Don't 'nothing' me when it's clear as the nose on your face something's bothering you. Don't be afraid to share with me. I'm far from fragile."

A pang of remorse shot through her and Kit reached out to squeeze Jamie's hand. "I know. It's not that. In fact, it's probably nothing."

"What?"

"Last night, I think someone was lurking outside my house."

Jamie's eyes went wide. "You think?"

"Yeah. I couldn't find any evidence, but my neighbor's dog went nuts."

White teeth came out to clamp down on her lower lip as Jamie breathed in. "You need to take that seriously. I wanted to shrug off my stalker, believe it was just in my mind, but it wasn't. So don't ignore last night."

Kit nodded. "I know. I won't."

"And you probably shouldn't jog alone anymore. Will you make sure someone's with you from now on?"

Her sister's concern touched her. "I'll be fine." She glanced around and saw nothing to disturb her. "Come on, let's go."

"Tell me what's new on the case," Jamie said.

So she did.

Walter Davis. A young man cut down before he could put into practice the ideals he held. That was one thing she'd learned about him. He'd wanted to change the world; defend the underdog. He'd been a little cocky, but charming and always willing to lend a hand.

All of this according to his girlfriend, Heather. His other friends had backed up her assessment.

Jamie whistled. "So, what'd he do to get this killer's attention?"

Kit breathed a humorless laugh. "That, my dear sister, is the question of the day."

Thoughts swirling, muscles warm and loose, Kit turned the corner and headed back to her house.

A light green car parked three doors down caught her attention. She'd never seen it on the street before. "I want to take a look at that car." She didn't say why.

Jamie kept pace with her as Kit jogged over and looked inside.

Empty. Except for the ashtray that overflowed.

Chain-smoker, she thought.

"Can I help you?"

Kit straightened and turned to see a young woman with dirty blonde hair and a baby on her hip standing on the porch.

"Sorry, I've never seen this car before and thought I'd check it out."

"My husband just bought it yesterday. Our other one died about a week ago."

Feeling a little foolish, Kit said, "I'm a cop. When I saw the strange car on the street . . ."

The woman grinned. "Ah, I understand. I have a brother who's a cop. Most paranoid individual on the planet."

Kit laughed. "Well, glad you know what it's like. Have a good day."

"You too."

She and Jamie headed back to her house where Jamie said goodbye, climbed in her car, and left. Kit grabbed a shower and got ready for the day. She'd give Noah until 7:00 a.m. and then give him a call. They had a case to solve.

The phone rang and she glanced at the clock. 6:46.

She snatched it up. "Hello?"

"Did I wake you?" Noah's deep voice caressed her ear and she closed her eyes. She really had to get over this attraction to him.

"Nope. I'm up. What's going on?"

"Another homicide."

"Where?" All business now, she clipped her cell phone to her side. She noticed he hadn't bothered calling that one—he'd gone straight to her home number, calling the phone she'd be most likely to answer this time of the morning.

"The old Peterson estate out on Cannons Road."

"Who is it?"

"A girl by the name of Bonnie Gray. A black-and-white unit is already there. The housekeeper called it in and was all hysterical. Meet me there?"

"I'm not familiar with that address. Give me some directions, would you?"

"Why don't I just pick you up?"

"I'll be waiting."

Five minutes later, he pulled into her side of the drive. Renting the little duplex near downtown had seemed like the best idea at the time. One day soon, she was going to make the time to go house hunting. Settling into the passenger seat, she said, "You must have been really close."

"Yeah, I always grab a cup of coffee at the little café over on St. John's. I was in the drive-thru when I got the call. That one's yours." He pointed to the steaming cup in the cup holder nearest her seat. "Cream and sugar are in the glove compartment."

"Coffee twice in the same week. Wow."

"Anything I can do to help, ma'am."

She shot him a grateful smile and opened the glove compartment. As she searched, she asked, "Okay, so what do we know about our dead body?"

"Just that it's a female with a single gunshot to the back of the head." He made a left turn, then a right. Took a sip of the steaming brew and replaced the cup back in the holder.

"Are Jake and his crew on the way?" Kit added one cream and three sugars. She placed the trash in the little bag looped around the cigarette lighter.

"They'll probably beat us there."

"What about Serena?" Kit had met Serena, the medical examiner, her second day on the job when she'd been called to a bank robbery. SWAT had taken out the robber and Serena had been called to clean up the mess. Tall, willowy, with straight as a stick, raven-colored hair, and ice blue eyes, she was gorgeous. In no way whatsoever would Kit have pegged her for an ME. And Kit thought she'd long gotten over making snap judgments based on people's looks.

"She'll be there."

Three more turns brought them to a large brick, middle-class home in what looked like a quiet older neighborhood. Noah parked behind the coroner's vehicle. Jake's van sat at the curb.

"Why is it called the old Peterson estate?" Kit couldn't help asking as she climbed from the car.

"Ages ago, the Peterson family lived out here. It was the biggest, nicest house on the block at the time. Residents still refer to it as the Peterson estate."

"So who lives here now?"

A frown crinkled his forehead. "The Grays. This case is going to be a sticky one." Before he had a chance to clarify, he was waved into the house.

Kit followed him up the front steps into a well-lit foyer. Seeing all the action taking place just in front of her, she scooted ahead while Noah stopped to say something to one of the CSU members.

Camera flashes nearly blinded her, but she ignored them and looked at Serena. "Hey."

The woman looked up, sorrow in her eyes. "She's so young."

Kit got a look at the victim for the first time. "Oh my."

"Yeah. Her name's Bonnie Gray. Twenty-five years old and getting ready to graduate from law school."

The gaping hole in the back of her head marred the once silky blonde hair. "What a waste." Forcing herself into objective mode, she asked, "Any sign of forced entry?"

"No, looks like she let the person in."

"So, it's possible she knew whoever killed her."

"More than possible. I'd say it's likely."

"Okay. Anyone else here?"

Serena turned the girl over and Kit gasped. "Did he . . .?"

"Yeah. Sick creep." Most of Bonnie's nose had been cut off. "Her mother's in the other room. She passed out when she saw her. The maid heard the ruckus. She had just entered the kitchen from the back door. When she came in the den, this is what she found. I managed to rouse the mother when I got here, but she wouldn't quit screaming. I know she has a bad heart. I don't know where she found the breath to scream like that. One of the paramedics finally gave her a sedative."

Kit took another look at Bonnie and shook her head. "If that was my kid, I'd need some drugs too. What about her father?"

"On a business trip to New York doing some research on a case. He's a criminal defense attorney."

"And a very good friend."

Kit turned to see a white-faced Stephen Wells staring down at Bonnie. His throat bobbed and she could have sworn there was a sheen of tears in his eyes. And of course, Edward, his intern, stood next to him, looking wide-eyed and a little uncertain.

And like he might have a weak stomach.

Raising a hand, he covered his mouth. Then he caught her eye and gave a weak grin around his hand. "I think I'm just going to wait outside."

Poor kid. She offered him a sympathetic smile. "Sure, there's no shame in that."

Appreciation at her understanding flashed. He left and she focused her attention on the DA. "Sir?"

"Bonnie's the daughter I never had. Her father is my best friend. We went through law school together." A heavy sigh. "He was so proud she was following in his footsteps." Another hard swallow. "This is going to hit him hard. Very hard."

"I'm so sorry."

"When the address came over the radio, another friend recognized it and called me."

Blowing out a sigh, Kit took another look at the dead girl. "We'll find them. Whoever did this."

He looked at her. "I'll be following this case closely. I want to know every detail when you and Noah know it. I'll have to keep her father in the loop."

"You bet." Compassion filled her. Along with a strong sense of responsibility. She'd never had a case that would be scrutinized to the nth degree. She'd have to make this personal. And she would. This is what Noah had meant when he said it was going to be a sticky case. She looked at Noah and the DA and said, "I'm going to see what I can find in her bedroom."

Noah watched his partner talking to Serena and marveled that two beautiful women would choose to wade through death on a daily basis. Not for the first time, he wondered if that was a sexist attitude. Probably. He was smart enough to keep those kinds of thoughts to himself, though. He'd hate to imagine how either woman would react if he voiced them aloud, but he just couldn't stop from wondering about it.

He'd already spoken to the DA before the man honed in on Kit and knew this case was going to be the cause of a few sleepless nights. Then again, he prayed they caught the killer before the sleepless nights had a chance to happen.

He turned back to Jake. "Found anything interesting?"

"A note."

"Really, what's it say?"

" 'I told you I was the best. Your nose isn't so high now, is it?' "

"So, he cut off her nose because he thought she was acting superior to him? And the best at what?" Noah asked no one in particular.

Jake shrugged. "Who knows? Maybe she beat him at tennis or something."

"Whoever did this knew her."

Kit walked up behind him, the DA on her heels. "Serena thinks that too. No sign of forced entry. I gave her bedroom a sweep and didn't see anything that would warrant murder. Some really nice pieces of jewelry that set somebody back a pretty penny."

"What kind of jewelry?" Stephen asked.

"You know. Things like a diamond watch, a gold and ruby tennis bracelet . . ." She shrugged. "The kind of jewelry any self-respecting debutante would have on her dresser." She paused and looked at Noah. "I did find a picture of a young man who could possibly be a boyfriend. It had been turned facedown on the nightstand."

"Lovers' spat?"

Kit shrugged.

An officer approached and held up a purse. "I found a student ID and a switchblade with the initials *JCM*. She went to Wofford Law College."

Noah lifted a brow. "Yeah. I know." He shot a look at the DA, who was still talking to Serena. "Interesting, isn't it?"

Kit looked at him. "Very. You think this murder is connected to the one that happened Monday? Walter Davis?"

"I don't know, but I sure think it's worth looking into."

"We need to know if the two victims, Walter and Bonnie, knew each other."

Noah blew out a sigh and nodded. "I guess we need to head over to the campus and do some digging, start questioning more friends. I want a list of every male student with those initials. Then we can try connecting her to any of them. The list can't be that long."

The officer said, "The knife was open and there's some blood on it."

"Really?" Kit frowned. "Hey Serena, any knife or cut marks on her besides her nose?"

Serena shook her head. "Not that I can tell. She's got some defensive wounds on her hands, but nothing that looks like it came from a knife."

"Wonder who the knife belongs to?"

Noah nodded. "We'll get all the prints we can from it and see who they match up to. In the meantime, I think it's time to go back to school." They let the DA know their plans and headed out.

Twenty minutes later, Noah pulled into the visitor spot in front of the registrar's office. They needed a schedule of classes in order to start tracking down students who were friends of Bonnie and Walter. Walter's family had said the young man didn't talk much about school and didn't come home often.

Bonnie's mother had been so distraught, she'd been able to give them nothing. The girl's father had yet to be reached.

Noah and Kit entered the building and gave twin sighs of relief at the blast of cool air. Noah smiled and approached the woman standing behind the barlike counter. Flashing his badge, he said, "Hello, ma'am."

Curiosity raised the woman's gray brows and she smoothed a hand down her khaki slacks. "May I help you?"

"I'm Detective Noah Lambert. This is my partner, Detective Kit Kenyon. I'm sure you've heard about the murder that happened Monday."

Sadness crossed her face. "Yes, I've heard. I'm Sandra Williams and I knew Walter, but just in passing. He seemed like such a nice boy."

Kit shifted beside him. "Do you know who any of his friends were?"

"No, not really. Like I said, I just barely knew him from when he would come in here for whatever reason. Very polite and well mannered."

"Could we get a printout of his schedule and one for Bonnie Gray?"

A phone rang in the background and the woman glanced at it before jerking her startled gaze back to Noah. "Bonnie?"

Noah and Kit exchanged glances. "Yes, why? Do you know her?"

"Yes. She helps out here in the registrar's office sometimes." She waved a hand. "Not that she needed the money, but she said she enjoyed the work."

"Hey Sandra?" a male voice from an unseen location called. "You've got a phone call."

She nodded and turned to head in the direction of the voice. A minute later, a young man in his early twenties came to the counter. "I hope nothing bad has happened. Sandra said you needed a couple of schedules."

"Please."

He nodded and sat down at the computer. Within seconds, the printer whirred.

Kit held her hand out for the first one. Noah grabbed the second. They placed them side by side on the counter and scanned each one.

"Huh. No classes together."

"Nope, not this time around. Some of the same classes, just different professors."

Sandra Williams came back to the counter. "Is Bonnie dead too?" Tears filled her eyes. Kit hadn't had to say a word. The woman read it on her face.

"We need to ask you a few questions, if that's all right."

"Sure." A white tissue dabbed at the corner of a red-rimmed eye.

"Do you know any of Bonnie's friends? Who she hung out with? Did she mention anyone when she was working with you?"

"She . . . um . . . had a couple of sorority sisters she was pretty close to. Megan Lee and Chelsea Bennett. If anyone could tell you what you need to know, it would be one of them."

Noah glanced at the young man still standing behind the counter hanging on every word. No doubt the story would be around campus the minute they walked out the door.

Kit smiled at the distraught woman. "Thank you. We may have some more questions later."

"That's fine. I'll be here. I'll want to know when the funeral is."

Compassion crossed Kit's face and Noah knew exactly what she was feeling at that moment. It never got easier seeing grief. "We know where to find you then. I'm sure the funeral will be announced in the paper."

She thanked them and turned to disappear into the back.

Noah looked at Kit. "Okay, so let's track down Megan and Chelsea and see what they can tell us."

The Judge banged his hand against the desk and let out a growl. The disrespect, the humiliation. How dare he? Couldn't he see she was his? The Judge had chosen her and now this.

Curses flew from his lips as he thought about how he would get even. And he would.

Various methods flittered through his mind. He would love to put the gun against the base of his head and pull the trigger.

But this man was different. Cops were difficult to take by surprise. He knew that from firsthand experience. And while they were easy to fool most of the time, he couldn't take a chance on messing up a cop killing—and he had to make sure he left no evidence behind.

It had to be fast, unexpected—and from a distance. A thought occurred to him. If he killed one, he'd have to kill two more. Because it had to be three. If he deviated from three, everything would be wrong.

The Judge rubbed his lips. So, he needed a plan. A different plan for taking out a cop. Then two more.

He'd come up with one.

Soon.

8

Kit's rubber-soled shoes didn't make a sound on the carpeted floor as they headed to find Chelsea Bennett. "Chelsea's on the second floor, room 208. Steps or elevator?"

Noah grunted. "Steps, I guess."

They found the stairwell and trotted up. Kit examined the numbers on each door and found room number 208 around the corner.

A quick rap on the door got the attention of the professor. He opened it, curiosity stamped on his aging features. Kit flashed her badge and asked, "Could we speak with Chelsea Bennett please?"

"Sure." He turned and said, "Chelsea, would you step outside for a moment?"

A young black girl in her midtwenties appeared. "Yes?"

Noah gestured at the empty classroom next door and asked her to take a seat. Kit and Noah flanked her in the desks on either side of her.

Kit said, "We need to ask you some questions about Bonnie Gray."

"Sure, what about her?" Fear flickered. "Is she all right?"

"Uh . . . no, no she's not." Noah cleared his throat. "She was killed sometime this morning in her home."

"What?" she screeched, as her eyes darted back and forth between the two of them. Kit laid a hand over the girl's clenched fist. Chelsea shook her off and bolted to her feet. Tears tracked their way down her dark cheeks. "He finally did it, didn't he?"

"What? Who did what?" Noah stood with her.

"That no good ex of hers. Justin Marlowe." She paced to the front of the room, then back. A tear teetered on the edge of her chin, then fell to the floor. "He told her when she broke up with him that if he couldn't have her, no one would."

"Did she file a restraining order on him?"

Contempt dripped from Chelsea's already black eyes. "Yes, she filed a restraining order." She snorted. "Fat lot of good that did her, huh?"

"Well, we don't know that it was her ex, but we'll certainly check him out. Do you know where we can find him?"

"Either strung out in his daddy's big ole house or on the golf course. He's into the drug scene. It was the reason Bonnie broke up with him. When she found out he was a user, she was livid. There was no way she was going to be connected with someone who might ruin her career before she even got started."

Chelsea's anger seemed to suddenly drain and she dropped back into the chair to bury her face in her hands. Sobs shook her shoulders.

Kit rubbed one and said, "I'm so sorry."

Without looking up, Chelsea murmured wearily, "You should be. You're supposed to protect people like Bonnie from people like Justin Marlowe."

"I know. You're right." Kit paused, her heart breaking for the second time that day in the face of such grief. "Our next stop will be to locate Justin and ask him a few questions."

Chelsea sighed. "Good luck pinning anything on him. He's the son of Judge Harrison Marlowe."

Bitterness bit the air around them and Kit looked at Noah. Disgust painted his features and she felt relief that they were going to be on the same page with this situation.

"Being the son of a judge isn't going to keep him out of jail if he's a murderer."

A laugh of disbelief escaped the girl. "Uh-huh."

Kit didn't bother to argue. Only by her actions would she be able to prove to Chelsea that just because Justin had connections didn't mean he could get away with murder—if he'd actually done it. "Is there anyone we can call for you?"

"No." She pulled in a deep breath. "I'll need to call Megan. She's been sick with the flu all week. If she's better, we'll go over to Bonnie's parents' house after everything settles down and see if we can do anything to help Mr. Gray with his wife. Bonnie was staying there until she graduated. Money wasn't an issue, but her mother's health was."

"We heard. Did Bonnie know Walter Davis?"

"Sure." She looked surprised. "You don't think Bonnie's death has anything to do with Walter, do you?"

"We don't know. We're trying to find out if there's a connection."

"Walter and Bonnie didn't have any classes together this semester, but they were friends. Bonnie and Heather were pretty good friends too, although Heather didn't like it when Walter and Bonnie got together without her there. She was a little on the possessive side."

Interesting. "Would she have done anything to hurt Bonnie?"

Chelsea shook her head. "No way. She might have been a little jealous of Walter and Bonnie's friendship, but she wouldn't have done anything to hurt anyone. She's not like that."

"Okay, thanks for your help. Here's my card. Give us a call if you can think of anything else."

Chelsea took it and turned to go. She stopped and just stood there for a minute.

"Chelsea?" Kit asked.

The girl did a slow one-eighty. "I can't not tell you this."

"What?"

Swiping her fingers under her eyes, Chelsea blew out a sigh

and looked at the ceiling. "Shortly after Bonnie broke up with Justin, she started acting . . . weird."

"Define weird," Noah requested.

Hands spread, Chelsea shook her head. "I'm not sure I can. Stuff like not being available for our usual girls' night out thing. Or saying she had to study, but not being home to do it."

"What do you think all that means?"

"I wasn't sure. When I questioned her about it, she got this little secretive look in her eyes and wouldn't say a word."

Kit raised a brow. "So Bonnie had a secret?"

"And expensive jewelry," Noah added. "From an admirer?"

Chelsea nodded. "I think so, but she never said who and I never saw her with anyone. And then two weeks ago, she just leaves town. She tells me she's got some crazy plans and one day she'll be able to tell me all about what's going on. Then she's just . . . gone. I hadn't seen her since."

Kit looked at Noah. "I saw some really nice pieces of jewelry in her room, but didn't think much about it. She comes from a wealthy family, so it's not unusual she would have that kind of stuff. But in light of what Chelsea's saying, I wonder if we could trace some of it."

"Possibly." He looked at Chelsea. "Thanks so much for your time. You have Detective Kenyon's card. Don't hesitate to use it if you think of anything else."

"I will, but I don't think you're going to need me anymore." The tears surged again, and she tried to blink them away, only to have them trickle down her cheeks. "Get Justin and you'll have your murderer. He's into drugs. Selling, using, whatever. He would have access to a lot of money from his father too. Don't let his good looks and charm fool you. He's a loser and wouldn't hesitate to resort to murder if he thought he could get away with it."

Without another word, she vacated the room. Kit looked at Noah. "Doesn't sound like Megan would be much help if she's had the flu all week, but we can give it a shot. Where to now? The ex-boyfriend?"

"Yeah. Justin Marlowe. Think that could be our *JCM*?"

"I think it's a real good possibility."

As they headed back to the car, Kit's eyes took in the campus. "Nice. They've really put some money into this place."

"Gotta give the kids a reason to come, I guess."

"What, an education isn't reason enough?"

Noah laughed and reached for the door handle. "Not in this day and age."

"The buildings are gorgeous." And they were. Tall and sprawling yet beautifully landscaped, surrounded with green grass, maple and oak trees. The campus had that wealthy neighborhood feel to it. She almost expected to see someone grilling steaks on the porch of one of the buildings.

Her phone rang as she slid into the passenger seat. "Hi, Serena."

Noah put the key in the ignition and waited. She turned the phone on speaker so he could hear.

"Hey, Kit." Serena's low alto came over the line. "I've been going over Bonnie's and Walter's bodies looking for any similarities."

"So, what'd you find?"

"They both had body parts removed with an extremely sharp blade. I think it's this knife you found. According to the lab, it's got Bonnie's blood on it and Walter's, although they think our killer tried to wash it. Walter's blood was in some of the harder-to-clean places like little nooks and crannies."

"So we can connect the two deaths."

"Absolutely. And under Bonnie's fingernails, I scraped out some skin. So we'll have some DNA to compare with any suspect you pick up."

"We're on the way to the ex-boyfriend's house now. Apparently they'd had an argument over his drug habit and she sent him on his way. It's probably his knife too. The initials match."

"Ah. Well, see if he'll offer up a DNA sample and the lab can compare it."

"Will do. Did you hear anything from the lab? What about prints on the knife?"

"I actually talked to one of the techs before calling you because I knew you'd ask. Candace said there were several prints. Some were Bonnie's. The others matched up to a Justin Marlowe. He's been in the system before."

"That's the ex-boyfriend."

"And while the scratches on Bonnie's hands looked like defensive wounds, they didn't come from the knife. When I asked Jake if there were any other weapons around that could have made the wounds, he said no, but the housekeeper told him she'd done some pruning in their rose garden the night before. The scratches are consistent with superficial wounds from the thorns on the roses."

Kit looked at Noah and he gave a little nod. Into the phone, she said, "Okay, that makes sense. Although, I will say I think it's a little strange that he brought a knife *and* a gun. Most killers pick one or the other and stick with it. Then again, if you wanted a quick death, you'd shoot someone. And if you wanted a body part, you'd need a way to cut if off. Hence the knife. Huh."

"I don't know, but I'd say it doesn't look good for Mr. Marlowe."

Kit hung up. Then she turned to the laptop mounted on her side of the car and typed in a few keystrokes. As she did so, Noah's phone rang. He backed out of the parking space as he spoke into the phone. "Hello? Oh, hello, Ms. Longfellow. How are you today?"

Kit looked at him and he winked at her. Curious, she listened unabashedly. He said, "Yes, ma'am. I understand. I can't make it over right now, but I'll call someone to swing by and check things out. All right." Pause. "You're welcome. Bye-bye."

When he hung up, Kit waited for the explanation she knew he'd provide. A small smile played around the corner of his lips. "That was Ms. Longfellow. She's eighty-two years old and is a sweet little old lady who thinks someone is breaking into her house about once a week."

"Oh. And she calls you?"

"Yes. And brings me a casserole every time to apologize for the inconvenience." He dialed a number and arranged to have an officer swing by Ms. Longfellow's house. Then he put the car in drive.

Kit just stared at him, then blurted, "You're like the sweetest guy I've ever met."

A red flush put in an instant appearance on his face. "You'd do the same for one of your friends."

She hesitated, thinking the first few times she would, but after that her patience might run out. "Hmm."

She dropped the subject to look at the computer screen in front of her. A picture of a mug shot popped up and Justin Marlowe stared back at her. "Nice-looking kid—even after being arrested."

"Kid?" Amusement deepened the corners of his mouth as he cruised to the stop sign. "He's not that much younger than we are."

Kit flushed. "Maybe not. Some days I guess I just feel a whole lot older than my thirty-two years."

He nodded, his smile fading. "Yeah. I know what you mean."

"Hey, look at this. He was arrested once two years ago for assault. Got it thrown out and was pretty clean up until about six months ago."

Noah flicked a glance at the screen and exclaimed, "Hey, I know that guy. I was part of the sting operation where he got caught in our net. I remember being furious because Daddy got him off."

She half turned in the seat to face him. "Huh. Well, not much Daddy can do this time if his kid committed murder. And if it was a violent assault, it's likely they took some DNA."

Just as Noah opened his mouth to respond, the passenger window beside Kit ruptured, glass flew, and Noah yelled as he yanked the wheel. The car spun a one-eighty and careened into a fire hydrant.

Kit gasped as the seat belt cut into her shoulder and across her lap. Shattered glass from the dash slapped her in the face along with a spray of water. "Noah!"

"Hold on!"

Another thwack sounded and the back windshield exploded. Kit felt something hit her arm, then pain radiated upward toward her neck.

A scream escaped before she could bite it back, and Noah cast her a split-second concerned look before spinning the wheel to round a corner. The car jerked and rocked up on two wheels before settling back down with a whiplash-inducing bounce.

Ignoring the pain coursing through her, she scrambled for her gun.

"I'm going for that parking garage," Noah gritted. "He's up on a building somewhere following our progress."

Kit tried to move her right arm and bit her lip in agony. That wasn't going to work. Placing the gun in her lap, she reached for the radio. "Officers need assistance. Rooftop shooter on the campus of Wofford Law College. Bullets coming from the direction of the mock courthouse building on Rochester Street. Shooter's location unknown." She threw the radio down and grabbed the gun again. She didn't have any idea who she was going to aim at, but just holding it made her feel better.

With a squeal of tires and the smell of rubber burning in her nose, Noah pulled to a stop under cover of the parking garage and scrambled from the car. Gun in hand, he raced to the edge of the deck and looked out.

Kit followed after him but paused as a wave of dizziness hit her. Sirens registered in her subconscious. She fought the urge to close her eyes and let the weakness in her knees win. With a determined effort, Kit made it over to stand beside Noah.

"Are you okay?"

His question echoed in her ears. "Yeah. Fine."

"You're bleeding."

She gave her arm a glance and winced. Blood saturated her shirt and dripped from the tips of her fingers. "And it hurts. But I'll worry about that later. Have you figured out where he's shooting from?"

"I think he was on top of the campus courthouse to your

left." He moved closer to examine her arm. "Is that from a bullet or glass?"

"I don't know yet. Do you see him?" Her eyes scanned the rooftops of the buildings. Nothing.

Officers and other police personnel swarmed the streets, evacuating them, searching the buildings, and looking for the shooter.

"No. Come on, he's gone by now."

Kit steadied herself against the concrete barrier. "I wonder if he's really gone or just blending in with the crowd?"

Noah frowned. "Good point." He turned and edged out to take another look.

"Noah?" She slid to the floor of the parking garage.

"Yeah?"

"I think I'm gonna pass out."

Her eyes shut and this time she couldn't shove the smothering blackness away.

9

"Kit!"

In one smooth movement, Noah caught her up in his arms, absently wondering how someone who weighed next to nothing could be so solid. Grunting, he wound his way through the ever-expanding numbers of police and emergency people.

Spying an ambulance to his left, he swerved and headed for it.

"Noah!"

He glanced over his shoulder but didn't slow his pace. Connor Wolfe, Kit's brother-in-law. "This way!" Noah shouted.

Connor broke away from the group he'd been consulting with and jogged toward him.

The paramedics saw him coming and immediately opened the back doors of the vehicle. Connor arrived just as Noah was passing Kit up to be placed on the gurney.

"What happened to her?" the fortysomething paramedic asked as he started checking her vitals. His partner, a young, fresh-faced kid who looked like she still belonged in junior high, grabbed the plastic oxygen hose and put it around Kit's head.

"I'm not sure. We were shot at and the window blew out. Glass hit her, but she seemed fine until she keeled over." Anxiety ate at him. Once again, a partner of his had been hurt. Fortunately, Kit's wound probably wasn't fatal and yet . . . "Check her arm."

The paramedic leaned over her and probed. Kit groaned and Noah breathed a silent sigh of relief. The man looked up. "She's got a deep gash here. Until I get it cleaned up, I won't be able to tell if it's from a bullet or a piece of glass. The way car windows are made now, I'm guessing this was caused by a bullet."

Noah flinched as the man continued his examination.

"She's lost a good bit of blood. Looks like the bullet may have nicked an artery. We'll get her patched up here, slow the bleeding, and transport her to Regional Hospital. Will you have someone meet us there? Family? A fellow officer?"

"Absolutely. I'm going to go back and see what they've got on the shooter."

"We'll take care of her."

With one last look at Kit, Noah exited the ambulance to hop down next to Connor, who asked, "How is she? What happened?"

"She's all right for now, I think. Looks like she got grazed by a bullet. Nothing life threatening. I'll meet up with them at the hospital when I'm done here."

The ambulance took off and Connor swept a hand over his mouth. Relief stood out on his features, and Noah realized how worried Connor had been.

"Good. I'm sure the family will want to know." Connor placed the call and told Sam what had happened, then he looked at Noah. "Samantha will call Jamie and their parents. They'll be bedside in twenty minutes."

Noah nodded, glad she had the kind of family that would be there for her. "Tell me about the shooter," he said.

"You pinpointed it. Taking your suggestion that he was up on the campus courthouse, we went there first. There was evidence someone had been up there. Didn't find any shell casings or any evidence to indicate the type of gun used, but CSU will get all that out of your car, probably."

"I don't think he knew what he was doing."

"Beg your pardon?" Connor lifted a brow.

"He was a lousy shot. Look up there." Noah pointed and Connor's eyes followed the direction indicated. "He had a perfect vantage point. He picked that well. The building's tall, but not so tall he couldn't see into the car. It's just three stories. But then he misses. He's not a marksman."

"Let's go see what he saw."

The two of them crossed the street, entered the building, and found the emergency exit stairs. The most likely way to access the roof. Taking the stairs two at a time, Noah reached the top first. He shoved open the door and stepped back out into the blazing sunlight. The city smells assaulted him. The campus diner sat to his left, a garbage dump in the small alley to his right, and the stadium about half a mile beyond that.

Making his way over to the edge of the building, he squinted and scanned the rest of the landscape—most specifically where he and Kit had been parked on the street.

Connor stood beside him and pointed. "Look at that."

"Yeah, I see it. A perfect view of the law building all the way down the street and around the corner."

"You were sitting ducks."

Noah paced over to the corner and looked down again. Stepped back three paces and studied the rooftop. "Right here."

Connor walked over. "Looks like knee prints." He pointed about a foot behind the scuffed dirt to a smaller set of marks. "Tips of his shoes. He was crouched here maybe?"

"Could be. The crime scene unit will be here in a few minutes. Don't know that they'll be able to find anything else worthwhile, but we'll give them the opportunity." Noah pulled out his phone and punched the one-digit speed dial number for Jake Hollister.

The man answered on the second ring. "What ya need, Noah?"

"We're up on the roof where we think the shooter knelt down to wait on Kit and me to leave the building. Wanna come take a look?"

"Be right there."

Noah hung up and told Connor. "I'm going to get to the hospital to check on Kit. You got this covered?"

"Yeah, let me know how she's doing as soon as you can, will you?"

"Sure thing." Noah made his way back down to street level and over to a car that had been delivered as a replacement for the one that had been shot to pieces. As he climbed in and cranked the vehicle, he wondered at the unrest in his heart. The agitation he felt when he thought about Kit and the danger she'd been in. Not willing to dwell on it, he made the ten-minute ride to the hospital, telling himself to think about something else.

Because if he continued to think about Kit, he'd have to admit his attraction to her.

And that just wasn't happening.

Yet.

10

Kit shifted on the hospital bed and winced at the stinging throb in her arm. She'd refused all narcotic painkillers and was paying the price.

Jamie handed her a cup of ice water and said, "Take a pill, Kit, you're not going anywhere anytime soon."

Resisting the urge to grind her molars, Kit said, "Well, I'm not staying here much longer. As soon as the doctor comes back and pronounces that I'm not at death's door, I'm outta here."

Samantha chuckled from her spot on the window seat. "You should have been *my* twin. You sound just like me."

Kit's lips curved before she could stop them. "Aw, you guys. You didn't have to rush right over here."

Jamie let out an indignant snort. "You were hurt. Of course we did."

"Where's Andy?" If she got Sam talking about her son, Kit would be able to fade into the background when it came to topics of conversation.

Immediately Samantha's eyes lit up. "Our next-door neighbor is retired and just adores Andy. Anytime I need a break or an emergency set of hands, she's always willing."

"You're so fortunate."

"You bet I am. Mom and Dad would be here too, if they hadn't taken a spur of the moment trip to the mountains this week. They're ready for cooler weather."

Kit grimaced. "Aren't we all?"

Before either sister could make a comment, a knock sounded on the door. Praying it was the doctor arriving to spring her, Kit called out, "Come in."

When Noah's reddish-blond head appeared around the door, her heart started pounding. What was he doing here?

Then he smiled and her stomach flipped. Wow. Where did that come from?

"Hey there, partner, glad to see you awake."

"Yeah, me too."

"How's the arm?"

"Just grazed by a bullet. It's fine and I'm ready to get back to work."

Sam snorted. "When the doctor releases her, she needs to go home and rest."

"Not a chance," Kit shot back. "I've got cases to solve. Especially two murders." She looked at Noah. "What did you find out about the shooting? You catch the guy?"

"No. He was on top of the law school mock courthouse, though. He had a real nice view of us as we left the classroom building."

She frowned. "So he was waiting on us?"

"Looks that way."

"But why? And how did he know we were going to be there?"

Noah sighed and Kit watched Samantha and Jamie bounce their attention back and forth between her and the man still standing in the doorway.

"As near as we can figure it, there are two options. The first: he followed us from the crime scene."

She grimaced. "I don't like the sound of that and what all that entails."

"Yeah, me either."

"And the second?"

"He was already here looking to take out another kid, saw us, figured we were investigating, and decided to shoot one of us instead."

"I don't like that one either."

"Right. You have any other thoughts?"

Kit wrinkled her nose. Did she? "Not really. Everything you said makes sense, unfortunately."

A short rap sounded on the open door and they all turned as one to see the doctor standing behind Noah. Noah moved aside to let the man in.

Kit smiled and did her best to look as perky as possible. When she shifted on the bed, she kept her grimace under wraps. "So, you ready to let me out of here?"

"With instructions to go home and rest."

"Sure." Agreeable innocence all the way. She ignored Sam's snort of disbelief and Jamie's giggle. Noah just rolled his eyes and shook his head.

The doctor took it all in, then eyed her, one side of his mouth lifting. "Right, I can see you're going to do exactly as ordered."

She couldn't lie. "Well, maybe not *exactly* as ordered, but I do promise to take it a little easier than normal."

He sighed and nodded. "Fine. You're not the first cop to cross my medical path."

"Any limitations on her job duties?" This from Noah.

Kit glared at him with a how-is-this-your-business look. He met her stare for stare. She finally looked away as she silently conceded he had a right to be concerned. She'd been hurt. If they got into a situation where she didn't have his back, he could be killed.

The doc shrugged. "Not really. She can do what she feels like doing." He looked at Kit. "The bullet just grazed you, really. There was a bit of blood loss, but you've recovered nicely in the few hours you've been here. By tomorrow you should be good to go."

"Why did she pass out?"

"Noah . . ."

"Come on, Kit, you can't go back to work if you're not really ready."

She snapped her mouth shut and looked at the doctor. He said, "Probably from a combination of shock and pain—and maybe some sleepless nights?" A pointed look.

"Maybe," she mumbled at his direct, questioning stare.

"I would recommend staying here tonight. Tomorrow, you can do whatever. I promise I'll let you go without argument—as long as you don't develop any complications overnight."

Kit groaned and Noah nodded. Sam and Jamie stared her down, arms crossed, expressions stern. The sudden swell of tears took her by surprise. The cocoon of their caring and concern surrounded her, and the fight went out of her.

Closing her eyes to hide her rocky emotions, she leaned her head back and said, "Okay."

A soft hand covered hers and she felt stable enough to look up. Jamie stood there, a small smile dimpling her cheek. It was like looking into a mirror. An exact replica of herself. She still wasn't used to it. "Rest, Kit."

"Right."

Noah patted her shoulder and the innocent touch made her tingle to her toes. "Connor's going with me to the Marlowe house. We want to see if we can pick him up for questioning."

She felt her lower lip push out and wanted to whine, "But I want to go." Instead, she pressed her lips together and nodded like the adult she was. "Okay, I guess I'm in no shape to do anything today." The aggravating throb in her arm pulsed in agreement. "Just keep me updated, will you?"

"You bet."

Noah left, and Kit felt two pairs of eyes boring holes into her. She lifted a brow. "What?"

Jamie flushed and Samantha shrugged. "Why are you being so stubborn?"

Kit set her jaw. "It's my case and I . . ." Why was she being so stubborn? "I don't really know. I just feel like I need to be the one . . ." She trailed off once more, looked away from her sisters' prying gazes, and stared out the window.

Why was she so antsy? So ready to push herself when she silently admitted her arm was killing her? Why wouldn't she just take the little pill and drift off into oblivion?

Because she was embarrassed? A little. But she'd had no more control over that bullet than she had Brian pulling that trigger at the hostage situation. But that wasn't all, she slowly realized.

It was also because, for the first time in her law enforcement career, she felt like she had to prove to her partner that she was good enough simply because of Noah's initial reaction to having a woman for a partner. The answer came out of nowhere, startling her so much, she physically jerked.

"Kit? Are you all right?"

Samantha had walked to the edge of the bed while Kit wandered around in her heavy thoughts. "I'm fine. A little tired." She didn't have to fake the yawn that took her by surprise.

"All right." Samantha leaned over and kissed the top of her head. "Get some rest and we'll check on you later."

Her sisters left and Kit sat alone in the sudden quiet of her room. She looked at the bedside phone. She really should call her mother. Her adoptive mom. But what would Kit say to her? Their last conversation had ended in recriminations and tears.

Was she up to that?

No.

She pressed the button to call the nurse.

A little pill sounded pretty good right now. But after a few hours of sleep and escape from the pain, she'd hit the ground running.

This was her case. She would work it and solve it. No one was going to take that away from her. Not her good-looking partner and definitely not some trigger-happy killer.

❖

Crumbling the third note he'd written into a tight wad, the Judge tossed it on the floor, muttering. "Get it right, idiot. Got to get it right. It's got to be perfect." It had to be. He had to make sure everything fell into place just as it was supposed to do. His son—the one he would someday have—would expect that of his father. He would look up to him and believe him to be a god. The Judge almost smiled at the thought.

Then he frowned. He'd gotten careless. He shouldn't have taken the shot when he did. As a result, he missed. He ground his teeth and berated himself. It was the rifle's fault, he decided. He would have to work with the sights. The old gun hadn't been fired in years. Not since his father, a sniper, had used it in the service. Yeah, that was it. The stupid rifle. It wasn't his fault after all. He'd fix the rifle and try again.

But for now, he needed to focus. He still had to finish his current mission.

Get rid of those who'd mocked him.

The Judge placed the pen to paper once more and scribbled his thoughts. When he was finished, he sang aloud, "Row, row, row your boat, gently down the stream. Merrily, merrily, merrily, merrily, let's see how loud you scream." He gave a little chuckle at his wittiness, then frowned as the rage built. "Laugh at me, will you? I'll teach you. I'll teach you all."

He slammed a fist onto the desk.

"Hey man, you okay?"

The Judge jumped and turned, slid his palm over the paper. "Oh, sorry, didn't hear you come in."

"Obviously." A backpack hit the chair next to the television. "Have you taken up talking to yourself now?"

The Judge forced a chuckle. "Just rehearsing."

"I thought you'd already given the big performance."

"No, that one was minor compared to this one." He pictured the moment the bullet would enter his next victim. Right after she begged for mercy and told him how superior he was.

The other man cocked his head, studied him for a moment,

then shrugged. "Whatever, man. I'm taking Allison out tonight. Catch up to you later."

"Right. Later."

His roommate was a likable guy. One who didn't question the Judge or his odd ways. He kept to himself, respected the Judge's privacy, and never, ever, mocked him.

Fortunately for him.

Once he had the place to himself again, he walked down the hall to his bedroom and reached under the bed to slide the cardboard box toward him. Picking it up, he set it on the bed.

Opening the lid with his left hand, he pulled the newspaper clipping from his back pocket and placed it on the right side of the box, the edge snug up against the ninety-degree angle. On top of that, he set the watch he'd taken from Walter. The watch Walter had tapped while rolling his eyes.

Should have plucked his other eye out too.

Then he chuckled. Oh yeah. He shot the other one out. No plucking required.

Then he pulled the school schedule from the left side of the box.

And smiled.

He flicked the paper and said, "You're next."

THURSDAY

THURSDAY

11

The next morning, Kit's release from the hospital went surprisingly fast, and before she knew it, she was on her way home, Jamie at the wheel.

Not the direction she wanted to go.

Her phone buzzed and she grabbed it. "Hello?"

"Hey Kit, how are you doing this morning?"

"Peachy."

His chuckle warmed her. "Connor and I went by the Marlowe house last night to find Justin. No luck. The kid was gone and hadn't come home yet, according to the officer assigned to watch the house."

"Rats."

"Yeah. We didn't knock on the door. We decided we wanted the surprise factor on our side."

"So you're not calling ahead, huh?"

"Nope, if the kid is guilty, we don't want Daddy shipping him off to some overseas friends, if you get my meaning."

"I get it."

"We're waiting on the call from the officer watching the house. As soon as the kid shows, we'll grab him."

"Sounds good. I'll meet you there."

"Are you sure you feel up to it?"

Her arm did feel much better this morning, and while she'd skipped the narcotic offered, she'd popped a couple of ibuprofen. It helped. Some. It was a good thing she'd qualified to use her weapon with either hand. Otherwise, she knew she'd be benched until her right arm healed.

"I'm fine. I promise." She paused, then said softly, "I may take a few risks sometimes, but I would never take one that put your life on the line. You have my solemn word on that."

For a moment silence was her only answer. Then, "All right. I wasn't worried about that, but thanks for saying it. Tell your chauffeur to drop you off at the station. I'll give you a lift home after we're done with Justin. Surely, he'll show up today."

"Great." Her adrenalin surged, almost knocking out the rest of the pain. She stuck her phone in the back pocket of the jeans Jamie had brought to the hospital this morning. Kit turned to her sister. "Drop me off at the station, will you?"

Jamie glanced at her. "You sure?"

"I'm sure."

Jamie sighed and said, "You really are a Cash. Same stubborn genes."

Kit winced inside but pasted a smile on her face. "Yep." It wasn't that she minded the reminder of her adoption or the fact that she didn't grow up in the Cash household, and yet . . . she did.

Guilt pressed in on her. She'd had a wonderful family. A loving dad who'd taken her fishing and taught her how to ride her bike, shoot her first gun, and gave her permission to belt any boy who took unwanted liberties. A pang of grief overshadowed the guilt.

Eleven months ago, he'd taken his last breath right after he confessed they'd kept her adoption a secret. Kit's birth father, he explained, had an addiction to pain pills. One afternoon he'd left several on the table. Samantha, arriving home from school in tears, followed her father's example and swallowed a handful of pills to dull the pain of her bad day.

After making sure Samantha would be all right, her father packed a bag and walked out, never knowing he left behind a wife pregnant with twins.

Kit closed her eyes, remembering the look on her birth mother's face as she told the story. The grief that twisted her features when she'd talked about finding out she was expecting twins. She'd been terrified. One baby was burden enough. But two? She couldn't imagine it. She called her best friend, who lived in Raleigh, and asked—would she take one of the babies?

Kit's adoptive mother agreed and Kit had grown up apart from her birth family, never knowing she had the siblings she'd craved through her entire childhood.

Anger twisted through her. Why had she been the one taken? Why not Jamie? How different would their lives have been if Jamie had been the one raised by the Kenyons and not Kit?

And why did it bother her so much? Cause her sleepless nights and tortured dreams? She'd had a *great* childhood, for the most part. And yet it didn't seem to matter. She remembered being lonely sometimes, desperately wishing for a sibling to play with on those rainy days when she was stuck inside with nothing to do.

And then there was her adoptive mother. Her sweet, hovering, overprotective mother.

"What's wrong?"

Startled, Kit jumped. "Huh?"

"I can hear your teeth grinding together all the way over here." Jamie quirked a small smile and Kit returned it. Weakly.

"Just . . . thinking."

"About?"

Did she want to say anything? How would Jamie feel if Kit told her the whole story? Glancing at her twin, she opened her mouth to find out, when her cell phone vibrated. Snatching it back out of her pocket, she saw that it was Noah. "Hello?"

"How far away are you?"

"About a minute and a half."

"I'll meet you at the car. We've got eyes on Justin Marlowe. He just pulled into the driveway and entered the house."

"Be there in a sec."

Kit clicked the phone off and looked at Jamie. Her sister. A young woman who'd suffered indescribable pain and terror at the hands of a deranged stalker—and come out a stronger person than Kit could ever hope to be.

And yet, she too had survived an ordeal that had caused her nightmares for years. A childhood ordeal she rarely discussed yet relived each time she walked into a hostage situation. Shuddering, she breathed a sigh of relief when the station came into view.

Not waiting for the car to stop, she opened the door and hopped out with only a bit of jaw-clenching pain running up her arm. Ignoring it, she waved goodbye to Jamie and headed for Noah, who was just climbing into the unmarked car.

She slid into the passenger seat and grabbed her seat belt. "Ready?"

"Ready."

Thank goodness he didn't ask if she was sure she was up to it.

"When did he get home?"

"Just a few minutes ago."

Ten minutes later, they flashed their badges at the guard who raised the gate and allowed them entrance to the subdivision. Noah followed the GPS directions and pulled up in front of a two-story brick house. Noah waved to the other unmarked car. She was glad they were there in case they needed backup.

Kit studied the house and observed, "The judge is living pretty well, isn't he?"

"I'll say."

"Don't suppose we'll get lucky and Justin will be just waiting for us to ring his bell so he can confess to killing his ex, do you?"

Noah quirked a smile. "Somehow I doubt it, but guess it won't hurt to try."

"Right." She drew in a deep breath at the smile and did her best to ignore the sudden surge of butterflies in the pit of her stomach. What in the world? She was investigating a murder, for crying out loud. Being attracted to her partner was not an option.

Was it? She'd never found herself in this kind of situation before and wasn't sure of the protocol.

She cleared her throat and climbed from the vehicle.

Noah had already started up the steps to the door. Before he could press the doorbell, it opened, and a good-looking young man in his midtwenties stood before them dressed in a green robe and matching slippers. Red-veined eyes, shadowed underneath with dark circles, widened in surprise. "May I help you?"

They flashed their badges, then Kit's eyes zoomed in on the area just above Justin's collar. "Yeah, how'd you get those scratches, Justin?"

The young man crossed his arms and leaned against the doorjamb. "None of your business."

"Heard you had a little argument with Bonnie."

"What? Who'd you hear that from?" He snorted. "Oh wait, don't tell me. Bonnie called the cops? Over our little tiff?"

"Not exactly."

"Then it was that little witch, Chelsea, huh?" He called her a few more choice names and ended his tirade with a vow to cut out her tongue.

Noah and Kit exchanged glances. "Violent, aren't you?"

"Just toward that—" He reined in his words.

Kit nodded. "We get the picture, Justin. You don't like her."

"She should keep her mouth shut."

"Why would you think we'd hear about your argument from her?" Kit shifted and Justin moved to close the door as he stepped outside onto the porch.

"Those two are thick as thieves. She's never liked me and never made any secret of that fact. Bonnie probably called her up and told her we had a fight and she called you guys." He shook his head. "Whatever."

"We need you to come downtown with us and answer a few questions."

Hesitation slid over him. "Why? I haven't done anything wrong."

"Because we need you to answer a few more questions about your relationship with Bonnie." She deliberately didn't say anything about Bonnie's death. She wanted him to trip over himself and his lies.

But he opened the door and stepped back. "Forget it."

Kit narrowed her eyes. "We can do this the hard way or the easy way. It's really up to you."

"Try *no* way." He attempted to shut the door in their faces, and Kit stuck a foot to block it from closing all the way.

"Hey!" Justin stuck out an arm and caught Kit in the shoulder. Her shoulder that was attached to a very painful upper arm.

"Ah!" She spun around, blinking back tears and another scream. Desperately, she gathered herself under control and hardened her expression.

Noah stepped forward and grabbed the guy's arm, spun him around, and cuffed him. "You're under arrest for assaulting a police officer. You're also a suspect in the murder of Bonnie Gray."

Justin went still as a stone. "What? Someone killed Bonnie?"

"Yeah, you."

The young man went still as he stared at Noah. "Wh-what are you doing? Bonnie's dead? I didn't kill her! You're making a huge mistake!"

"Right," Kit snorted and stepped in front of him, keeping all signs of weakness or pain hidden.

Justin stared at her, fear igniting in his eyes.

Kit kept her guard up even as she confronted him. "So how'd you get those scratches from your ear to your collar?"

Nostrils flared. "I can explain those."

"So can I. You went to Bonnie's house to kill her and she put up a fight."

"No, that's not what happened."

"Save it. You have the right to remain silent . . ." She read him his rights.

Anger flushed away his shock and two bright red patches appeared on his cheeks. "Stop reading me my rights. I didn't do anything. I went there because she was seeing someone else and I wanted to know who it was!"

"Do you have a lawyer you want to call?"

"No! I don't need a lawyer! My dad won't let you get away with this."

"We'll talk downtown."

They listened to him protest his innocence all the way to the jail. By the time Noah pulled into the parking spot, Kit was ready to stuff cotton in her ears—or slap duct tape over Justin's mouth. Instead, with her good arm, she hauled Justin from the backseat and led him toward the door.

Once inside the interrogation room, Justin took a seat, his back ramrod straight, jaw clenched. "I didn't kill her."

Just as she was getting ready to fire off a few questions, a knock on the small square window of the door brought her up short. She shot Noah a look and he shrugged. Hiding her irritation, she muttered, "Hold that thought. I'll be back."

Stepping from the room, she came face-to-face with District Attorney Stephen Wells and the young intern Edward Richmond. Neither of them looked happy. Raising a brow, she asked, "May I help you?"

Noah exited the interrogation room and planted himself beside her.

The DA sighed. "Do you know who you have in that room?"

Noah gave a half laugh, half grunt. "Yes, I do. The question is, how do you know who's in there?"

"A neighbor witnessed the arrest and called Judge Marlowe, who in turn immediately called me to tell me to get my officers under control."

Noah crossed his arms and Kit felt her blood pressure kick it up a notch. "And your response?"

"I told him I was sure there was a good explanation and I'd look into it."

"There is a good explanation. The kid shoved a police officer. Not only that, he probably killed his ex-girlfriend. Unfortunately, being a judge's son isn't going to get him off of facing the consequences for all of that."

Thus far Edward, the intern, had kept his counsel. Now he asked, "What kind of evidence do you have?"

Kit jutted her jaw. "A knife with his initials and prints were found at the scene connecting the deaths of Bonnie Gray and Walter Davis. Not to mention the scratches that are going to match up with the DNA found under the victim's fingernails."

"But you won't know that for sure until you get the test results back."

Snotty kid. Kit kept her lips clamped and said, "He already admitted he could explain the scratches. Let's give him a chance." A chance to hang himself.

"Not without representation," Stephen was adamant.

"Where's the judge then? He can sit in and offer advice to his son."

"I believe he was wrapping up a court case and then heading straight over."

"Well, as soon as he gets here, let us know."

Kit stomped off with one last glare toward the DA and his sidekick.

12

"Are you going to press charges for assault?" Noah asked.

Kit snorted as she sat at her desk chair and propped her feet up on the top drawer that was stuck in a permanently open position. "No. What's the point?"

"Might teach him a lesson." Noah leaned against the desk to face her and crossed his arms. She really was a beautiful woman. Even with anger flushing her cheeks.

"Somehow I doubt it. In this case, it's no big deal." Her phone rang and Noah watched her good hand dart out to grab the handset. "Hello?" She listened, then a smile crossed her face. "Thanks, Serena. I'll pass that along."

When she hung up, Noah couldn't resist. "What?"

"Serena said Bonnie died sometime this morning between the hours of midnight and three."

"Then we need to find out where Justin was during that time."

"You bet. We also need to find out where he was at the time of Walter's murder."

They headed back down to the interrogation room to find the judge holding court with his son. A big man topping six feet two, with bushy gray hair, dark penetrating eyes, and a booming bass voice that carried well, he yelled and Justin drooped.

Noah rapped on the door, cutting the judge off mid-yell. He turned and glared. Seeing Noah, his brows shot up and some of the red in his face receded. He strode to the door and pulled it open. "What is it?"

"Hello, Judge Marlowe." Noah motioned for the man to step out of the room. He shut the door so Justin couldn't hear the conversation.

"Don't hello me." Judge Marlowe narrowed his eyes, fury still spitting from his blue eyes. "Tell me what you think you have on my son."

"Evidence," Kit snapped. "We need to know where Justin was from midnight on."

"At home. Asleep. Just like he is every night at that time."

"Do you mind if we hear that from him?" Kit placed her hands on her hips.

Noah figured he was the only one who noticed the flash of pain in her eyes as she ignored the pressure on her wounded arm.

Judge Marlowe narrowed his eyes and crossed his arms across his chest. "Yes, I do mind."

Noah rubbed his jaw, then said, "Look. We had a car on your house all night. Justin didn't get home until about seven this morning. We need to know where he was. Because he wasn't at home."

The man blanched and dropped his arms. "He wasn't?"

"No sir."

"Well, he isn't a kid anymore, he probably spent the night with a friend."

"Then let him tell us that."

Hesitation. "All right, but I'm in the room with you."

"Absolutely. We've already offered him a lawyer. He refused."

The man's face hardened. "He doesn't need a lawyer, he has me."

The three returned to the room to find Justin with his head in his hands. He didn't bother to look up when the door opened.

"Justin." Kit's voice was soft. Noah looked at her in surprise. She flicked him a glance and he let her lead.

"Justin," she repeated more firmly.

He looked up. "What?"

"Where were you last night?"

His bloodshot eyes darted to his dad, then back to his clasped hands. With his right thumb and forefinger, he started picking at a hangnail and mumbled, "At . . . at . . . home."

His father blew out a breath, slapped a hand on the table. Justin jumped and glared at the man. Judge Marlowe kept his voice low, controlled. "No, you weren't. They had a car on the house all night, Justin. They watched you drive up and go inside early this morning."

Justin flushed and looked at the door, his desire to escape clear. "Fine. I was with some guys. We were just hanging out. Went to a few bars." He scrubbed his eyes. "Then I came home to go to bed."

"What time did you go to Bonnie's?" Kit asked. "And don't deny you were there, we have evidence. We're just waiting for the DNA results to come back from the lab. I'm sure it's going to match up with the sample you're going to give us. What do you think?"

More fidgeting, another glance at his father, then back at Kit. He raised his hand to touch the fresh scratches on his neck. "All right. I went to see Bonnie around midnight."

"And she wasn't happy to see you, was she?"

"No." He clipped the word, then continued without further prompting. "We fought. She scratched me. I left. That's it." He stopped, rubbed his eyes, and sighed. "Oh, and you'll probably find bruises on her upper arm. Her left one, I think. She kept walking away from me so I grabbed her pretty hard to get her to look at me. That's when she slapped me and scratched my face."

"What about her mother? Did she hear this argument?"

"No, I don't think so. She was already in her room. Plus she's so sick and with all that medication she takes . . ." He rolled his eyes. "No, she wouldn't have heard anything."

"Was anyone else in the house last night?"

"No. When her father's out of town, Bonnie pretty much takes the night shift with her mother, checking on her and making sure she doesn't need anything during the night. Then in the morning, the housekeeper comes in." He shifted and looked at Noah, then Kit. Kit noticed he avoided eye contact with his father. "Look. When I left her, she was still shouting obscenities at me and was very much alive. I'm not going to say I wasn't mad enough to belt her one, but I didn't." He spread his hands. "I can't help it if you don't believe me, but that's all there was to it."

"Why did you think she was seeing someone else?"

"Because she said she was. Told me we were finished, that she didn't need me anymore."

"Did you buy her expensive jewelry?"

A frown creased the skin between his brows. "No, why?"

"Are you still doing or selling drugs?"

"No!" his shout echoed around the room. This time he did look at his parent, a cross between a glare and a plea. "No. I'm clean. Dad makes me test once a week." Justin's jaw worked. "If I use, I'm out of the will—and the house." He tried a smirk, but it fell into a grimace. "I can't afford to use."

"What about a pocketknife we found at the scene with Bonnie's and Walter's blood on it?"

His head snapped in Kit's direction as she pulled out the plastic bag containing the knife. She tossed it on the table in front of father and son.

Justin looked at it. "That's mine."

"We figured. The initials kind of tipped us off."

"Where did you find it? I haven't seen it in a while."

"How long is a while?"

His Adam's apple bobbed and he shot a nervous look at his father. "I'm not sure. It must have fallen out of my pocket somehow. Um . . . a couple of weeks ago or something."

Kit narrowed her eyes. She didn't believe that for a minute. "You're lying."

Justin raised a hand to rub it across his lips. Then his jaw firmed. "I'm not lying. I don't know where I lost it or why it turned up in Bonnie's house."

She wasn't going to get him to admit anything. That last look at his father told her plenty. "How did you and Walter Davis get along?"

He shrugged. "Fine, I guess."

Noah leaned forward. "Look, Justin, I'm going to lay it out for you and your dad. We've got two dead college students who knew each other and hung out. One of them is your ex-girlfriend. The other a guy whose company she seemed to enjoy. She ditched you and was moving on. That can be hard for the one left behind."

But Justin was shaking his head. "I know where you're going with this and it's not true. No, I didn't like the fact that Bonnie wouldn't even talk to me about the possibility of giving me another chance. The only reason I went over there was to beg her to talk to my dad so he could tell her I've been clean. She went crazy, told me to get out, that she couldn't be seen with me. She just wouldn't"—he held his palms up in a little-boy gesture—"give me one more chance. How can you not give someone a second chance?" A single tear spilled over, ran down his cheek and dripped to the table.

Kit exchanged a look with Noah and he asked, "Is there anything else you want to add?"

"No, nothing. I swear I didn't have anything to do with Bonnie's death." His voice cracked on the last word and his breaths now came faster, in short pants. "I swear. You have to believe me." Then he dropped his head into his hands and sobbed.

Kit walked from the room and grabbed a cup from the water cooler. Filling it up, she took a long drink, popped two ibuprofen, then turned to find Brian Sands standing beside her.

The one who'd pulled the trigger and killed the man she'd talked into surrendering.

Spinning on her heel, she started to walk off, but his voice stopped her. "Kit."

Without turning to look at him, she said, "I'm not a good person to talk to right now, Brian."

The SWAT member stepped in front of her. "Look, we're going to have to work together in the future. We've got to get past this. That man was lifting his gun to shoot. You didn't have on a vest . . ." He blew out a sigh.

"He wasn't going to shoot. And nothing," she jabbed a finger at him, "that you say is going to convince me otherwise." She paused and sighed. "However, I suppose I need to apologize for blasting you in front of everyone." She swallowed and met his eyes. "I shouldn't have done that."

"I don't care about that. What I care about is our working relationship, because the way it is now . . ." His brows furrowed and he sighed. "Can we agree to disagree on this and move on? Because we've got to figure out how we're going to be able to work together."

"We're not. If you get a call and I'm the negotiator, pass it to someone else. I can't work with someone I can't trust to read my signals and trust my judgment."

Impatience stamped his face. "I don't want to do that. I might not be *able* to do that." Something else flickered across his face and she narrowed her eyes. He reached out a hand and touched her arm. "Kit . . ." He broke off and she realized with a start he was struggling to tell her something personal.

Oh no, he wasn't going to ask her out or anything, was he?

She watched his lips press together, then, "I wanted to ask if you would meet me for a cup of coffee or something sometime. Soon. You know, maybe across the street at the little café or . . ." He shrugged and flushed.

Kit wanted to groan. Instead, she tossed her water cup into the trash can and saw Noah approaching. "Brian, you're a nice guy, but one I'm very frustrated with right now . . ." It was her turn to cut herself off. "Look," she sighed. "Maybe we do need to sit down and talk, but now's not the time. I've got a case to solve."

He stopped her one more time. "Fine, I understand that, but what happens when we get a call and I'm the only one who's available to be your gun?"

For a minute she didn't answer, then said in a low voice, "You'd better obey my signals."

Brian swallowed hard and looked away. Finally, he tossed her an indistinguishable look and headed down the hallway without another word.

Noah had slowed his approach and studied the walls. Now he stood beside her. She looked at him and asked, "What do you think?"

"About Marlowe or Brian?"

"Marlowe. Brian is a taboo topic."

"I believe him. Except for the part about how he lost the knife."

"Why do you believe he didn't do it?"

"I don't know. I'm generally pretty good at reading people. He's coming across as telling it straight. Except for the part about the knife."

"Rats."

"You were hoping I'd disagree with you."

Surprise lifted her brow. "You *are* good at reading people. And yes, I caught the thing with the knife too."

"So, I guess we cut him loose and see if we can track down the real bad guy."

She grimaced, not just because they had to cut the creep loose, but because her arm throbbed. "Have at it. I'm going to make a phone call."

He saluted and turned to walk back into the interrogation room. Kit glanced at her phone. It had been vibrating off and on for the past two hours.

Her mother was calling her. Her adoptive mother.

Not that that was terribly unusual, but the woman had sworn she'd wait on Kit to call. A brief sliver of concern shot through her. Had something happened? Was she all right? Was something wrong with her healthwise?

But she hadn't left a message.

As angry as she was at her mother, she didn't wish any ill will toward her. Quite the contrary.

Kit hit the speed dial.

Three rings later, her mother's familiar voice came on the line. "Hello, Kit."

"Hi, Mom." Sudden tears clogged her throat, taking her by surprise. She cleared them away and said, "You called?"

"I did. I wanted to . . . ask when you thought you might come home?"

"Not anytime soon, Mom. I told you why I was here. That hasn't changed."

"How are . . . they?"

"You mean Charles and Claire Cash? The two people who gave me up for adoption so you could have a child?" A swift indrawn breath told Kit her arrow had found its target. Remorse followed. "I'm sorry. I'm . . . sorry. I'm just . . ."

"Angry," her mother finished with a whisper.

"Yes. I am." But the pain in her mother's voice pierced her. She'd been cruel. And that was uncalled for. "I'm sorry, Mom. I shouldn't have said that. No matter how angry I am, there's no reason to be mean about it."

"I understand your anger . . . and truly, I don't suppose I really blame you."

Love for the woman who'd raised her swept over her, blindsiding her for a brief moment. "Regardless, I need to work through this and I believe this is what I have to do. We've talked about this. You agreed not to interfere. To let me get to know them without heaping guilt on my head."

"I know." Subdued and quiet, her mother said, "I just wanted to hear your voice, Kit. I miss you."

"I . . . miss you too. I really do. I miss the way things used to be," she whispered. Then the anger returned and she swallowed before she said something else she'd regret. "Look, Mom, I need to go, all right? I'll call you later."

A pause. "All right, Kit. I'll be praying."

A lump formed in Kit's throat. Of course she'd be praying. That's what her mother did. Kit hung up without another word. When she went to hook the phone on the clip at her waist, she noticed her hand trembled. Emotions she'd kept under lock and key for the past six months seemed ready to spill over and cause a mess if she wasn't careful. Since finding out about the adoption, speaking to her mother had become such an effort. Kit hadn't lied. She did miss the way things used to be. The easy companionship she and her mom found in just being together, the fun they had shopping, joking and laughing.

Her mother's teasing about settling down and making her a grandmother.

"Hey Kit, we're finished up here. You ready to head out and find our next suspect?"

Noah's voice pulled her from her unhappy thoughts and she made a huge effort to push the anger aside. Clearing her throat, she said, "Sure."

"Everything okay?" Concern tinged his voice.

Forcing a smile, she said, "Yep."

Doubt lingered in his eyes, but he didn't press her. "I just got a text that Bonnie's father is home. I thought we'd go back by Bonnie's parents' house, talk to her father, then get some pictures of the jewelry to see if we can find out where it came from."

"Sounds good."

13

Noah pulled into the driveway of the Grays' house and shut off the engine. He looked at the front door and frowned. "I hope our coming here doesn't upset Mrs. Gray any more than she's already suffered."

"There were two cars parked around the side in front of the garage. I'm guessing she has someone, a family member, with her."

"Bonnie's father, I hope. Let's go."

They walked up the steps and Noah rang the bell.

Seconds later, footsteps sounded in the foyer followed by the door opening.

A tall, gray-headed man stood there, eyeing them. "Can I help you?"

Noah and Kit flashed their badges and the man's face hardened. "Did you catch the man who killed Bonnie?"

"No sir, not yet." Kit's voice oozed sympathy. "But that's why we're here. Are you Bonnie's father?"

"Oh yes, yes, I'm sorry. I'm Robert Gray. I just arrived home a few hours ago."

"We need to ask you a few more questions if that's all right with you," Noah requested.

The door opened wider. "Fine. We can talk in my office."

They followed him through the house and down a back hall to a room that looked like a professional office—plush carpet, large mahogany desk, and a comfortable leather chair took up most of the area's space. Pictures lined the walls and smaller framed photos were proudly displayed on the hutch behind the desk.

Mostly pictures of Bonnie, Noah noticed. Sympathy for the man's grief twisted inside him.

He and Kit took the seats Robert gestured to, and the man seated himself on the couch opposite them. It said a lot to Noah that he didn't sit at his desk. This wasn't business. This was about a daughter he'd obviously loved.

"How can I help?"

"We talked to several of Bonnie's friends at the law school, and one of them seemed convinced Bonnie was seeing someone. Do you know who that might have been?"

Bonnie's father frowned. "No. I know she was seeing that Justin kid," he grimaced as he said the name, "but she came to her senses pretty fast when she found out he was involved in drugs."

"You knew about that?" He couldn't see Bonnie sharing that information. Then again . . .

"Bonnie didn't tell me, if that's what you're wondering. I overheard an argument they had right before they broke up. Justin came over here and he was high. I was going to order him out of the house, but before I had to intervene, Bonnie was yelling at him to leave and never come back, that she was finished with him. I simply faded back into my office to wait until it was over—and was there to step in if I needed to. I didn't."

"Okay, so she gets rid of Justin. How long after that until you noticed she wasn't so down anymore? She wasn't sad and moping around?"

The man steepled his fingers and placed them under his chin. "I left on a business trip not too long after that, but it seems to me when I got back, she seemed almost like her old self. Smiling, excited about graduating." He shrugged. "I figured she'd just determined to put that bad experience behind her and moved on."

Kit clasped her hands together in front of her and said, "When we were in your house right after Bonnie's death, I took a look at her room. She had some nice pieces of jewelry on her dresser. Any idea where those came from?"

"Bonnie has a lot of nice jewelry. Could you be more specific?" He stood. "Or better yet, why don't you show me?"

They exited the room and made their way to the stairs. At the top, they made a left turn. At the first door on the right, Bonnie's father stopped and took a deep breath before he pushed it open and stepped into his daughter's room.

It still smelled like the expensive perfume she must have used every day. Noah decided he preferred Kit's combination of vanilla soap and strawberry shampoo.

Kit moved to the dresser. "It's not here. Did you move it?"

He frowned. "No, I haven't been in here since she died."

"What about your wife?"

Shaking his head, he said, "No. She can't climb the stairs."

Kit and Noah exchanged a glance, and Noah asked, "What about your maid? Mary, isn't it?"

"She hasn't been here since she found . . ." He trailed off, clearing his throat.

"But you've had visitors, right?"

"A lot. Too many to count."

"So any of them could have come up here."

He sighed. "Easily."

"Do you mind if I look around and see if I can find the boxes they came in?"

"No, not at all."

Kit started her search, opening drawers, going through Bonnie's closet, and looking under her bed. She sat back on her heels and sighed. "Nothing."

Then she spied an end table and pulled open the bottom drawer. "Bingo."

"What did you find?" Noah asked.

"A box from Roxanne's." She held it up. "Looks like it might have held that sporty emerald and diamond tennis bracelet."

Noah let out a low whistle. "Roxanne's isn't cheap."

"No kidding."

Satisfaction gleamed in his eyes. "Let's go find out who bought it."

14

Noah parked on the street in front of the jewelry store. Kit pushed open the door and stepped inside, and a little bell sounded a warning that she'd entered. Noah followed behind.

A small Asian woman of indeterminate age hurried to greet them. "Hello. Welcome to Roxanne's. What can I help you with?" A sly grin crossed her smooth face. "A ring perhaps?"

Kit felt a flush start and wondered at the brief pang she felt in the vicinity of her heart. What would it be like to pick out a ring with the man beside her?

Clearing her throat, she pulled out her ID and said, "No ma'am, we just wanted to ask you a question about a piece of jewelry that was purchased from your shop."

"Oh." She frowned. "Certainly."

Noah handed the box over and she took it, studying it. "This box? Yes, it came from here. What was in it?"

"We're not sure, but we think it was an emerald and diamond tennis bracelet."

"Ah." The light went on in her eyes. "Yes, very expensive. A man came in and said he was looking for something for someone special. I suggested that piece."

"And you remember this?"

"Oh yes. Because he pulled out a wad of cash and paid for it with one-hundred-dollar bills."

Kit felt her hope deflate. Cash. Untraceable.

"Did you know who the man was? Get his name?"

"No. Just a very nice-looking gentleman. Probably about fifty years old or so. But he had a baseball hat on and he kept his sunglasses on. I couldn't see his eyes. He said he had just come from the eye doctor and the light still hurt his eyes." She gave a little laugh. "At first I thought he might be here to rob me so I kept my hand on the alarm button, but then he pulled out all that money, paid for the bracelet, and left."

"So Bonnie was seeing an older man," Kit murmured.

"Married?" Noah wondered.

"Hence all the secrecy."

"When was this?" Noah directed the question to the woman.

"Hmm." Michelle rubbed her chin as she thought. "Maybe three or four weeks ago?"

Spying the camera in the corner of the shop, Noah asked, "Would you have security footage from that long ago?"

"No, I'm sorry. We keep about a week at a time, then recycle. That long ago would be gone by now."

"Well, thank you for your time."

"I will see you again."

"You will?"

"Someday. Have a wonderful day."

They exited the store and Noah gave a grunt. "Huh, wonder what she meant by that."

"Maybe when she has to finger the guy at the trial after we catch him. Because I have a feeling whoever bought Bonnie that jewelry is somehow involved in her death."

In May, the sun hung in the sky longer, making the days seem like they would never end, even at 7:30 in the evening. However, the sky had turned overcast, the clouds swelling with their liquid burden, ready to burst and empty their contents onto the world below. Excitement tingled through him. Number three. The perfect number.

The Judge watched the woman toss her backpack into the back of her truck and climb in. She'd just finished taking care of her grandchildren. Her class started at 7:50 and would end at 9:15. She cranked the truck and spun out of the driveway. The killer followed at a distance, his mind humming.

Could he do this? She was fifty-three years old and had probably never done anything wrong in her life.

Except what she'd done to him.

He almost hesitated as he hefted the gun in his right hand. Walter and Bonnie had been easy. But this one . . .

He thought about his own grandmother. She'd been kind when she'd come to visit. Had made him feel like he was important. But even she hadn't saved him from his father.

He thought about the time she'd come over on a surprise visit. He'd been up in the tree, desperate to get away from the swinging fists and blistering, soul-shattering words. She stood at the bottom of the tree and talked him into coming down. Then she took him inside and bandaged the cut above his eye and the scrapes on his hands and knees caused by the rough bark.

She cupped his cheeks. "Now, darlin', what'd you do to make your dad so mad at you?"

"Nothin'," he muttered, eyes downcast. "He just hates me."

At that, she'd blinked really fast and turned around for a few minutes. When she turned back, she wiped the back of her hand across her nose and said, "I wish I could take you with me, little one, but my house ain't much better. You know your granddaddy is twice as mean as your daddy."

As far as he was concerned, any place was better than his home. "Take me with you, Nana, please."

"I can't, boy. Now come on and I'll tell you a story. Your

daddy's passed out for the next few hours and won't bother us none."

So, he'd climbed into her lap, thinking he was getting too big to be sitting there. At eleven years old, he shouldn't want hugs and kisses and stories.

But he did.

And he listened to her talk about men who grew up and had money. Men whom everyone looked up to.

Men who commanded respect and oozed power.

The kind of man she wanted him to be one day.

The kind of man who was exactly the opposite of his father.

The kind of man who would have a son who would look at him with love in his eyes.

Respect. That was very important to her.

And the Judge determined he'd have respect. Because that would be important to his child one day. He had to make a name for himself so his son would be proud.

He watched the grandmother's truck sputter to a stop on the side of the highway. She'd managed to go a little farther than he'd anticipated. But there were enough trees to give him the cover he needed. Oh yeah, when he held a gun to her head, she'd respect him then, wouldn't she?

He remembered his own grandmother leaving him alone that night and his father waking up. The thundering curses, the crash of fist on bone. The hospital emergency room and his father stating his idiot kid had crashed his moped.

He flashed to another scene and remembered their looks of impatience, the tapping of the woman's toe against the wooden floor. If he closed his eyes, he could hear the sighs of disrespect and the little snickers of mockery that had come from the woman who now stood at the hood of her truck looking for help. He checked the gun and slid it into the waistband of his jeans.

Yes, his grandmother had messed up that day. She should have taken him with her. He remembered the last conversation he had with her before she'd had a massive stroke and died the next week. "Now you get your education, you hear me? You must have an education to grow and be someone important, then you'll be able to have that family you want. You'll have the perfect family, darling. You'll be the perfect daddy with the perfect wife and the perfect child."

"I want a sister too."

She gave a little laugh. "Well, that might be a little hard to manage, but I'm sure you'll find a 'girl' friend who'll feel as close as a sister. One day, boy, one day. I expect great things from you, ya hear?"

"I hear, Nana."

And then she'd died, leaving him in the vicious grip of a man who hated everything and everyone.

But that wasn't important now. The woman leaning over the engine of her truck needed his full attention.

"You need some help, ma'am?"

She looked up and smiled her relief, and satisfaction surged through him. Recognition blipped in her eyes and that's when he struck.

Two minutes later, the Judge stared down at the woman who now lay at his feet. Her wide eyes blinked nonstop. The hysteria had finally shuddered to a halt.

"Now, I'm going to remove the gag. You scream and I'll slit your throat. Understand?"

A hesitant nod. Slight hope lit her eyes. He chuckled silently to himself. Ah well, he could let her hope for a brief moment. It would make watching the hope fade all the more titillating.

He pulled the gag off. "Now, do not say my name, do you understand? You don't deserve to be allowed to say my name. Are we clear?"

"Yes. W-w-why are you doing this? I have grandchildren who need me. Please don't hurt me." More tears. The Judge ignored them. He knew she couldn't help it.

"Do you know why you're here?"

"No," she sobbed, "please don't kill me. Please!"

"Shut up and don't say that again."

More sniffling. Then she caught her breath. "O-okay."

Good. She was showing him respect. He relaxed a bit. "Let me just tell you that this trial is now in session."

Confusion waded through the fear. He watched it play out on her face. "Trial? What do you mean?"

"You disrespected me," he hissed. "Tapping your foot, sighing impatiently, do you remember?"

The light went on. "You . . . you mean when you were arguing about—"

"Yes."

"That's what this is about? Because I was having a really awful day and I disrespected you?" Anger made it to the surface. Disbelief coated her face.

"Yes." Good, she admitted it. "The jury finds you guilty."

"Jury?"

"Yes. Me."

"You're crazy," she finally whispered, understanding now that there was nothing she could do to get through to him. He already had her death planned. Desperation and despair flooded into her eyes. "I'm sorry." She began to weep. "I'm so sorry. I . . . I should have been more patient, I shouldn't have—"

"Good, that's good. Repentance is good." He cocked the gun. "Any last words?"

"Stop, oh please, stop."

He placed a foot against her hip and rolled her over so she lay facedown, settled the gun against the back of her head, and pulled the trigger. She jerked, then was still.

"At least I'm merciful. You were granted your right to a speedy trial . . . and to be humanely executed. You were." Briefly he wondered what his father would think of him. Would he be proud? Happy that his son finally learned to stand up for himself?

Or would he find fault like he always had? Laugh and mock him and make him feel small and unworthy?

It didn't matter, he decided. His father didn't matter.

Only this mattered.

Then he pulled out the new knife he'd purchased just this morning and cut off the first three toes of her right foot.

Twenty minutes later he dropped the miniature gavel on the ground and laughed. She'd be doing no more toe tapping.

Calm filled him. He'd completed his mission. One. Two. Three. Now for the next three.

By nine o'clock that night, Kit and Noah were both wired and starving. After what amounted to a pretty fruitless search for their elusive killer, she'd been on edge and cranky. But a pair of sweats, an oversized sweatshirt, and fuzzy socks were a good start to putting her world back on its axis.

And Noah was here. That helped too.

For some reason, she'd asked him to come over to her house, and for some reason, he'd accepted. The pizza had arrived five minutes ago.

"One thing I'll miss when I move into my new house. Home-made Mama Linelli's Pizza."

"New house? When are you moving?"

"As soon as I find the time to find one and buy it."

He laughed.

Kit placed a slice of pizza on her plate and watched him do the same.

She waited.

He looked at her. "What are you waiting for?"

Kit shrugged. "I figured you'd want to say the blessing."

A strange light entered his eyes and he reached out to take her hand in his. "I would love to."

He said a short prayer of thanks for the food and added a request for wisdom and safety in solving the case they were working on.

When he looked up and met her eyes, she shivered at the soft look there.

Then he broke contact and asked, "How'd you get into this job anyway?" Noah picked up a slice of the pizza and guided it to his mouth.

Kit watched his teeth sink into the gooey mess and felt her heart stutter a beat. She closed her eyes briefly and told herself they were partners. Love and partners were not a good combination.

Why? The little voice inside her whispered. *Why would it be so bad? At least he would understand the job. Unlike the last guy you picked.*

She shut off the little voice and concentrated on Noah's question. Did she want to explore the past that closely with this man she was trying not to drool over? She hedged. "I found something I was good at."

"And how did you find out you were good at it? Why become a cop in the first place?"

Kit let out a small sigh and set aside her soda. She picked up a napkin and cleaned her fingers of the grease. He kept his gaze on her, waiting patiently for her answer.

"When I was eleven years old, I was taken hostage by a friend's father."

Noah jerked and the slice of pizza that was headed toward his mouth again bumped his chin, then hit the plate. He ignored it. "What?"

"I was visiting a friend after school. Her mother had picked us up, taken us for ice cream, and then we went back to her house, where I was going to spend the night."

She stole a glance at him. He was totally absorbed in her words. "Anyway, her parents had been separated for a while, and her dad chose that night to come home and demand a reconciliation with his wife."

"Did he know you were there?"

"No. In fact, we were actually supposed to be at my house that night, but we ended up at Julia's house instead."

"Oh man. So when he came home . . ."

"He'd been drinking, wasn't really in his right mind. Apparently he'd tried to call all day and Julia's mom wouldn't answer the phone. When he got there, Julia heard him come in the door and went running out to see him. In spite of all of his faults, she loved her dad."

"Of course, every kid does."

"Then the arguing started." She drew in a deep breath. As always, the memory of that night was never too far from the surface. She could now remember it, talk about it with some detachment, yet every once in a while the emotions from it would blindside her.

"When they started yelling at each other, I hid out, scared, hoping they'd stop."

"Did they?"

"No. I . . . I could hear Julia crying, so I crept to the edge of the hall just about the time her father pushed her aside and slammed her mother up against the wall."

His warm hand covered hers. She shivered. Reliving it like this, not just thinking about it, but actually saying the words out loud . . .

"You don't have to tell me the rest of it. I have a pretty good idea what happened."

"No, it's all right." She curled her fingers around his and let herself enjoy the sensation, the feeling of safety he offered. How strange. She was the one who usually provided that to other people. To be on the receiving end felt . . . nice. "I darted back down the hall into the master bedroom and dialed 911."

"So, the cops arrived?"

"Yeah. And after a series of events, her dad grabbed a shotgun from somewhere and blew a hole in the door." She shook her head. "I'm still not sure where the gun came from. It seemed like it was just there all of a sudden."

"Did he hit the cop?"

"No. Fortunately. But he wasn't ready to surrender either."

"How long?"

"Seven and a half hours."

His fingers squeezed hers and she realized he still had his hand tucked around hers. "What an awful experience for a kid."

"For anyone."

"Yeah, but especially for a kid."

It had been awful. She'd had horrible nightmares for several years after that. It wasn't until she'd become a certified hostage negotiator that the dreams stopped.

Weird.

"Anyway," she continued, "I remember listening to every word that negotiator said. Intently. I didn't eat, didn't sleep, didn't hardly breathe. I think I tried to become invisible, because if he couldn't see me, he couldn't kill me, right?"

"Right."

"I didn't even go to the bathroom. I just wet my pants where I sat." She gave a low chuckle. "That's one thing I remember clearly. I hated that. Almost as much as I hated the helpless feeling of being out of control."

"That's understandable."

"I went through several years of therapy and belonged to an amazing . . ." She paused and cocked her head. "Huh."

"What?"

"I was going to say an amazing church. But I just remembered that church part." Memories flooded her. "We had a great children's minister. He and his wife practically adopted me after that. He was a trained counselor. Not the one I saw on a regular basis, but he helped . . . a lot." She shifted, agitated. "I can't believe I didn't remember that until now. How weird."

"Not so weird. You've already said you're mad at God."

"Yeah, I am. Sort of."

"Anger is a powerful emotion. You've probably suppressed some good things about God in order to hold on to that anger. The question is, why are you so mad at him?"

She stiffened, then stood to gather the pizza leftovers. "Are you done?"

"I guess." He tossed his napkin onto the box and leaned back. "So what kind of house do you want?"

Startled at the welcome subject change, she just looked at him. "What?"

"You said you needed to go house hunting. What are you looking for?"

She sat back down and let the box fall back onto the table. "If I close my eyes, I can see it so clear. It's more like a farm. I want something with a little land. A couple of horses, a dog." She laughed. "I want a dog. My dad was allergic to everything and animals were not welcome in our house when I was growing up."

"What else?" His voice was soft and his eyes caressed her face.

A little self-conscious, she shifted. "I don't know. I don't have a particular color or shape for the house, just the idea of it. What it represents."

"Do you want to get married?"

Kit sat up with a jerk. "What?"

He flushed as he realized how that question sounded. "No, I'm not asking if you'll marry me, I'm just asking if you see that in your future."

She studied him. "If I do, it'll have to be to someone who understands my job. Not just the crazy hours, but the emotional toll it takes on me." Kit shook her head. "I dated a guy a couple of years ago who couldn't handle it. I can't go through that again."

"So you'd like to be married one day?"

"Yeah." She looked him in the eye. "I would."

His lips curved in a slow heart-stopping smile. "Good."

Break-dancing butterflies cut loose in her belly and she swallowed at the crazy sensation. "So tell me about you, Noah. What was your childhood like?"

His eyes dropped to study the table. "It wasn't a great one, to be honest. But I overcame it. I'll tell you about it one day."

"What's wrong with right now?" She picked up the pizza box

once again and placed her other hand on her hip. Why was he so reluctant to talk about his past, his family? She'd spilled her guts to this guy and he was like a clam. She didn't like it.

Instead of answering her question, he raised a brow, stood, and reached out a hand to take the box from her. "Want me to get rid of that for you?"

With her good arm, she held it up out of reach. "I can take it out. It won't fit in my little trash can. Now, prepare to tell me your life story."

Surprise pierced her as neatly as the bullet that crashed through her kitchen window, cutting a path through the pizza box she still held above her head.

15

Noah slammed himself to the floor and hollered, "Kit, are you okay?" He'd seen her dive to the floor two seconds before he did.

"Fine," she grunted.

He turned his head to see her army crawling toward the phone, wincing each time she put weight on her still sore arm. "I've got my cell phone, Kit. Stay still!"

"You call Dakota. I'll call 911." She had a landline on the kitchen counter. He stuck around long enough to see her grab the cord to pull it off the counter. It landed on the floor in front of her.

While she took care of calling the authorities, Noah stayed low and raced toward the back door that led to a screened-in porch. Briefly he paused at the window and scanned the area.

Nothing.

He snatched his cell phone out and punched in Dakota's number. He wanted someone he trusted on his way over here.

Footsteps sounded behind him and he whirled. Kit crept toward him, gun held ready, face intense, anger visible.

Dakota came on the line.

"We're at Kit's house and need backup. Someone decided to take shots at us again."

"What?" Dakota's voice thundered through the phone. "Connor and I'll be there as soon as we can. Do you have backup on the way?"

"Kit called it in. Should be here shortly. Be careful, I have a feeling our shooter is still out there."

"Hunker down and stay out of bullet range."

Kit reached for the doorknob. "I'm going after this guy."

"Are you crazy?"

Through gritted teeth, she ground out, "No, mad."

Panic hit him. He couldn't let her go outside. "As soon as you set foot outside that door, he's going to put a bullet in you."

"Come on," the Judge whispered to the cops inside. "Come on."

He had the perfect view from the roof. Even in the darkness, the lighting from the street and Kit's home provided enough of a visual that if Kit came out the front door, he'd have to squirm around a bit to get his sights on Detective Lambert, the one he wanted dead. But if Lambert came out of the back door from the porch, all he had to do was pull the trigger.

A plan a son could be proud of. How he wished he could have been proud of his father. The familiar sick rage built in him and he pushed it down. Now wasn't the time to think about that. "Come on."

The rifle still felt odd in his grip. Heavy, bulky. He was much more comfortable with the small Walther PPK/S. The one he'd used to kill Walter.

Still no movement from the house.

Why weren't they racing out of the house to find the shooter? What kind of cops were they?

The Judge wasn't concerned about someone seeing him. He had a great spot behind the chimney.

Then a car pulled into the subdivision and the Judge cursed.

What were they doing home so soon? She'd said her parents would be out of town until tomorrow. He had to get down now before they came inside. Otherwise he'd be stuck up here until they left again.

As much as he wanted to stay and watch all the action, recording it in his mind for a story to tell his son, he definitely had to leave before the cops figured out where the bullets had come from.

He scrambled for the rope he'd pulled up after him. The climbing gear had come in handy. He smiled as he thought about it. It had been so easy. Just toss it up and over, the hook on the end of the rope had grabbed and held. And with the rifle strapped to his back, like Spiderman, he'd scaled the building.

And waited.

Only now, sirens sounded in the distance. He'd shot through the window. And missed. He wanted to scream out his frustration. How had he missed again? He shook the rifle. Stupid, ancient weapon. He should have invested in a newer one. But he hadn't wanted to spend the money. So he'd worked with the sight and got it lined up the way he wanted. Or so he thought.

And he'd shot and missed. Again.

And they called for backup instead of racing out the door. They were smarter than he gave them credit for. He'd thought if he kept his distance, he'd be able to take out the one he wanted without any trouble, but this was twice now that he'd missed.

He wouldn't make that mistake again.

Kit paused. Heard the sirens. "Help's on the way." She still itched to open the door and search the neighborhood until she found the creep who shot out her window.

But she could tell the thought of her sticking her head outside completely unnerved him.

Noah looked out the window one more time. "Good."

"I wonder who he's after," she mused, grudgingly giving in to Noah's rational argument that going out the door before backup arrived would be incredibly stupid.

He looked back at her, his brow lifted. "Um . . . us?"

She shot him an aggrieved look. "Funny. I mean, is he after both of us? Or just one of us?"

"He's struck twice."

"And we were together both times."

"But the bullets came closer to you both times."

"On purpose or because that's just where they ended up after he pulled the trigger?" She pursed her lips. "And why is he shooting at us anyway? Who is it? Someone who doesn't like us investigating this case?"

"A psycho who just got out of jail and is out to get the person who put him there?"

The back-and-forth dialogue helped her think.

He looked out the window. "Good questions. We'll have to figure out the answers later. Our backup is here."

"Once they decide the scene is secure, they'll be all over the place." She rubbed her head. "Great." Another thought hit her. "Alena!"

"Who?"

"The girl who lives in the other half of the duplex."

A knock on her front door had her crossing the room to open it. Connor swept in, followed by Dakota and three other officers.

"Are you okay?" Concern creased Connor's eyes as he placed a hand on her shoulder.

Kit nodded and turned as Noah came up behind her. "Yes, we're fine. We were just trying to figure out who the actual target with this guy is and what we've done to earn his attention. I need to check on Alena."

One of the officers heard her. "Is that the person who lives next to you?"

"Yes."

135

"No one's there. We already checked."

"Oh, thanks."

Which explained the lack of barking. Roscoe would have been going nuts.

Dakota, Noah, and Connor stepped outside. Kit walked into the kitchen. The broken window gaped a jagged grin, allowing the heat of the night to roll in.

Glass lay in her sink, over the countertops, and on the floor. Upon the bullet's impact, the pizza box had flown from her grasp, hit the wall, then fallen to the floor. She left it there.

Approaching the window, she ignored the crunching under her shoes and examined the entry point of the bullet. Her eyes judged the angle and followed the invisible line to her wall. She could see the hole it made from where she stood.

A sound behind her whipped her attention to the doorway. "Hey Jake."

"Hey Kit Kat. Whatcha got?"

"A bullet in my wall over there. Feel free to dig it out. I'm trying to figure out where it came from."

"You know I'll figure that out with all of my handy-dandy investigative tools."

She smiled at him, and it felt strange, the upward tilt to her lips. Her jaw felt frozen in place, like she'd kept it clenched too long. When she moved it, it ached. "I know, Jake."

"The team is working on that as we speak." He walked over to the wall that held the bullet and began extracting it.

Noah came back in and looked at her. "From the angle of the bullet, and this is just a rough estimate until Jake does his thing, we think the bullet came from across the street. Guy was up on the roof of the house."

"And yet once again, he missed," Kit murmured.

"You think it's the same guy that killed those two college students? Maybe warning us away?"

"Could be, I guess. It's no secret we're the ones investigating the cases. But, it just seems odd that this guy plants a bullet in the brain of two people at close range, but both times that he's used a rifle, he's missed."

"Assuming it's the same person."

"True."

"I think it might be a good idea to look into past cases and see who's recently been released from jail who might have a grudge against you or me."

Noah nodded. "After we were shot at, I asked the captain if he would have someone start looking into that."

Surprised, Kit looked at him. "You did?"

"Yeah, sorry, forgot to mention it." He looked away.

"So, has anyone found anything?"

"Nothing as of this afternoon. He promised to call if anyone came across something interesting."

She studied him. "What are you not telling me, Noah?"

Rubbing a hand across his eyes, he said, "I'm wondering if I know who is doing this. Then again, it just doesn't seem possible."

Her brows reached for her hairline. "Care to share?"

Noah blew out a sigh. "I wanted to be sure before I said anything."

For the first time since they'd been partners, she felt anger with him. Keeping her cool, she stated, "Well, one of us might not live that long, so why don't you fill me in."

"Of course, you have the right to know." He stepped to the wall to watch Jake pry the bullet from its plaster coffin. "You remember what I told you about my former partner and how she died?"

"Yes."

"Her husband wasn't convinced I wasn't to blame for Lisa's death."

"Ouch," she sympathized. "Does he have a history of violence?"

"No. Nothing."

"Then what makes you think it's him?"

"I don't know that it is. I just think we need to cover all of our bases, and he seems like a good place to start."

She thought about that and asked, "What's his name?"

"Skip Cooley."

"Then let's make him our first stop in the morning."

"Sounds like a plan. So," he looked around, "where are you sleeping tonight?"

Kit turned and scanned the mess in her kitchen. "I'll pack a bag and head over to Dakota and Jamie's. They'll let me hang out with them tonight." She gestured toward the window. "I guess I could tape it up and stay here, but that wouldn't offer much security."

Noah rubbed his nose. "Let's do it to keep the bugs out." He slapped at a thirsty mosquito as Kit found the necessary supplies to close the hole in her window until she could call the glass company. "About your security around here . . ."

She held up a hand to halt him before he got started. "I know, I know. But this is a rental. I refuse to put money into a security system when I plan to buy a house."

"Then we need to go look."

She sputtered. "We?"

"Sure. Why not? We're going to be together day in and day out until we solve these murders. When you get a little time to look at a place, I'm probably going to be with you, so . . ."

She shook her head. "I don't even have time to find anything to look at."

"That's where friends come in handy. I know a guy."

Of course he did.

FRIDAY

16

Noah followed Kit up the walk to a place he used to think of as his second home. Set in a middle-class neighborhood, the two-story brick house looked forlorn. Neglected. The grass needed cutting, the bushes needed a good trim, and dead leaves crackled underfoot as he climbed the steps.

He'd tried to visit in the days right after Lisa's death, but Skip wasn't receptive to the idea. Had been quite resistant to his presence. So Noah had stayed away. But that didn't stop him from hurting for his grieving friend.

Kit knocked on the door. "You don't think he'll be at work?"

"Nope. He could be with a client, although he generally doesn't work on Fridays."

"Did you meet him through Lisa?"

"No, I knew him from church."

"Church, huh?"

"Yeah." A pause. "What about you? Are you ready to see what it's all about yet?"

"Nope."

"Why not?"

"Because I'm still not real happy with him right now."

"Hm. So, how are you going to get happy with him if you don't give him another chance?"

Another pause. She fidgeted, uncomfortable with the topic. "I don't think he's going to answer the door."

"Who? God?"

She laughed. He was glad to hear it. "No, you idiot. Skip."

Noah felt his smile slide from his lips. "I guess not. We'll have to check back later."

Kit led the way back to the car, keys dangling from her fingers. "What does he do for a living?"

"He's a realtor."

She froze. "Not the I-know-a-guy realtor."

"He'd be the one."

Her frown remained as she opened the door to the car. "Is that wise?"

"I don't know. Thought I'd find out." His cell phone rang and he pulled it out as he slid into the passenger seat.

Kit cranked the car and put it into gear. "Who is it?"

"Lyle, the ballistics expert." He pressed the answer button and spoke into the phone. "Hi, Lyle, what do you have for me?"

"Bullets. Two bullets specifically."

"Do they match?"

"Negative. The one from Walter's head was from a Walther PPK/S." He paused, snickered. "Weird. Walter shot with a Walther."

"Lyle . . ."

"Yeah, sorry, disrespectful. I know. Sorry."

He didn't sound very repentant, but Noah didn't bother to call him on it. "So what about the other bullet? The one from Kit's house?"

Noah could hear papers shuffling in the background. Then, "That came from an M21 Sniper System rifle."

"And the guy missed?" Incredulous, he looked at Kit, who lifted an eyebrow at his tone.

"Lucky for you," Lyle retorted. "The bullet retrieved from the car matched the one in Kit's house."

"I'm still reeling at the fact that the guy missed."

Lyle snorted a choked laugh. "Just some background information. The gun isn't manufactured anymore. Typically it was used by Navy SEALS back in the eighties before it was replaced by the M24."

"So, it's not one you'd walk up to a guy on the street and buy?"

"No. Maybe a pawn shop. Someone cleaned out daddy's attic, came across it, and decided to make a few bucks. But it would have to be registered. I'm guessing he used that gun for a reason."

"Because it couldn't be traced back to him."

"Exactly. There's really no way to tell how the shooter got his hands on it. Could be a zillion possibilities."

"All right, thanks." He hung up and looked at Kit. "One 9mm, one Walther PPK/S, an M21 Sniper System . . ."

She glanced at him. ". . . and a partridge in a pear tree?"

"Something like that."

"So, are we looking at a weapons expert?" she asked, then answered her own question. "Probably not. He missed. Twice."

"Thank God."

"Hmm."

Noah rubbed his head. "Okay, back to the case. None of Bonnie's friends seem to have any motive to kill her. I personally would have put my money on the ex-boyfriend. However . . ."

"I know," she said and pursed her lips. "His alibi checked out. If you can believe his friends." Kit passed a slower-moving vehicle and headed toward the campus. "As weird as it sounds, I don't think he did it. I think it happened just the way he says it did."

"Except for how he lost the knife."

"Except that." Kit's phone rang. She snatched it from the clip on her side. "Hello?"

Noah watched her listen. Her eyes cut to him and she said, "Thanks."

"What?"

Kit flicked her blinker on and made a left turn. "Another body they think might be related to this case. Another miniature gavel found at the scene." She blew out a sigh and slapped her hand on the wheel. "I think it's safe to assume that we have a serial killer on our hands."

"Who and where?"

"Susan Chalmers. A fifty-three-year-old woman found in the trees off I-85. She was buried pretty deep."

"Fifty-three? That's too old. How does she fit in with Walter and Bonnie?"

"She was on her way to her 7:45 law class last night and never showed. Her husband called in a missing persons report when she didn't come home and wouldn't answer her cell. The police went looking for her and found her truck broken down on the side of the road. Cell phone was in the truck."

"When did they find her body?"

"This morning. A cadaver dog sniffed her out."

"They brought in a cadaver dog? That fast?"

"They found the toes from a right foot. Hot pink nail polish." She grimaced. "They figured the body might be nearby, so they called in the dog. Took him about a minute and a half to sniff her out."

Noah studied the road before them. "That means there might be some other motive besides a jealous lover's quarrel. If this killing is related somehow to the other two, then we need to talk to Captain Caruthers about setting up a task force."

"I was thinking along those lines myself."

"I want Connor and Dakota in on this."

"Along with anybody else you can think of. This guy is killing people left and right." She paused. "These are all law-school related. I wonder if we should suggest shutting down the campus until we catch this guy."

Noah shrugged. "I don't think shutting the campus down would do any good. The first victim was killed in his dorm room. The next two—assuming this killing is related—were done off campus."

"True. But they're all law students. I wonder if that's the connection somehow."

"Possibly. It's certainly an educated deduction."

Within minutes, they arrived at the scene. One lane of the highway had been closed off. A flashing neon arrow pointed traffic to the other lane.

Dakota stood to the side, talking into his phone. Serena's vehicle sat parked next to the wooded area. Kit and Noah exited the vehicle and walked toward the scene. Dakota hung up and greeted them with a grim look. "The captain called the FBI in officially. They gave me the case and the orders to set up a task force."

Noah and Kit exchanged a look. Noah returned the humorless smile. "Great minds think alike. Kit and I were just discussing that on the way over here. Because it looks like we've got a serial killer on the loose, it's time for the FBI to give us a hand."

"Looks that way. I've only been here for a few minutes. Serena's checking out the body."

A sleek black SUV pulled from the highway onto the grass and stopped behind a gray and blue highway patrol vehicle.

❖

"Who . . ."

Before Kit could finish her question, District Attorney Stephen Wells opened his door and stepped out.

"Oh boy," Noah blew out between pursed lips.

Oh boy was right, Kit thought. Then the passenger door opened and Edward Richmond, the intern, followed the DA over to them.

He eyed Kit, then smiled at Noah and held out a hand. "Good to see you again, Detective."

"You too."

Stephen looked like he'd lost a few pounds in the few days since Bonnie's death. He said, "Anything new?"

"Not yet, we just got here. What are you doing here?"

This wasn't the first time the man had been to a crime scene, Kit knew, but his deep involvement in the case had her aware that they needed to make sure their t's were crossed and their i's dotted. Not that they didn't do that for every case, but they didn't usually have the DA breathing down their necks either.

Stephen said, "I promised Bonnie's father I'd stay on top of things. When I heard this come across the scanner, I decided to stop in and see if there was a possible connection to the first two murders. Do you have anything?"

"We were just getting ready to see what Serena had. The victim is Susan Chalmers. She's a law student."

The foursome walked over to see Serena bag something she considered evidence. Noah asked, "Single gunshot to the back of the head?"

Serena glanced up. "You got it."

"Who found her?"

"Officer Abbott and a cadaver dog."

Kit frowned. "Anything else?"

"Whoever killed her cut off three of her toes from the right foot. The rest were left alone."

"Why not cut them all off? Does the fact that he just cut off three mean anything?"

Noah pondered out loud. "Maybe he was interrupted. Someone drove by and he was afraid of being seen."

"Possibly." Serena shrugged. "Whatever, this is one sick dude."

Kit sighed. "So Officer Abbott was the first one on the scene."

"Yeah, that's me," Officer Abbott spoke up.

"Can you tell us how you found her?" Edward asked unexpectedly. Kit shot him a glance, but the question was a valid one, so she let it pass.

"According to her husband, she was supposed to be in class from 7:45 to 9:15. Around 10:00, her husband started getting a little antsy that she wasn't home, so he started calling her cell phone. She never answered."

"Because it was on the front seat of the vehicle." Noah stood by the open door of the truck. In his right gloved hand, he held up the phone he'd dropped into a paper bag. "So it was unusual for her not to answer?"

"Yeah." Officer Abbott nodded. "She always called when she started home. Sometimes she stayed after class to talk to her professor, but was almost always home by 10:00 or 10:15 and she always called way before then."

"So around 11:00, her worried husband gets in his car and goes looking for her."

"Driving the route she normally would have taken," Kit guessed.

"Yes ma'am. He didn't see the truck when he passed by, but it's hidden pretty well under those trees. Plus it was dark." He gave a shrug. "He missed it. When he gets back home, it's around 12:30 or so, and he calls her in as a missing person. He's already called every friend he could think of, but no luck. No one's heard from her."

"So he reports her missing."

"And I get the call. I drive over to his house, take the report, and decide to drive by myself. I never saw the truck either, unfortunately. Then on my way home I decided to give the route one more drive-by and noticed something shining in the morning sun. When I got out to look, it was the mirror of the truck. A little more investigating and I found—" He swallowed. "I found a toe. It was . . . ah . . . fresh. So I called it in. I looked around to see if the owner of the toe might still be alive, but didn't want to go tramping around too much and mess up the crime scene. I hollered, but no one answered . . ." He gave another shrug.

"Where's her husband?"

"Over there." The officer pointed to a man who looked shell-shocked. "Bud Chalmers." Bud leaned against one of the police cruisers. In his midfifties, his pasty complexion didn't bode well. Kit wondered if he had heart problems that went beyond the brokenness of losing a loved one.

The DA had been quiet for the most part. Edward had apparently taken his cue and kept his mouth shut after that impromptu question. Stephen motioned that they were leaving and said to keep him updated. She nodded that she would.

"Mr. Chalmers?" She approached the man, compassion crimping her heart. He shouldn't be at the scene, but she didn't have the heart to force him to leave if this is where he needed to be. As long as he stayed out of the way . . .

He looked up and the lost devastation that stared back at her made her want to weep.

I'm going to get you, you creep. I will.

Taking a deep breath, she said, "I'm so sorry for your loss."

He nodded. "It's not right." An almost pleading look entered his eyes. "What's this world coming to?" Tears swam and he blinked them back, but not before one trickled down a weathered cheek that needed a shave.

"I'm so sorry, sir. We're going to do everything we can to get this guy." She paused when Noah walked up and offered his own condolences. Then she asked, "Can you think of anyone she might have made mad? Had an argument with? Any enemies?"

"No." The gray head waggled back and forth. "No. I mean she seemed a little more distracted than usual, was tense and uptight, but I just chalked it up to school nerves."

"But no threats or anything like that?"

"No, not my Susan. Everyone loved her."

Noah blew out a sigh, then turned to Kit. "What do you say we talk to a few people around campus about Mrs. Chalmers."

"Like you said earlier, great minds think alike."

17

"It feels weird being back here. I feel like I have a red bull's-eye stamped on my back." Kit shuddered and looked around.

Noah's gaze followed hers. "I know what you mean. Look at these buildings. They're a sniper's dream."

"I'm sure the architects took that into account when they designed them."

"Cute." And she was cute. Too cute for his peace of mind. Not only was she cute, she was smart, savvy, and he liked her sense of humor. And that dimple . . .

He sighed. Then nearly choked as he realized he was behaving like a lovesick schoolkid. He really needed to focus. Clearing his throat, he asked, "Okay, so where is his office?"

"Who's office?"

"The good professor you called and asked if we could visit."

"She," Kit said with a straight face.

"Huh?"

"Dr. Francine Bowden. She."

"Oh."

She paused. "So are all the doctors and truck drivers in your life of the male persuasion too?"

Noah felt the heat start around the base of his neck and travel north. "Aw, knock it off. I'm not a chauvinist. It was just a slip of the tongue."

"Uh-huh."

"Quit it." He gave a yank on her ponytail and she grinned at him. Noah groaned. "I'm serious. Now where's her office?"

"Over there. In the building to your left."

Noah made a left turn and opened the door to let Kit walk past him. They made their way to the elevator and he pressed the button. On the second floor, the doors slid open and the two stepped off.

"Which way?" Kit asked.

"Right."

"How do you know that?"

"The sign on the wall with the arrow that says 'Dr. Bowden' was my first clue," Noah said, copying her earlier deadpan expression.

It was Kit's turn to flush. Noah laughed out loud and led the way.

At the door Noah raised his knuckles and rapped.

"Come in."

He turned the knob and they entered the neatest office he'd ever seen.

Even Kit blinked.

"Wow."

Francine Bowden laughed, immediately understanding their shock. "I know. Not exactly the office of the absentminded professor, is it?"

"No. It's . . . immaculate." Kit glanced around.

Noah did the same. "Impressive," he said.

The fortysomething lady shrugged. "I like organization. I want to be able to find anything I need when I need it." She gestured to the two chairs in front of her desk. "Have a seat, detectives, and tell me what I can do to help."

Noah settled himself into the chair and clasped his hands between his knees.

"What can you tell us about Susan Chalmers?"

Grief flashed briefly. "Yes, I heard about her murder, of course. And the others too. Such a shame."

"What kind of student was she?"

"A fabulous one, much to my surprise."

"Why surprise?"

"Because when she first started taking classes, she had no confidence. She would often ask me if she was wasting her money, if she was too old, that kind of thing. I always did my best to encourage her, because she had so much potential." The professor shook her head. "If she could have gone to school twenty years ago, she would have already made a name for herself in the law profession."

"Did she have any enemies?"

A brow raised. "Susan? Goodness, no. She was one of the sweetest, most giving people I've ever met. She had a gift for writing and was most willing to share that with some of the other students who weren't quite as gifted. She often edited papers or made suggestions how to make them better."

"So she didn't seem distracted or anxious or anything that you would have deemed out of the ordinary?"

Dr. Bowden shrugged. "No. I mean, it's time for final exams. There's plenty of anxiety going around. But nothing . . ." She frowned and tapped her lips with a finger. "Wait a minute. There was one thing that was a little odd, but I don't know if it has anything to do with anything."

Noah leaned forward. Kit did too and he could smell the fresh fragrance of her shampoo. Doing his best to ignore the effect she had on his equilibrium, he raised a brow and encouraged, "You never know. What was it?"

"It was about two weeks ago. We finish class pretty late, but I always offer to stay in my office until 10:00 so that if anyone needs anything I can answer questions, et cetera. That night after class, Susan stopped by my office to ask if we could talk. I told her sure."

"What did she want to talk about?"

"I don't know. We never got to that. She came in and sat

down. I had just settled into my chair behind my desk when another student came to my door." She pointed to it. "I always leave it open. I don't care if you're male or female, the door stays open. My policy."

"A smart one," Noah approved.

"Unfortunately, you can't be too careful these days."

"I agree. So what happened?"

Professor Bowden frowned and sighed. "Susan saw the student, excused herself, and got up and left. But it struck me that the expression on her face was one of sheer terror. She was scared of him."

Noah exchanged a look with Kit, who asked, "Who was the student?"

"Gordon Childs."

"Where might we find this young man?" Noah queried.

Professor Bowden laughed. "I haven't got a clue. I don't keep up with my students' social or class schedules."

"Do you have any idea who he hangs around with? Names of friends?" Noah hoped she had at least one name to give them. It would cut down on the chase.

She tapped her lips. "It's Friday afternoon. You might try the student center. I believe Gordon likes a good game of pool. He often finds fresh blood there on the weekend."

Kit narrowed her eyes. "A hustler?"

Dr. Bowden nodded. "From what I hear, more than one new kid on the block has lost the contents of his wallet to young Mr. Childs. But I'll be honest, I like Gordon. I haven't had any deep, meaningful conversations with him, but he seems like a good guy and he's an excellent student. I've often wondered if the hustling reputation is overblown." She shrugged. "Maybe it's how he pays his tuition. Who knows?"

Noah stood. "All right, thanks so much for your time."

She sobered. "You're quite welcome. I do hope you catch this person. It's pretty nerve-wracking having your students picked off one by one."

Grimacing, Noah nodded. "Believe me, we're doing everything we can."

She stood and they all shook hands. "Please let me know if you think of anything else," Kit said as she headed for the door.

"Certainly."

Noah's phone rang and he grabbed it as they reached the elevator.

Back outside on the sidewalk, Kit listened to Noah wind up the conversation. She glanced over at him as he slid his cell back into its holder. "So no one came up with someone who's recently been released from prison that would be out to get you?"

"There's one or two possibilities that the captain's checking out, but I don't think they'll pan out. I know who he's talking about, and while one of them has a history of violence, it was all domestic."

"Let me guess. You got the wife and kids into a safe place."

"Um . . . actually, it was the husband and kids. The wife was a raving lunatic. Who's showing chauvinistic tendencies now?" he asked, tongue in cheek.

Kit burst into laughter. Noah joined in, and Kit realized how bad she needed to laugh. It felt good. "Okay, okay, you got me." Turning serious, she said, "I guess we'll find out soon enough. Okay. I suppose we should have asked for directions to the Student Center."

"No need." He held up a folded piece of paper.

"What's that?"

"A handy little map I picked up in the lobby back there."

They started walking and her eyes scanned the building rooftops as she walked. Was their shooter still out there somewhere on campus? Did he know they were back? And would he try again at some point? Something told Kit they hadn't heard the last of him.

"Has your handy little map told you where we're going yet?"

"I think we take a right up there."

"No, we're here."

He studied the map without looking up. "I don't think so. According to this, we're supposed to turn beside the Irons building."

"All right, if you say so, but I really think we're here, Noah."

He lifted his nose from the map, saw the direction of her gaze, and followed it. "Huh. You think?"

One shoulder lifted in a lazy shrug as she did her best to keep her chuckles under control. "I could be wrong," she deadpanned.

The building just ahead of them had a sign above the front door. He read it. "Student Center."

"Just a wild guess here," she offered, "but I think we found it."

He tossed the map into the nearest garbage can. "You're a riot a minute, Kenyon."

"I know. Just one of my many assets."

He broke down and grinned at her. "I can't tell you how much I'm beginning to like your assets."

A snort escaped her and she couldn't keep the laughter inside anymore. "Noah Lambert! I can't believe you said that."

"What?" All innocence stared back at her. Then a flush started at the base of his neck and he shook his head. "Aw, Kit, I didn't mean anything disrespectful by that comment."

"I didn't take it that way." She gave his arm a little push. "Now, let's get in there."

His face still beet red, he stepped toward the building, and she covered another smile. She really liked him. She liked his smile and the way it spread crookedly across his face, deepening the lines around his eyes. She liked the way they could bounce teasing off each other like they'd been doing it for years. She liked the way she could make him—a cop who'd seen way more than the average person and hadn't become hardened—blush. She liked just about everything about him except that stubborn streak he let out occasionally. And even that wasn't too bad. Definitely kept things interesting.

She cleared her throat. "What do you think about the whole miniature gavel thing? It's obvious that the killer is leaving them. Why do you suppose that is?"

"I don't know. I mean, I have my thoughts, but our FBI profiler is supposed to be working on that."

"Before we go in, share some of your thoughts, will you?"

He paused as though gathering his thoughts. "I guess you could go with it several ways. One: he's mocking the justice system. He kills them, then leaves the gavel to snub his nose at the law students he's killing."

"Two?"

"He somehow sees killing these people as a form of justice."

She thought for a moment. "That sounds more plausible for some reason."

Then she didn't have time to think about it anymore as they walked into the Student Center. Chaos, chatter, and laughter greeted them. "Hey, did you get a picture of this guy?"

He pulled out his iPhone and tapped the screen a few times. "Here. Straight from the law school directory."

She took a good look. "Got it. Where to?" she yelled over the noise.

"Didn't Professor Bowden mention something about pool?"

"Yeah." Her eyes traveled around the room. To her left there were several bar-style restaurant choices from McDonalds to Chinese. To the right, tables and booths covered an area equal to the square footage of her duplex. Straight ahead was the game room.

Single file, they made their way back through the throng of students to the game area. There they dodged darts and the Wii antics of those playing a rousing game of tennis to arrive in a more open space.

Three pool tables, four air hockey tables, and a corner reserved for the board games filled the back room. For a minute, they stood there taking it all in.

"Hey, isn't that the DA's intern?"

Noah looked in the direction she indicated. "Yeah, that's Edward, all right."

"Looks right at home here, doesn't he?"

"I'll say." The young man leaned against a window, pool stick in his left hand, soda in his right. When he saw them coming, he straightened and set his drink on one of the side tables. "Detectives." He reached out a hand and they took turns shaking it. "What are you doing here?"

"Looking for someone," Kit offered.

"Who? Maybe I can help."

Noah showed Edward the picture on his phone. Edward nodded. "He's here somewhere, I just saw him. He said something about being hungry and went to get a sub, I think."

"Thanks, Edward," Kit said, then she paused and added, "Hey, I'm sorry for blasting Brian in front of you. That had to be a little embarrassing and I'm sorry for doing it."

Edward shrugged. "Don't worry about it. I agreed with you. He should have followed protocol and obeyed the orders you sent him."

Kit shifted. "Yeah, well, I just wanted to apologize."

"Well, thanks, but you didn't have to." He gave a small smile and lifted a hand to rub his lips as he offered her a shrug.

"Right." She turned and took a deep breath. Apologies didn't come easy for her, but when she was wrong, she was wrong—and she was big enough to admit it.

So when are you going to apologize to your mother, her conscience mocked her. *I'm not wrong about that*, she argued back.

She looked at Noah. "Let's go check the food lines again."

He turned and led the way.

Back in the food court area, Kit drew in a deep breath and realized she was starving. The toast and peanut butter she'd scarfed down this morning was long gone.

After they snagged Gordon for a couple of questions, she'd be putting in a request for a late lunch.

"Hey." Noah tapped her arm and goose bumps broke out. "Is that him?"

Ignoring her crazy physical response to a man she wasn't sure she should be attracted to, she looked around him.

And there stood Gordon Childs second in line at the sub station. Together, they approached him.

Kit didn't know what it was, but some sixth sense must have tipped him off, because he looked up when they were about twenty feet from him.

Puzzlement flared briefly in his eyes, then they widened as he took in the badges they'd decided to openly display on their belts.

"He's going to be a runner," Kit said.

"I think you're right," Noah said. "Hey, Gordon!"

Gordon spun from the line and headed for the emergency exit.

Kit bolted after him, yelling to Noah, "You go to the right!"

The emergency door ruptured open and alarms spilled into the student center. Bodies pressed in on each other to see what was going on, but it was too late.

Kit was hot on the kid's heels, could hear his hurried steps rushing down the stairs. "Gordon, wait! We just want to talk to you!"

18

No answer.

He either didn't hear her or didn't care. At the bottom of the steps, Kit heard the door bang open and gripped the rail to propel herself faster down after him.

Reaching the door that had yet to swing shut, she threw herself through it in time to see Gordon round the corner of the building. Giving chase, she heard a yell and a curse.

"Noah! You got him?"

Flinging herself around the corner, she came to a screeching halt when she saw that Noah had the situation well under control.

Placing her hands on her knees, ignoring the renewed throbbing in her injured shoulder, she bent double and huffed, "Good job."

Noah slapped the cuffs on the still struggling young man. He was thin and wiry, while Noah had the build of an agile, seasoned weight lifter. The poor college student was no match for him.

Lifting Gordon to his feet, Noah turned him around to face them. "Why did you run?"

"What do you want?" Fear flared his nostrils and his eyes darted back and forth between Noah and Kit.

Kit stepped forward. "We just wanted to talk to you. Ask you a few questions."

"About?"

"A woman named Susan Chalmers."

His shoulders slumped. "Oh."

Kit raised a brow and wondered what *he* thought they were there for.

Gordon lifted his eyes and said, "I heard she was dead."

Noah nodded. "Yeah, and we heard you knew her pretty well."

Wariness flashed. "She and I talked some, yeah, but I mean we weren't buddies or anything."

"What'd you talk about?"

"Class mostly. Papers and just stuff like that."

Kit bit her lip against the pain from her shoulder, wondering how long before it would settle down this time. "Okay, I've got a couple of questions I need to ask you, and I'm not doing it without reading you your rights." Over his protests she did.

"What? Yes, I understand the rights, but you don't need to—"

"Did you kill her?" Kit asked, deciding to go with the direct approach.

He paled and began to tremble. "No, I didn't kill her! Do I need a lawyer?"

Noah shrugged. "I don't know. Do you?"

The young man shook his head. "No. Why would you think I'd kill her?"

"Because she was scared of you. Why is that, Gordon?"

Gordon shifted. His eyes darted as though trying to figure a way out. Kit hated to tell him he didn't have a chance of getting out of this one. But did he kill Susan? That was the question.

He swallowed hard, his Adam's apple doing a dance up and down his throat. "I swear I didn't touch her."

"Make us believe that." Noah pulled the keys to the cuffs from his pocket. "If I let you loose, will you promise not to take off again?"

A sigh rippled from him. "Yeah. I guess I knew this day was coming sooner or later."

"Really?" Kit asked as Noah released the cuffs. "Why do you say that?"

Gordon brought his right hand around to massage his left wrist. "Just a hunch."

Kit looked around and spotted two benches facing each other under the shade of an old oak tree. "Let's go sit over there and have a chat." It would be quieter than going back inside. A crowd had gathered at the commotion and Kit waved them off. Once the handcuffs were removed, the gawkers seemed to lose interest and filtered away.

The trio made their way to the benches and Noah slid down on one, legs stretched out before him, ankles crossed. His relaxed posture didn't fool Kit. She'd been around him enough to know he was ready to move should the need arise. She sat beside him and Gordon chose the opposite bench.

"Okay, Gordon, why was Susan scared of you?" Kit repeated the question.

"Because I'm an idiot," he blurted out.

Noah lifted a brow. "Explain that, please."

With a heavy sigh, Gordon buried his head in his hands, then looked up. "I asked her to write a paper for me."

Without blinking, Kit stared at him, silently urging him to hurry it up.

"She thought I was asking for her help and said sure, she'd be glad to."

The light went on for Kit. "Ah. But you didn't want her help, you just wanted her to do it."

A guilty flush made its way up his throat and into his cheeks. "Yeah. When she realized what I meant, she refused."

Noah rubbed his chin and studied Gordon. "Let me guess, she threatened to squeal on you."

"Yes, she did. And I flipped out. I've never done anything like that before. Ever. I'd worked so hard to get to this point. I'm so close to graduating, and because of one dumb mistake, she could blow it all for me." He blinked rapidly as though trying to keep tears at bay.

"Sounds to me like you just presented us with a pretty good motive for murder."

Gordon jumped up and Noah tensed. Kit found herself ready to pounce too. But there wasn't any need. The student just raked a hand through his hair and said through clenched teeth, "That's not why I'm telling you this. I'm trying to make you understand . . ." He looked away.

Kit pushed again. "So you killed her to keep her quiet."

He snapped his attention to her and stalked back to the bench. He sat with a thud and held his hands out in a beseeching manner. "No! Absolutely not. But I did . . . um . . . threaten her . . . sort of."

"How did you sort of threaten her?" Noah leaned forward, elbows on his thighs, hands clasped between his knees. His eyes lasered into Gordon.

Palming his eyes like a two-year-old, Gordon said, "I told her it would be a shame if something happened to one of those grandkids she was always yakking about simply because she couldn't keep her mouth shut."

"Holy . . ." Kit broke off and stared at him. "No wonder she was scared of you."

Gordon groaned and leaned forward to cover his face with his hands. "I know! I know." He looked up and tears glistened. "It was totally wrong. But I was just under so much pressure. I have all these graduating expenses and finals coming up and that stupid paper was due . . ." He swallowed again and lowered his voice. "My dad had a doctor's appointment. He's dying and it's just him and me. I have to take him, there's no one else."

"That's rough," Kit said, "but no excuse to threaten a woman's grandkids."

Gordon nodded and swallowed. "I know." He paused, then sighed. "My dad knows he doesn't have much time left. His one remaining wish is to live long enough to watch me walk across that stage and receive my law degree. But I'm also working full-time and doing my best to fulfill my intern requirements, studying for exams . . ." He held up his hands in an expression of helplessness. "I kept getting called in to work for this one girl who never shows up like she's supposed to. I needed the money. I mean between the medical bills and everything I just couldn't say no. I make close to three hundred dollars a night bartending. As a result, I was getting so far behind in school . . ." He stopped again and blew out a breath. "And that paper was huge. There was no way I couldn't *not* turn it in. I thought if I could just get her to write that paper for me . . ."

He closed his eyes and leaned his head back to stare at the overcast sky. "I couldn't let her say anything, but I only threatened her—and that just kind of . . . um . . . popped out. I spoke without thinking. But I would never have laid a hand on her—or her grandkids." He shuddered and sincere regret twisted his features. "I couldn't. I just messed up royally and I couldn't fix it."

Compassion darkened Noah's features, and Kit could understand that, but she also felt sorry for a poor woman whose only fault had been not only to be one of the best students in her class but to have a backbone full of integrity too.

"So why did you run when you saw us?"

Another guilty flush. "Oh yeah. That. Um . . . I thought you were here about the drugs."

Noah sat up straight. "What drugs?"

"The ones I bought when I thought I was going to explode if I didn't get some relief from all the stress and pressure."

Kit and Noah exchanged a look. "All right," she said, "where are they now?"

"I flushed 'em."

She sat back. "Why?"

Gordon looked off into the distance. "Because of my dad. He didn't raise me that way and would have been terribly disappointed. Every time I tried to swallow one of the pills, I'd see his face, his eyes. I'd hear his voice telling me to be better than those who were weak and turned to drugs." A shrug. "I couldn't do it. I finally tossed them in the toilet." A slight smile crossed his face at that statement and he looked her in the eye. "I slept great that night."

Kit smiled back. "Good." She changed the subject. "Did you know Walter Davis and Bonnie Gray?"

"Sure." His brows pulled together. "Everyone knew them. We were all getting ready to graduate. Why?"

"Do you have any idea who would want to kill them?"

"No. And I promise if I did, I'd tell you." He thought for a moment. "I know that Justin Marlowe had it bad for Bonnie. She dumped him and he just couldn't stand it. He was into the drug scene and she didn't want anything to do with that." He shifted and the guilt flashed over his features again. "That's who I got the drugs from."

"Really? That's pretty interesting since Justin told us he'd sworn off them."

"I think he did. I mean, I haven't seen him using lately. Just selling."

Noah glanced at his phone and pulled in a deep breath. "All right, Gordon, you've made a couple of dumb decisions over the last few weeks, but it looks like you've made a couple of good ones too."

Gordon looked at Noah, then swiveled his gaze to Kit. "I tried to apologize to her—to Susan. I tried to tell her I didn't mean it and that I was sorry, but she wouldn't listen. She'd just start crying and get as far away from me as she could." He barked out a humorless laugh. "Not that I blame her, but I hope she knew. I was dumb, thoughtless, and about to explode from the stress, but I . . ." He shook his head.

Noah clapped him on the shoulder. "Here." He pushed a card into the young man's hand. "It sounds like you have an awful lot on your plate and that you're doing a lot all on your own. This is my cell number. Call me if you ever need to. My pastor's number is on there too. You don't have to be a member of the church to get help from them."

Gordon looked shell-shocked.

Kit felt a little off-kilter herself. Who was this guy? This cop who seemed to reach out to everyone he came in contact with? This man who turned her insides to mush and had her dreaming of a possible relationship? What in the world?

After Gordon left, Kit stared at him. "First Heather and now him?"

He just smiled. "One by one, Kit. One by one."

19

"Who texted you?" Kit asked.

"We have a task force meeting in thirty minutes." Noah punched in a response and climbed into the car.

"So we're going on the assumption that we have a serial killer on the loose," Kit stated as she clicked her seat belt into place.

"Looks like it."

They made it to the station with a few minutes to spare. Kit walked to her desk and wondered how many messages she'd have to wade through. Her message light flashed like she knew it would.

While Noah took care of his own business, she got started on the messages.

Three were from her mother. Her adoptive mother. But she hadn't left a message to call her back, just three hang-ups with her number on the caller ID.

"You ready?"

Kit jerked. "Oh yeah. Right. Coming."

"Are you okay?"

She shot him a bright fake smile. "I'm great."

When his right brow went north, she let the smile slide from her face. She didn't have to put on an act with him. "I don't know," she finally admitted. "My mom called."

Concern creased his forehead. "I can cover for you and fill you in later if you need to call her back."

Kit considered it, then shrugged. "No, if it was an emergency, she'd have left a message. I'm good."

"Okay, if you're sure."

"I'm sure. Let's go."

They headed down the hall to the conference room where Captain Caruthers was already standing at the head of the large table that could seat about twenty people. She spotted her brothers-in-law, Connor Wolfe and Dakota Richards, seated to the rear of the room. She offered a wave and received one in return. Next to them sat two people she didn't recognize. Probably more FBI.

Up at the front someone had transferred all of the photos and information on the three victims. Seated next to Noah, Kit studied the wall, her eyes taking in each detail, willing them to speak to her, to tell her what they were missing.

What was the connection between the three?

And she had no doubt. There was a connection. Even if she couldn't see it yet. The bad thing was, it was probably as obvious as the nose on her face.

The captain started speaking and she forced herself to tune in. "All right, listen up, folks, it appears that we've got a serial killer on our hands. As a result, we've brought in some help. Some of you will know them. Connor Wolfe and his new partner, Page Duncan, will be joining the investigation. Welcome, Page."

Everyone murmured their hellos and nice-to-meet-yous.

The captain went on. "Also, FBI Special Agent Dakota Richards is back and has brought a couple more agents to help us out. Dakota, you want to make the introductions?"

"Sure." Dakota stood, pushed his trademark Stetson back on his head, and motioned to the man and woman seated next to him. "This is Special Agent Drake Mitchell and Special Agent Olivia Clark. They've been assigned to help out with the task force. Olivia specializes in profiling and Drake here can do whatever else needs doing."

The captain nodded. "Glad to have you here. We've got you a temporary office space setup. Dakota's probably shown you where you'll be working out of." They nodded. "All right, here's the rundown. We've got three dead law students, all with body parts that have been cut off. We have a weapon, a pocketknife that may have been used in the first and second murders. We know who the knife belongs to, but no evidence to suggest he was the one who used it on the victims and no prints for us to run."

An officer seated near Kit raised his hand to question. "What about a press conference? We need to let the public know what's going on."

"I'm already on that. I'll be holding that press conference around four o'clock this afternoon. It'll be replayed on the six, ten, and eleven o'clock news tonight. FOX and CNN and every other news station will probably be picking up the story as soon as the words 'serial killer' get out."

Kit made note of that on the lined pad in front of her.

"Has the lab come back with any more connections between the three murders?" This from Dakota.

"Negative. The only connections are"—he ticked them off on his fingers—"one: the fact that they were all killed execution style with a bullet to the back of the head. Two: they're all law students. Age and gender don't seem to matter. Three: they all had body parts removed and left at the scene."

Kit murmured to Noah, "We need to focus on the body part thing. That means something to him. If we can figure that out, we'll have a lot."

"Could mean anything, but we could brainstorm some ideas. Maybe Special Agent Clark will be able to shed some light for us."

Shifting their attention back to the captain, who'd just shot them a glare, Kit raised a hand.

He nodded. "Something you want to share with the group?"

"Sorry, sir," Kit offered. "I was just saying I think we need to focus on the meaning of the body parts thing." She looked at Olivia Clark. "Could you work on that first? Try to figure out why he's chopping off different parts from each victim? Or at least give us some ideas to start with?"

"Certainly. I'll review all of the information and keep that in the forefront of my mind."

Kit smiled her thanks.

The captain wrapped it up. "That's all, folks. Get out there and get this guy. I don't want him killing anyone else."

Kit didn't either, but she was desperately afraid the killer would strike again before they could catch him. Was he even now scoping out his next victim?

The Judge laughed as he crossed the street and entered the building. He knew after finding the third body they'd be calling in reinforcements. Maybe even a task force. But they'd never catch him.

At least not until he'd fulfilled his duty, which included passing judgment on those who didn't deserve to share his space, much less his profession.

Law students. And cops.

He smirked. They thought they were so smart, were so full of themselves. It wasn't until it was too late that they finally realized they'd never be as smart as he.

And the cops. He hoped he had them chasing their tails.

Bonnie Gray had been killed with a stolen gun. A 9mm he'd fallen in love with the minute he'd held it in his hands. The Walther PPK/S, he'd purchased on the black market for about five hundred dollars. Two similar murders, but two different guns.

He almost laughed aloud as he imagined their consternation at the ballistics reports. The ones from Walter, Bonnie, and the bullet he was sure they found in Kit's house. Not to mention the one he'd planted in Susan.

Really, the only reason he'd used two different guns in the executions was because he wanted to see which one he liked better. He thought he might stick with the 9mm. Or maybe he'd just alternate. Whatever. It didn't matter. The ones to be punished would be dead either way.

That was the priority. That they paid for their grievous sins. That they were punished like they deserved.

Although, one was different. Excitement flooded him. He may have found the perfect woman. The perfect wife. The perfect mother for his son.

She was smart. She always seemed to smile and she never, ever mocked him.

Shaking his head, he looked toward the game room. Then again, business could wait. A game of pool might be fun. Might help him relax a little before he tracked down the next guilty one and served up the justice they deserved.

Alena smiled up at Corey as he held the door to Flannigan's. "Thanks."

His tired eyes seemed to sparkle a little brighter. "You're welcome."

Once settled in the booth, Alena pulled the menu toward her. "How did you find this place?"

"My uncle told me about it. He and I eat here occasionally."

"What do you recommend?"

"The fried chicken and veggies. They're good for you." He flashed her a rare grin and her stomach twisted into knots. She realized how much she liked him all over again. Which was why she had to ask him a tough question.

Resting her arms on the table, she leaned forward and asked, "Okay, we said we'd shoot straight with each other, right?"

"Yep."

"Am I the only girl you're seeing or are you dating others?"

He frowned and the light in his eyes dimmed. "Why do you ask that?"

"Because you had your arm around Leslie Pritchard while you were walking across campus yesterday. And you don't even go to school there. So, what's the deal?"

"Ah." He took a sip of tea. "I did have my arm around her." He reached out, took her hand, and stared deep into her eyes. "But I promise, I'm not dating her. You're the only girl for me, Alena."

Pain darted through her. Could she believe him? Did she dare not believe him? "Then what were you doing with her?"

He sighed. "I've known Leslie since we were kids. She's my uncle's best friend's daughter. Is that confusing enough for you?" He smiled, then sighed. "She asked me to come to the campus to help her out with something."

"What?"

Corey studied her, and she wanted to squirm, but she also wanted to hear his explanation.

He rubbed a hand across his face, then said, "She wanted to make her boyfriend jealous, so I helped her do it. I also gave her a little kiss on the lips in front of him. Okay?" He spread his hands. "That's all it was. I promise."

Alena bit her lip, then drew in a deep breath. Forcing a smile, she nodded. "All right, if you say so."

"I say so."

Noah led the way to Flannigan's Fine Food. He and Kit were both starved. After the task force meeting, they'd met up with Connor and Dakota, inviting Olivia, Page, and Drake to come along.

When the group settled into the corner booth and put in a drink and appetizer order, Kit looked across the restaurant and saw her neighbor, Alena, sitting with a good-looking man.

Catching her eye, she waved. Alena waved back, but Kit

thought she looked a little strained. Making a mental note to ask her about it, she turned back to the group and brought up the case. "Okay, how are we going to go about catching this guy? It's not like we can put a cop on every law student on and off campus."

Noah narrowed his eyes. "No, but what if the students did their part and made sure they went out only in pairs or groups?"

"They're going to have to."

"They're also going to have to be careful about who they trust."

Kit sighed and took a sip of her soda. When the waitress came back, she took their order. Kit asked for hers to go, then turned to Dakota. "I hear you had some excitement in this restaurant not too long ago."

He gave a grunt. "Yeah, I'll say."

"What are you talking about?" Page asked.

Kit took a sip of water then said, "My sister"—how she loved the way the word rolled from her tongue so easy now—"had a stalker. He sent her a gift to this very restaurant. Everyone thought it was a bomb."

"It wasn't," Dakota clipped.

Kit bit her lip and raised a brow. "Sorry, I didn't mean to talk about a taboo subject."

Dakota sighed. "Sorry. I didn't mean to snap. It's not taboo, just not a pleasant memory for any of us who were here."

"Right. Sorry. Jamie was just telling me about it the other day on the phone when I mentioned eating here."

Her brother-in-law looked startled. "She told you about it?"

"Yes," she stared at him, "why? She tells me lots of things."

With a rueful smile, he said, "It's my turn to apologize. Jamie just doesn't normally talk about it that much. At least not in a general discussion. She talks about it so much with some of the people that she helps counsel that . . ." He trailed off. "Anyway, sorry. Didn't mean to snap."

Kit shrugged. "It's okay. And just for the record, I didn't ask her about her past. She brought it up."

"No, that's cool." He looked at his captive audience. "And before you ask, yes, we caught the guy."

"Thanks to Kit," Connor said. "She distracted him, talked him into staying calm while we got into place to bring him down."

She flushed. "I wasn't looking for kudos. Just making conversation."

Noah shot her an admiring glance. "That had to be tough."

A shrug. "At the time, yeah. But it's what I do and I wanted to do it. I'd just found my sisters and I wasn't about to lose one of them." She changed the subject. "So, how do we go about getting this guy who's killing our law students? Olivia," she addressed the profiler, "what are your thoughts on our killer?"

"I studied the notes he's left. He's talking directly to the victims. For example, the first note, 'Life's a laugh. How does the death penalty feel? An eye for eye . . .'" She shook her head and her short black curls bounded around her head. "The first sentence: 'Life's a laugh.' I think he may believe Walter had it too easy. The killer is jealous of Walter's ease. Did he have money?"

Noah nodded. "His parents were well off. But he also seemed to cruise through school and classes with no problems. I talked to one of his professors on the phone the other day, and he said Walter was brilliant and that the legal profession had lost out big-time with his death."

Page eyed the group and offered, "So, maybe this guy was jealous of Walter's money and the fact that school came easy to him."

"Or maybe there was some professional jealousy? The killer didn't like being second or third best?" Dakota interjected.

Olivia nodded. "Any of that would fit. But the 'eye for an eye' comment intrigues me the most. An eye for an eye indicates that Walter did something to our killer that deserved retaliation or revenge."

Drake took a long drink of his tea. "But what?"

"If we figure that out, we'll be able to find our killer."

"Hey guys."

Kit looked up to see Brian Sands and Johnny Nance standing beside her. "Hey guys, what's up?"

Brian eyed her. "Just saw you sitting here and thought we'd stop by to say hey."

Kit introduced them to everyone. After a round of handshakes, Brian and Johnny moved on and planted themselves in a booth opposite from where Kit sat. She shifted as she felt Brian's eyes bore into her, but did her best to ignore him. Now that she knew he was interested in seeing her outside of work, she felt uncomfortable and a little angry at him for putting her in this situation.

When their order came, she told herself not to worry about Brian and focused on the conversation. She was just about to ask what Olivia felt would be her next step in the investigation when her phone rang.

Captain Caruthers.

Turning her head away from Brian's stare, she slapped the phone to her ear. "Kit Kenyon."

"We found something."

She sat up and shot a look at Noah. "What is it?"

"It doesn't have anything to do with the murders. This is about whoever was up on top of that house across from yours taking shots at you."

"Really? And what did they find?"

"The CSU team missed it."

Noah leaned over and placed his cheek next to hers so he could listen. She'd put it on speakerphone if they weren't in the restaurant. As much as she tried not to, she couldn't help the deep breath that allowed her to breathe in his scent any more than she could stop that funny swooping thing her stomach did whenever he got too close. Captain Caruthers was saying, "Your shooter stuffed some rappelling gear down the chimney."

"So who found it?"

"The owner."

"It's May. What's he doing cleaning out his chimney?"

"Apparently his kids were throwing a Frisbee and it landed

up on the roof. He went up to get it and noticed something not right about the chimney cover. When he went to investigate, he pulled up a rappelling rig."

"Then how did our guy get off the roof if he left that stuff up there?"

"Jumped is my guess. Probably found himself a nice bush to land in. I'm not saying it wouldn't hurt, but it sure wouldn't kill him."

Kit let out a sigh. "All right, thanks. Let us know if you figure out who it belongs to."

"Absolutely."

She hung up and looked at the group. "Well, that was interesting." She relayed the conversation, then took a sip of soda.

Dakota grunted. "The lab will run prints."

"Yep." She rested her chin on her palm. "And the computer will spit out a bunch of matches."

Noah nodded and sighed. "And then the human eye will have to analyze."

"Right. It'll take some time." She looked at him. Noticed the little lines around his eyes and the scar on his chin. She wondered what he'd do if she leaned over and kissed it.

Whoa. You're not exactly alone here, remember? Grabbing her takeout, she said, "I've got to get to that training exercise." The others moved so she could slide from the booth. Without looking Noah in the eye, she flung a smile in his direction. "Catch up with you later."

"You bet."

"See you later, Kit." Dakota lifted a hand in a wave. "Don't forget Sunday lunch with Ma."

"Right." She waved and practically ran for the door.

She really had to get her emotions under control, because she had a feeling Noah had read her thoughts like an open book.

A glance in Brian's direction showed a frown on his face and disappointment in his eyes.

Great.

20

Noah knew Kit would be busy with a training exercise with the SERT members that afternoon and well into the evening. He'd be on his own. Which was fine with him. Space between him and Kit was exactly what he needed, since it seemed he was determined to keep finding reasons to get close to her, to touch her.

To wonder what it would be like to kiss her.

Any excuse to be in her presence.

And it wasn't hard to do, seeing as how they spent nearly all of their waking hours together.

And as much as he found himself wanting to spend some sleeping hours with her, he figured he had some thinking—and some praying—to do. He had desires like any normal red-blooded male, but when he'd committed his life to Christ, he'd vowed to keep himself for his wife.

For a woman like Kit.

A woman he'd actually envisioned wearing a white gown.

And after only a little more than three weeks.

It scared him to death.

And while his attraction grew with each passing moment in her company, he couldn't do a thing about it now—while she and God weren't on speaking terms.

It hurt to think that she might not ever come back to the God he loved, but . . . no, she would. She had to.

Because his heart was already so involved he didn't know what he would do if he had to keep their relationship on a friendship/partner level for much longer.

God, I don't know what you have in mind for the future, but I'm praying it involves Kit. You've blessed me so much, and you know I'm ready to settle down and have a family. Draw Kit close to you. Bring her back to you. Let her see that while my arms are open to her, so are yours—and those are the ones she really needs.

Finished with the prayer, he felt better. But at the same time he had to get his mind on something else or go crazy.

Which is why he found himself at the lab, pushing to hear about the fingerprints on the rappelling gear.

Shorty Macguire, the young lab tech, who stood six feet three inches tall, had fiery red hair, a Scottish brogue, and a desire to help. "I've got the results right here."

"Great. Who do we need to find?"

"There are prints from a girl named Heather Younts."

Noah felt the air punch out of his lungs. "Heather?"

Shorty cocked his head. "Yeah, why? Does tha' name ring a bell?"

"It sure does. Her boyfriend, Walter Davis, was the first victim of our serial killer."

"Um . . . wow, then tha' means you have a connection between the guy tha' tried to kill you and . . . wow."

"Yeah, wow," Noah muttered absently, his mind spinning with all kinds of possibilities. He snapped back to who the prints belonged to. "Why was she in the system? Anything other than being a law student?"

"Uh . . . apparently, she was arrested for shoplifting when she was seventeen. A onetime thing tha' got her a slap on the wrist and some community service."

"Okay, I think I need to have another talk with Heather."

"There were a couple of other prints on there tha' didn't show up. They weren't in the system. But," he shrugged, "if you come up with some other suspects, send 'em my way and I'll be glad to see if I can match 'em up."

Noah clapped the man on the shoulder. "Thanks, Shorty. I'll be in touch."

His phone rang just as he pulled it out to give Kit a call. A glance at the caller ID made him smile. He answered on the third ring. "Hello, old man, what can I do for you?"

"You could learn proper phone etiquette. Seems all my teaching was in vain. The boy don't even answer the phone right."

Noah couldn't help the fond chuckle that escaped him as he pictured the grizzled man who looked like he belonged to the Mafia. Six feet four inches, the man could intimidate the most fearless street hardened youth. He'd sure put the fear of God into Noah when he'd been an angry, jail-bound sixteen-year-old. "Myles Cleary, you're a bright spot in a dark day. Good to hear from you."

"You've been noticeably absent around here at the boys' home. I'm just calling to check in on you and see if you need anything."

"Naw, just working hard. I'm trying to solve a couple of murders."

Myles turned serious. "I've heard about all that. I'm sure sorry." He paused, then said, "But if you're the one working the case, it won't be long till you get him."

Noah's heart filled with pleasure at the pride in the man's voice. He'd been a father to Noah when he'd needed one the most. "Thanks, Myles."

"So tell me about this new partner of yours."

He held his breath a moment, then let out a laugh. "You've been talking to the captain again, haven't you?" Not only was the captain a member of the same church, he was also one of Myles's closest friends.

"Yeah. Said he partnered you up with one of the best."

Noah pictured Kit's smiling face. "Oh yeah, she's definitely one of the best."

"What's that I hear in your voice, son?" Noah could tell Myles was only partially teasing and there was no way he was getting into a discussion on his feelings for Kit right now.

"Ah. Nothing, Myles, nothing. Listen, I've got to go. I'll catch up to you later, all right?"

Myles let out a belly laugh that made Noah wince. He hadn't fooled the old man at all. Disgusted with himself for wearing his feelings on his sleeve, so to speak, he groaned. "Leave it alone, Myles, I'll introduce you to her soon."

"I expect you will, son, I expect you will."

Shaking his head, Noah hung up and dialed Kit's number to ask her if she'd like to make a visit to Heather Younts to see if the girl had more to add to her story.

He told himself the sudden thud in his chest area had nothing to do with seeing Kit again and everything to do with the cheeseburger he'd wolfed down earlier.

Unfortunately, he'd never been a very good liar, especially when it came to lying to himself.

21

Kit shook her head and crossed the parking lot. Half the unit was down with a virus, so training would take place next week. A phone call to let her know would have been nice, but she didn't sweat it. In a way she was relieved. That meant she had more time to spend on the murders—and catching their killer. And she wanted to find Justin Marlowe to press him about the pocket-knife. Why that piece of evidence nagged at her, she wasn't sure.

But it was her conviction that Justin could provide an answer.

Her phone rang as she was climbing into her car. Noah.

Did her heart actually *skip* a beat? Could she really do something that cliché?

One thing she'd thought about, as she'd waited for the team that never showed, was the fact that she and Noah seemed to be getting closer with each passing day—and she knew absolutely nothing about his family.

Making a mental note to ask him, she answered on the fourth and final ring. "Hello?"

"Hey, what time do you finish your training?"

"Five minutes ago. It's been postponed. What's up?"

"The prints on the rappelling gear came back belonging to Heather Younts." Satisfaction echoed in his voice.

"Wow. Wasn't expecting that one."

"Yeah, I've heard that word a lot today. So, you up for making a visit to Heather?"

"Sure. Have you tracked her down yet?"

"Just getting around to that," he said. "It's Friday afternoon. I wonder if she's hanging around campus or heading to her parents' house. Or a friend's." He paused and she heard rustling come over the line. "I've got her number written down somewhere." Another pause. "Okay, here it is. I'm going to give her a call. Why don't you meet me back at the campus? If she doesn't answer, we'll start asking questions."

"I'm on my way. I'll meet you in front of her dorm unless I hear back from you. Oh," she added, "I'm going to see if I can track down Justin Marlowe. I want to ask him a few more questions about that pocketknife. If he didn't use it on Bonnie, someone did."

"What if it fell out of his pocket like he claimed?"

"I'd have less trouble believing that if it wasn't covered in her blood."

"Right. See you in a few."

Fifteen minutes later, she pulled into the campus and wound her way through the streets to park in front of Heather's dorm building.

Noah hadn't called, so he must have gotten in touch with her.

Climbing out of her car, she saw Noah heading her way. He'd already parked in the almost deserted parking lot. The weekend for the law students had started, and no one wanted to hang around school when there were stresses to party off.

She almost smiled. It reminded her of her one week of wildness.

"What are you thinking about?" he asked as he caught up with her.

"My junior year of college."

"What's so funny about it?"

"It was the year I decided to quit being a nerd."

He snorted a laugh. "You're the last person I'd call a nerd."

She cut him a glance, then said, "You'd be surprised. I may

not look like one, but I was so focused on getting straight As and getting my degree, I didn't have much time for fun."

"But that changed your junior year?" They entered the building and noticed no one at the desk. "I'll call up and tell her we're here. We can talk in the lobby."

Kit nodded and waited for him to finish his phone call. He hung up and said, "She's on her way. She said I just caught her as she was finishing up packing."

"Going away for the weekend?"

"Yeah. A camping trip to the beach with some friends."

"Ah. A weekend of roughing it, I see."

Noah raised a brow and then reminded, "Your junior year?"

She shrugged. "I went to a party, got drunk, woke up sick, and wondered where twelve hours of my life had gone. I didn't like it much and decided to go back to being a nerd."

He frowned. "That could have had a really bad ending."

"I know." She sighed. "Thankfully, it didn't."

Knowing what she knew now about date rape drugs and how easy it was to make a person disappear, she shuddered at her youthful naiveté. But all that was in the past. She was a quick study and she'd never again touched more than the occasional glass of wine.

The elevator slid open and Heather Younts entered the lobby, pulling a carry-on-sized suitcase and an overnight bag with her.

Setting the luggage aside, she came right to the point. "You said you had some more questions for me. I don't know what else I can tell you, but . . ." Trailing off, she waited for them to speak.

Noah picked up the questioning. "We found some rappelling equipment at a crime scene. It had your prints on it."

The girl frowned. "Well, I'm a member of the rappelling club here at school."

"Do you have your own equipment?"

"No, I just borrow it from whoever's not going. There's always someone who can't go every time. We switch equipment around all the time."

Noah blew out a sigh. "So there's no way to tell whose equipment it is just by looking at it?"

She laughed. "No way. I mean, not unless it's someone's special stuff and usually that doesn't get loaned out to anyone."

Kit spoke up. "But that means that whoever we're looking for might be in the rappelling club."

"Or not," Heather said. "Sometimes we take people who are simply interested in the club. Let them try it out, see what we're all about. Some join, some don't."

Grimacing, Kit said, "A needle in a haystack."

"Whose equipment did you borrow the last time you went rappelling?"

Her brow furrowed. "Um . . . I think it was Lee's."

"Lee?"

"Lee Travers."

"Where can we find Lee?"

"He probably went home. He's not big on staying around campus during the weekend."

"Do you know where he lives?"

"He's not a local. He's from North Carolina. Somewhere around Raleigh, I think."

Kit nodded. "My stomping grounds." She looked at Heather. "Do you have his address?"

"No, but you should be able to find it pretty easily." Heather stood. "Look, I need to get going. My friends are waiting on me. If I think of anything else, I'll call, but I just want to get away from here for a while. The memories . . . Walter . . ." Tears welled and she looked up at the ceiling, trying to blink them back.

"Go on," Noah said, "we've got your number."

The girl grabbed her bags and hurried for the door.

Noah looked at Kit. "You've got that look on your face."

Perturbed, she frowned. "What look?"

"That look that says you're thinking too hard. What are you planning?"

"A road trip. Justin's going to have to wait."

SATURDAY

22

Saturday morning dawned reluctantly. The clouds looked ready to release their burden at any moment. Kit threw her duffle bag in the back of her Toyota 4Runner and climbed in the driver's seat. She'd called her mother late last night and hadn't received an answer. Worried, she'd tried her mom's best friend, Brigitte Hathaway.

Brig, as Kit had called her since she could speak, informed her that her mother had been admitted to the hospital yesterday.

"Why? What's wrong with her?"

"Do you really care?" the woman asked coolly.

Hurt, Kit kept her cool and wheedled, "Brig, come on. You know I care. I love her, I just have some . . . issues I need to work through."

"I know all about your issues, Kit. But you're mad at a woman who never did anything but love you."

"She lied to me my entire life!" Kit snapped as the hurt faded back into anger.

Brig went quiet. Then, "Are you coming to see her?"

"Yes. Tell her I'll be there in a few hours. Please."

As she started to back out of her driveway, a car pulled up, blocking her exit. Stepping on the brake, she waited.

Noah climbed from the vehicle and walked up to the window

she'd just lowered. "I talked to the captain. He said you'd asked for a couple of personal days."

"I did." She clenched her jaw. "I know now's not exactly the best time since we're in the middle of an investigation, but this is something I have to do."

"Where are you going? Is everything all right?"

Was this any of his business? But she could see the concern in his eyes. "My mom is having some minor—if there is such a thing—heart surgery this afternoon. I'm going to Raleigh to check on her."

"Your mom?" Confusion flickered. "I thought . . ."

She knew what he thought. "It's a long story I'll have to bore you with one day."

Curiosity gleamed in his gaze, but all he said was, "Would you be opposed to having someone come along?"

"You?"

"Who else?" He flashed her that grin that seemed to make her knees grow weaker each time she saw it. Pretty soon, she'd just melt into a little puddle every time he smiled at her.

"Why would you want to do that?"

"Because I like being with you." Innocence and amusement stared back at her.

She paused, then cocked her head. "And?"

He laughed. "And I'm pretty sure you're going to turn this into a working trip by chasing down Lee Travers. I want to be there when you do."

Kit gaped at him. How had he known? "Yep. He lives on the outskirts of Raleigh, not too far from where I'm going."

"I know. I checked. So did you call him yet?"

"Yes, no answer. I can keep trying on the ride there." Her heart twisted at the thought of spending so much unofficial time in his company. She kept her expression neutral, hoping he couldn't read her sudden pleasure. "All right. Climb in."

"I'll drive if you like."

"Why? You don't trust me?"

"With my life. Now come on."

With a shake of her head, she pulled back into her spot, grabbed her bag from the backseat, and joined Noah in his car.

She buckled up and looked at him. "You just caught me."

"I see that. You didn't answer your cell phone."

Frowning, she reached into her back pocket and pulled it out. Missed 3 calls. "Oh sorry. I left it on silent." She changed the setting to vibrate and slipped it back into her pocket.

"I guess I should apologize."

She startled. "What for?"

"For making you work when you should be focusing on your mother."

Kit shrugged. "It's no big deal. I mean it's not like I'm going to be able to do anything but sit in a hospital room." And avoid conversation. Work would be a welcome relief.

"Not to be nosey, but I thought your mom was the same woman as Jamie and Samantha's mother."

"She is. My biological mother. I was adopted as an infant."

"Does that have anything to do with the statement you made back at the restaurant the other day?"

She frowned. "What statement?"

"Something along the lines of 'I just found my sisters and I wasn't about to lose one.'"

"Oh. That statement. Yeah. It does."

"Okaaaay." He frowned as he drew the word out. "Why don't you bore me with that story on the way there?"

"I need to stop at an ATM. I don't have a bit of cash on me."

"Kit . . ."

"Oh fine. But don't get too comfortable, I don't want you dozing off on me."

The Judge watched his prey pull out of the driveway and head down the street. Where were they going? He'd seen her and the other detective talking to Heather again. What did they want with her? Did she know anything? Obviously not. They hadn't come after him.

Instead, they were heading out of town. Interesting. He followed, curiosity and anger warring within him. Curious about where she was going. Anger because it was with the cop. What was she doing with him on the weekend? Oh, yeah, sure, cops worked weekends, but she was in his personal vehicle. Not the cop car that said she was working.

This wasn't good.

He'd already failed to get rid of Noah twice. Now it looked like he might have a chance to try again.

Or warn Kit.

That was it. He'd give her a warning. After all, she didn't realize what she was doing.

He watched the car speeding along in front of him on I-85 and felt the fury burn in his chest as he pictured them together. It was wrong. How dare Noah put his hands on her? She was *his* future wife. The one who would be the mother of his children. Fingers clenched the steering wheel as he continued down the highway.

His fingers itched to place the gun against the back of the cop's head and pull the trigger. Signaling to switch lanes, he stayed two car lengths back. Patience, he told himself. The time would come.

He checked his Blackberry. Nothing pressing this weekend. A spur-of-the-moment decision had sent him after them. Now he couldn't seem to stop himself. He'd follow them and see what they were up to. But he wouldn't stay long. He had another trial to get under way. And an execution to carry out.

The first in his next series of three.

"So, your mother was pregnant with twins. Your biological dad had left before she found out she was pregnant. She went through with the pregnancy without telling anyone she was having twins and gave one of the babies away."

Kit sliced him a glance and he could see the hurt in her eyes. "Yep. That about sums it up."

"And when your biological dad came home . . ."

"He'd been in a rehab facility part of the time, getting himself cleaned up."

"Because of the back injury that led to his painkiller addiction."

"You follow a boring story pretty well, Lambert." Kit's voice was monotone, without inflection. But deep down, Noah could hear the hurt behind the words. "Yes, he felt he was a danger to his family, especially when Samantha followed his example and popped a few of his pills because she thought they would take away the pain of her bad day at school. She had to have her stomach pumped and almost died."

Noah winced. "That had to be awful."

"It was his wake-up call. So he woke up and walked out without a word. They found out later he left to clean himself up."

"But he left his wife pregnant with twins."

"He didn't know. My biological mother didn't have much family or support, so it wasn't too hard to hide. As a result, I went to live with my biological mother's former best friend, Faith Kenyon, and Jamie went to live where she was supposed to."

For a minute, Noah didn't speak. Then he told her, "I think you were probably right where you were supposed to be too, but it's obvious you don't feel the same."

"Just don't go there, okay?"

"Come on, Kit—"

"Change the subject. Let's talk about you."

A sigh filtered from him and he was silent for a moment. "Okay, so are you close to your adoptive mom?"

She shot him an annoyed glance. "That's not about you. If you don't want to tell me about your sordid past, then can't we just talk about the weather?"

"I don't care about the weather. I care about you."

A car moved over into their lane causing Noah to jerk the wheel to get out of the way. The car swerved a bit and he could have sworn she bit off a curse. "Excuse me? I didn't catch that."

"I said, 'Darn it.'"

"Are you sure that's what you said?"

A low groan of exasperation erupted from her. "Why do you like to aggravate me so much?"

"Kit, it's not that I like to aggravate you, it's just that I think you have a lot of stuff going on inside you that you need to let out. Pushing you seems to help you break down some of those walls."

She went still, and he wondered if he should have been quite so blunt. Then she shot him a sideways glance. "And what about your walls, Noah? Do you ever let anyone past those?"

He flinched and opened his mouth to say something, then shut it. What could he say? What could he tell her without making her feel . . .

Nothing.

He couldn't say anything yet.

When he didn't respond, she gave a small sigh and looked out the window for the next thirty minutes.

Out of the blue she asked, "Are we being followed?"

Snapping his attention away from his attractive partner, he glanced in the rearview mirror. "Which car?"

"The black Mustang about two car lengths back. It's been right behind us since we left Spartanburg. Keeping about the same distance and everything."

"Somehow, it wouldn't surprise me."

"Slow down a little and let's see what he does."

He let off the gas. Pressing the brake would alert the perp they were on to him. Noah pursed his lips and looked in his side mirror for a second before looking back ahead at the road. "Can you make out any details?"

"No. The windows are tinted and it's too far back. The car is an older model black Ford Mustang. Probably early nineties.

But it does have an emblem on the hood. Looks like some kind of bird or something."

"Wish I could get behind him and get his license plate."

"You could try."

"Yeah, but I don't want to tip him off that we know he's back there."

She pointed. "There's our exit. You want to see if he keeps following or we're just being paranoid?"

"Sounds good to me." He accelerated and moved over into the right lane. The black Mustang stayed in the left. Noah moved on over and started up the exit ramp. The black Mustang kept going.

Kit rolled her eyes and looked at her partner with a wry smile. "Guess I'm losing it."

He shrugged. "Maybe. I don't know." He shot her a look. "Then again, who would blame you if you were?"

"Thanks a lot."

"Any time."

She pursed her lips. "He could have been after you, you know."

"Possibly, but look at it this way. We've been partners now for about three weeks. Before you came along, no one was shooting at me. At least not snipers from on top of buildings."

He had a point, but she wasn't going to give him the satisfaction of agreeing with him. Although it did make her wonder what she'd done to make someone that mad at her.

Before she could finish a mental list of possibilities, she'd directed Noah to the hospital. "You can just drop me off at the door."

"Are you sure?"

"Quite. Leave me here and see if you can track down Lee Travers." She sighed. "This is something I've been putting off for about six months now. I'll call you when I'm done."

He nodded. "I'll be praying for you."

She froze. Then looked back at him. "Thanks."

Climbing out of the car, she headed inside the building. A stop at the nurses' desk got her a room number. Kit slipped into the elevator and made her way to Faith Kenyon's room. Her mother. Adoptive mother.

Taking a deep breath, she rapped her knuckles on the door and pushed her way in.

Brig sat in a chair next to her mother's bed.

Looking at the frail woman in the bed, Kit couldn't hold back a startled gasp. "Oh Mama." She hurried to her side and picked up the hand that had become gnarled with arthritis much too soon. Just one look at her mother's face brought a cascade of happy memories. Good-night kisses and after-school snacks and her daddy pushing her on the swing. Chocolate chip cookies and Christmas morning squeals.

Brig looked at her, one eyebrow raised. "'Bout time you got here."

"I'm sorry." And she was. All the anger she'd been holding on to faded in light of her mother's illness. She laid the hand she held back on the bed and faced her mother's friend. "She didn't tell me."

"No, she didn't."

"That was you calling and not leaving messages, wasn't it?"

A flush stole over the woman's creased cheeks. "Guilty as charged. I kept hoping if you saw her number come up enough times on your phone, you'd call to check on her."

"It worked."

Satisfaction gleamed for a brief moment, then Brig looked at her sleeping friend. "I think her heart just broke when you took off."

Shame slammed Kit and she blinked back a surge of tears. "You're right," she said softly. "I shouldn't have done that. I was just . . ."

"Very angry," came a small voice from the bed.

Kit turned. "Mom. Hi."

"Hello, darling."

She gripped the bed rail. "Yes, I was angry."

"I may be sick and laid up, but I haven't lost my sight. You're still angry."

Kit dropped her eyes. "Yeah, I am, but I also love you very much and want you to get better fast."

A single tear slipped down her mother's cheekbone to disappear into her hair. Kit reached out to wipe it away. "You should have told me," she whispered.

"Maybe so."

"I'm working on it, though. I won't stay mad forever."

"You need to take it to the Lord, darling."

Her jaw firmed, then relaxed. "Maybe so. I've been giving him a lot of thought lately too."

Joy ruptured in her mother's eyes and Kit leaned forward to press a kiss to the woman's forehead. "Get better fast, all right?"

The door whooshed open and a young man entered, followed by a nurse with medicine for the IV. "Hello, Mrs. Kenyon. This handsome man is your ride to surgery. Are you ready to go get a couple of arteries unclogged?"

Kit looked up. "It's time already?"

"Got to do the prep stuff and then get in line."

The nurse smiled and Kit found herself smiling back. Looking back down at her mother, she said, "I'll be here when you get out."

Kit stood by as an orderly wheeled her now groggy mom out of the room and regret filled her. Was she wrong to have reacted the way she did? But how else was she supposed to feel? Her emotions twisted inside her, and she desperately wished she could talk to her dad.

"Are you okay?"

She'd forgotten all about Brig. Kit nodded. "Yes, or I will be. I need to run an errand, though. Will you call me the minute she comes out of surgery?"

"Of course."

Kit gave the woman her cell phone number.

"But where are you going?"

"I need to go see my dad."

Sympathy and understanding flashed, and Brig simply nodded.

One minute later, Kit was hurrying down the hall to catch the elevator. At the lobby, she turned left and exited the hospital. Several taxis waited in their area and she waved one over.

Climbing in, she said, "Wilmington Street. Montlawn Memorial Park."

Twenty-three minutes later, she stood at the foot of her father's grave. She'd asked the cabbie to wait, as she didn't plan on staying long. Just long enough.

Her father had been buried toward the back of the cemetery. As she walked the winding path, the trees shielded her from the light, misty rain that had started to fall.

Finally, she arrived at the grave. PAUL ALAN KENYON. 1950–2009. LOVING FATHER TAKEN TOO SOON.

Kneeling, she pulled a few weeds and tossed them aside. Other than those, the grave had been well-tended. Fresh flowers had been placed in the weatherproof vase.

Her mother? Brig? Or her dad's brother?

It didn't matter.

Kit felt the tears well up and choked them back. "I miss you, Dad." And she did. Part of her was glad he'd told her the truth about her birth. And part of her wished he'd just kept his mouth shut.

Then again, she loved the memories she had with her adoptive parents.

And wondered what kind of memories she'd have if she'd been raised in the Cash family.

Did it matter? *Why did you let this happen, God?*

A rustle of leaves was the only answer she heard. The snap of a twig. Her nerves jumped and she spun, eyes darting from one area of the cemetery to the next.

Chills broke out on her arms.

Was someone there?

Watching her?

Nothing moved.

Silence reigned.

She looked around and realized she was pretty isolated. A tall headstone loomed to her left. Her father's was simply a rectangle with a curved upper edge that had been set into the ground.

All different sizes and shapes, the headstones lay in a scattered pattern, and she noticed for the first time that she really couldn't see the area around her very well.

That made her nervous. Frustrated with herself for being spooked, she nevertheless decided to hurry up and get out of here.

"I wish you were here to give me some advice—and help me get over this anger I feel toward you and Mom. And, of course, because I'm angry at you, I feel guilt too. Like it's really stupid being mad at a dead person. But I can't seem to help it and don't know what to do with it."

For some reason Noah's voice sounded loud in her mind. Try praying, he'd probably say.

God?

Nothing.

She sighed again.

Then something hard jammed itself into the back of her head. She jerked, then froze as a voice said, "You're very hard to find alone."

23

"What do you want?" The adrenaline surge made her light-headed, then she pushed past her shocked surprise, mentally slapping herself for letting her guard down, ignoring her instincts, and focused on the person behind her.

"To warn you."

"About what?" she gritted.

"In order to fulfill your true purpose, you must not engage in any more flirtation with the good detective." Sarcasm dripped when he referred to Noah. "Should you continue to do so, you will find yourself judged guilty."

"Guilty of what?" Flirtation? With Noah?

A chill shuddered through her.

Who was this guy?

Her mind clicked with escape ideas.

None of them would enable her to outrun a bullet.

"Guilty of adultery should you continue the path you're on." He gave a low laugh, and Kit heard the evil lurking beneath it. She felt him reach out and stroke her hair, the soft caress causing her stomach to lurch.

"Who are you?"

"Just call me the Judge. But one day soon, you'll be my wife.

The perfect wife. The perfect mother to our child. So no more flirting with that cop. You understand?"

"You're crazy," she muttered in a low voice. Then wanted to kick herself. *You're trained to talk to the crazies, remember? Use your skills and save yourself.*

The gun jammed harder.

She winced as her fear level tripled.

"The Judge has determined that should you choose to ignore this warning, you will die."

"You killed Walter and Heather and Susan, didn't you?"

Another low laugh. "Yes, I did. The series of three. They were executed for their sins."

"What kind of sins?"

"Sins against me."

"What does that have to do with me?"

"Nothing. But in the process of your investigation, I've watched you. And you're exactly the kind of woman I've been looking for. You show respect to those around you. You defend the defenseless, you stand up for what you believe in, and I believe you would die for those you loved. You would never . . ." He cleared his throat and she flinched. "Just know that you were chosen." From the corner of her eye, she caught a glimpse of a black mask.

Heart thudding, pulse racing, she demanded through her fear, "Chosen? You chose me? But I didn't choose you. How can you possibly believe I would choose someone like you?"

"Is that disrespect I hear in your tone?" His voice hardened, chilled her to the bone.

Easy, Kit. Tell him what he wants to hear. "All right. I'm chosen. Why did you decide to confront me this way?"

"Because you needed to be warned and I couldn't get you alone. Finally, here—paying respect to the dead like the good daughter you are—I can see that you know your place, your duty to your father. You would do the same for a husband, wouldn't you? And a child?"

Stumped, Kit winced as the gun pressed harder.

"Wouldn't you?" he yelled in her ear.

"Yes! Yes!"

"That's what I thought." Satisfaction resonated. "We shall one day be one, Kit. The two shall be one. Then we will be three. You've been warned."

She opened her mouth to respond, but didn't get the chance.

"Hey! Hey, what are you doing?" The voice came from behind her. She felt her attacker shift to see who'd yelled and she grabbed the moment to swing an elbow back as hard as she could. But he'd moved again and her aim was off. She caught him in the knee. He hollered and swore.

Running footsteps sounded in her ears, and she knew this guy wouldn't hesitate to kill whoever was coming to her rescue.

"Stay away from him," she yelled to the good Samaritan. "He'll kill you!"

"What's going on over there?" another voice called out. "Kit?" Noah?

Then the gun cracked and Kit waited to feel the bite of the bullet, had a mere second to wonder where she would spend eternity, then pain exploded behind her left ear as the butt of the gun connected with the side of her head. She landed on the ground with a thud, her head spinning. Where had the bullet gone? It took a full second to realize her attacker had been shooting at Noah, not her.

She rolled to her left, caught his leg with a foot and knocked him off balance. Kit heard the pop of the gun again, and a bullet landed on the ground beside her. Great, her maneuver almost got her killed. She rolled and from the corner of her eye, she caught a glimpse of the man scrambling to his feet.

With one last glare in her direction, he said, "This isn't over."

And he took off firing his weapon in Noah's direction.

Noah returned fire once more. She rolled again, scrabbling behind the nearest tombstone that would shelter her.

Her fingers shook as she grabbed for the weapon under her

left arm. Palming the gun, she felt a surge of weakness shudder through her as her head protested her movements. Shoving it off, she peered around the stone to see her attacker running in a zigzag pattern toward the woods.

Sirens sounded along with the squeal of tires on asphalt.

She gave chase, heard Noah yell at her, but couldn't process what he said. How did he know where to find her? How had the killer known where to find her?

The questions flittered through her brain even as her feet stumbled after—what had he said to call him? The Judge?

More yelling from behind her.

She tripped, swayed, and sank to her knees, her head spinning. She saw Noah dart toward the trees, aiming to cut off her assailant.

Officers descended on the area and Kit forced her throbbing head to think.

"Put the gun down, ma'am," she heard behind her.

Kit whipped around to see an officer holding a gun on her. She immediately put her hands in the air. "I'm a cop."

"I need to see some ID, but please just put the gun on the ground, first."

Slowly, she lowered the weapon to the ground and kicked it over to the officer. He kept his gun trained on her. "Okay, show me your badge."

"It's in my pocket. I'm going to reach for it, all right?"

"Just move slow."

She did and pulled out her badge. Flipping the cover back, she held it so he could see it.

With a sigh, he lowered the gun, picked hers up, and handed it over to her. "Sorry about that."

"You didn't know. You did the right thing." Kit looked toward the woods and felt a growl of frustration form in her throat. She should have had him. He'd been right there and she'd let him get away.

"I'm going after him," he said, "if you're all right."

"Yeah." She waved in the direction the man had escaped. "Go, go. But be careful, he's already killed three people." She got to her feet and started to go with him, but the throbbing in her head made her nauseous. She bent over and grasped her knees, waiting for the wave to pass. Dropping to her knees, she ground her teeth in frustration.

The officer paused. "Stay put. Help's on the way." Then he took off.

Watching him go, a thought chilled her. She was in North Carolina. This shouldn't have happened here.

This guy had followed her and found her. He'd also made his purpose clear. He was determined to make her one of his victims.

Noah raced back to find Kit, who still knelt, head lowered. "Kit, are you all right?"

She looked up and winced. "Yeah, he hit me with his gun, I think. Who was he shooting at?"

"The person who probably saved your life. Fortunately, the guy ducked. Who was the shooter?"

She stared at Noah. "The Judge."

"Huh?"

"You remember when I said we were being followed?"

"Yeah. The black Mustang."

"I was right. He admitted to killing our three victims back in Spartanburg. Said to call him the Judge."

Noah blew out a sigh. "The Judge? What? As in judge and jury?"

"Yes. That's kind of what he sounded like." She swallowed and shook her head. Wincing, she held a hand to it. "That was so weird."

"Weird how?"

Kit looked at Noah. "He said to stop the flirtation with you because I was chosen by him to be his wife. The perfect wife, no less."

He blinked. "Huh?"

"Exactly."

"That's not good, Kit." Noah breathed a worried sigh. "He's definitely targeted you."

"You want to hear something even more weird?"

"No, but lay it on me."

She shuddered. "He quoted the Bible and said, 'the two shall be one, then we will be three.' Or something like that."

Noah's nostrils flared and he drew in a deep breath. "I really don't like the sound of that. We need to get this information to Olivia. I want to hear what she has to say about all of this."

"I agree." She rubbed her head. "At least we know who those bullets at my house and the college were meant for now." She looked at him, her face reflecting her fear. "He means to get you out of the way to get to me."

Noah's lips thinned. "I can take care of myself." A sigh. "Come on. We need to get back and meet with the task force. I'll call in a BOLO for a black Mustang traveling back toward Spartanburg on I-85 and all of the back roads. Surely someone will spot him." He placed the call, then with a hand under her arm, Noah helped her to her feet. She swayed, then got her balance. Reaching up, he felt the back of her head, just under her ear, and felt anger eat at him. "That's quite a goose egg you've got there."

"It'll heal."

"Hey, are you guys okay?"

Her good Samaritan. Noah turned and held out a hand. "Thanks so much for calling out like that. You saved her life."

A flush covered the man's cheeks. "I couldn't believe my eyes. I turned around and there was this guy with a mask holding a gun on her head." He swallowed hard. "I wasn't sure what to do so I just yelled."

Kit grasped the man's hand and squeezed. "Thank you. I know the police will want a statement from you."

"I already gave it but wanted to make sure you were all right before I left."

"I'll be fine. Thanks."

Her rescuer gave them a two-fingered salute and took off.

Noah looked at her. "Between your arm and your head, I'd say you're having a bad week."

She gave a small smile. "I'm alive. I'd say that makes it a pretty good one."

He barked out a short laugh. "Yeah, I guess that's one way of looking at it."

"So, what are you doing here?"

Sobering, he said, "I called Lee Travers's home before I left the hospital parking lot. He's taken a weekend trip to Florida with his niece and nephew. Apparently they go quite often."

Kit nodded. "It's just an hour by plane. What a fun weekend."

"Guess that's why he didn't answer. I managed to scrounge up his grandmother's number and she gave me the information."

"Sorry you wasted your time."

"Definitely not a waste of time." He gave her a slow smile. "I'd hitch a ride with you anytime."

Pink suffused her cheeks. "You didn't hitch, you drove, re-member?"

"Right. I kidnapped you. Anyway, I felt bad about just dump-ing you at the hospital. Since you weren't answering your phone again, I went back to find you and ran into your mother's friend. She told me where to find you and how to get here."

With a wry shake of her head, she looked at him. "In detail, no doubt." She pulled out her phone.

"In detail. Even drew me a little map on how to find the grave." He paused. "So, are you done here?"

Kit heaved a sigh. "I guess." She shook her phone. "My bat-tery's dead. I forgot to grab my car charger."

"We've got the same phone. Mine's in the car." A pause. "Did it help coming here?" He sure hoped so. She needed to find some peace with everything going on in her life.

And you don't? his inner voice snickered.

Yes, he did too. But at least he knew where to find it and was working on it. So far Kit was relying on herself. And that would get her nowhere fast.

"A little. Maybe."

"Then what is it? You have this weird look on your face."

She gave him a little glare. "I think I'm entitled. I was almost killed, remember?"

"Yeah, but this look doesn't have anything to do with that. It's more like—" he shrugged, "—I don't know. Sorry."

A sigh slipped from her and she looked at the sky. "Do you know what I was thinking when I thought he was going to kill me?"

"What?"

"I wondered where I'd spend eternity."

Hope leapt inside him. "And?"

"I wasn't sure. And that scared me. More than the guy standing behind me holding a gun to the back of my head."

Noah went silent, then said, "Huh. Something to think about then."

"I prayed too," she went on as though he hadn't spoken.

"You did?"

"Yeah. It was like I could hear you whispering in my ear that's what I needed to do."

Noah wrapped an arm around her shoulders and pulled her into a very un-partnerlike embrace. "Sounds to me like God's given you another chance to start talking to him."

With her nose buried in his chest, he could smell the fresh scent of vanilla shampoo mingled with the odor of sweat from her ordeal.

Concerned the killer might be hidden somewhere in the shadows, watching, waiting, laughing as they searched without finding anything, Noah pulled her to the safety of the car. Right now, he needed her to be away from the commotion of the crime scene team and any other prying eyes.

Once inside the relative privacy of the car, she leaned her head back against the headrest and closed her eyes.

His heart clenched at her drawn features. The need to comfort her gripped him. And the need to kiss her nearly overwhelmed him. Definitely not something two partners should do.

Should they?

In one sudden, smooth move, she turned, maneuvered around the gear shift, and slid her arms around his neck, tucking her head under his chin. Feeling her warm breath fan across his throat made him cave.

He tilted her chin and placed his lips over hers.

She went completely still, and he froze for a brief moment, wondering if he was going to get a fist in his gut.

Then he felt her respond, her soft lips moving under his and sending his senses reeling.

His hands crept up to cup the back of her head to bring her closer and she gasped.

In pain.

The soft sound brought him back to earth with a thud.

He pulled back and sucked in some much needed oxygen.

She stared up at him and blinked. "Wow."

He gave a little laugh. "Uh, what just happened?"

"I don't know, but if you say you're sorry, I'm going to have to hit you."

"Sorry's the last word on my mind right now."

A little grin pulled at the corners of her lips. "Good." Then she frowned and scooted back against her seat, her gaze flicking to the window to study the woods and the surrounding area. "What if he's watching?"

Drawing in a deep sigh, Noah grasped her hand. "Then he's going to be mighty upset with you. Let's get out of here, I don't like it."

"Right. And I need to get back to the hospital to check on my mother."

"Sounds like a plan. I have an idea too."

"What is it?"

"There's an ATM right across the street from that little jewelry store Bonnie's bling came from."

Realization dawned. "And ATMs have cameras."

"Then there's that pawnshop next door. It probably has a camera on the outside."

"And another ATM about three doors down."

Excitement lit her features in spite of the pain she must have been feeling. "He may have walked past one of them."

"I'm guessing if he went to all the trouble to dress up in a hat and sunglasses, he wouldn't park his car right out front."

"I'll call Dakota and tell him to get the video from those and any others in the area. With Jazz on it, we should have access to them by the time we get back to Spartanburg." Jazz, the computer expert located at the FBI's home base of Quantico. She could find anything needed in the blink of an eye. Getting videos from an ATM would be a walk in the park for her.

24

Kit still felt a little light-headed, but she had a feeling it didn't have a thing to do with getting knocked on the head. In fact, she was quite sure it had to do with getting knocked off her feet. Even though she'd been sitting down.

That kiss had left her reeling and she wasn't quite sure what to think about it.

Or do about it.

Then again, did anything need to be done?

Apprehension curled inside her and she wondered if he'd just ignore it—or do it again.

She wasn't sure which option she wanted to happen.

"You're awfully quiet."

"Sorry, I've got a lot on my mind."

"Thinking about that kiss? Because I sure am."

Okay, so he wasn't going to ignore it.

She breathed a little laugh. "Oh yeah, I'm thinking about it."

"And wondering how it's going to affect our partnership?"

"That too," she admitted.

He shrugged. "We just won't let it."

She raised a brow at him. "You think?"

He shot her a warm smile. "I think. I don't regret it and plan on doing it again. Now, how's your head?"

She didn't know how to respond. To the comment that he wanted to kiss her again or answer the question about her head. She chose the latter and winced. "Throbbing."

Sympathy made him frown. "I'm sure. We'll find you some ibuprofen or something when we get back to the hospital."

"I'll take it."

At the hospital, Kit and Noah went straight to the surgery waiting room. Brig sat next to the window, knitting needles clicking away. The needles paused as Kit slipped into the chair next to her and asked, "How's she doing?"

"So far so good is what they tell me," she reported, her eyes taking in Noah, who sat next to Kit. Then her eyes narrowed back on Kit. "What happened to you?"

"I had a little run-in with a bad guy."

Brig put aside her knitting and pushed her glasses up. Leaning in, she examined Kit's head, then made a tsking sound. "You should have that looked at."

"I just need to take some ibuprofen. I know you have some in that monstrosity you call a purse."

Brig gave an affronted frown. "That 'monstrosity,' as you call it, is the best purse I've ever had. I can fit anything in there and always have what I need." So saying, she rummaged through it and came up with a bottle of Motrin. She shook it and handed it over with a smirk. "And what everyone else needs too."

Kit popped two dry and leaned her head back against the wall.

A cup of water made its way into her hand and she looked up to see Noah standing in front of her. Grateful, she took several swallows, then looked at Brig. "Guess you already met my partner, huh?"

"I did."

Kit made the formal introductions anyway, and Brig went back to her knitting with a speculative gleam in her eye.

Noah's cell phone rang and he excused himself.

Brig took the opportunity to cast a questioning glance at Kit. "Well?"

Kit played innocent. "What do you mean?"

"He means something to you. What?"

"He's my partner. That's it."

"Uh-huh, right." Back to the knitting. "That's why he looks at you like he'd like to stake a claim on your heart."

"Brig!" Refusing to squirm or say another word about it, Kit pressed her lips together.

Noah came back in, the grim look on his face causing her to sit up straight. "What is it?"

"They spotted the black Mustang."

"Are they sure it's the right one? Where?"

"They're sure. It has that yellow eagle on the hood. At a diner off I-85. Units are responding even as we speak."

Kit bit her lip and looked in the direction of the operating room where her mother would be for another hour or so.

"Go," Brig said.

"What?" Kit jerked her eyes back to her mother's friend.

"Go. Your mom will understand." She glanced at Kit's head. "And seeing that won't be a good thing for her. You know how she worries about you."

On impulse, Kit leaned over and hugged the woman who'd been another mother to her growing up. "Thanks. Give her my love and tell her I'll be in to see her as soon as I can, okay?"

"Are you working that serial killer case?"

Surprised, Kit cocked her head. "Yes, why?"

"Thought you probably were. Your mom would want you to get that guy off the streets. You know she would. So go take care of it."

"Thanks, Brig."

Kit and Noah rushed from the hospital, Noah snagging the keys from his pocket. "We're about twenty minutes away from him."

Once in the car, he put the siren and the light on and they raced to the location Noah had been given.

Four police cruisers sat in the parking lot. Several patrons stood outside watching the excitement.

Kit climbed out of the car and flashed her badge as Noah did the same.

The officer in charge came up. "I'm Gage Wilder. Your man is long gone. He left this Mustang here and stole a motorcycle."

"Who's the car registered to?"

Officer Wilder consulted his notes. "A Zachary Hadley. He reported it stolen from the Wofford Law College early this morning."

Kit paused, then drew in a slow breath. "He was watching me even then."

Noah lifted a brow. "What?"

"This was a spur-of-the-moment trip. In order to follow me, he had to have been watching me."

"Why would he follow you in a stolen car?"

Shoving her hands in her pockets, she walked a few steps away then back. "I don't know. That doesn't make sense."

"Unless," Noah said slowly, "he has another target in mind and was going to use the stolen vehicle in some way."

"Like to avoid getting caught?"

"Yeah."

"But he was watching my house, saw me—us—leave, and made a last-minute decision to follow."

A hand reached up to rub his neck and Noah frowned as he thought. "But he stayed on the highway when we turned off. How did he know you were going to be at the cemetery?"

She blew out a sigh. "Good question. But right now, I'm more concerned with another question."

"Who is his next victim? The one he's already got picked out and was ready to snatch this morning before he decided to follow us?" Noah guessed.

"You got it in one."

25

The Judge grunted as he pushed the weights above his head. He'd arrived at the gym an hour ago and he was furious with himself. He'd failed. He'd been so exhilarated to finally have his wife where he wanted her, he'd gotten careless. Too much talk, not enough action. He should have forced her to go with him.

No matter, he'd have another chance. He still had too much to do before he was ready for a wife and child. He looked at the clock. Almost time.

He hated having to give up the Mustang, but he'd found another car once he'd gotten back into town.

Soon the party would start and the Judge would find the one whose time was up. It was time to face the consequences for his actions.

Soon, Corey, soon.

After all, you do have the right to a speedy trial. But before he paid Corey a visit, he needed to check in on someone. Someone who had the perfect son. Settling the weights on the bar, he grabbed the towel and dried the sweat from his face. He'd done his homework, he knew where Kit lived. And he knew where to find the perfect son.

❖

Thirty-six-year-old Corey Samples tipped the beer to his lips and took a pull. Music blared and he wondered how many of the girls were actually of age to be doing the things they were doing with the college guys they were doing them with.

Then decided he didn't really care.

One hand in his pocket, the other wrapped around the bottle, he sauntered to the door and slipped outside.

So this was college.

He'd signed up for the army when he was eighteen. He'd just gotten back from Iraq and taken an honorable discharge. He looked down at the disfigured left hand and shuddered.

Depression weighed on his shoulders and he blinked at the images his mind conjured up at the most inappropriate times.

Law school.

Is that what he should do?

His uncle sure thought so.

Sitting in on the mock trial had been interesting, but most of the students were just kids. Kids who'd never experienced a day of going hungry. Never experienced a fear so intense you thought your insides were going to shrivel up and die just from the adrenaline rush. These kids thought they were going to change the world. What did he have in common with them?

On the other hand, he'd always liked to be right and could argue like a pro for something he believed in.

Maybe his uncle was right. Maybe law school would give him direction and a purpose in life. Maybe it was worth a try.

Blowing out a sigh, Corey rubbed his head.

And felt the hairs on the back of his neck raise, his finely tuned sense of being watched setting off his internal alarms.

Keeping his back toward the frat house and his eyes on the parking lot beyond, he backed slowly, steadily . . . until he felt something gouge him in the lower back.

Whirling, fist ready, he dropped his hand when the guy with the beer bottle started laughing. "Dude, you're so uptight. Loosen up and have a little fun."

Corey forced a smile. "Right. Right."

But he glanced back over his shoulder.

And saw something move in the shadows beyond.

❖

Dakota met them in the office. Dusk approached but Kit didn't care. If this was going to help nail the psycho who was going around cutting parts off the people he killed, she'd stay up all night.

"What did Jazz come up with?" Noah asked.

Dakota waved them over to a wide-screen monitor, and Kit smiled when she saw who was there.

"Hey Samantha, what are you doing here?"

"I was told my computer expertise might be needed." She gave them a quick grin and clicked on the frozen image on the screen. "Mom and Dad are keeping Andy so Connor brought me over. Jamie's working late. Dakota decided he was lonely and thought we could all go grab a bite to eat after you find what you're looking for."

The video played and Kit leaned in for a closer look.

"Our regular guy had to leave. Sam said she'd come in for us," Dakota explained.

"I think this may be who you're looking for," Sam said and zoomed in on an individual with a baseball hat and glasses. She froze the image, and with a few clicks of the mouse, she cleared it up as best she could.

Kit pulled in a deep breath and let it out slowly. "Is that who it looks like?"

Noah met her eyes. "I sure hope not."

Sam squinted at the picture. "He looks familiar."

Connor came from his office and took a look. "Hey, that's Stephen Wells. Why are you guys investigating the DA?"

❖

LYNETTE EASON

The Judge approached his next victim, his heart pounding in anticipation of the upcoming trial. He had more reasons than one to want this guy out of his way. He'd been paying way too much attention to Alena. Alena was a good friend. Like the sister he never had. She was family. And he had to protect her. Like him, she'd grown up with an abusive father. Just the other day she'd confided to him that she'd wished for a big brother. One who would have protected her against the abuse.

And now she was seeing an older guy.

And that just couldn't happen. He would corrupt her sweet innocence with his worldly ways. Just the other day when the Judge had called her, she turned down his offer of a dinner out.

Because she was going out with Corey.

It made him sick to think of it.

And just gave him one more reason to get rid of the guy.

"Hey Corey, how's it going?" He passed over the beer he'd just opened and handed it to his "friend."

"What are you doing here?" At first he frowned at the bearer of the alcohol, then shrugged. Mimicking his earlier actions, he tilted the bottle and took a swallow. "So, what do you think of this shindig? I wouldn't think this would be your kind of party. I noticed you're not real popular with a lot of the people here."

From the edge of the rail, the Judge looked through the open French doors into the living area beyond. And while his fingers tightened around the neck of his beer bottle, he ignored the last comment. It didn't deserve a response. "Nice place. I'm going to have me something like this one day."

"After you make all your money freeing the criminals?" There went the lip curl.

The fury he'd held inside for so long bubbled near the surface. He swallowed and forced himself under control, but one hand curled into a fist.

Keeping himself under control, he waited. It wouldn't be long now. "So, are you thinking of going to school here?"

Another swig on the bottle and Corey turned to look back

213

out into the darkness. "Maybe." A pause. "Why do you act the way you do?" He shifted to look at the Judge.

"What do you mean?"

"So arrogant. Like you're better than everyone else. I mean, when you were talking . . ." His prey stumbled and leaned into the railing of the porch. "Whoa. I think I've had one too many."

"You need a ride home?"

Corey blinked and the Judge figured he was probably seeing about four of everything right now.

"Um . . . yeah. Yeah, I'll get someone from inside."

"Now Corey, what's wrong with accepting a ride from me?"

"'Cuz I don't like you." Corey's words slurred and the Judge knew it was almost time. Time for the fun to begin. Time to exact his vengeance. To prove who was the best and wipe the smirk off Corey's face.

He remembered the look on the man's face as he'd wound up his argument. An upper lip curled in disgust, his knowing look that the Judge was an idiot and he could do a much better job. A look that had haunted the Judge's dreams for several weeks.

Only now the time was here.

"Come on." He placed a hand around the man's waist and hoisted him from the rail. "Let's go."

"No, don't wanna go wid you."

"Too bad, big guy, you can't drive."

With the drug running through his system, Corey was in no shape to argue. The Judge easily pulled him along down the back steps and never saw another individual on his way to his stolen ride. He glanced at his now unconscious passenger. The seat belt held him in, and with his head lolling against the window, he simply looked like he was taking a nap.

The Judge looked at Corey's mouth, imagined those lips curled into a sneer. Then imagined that sneer permanently removed.

One by one, he was getting the bad guys. The ones who didn't deserve to breathe the same air as he. The ones who thought they were so much better.

The ones who had laughed—and the ones who'd interfered with his plans for the perfect family.

Corey had watched him during his argument, his eyes following everything going on. And then Corey had met his gaze and curled his upper lip. In disgust? Shocked, it had thrown the Judge for a brief moment, had made him stumble. And that angered him, infuriated him, not only with himself, but with Corey and his superior attitude. One the Judge was getting ready to wipe off his face.

He leaned in close and whispered in an ear that wouldn't hear him. "Because I am better than everyone else and it's time everyone saw that."

Kit's eyes popped open and she lay still, barely breathing. She'd fallen asleep in the recliner after Noah had dropped her off around midnight. Unable to sleep, she'd turned on the television and curled up with a blanket in her favorite chair.

And dozed off.

Now she held still.

Listening.

Waiting.

The television, still on mute, flickered.

What had awakened her?

The phone?

No.

A soft noise.

There!

A subtle rustling near her front door.

Adrenaline surged and she groped for the gun she'd placed on the end table. Instant comfort suffused her as the butt of the gun slid against her palm.

Shrugging off the blanket, she considered her options. Lowering the footrest of the recliner would make noise, so she placed a foot on either side of it and stood.

Another noise reached her ears.

A scrape.

A curse?

Her heart thudded. She reached for her phone and called Noah's number as she moved on socked feet across her hardwood floor.

Noah answered, his voice raspy with sleep. "Kit? What's wrong?"

"Get over to my house," she whispered.

"Do I need to call for backup?"

"Yes."

She could hear him moving, then seconds later she heard a car start. "Are you still there?" he asked.

"Yeah." And so was whoever was outside her door.

She paused at the edge of the kitchen and looked at the clock. 2:06.

Barking sounded from next door.

Roscoe.

Great. He was going to scare the guy off. And bring Alena to the door to see what was going on.

Which meant Kit had to move now.

The blood rushed triple time through her veins. Kit gripped her gun with her right hand and the doorknob with her left.

Sucking in a deep breath, she twisted and threw open the door. "Freeze!"

The figure darted toward the parked car he'd left just down the street. Kit hollered again. "Stop or I'll shoot!"

This time the fleeing man stopped and put his hands over his head.

Kit moved forward and her foot snagged on something in her path. Stepping over it, she squinted. "Turn around, and if you have a weapon, you'd better drop it and keep your hands where I can see them."

The man's shoulders drooped and she thought he looked vaguely familiar even before he turned around and faced her.

"Brian!"

He stepped toward her just as Noah's car screeched to a halt in front of her house. He shot out of the car, weapon ready.

A groan escaped Brian as he moved into the light coming from her open front door. An embarrassed smile crossed his face. "You caught me."

"What are you *doing*?" she nearly screeched. "Do you know what time it is?"

Noah shoved his gun into his holster and watched the scene with a frown. He made a quick call to cancel backup.

Brian swallowed. "Can I put my hands down now?"

Kit lowered her weapon almost as an afterthought. "Yes, of course."

She looked around at the neighboring houses and saw porch lights on and curtains moving in the windows. Shaking her head, she said, "Come in. We're making a spectacle of ourselves in front of everyone."

As she moved to let them in, she kicked the object at the base of her door again.

"What . . ." Leaning down, she looked at the rectangular box and hesitated. Did she need a bomb squad? After all she'd been through lately, she wasn't sure she wanted to take any chances.

"It won't bite you," Brian said.

She looked up at him. "It's from you?"

A guilty flush reddened his features. "Yeah."

She picked up the box and looked at her partner. "I think I can handle it from here. Thanks for rushing over."

Noah didn't look like he was in any hurry to leave, but she needed to have a serious conversation with Brian and she wasn't going to do it in front of Noah. "I'll talk to you tomorrow—er, today. Later."

"You're sure?"

"I'm sure."

Noah gave them one last glance, then headed for his car. Her heart warmed at his willingness to jump to her defense. Not that she necessarily needed him to.

But she had to admit—it was nice. Very nice.

Brian shuffled behind her, pulling her attention from Noah's departure.

She shut the door and handed the box to Brian. "Flowers?"

He dropped his head. "Dumb idea, huh?"

Kit sighed and motioned him into her den. "No, Brian, it's not dumb. It's very sweet. Strange to do it at 2:00 in the morning, but," she shrugged, "sweet. I guess."

Instead of sitting, he walked over to her mantel and leaned against it, studying the pictures she had there. "You have a beautiful family."

"Thanks."

"Cute baby too."

This brought a smile. "Yeah, he's great. That's Andy, Connor and Samantha's little boy."

"I've seen them around the station."

Okay, time to focus. "Look, Brian, you're a great guy."

"But I'm not the guy for you," he interrupted her. "I get it now. Noah's arrival pretty much cemented what's going on."

She couldn't help the flush. "He's my partner."

Brian just gave her a knowing look. "Right." Rubbing a hand through his hair, he sighed. "You don't have to worry about me anymore. I've just admired you for a long time and thought I'd better do something about it before you got snatched up." He gave a rueful smile. "I guess I waited too long."

Kit held up a hand. "I'm sorry . . . I . . ."

"No, it's okay. I'll leave you alone." Brian walked toward the door. "See you around."

"You'll find someone, Brian. Someone just right for you."

His eyes hardened for a brief moment, then he nodded his head. "I know."

And then he was gone, and thanks to the adrenaline ebb, Kit felt like her knees wanted to give out.

She made it to her bed and crashed on top of it. Sleep finally crept in.

SUNDAY

26

Kit rolled over and snatched the phone from the hook. "Hello?"

It was Brig. According to Brig, her mother had come out of surgery and was recovering nicely. Kit planned to return to see her sometime in the following week. Right now, she had to focus on this case.

Deep down, she was afraid if she stayed near her mother, she might lose the small hold she still had on her anger. Anger that she was beginning to realize was serving no purpose except to make her look—and feel—petty and childish. She needed to move on. But how?

The phone rang again. Apparently, she wasn't destined to sleep in this morning.

"Hello?"

"Kit? It's Jamie."

Clearing her throat, Kit blinked and rubbed more sleep from her eyes. "Hey there, what's up?"

"Not you, obviously. Sorry for the wake-up call."

"It's all right. Brig actually woke me up to tell me my—um—mother was doing better. And I need to get up anyway and go for my run if I'm going to do it. I've got a very unpleasant task ahead of me either this afternoon or first thing tomorrow morning."

Questioning the DA as to why he was buying expensive jewelry for a girl half his age was not on her list of fun things to do.

Unfortunately, she had a feeling she already knew the answer. They were just waiting to hear back from the captain about whether or not he wanted to be in on the questioning. They'd received word that he'd taken the day off to go hiking in the mountains with his son and grandson. She had a feeling cell coverage wasn't very good. But as soon as he got the message, he'd be all over it. And so would the higher-ups. This thing would be handled with kid gloves.

She focused back in on what Jamie was saying. "Sam and I are going over to Mom and Dad's after church for lunch. You want to join us?"

For a minute, Kit didn't respond. She'd been so caught up in the case, she hadn't had time to breathe, eat, or sleep. She had pushed all thoughts of her personal life aside—except for the brief visit with her mother—while the window of opportunity to catch a killer was open wide.

Unfortunately, that window narrowed with each passing hour. But lunch with her sisters, biological mother, and sweet little nephew . . .

"Um, sure. At least until I hear back from my captain, which means I don't know how long I'll be able to stay. Uh . . . what day is it?"

Jamie laughed. "Sunday, silly. Church day, remember? And you can stay as long or as short as you need to."

"Right. So you want me to meet you at the house or what?"

"That'd be great. Or I can swing by and pick you up." A pause, then a hopeful, "Or you can come to church and ride with me."

"Not today, thanks." She heard the silence on the other end, could feel the disappointment. But she wouldn't go to church to make someone happy. If she went, it would be because she wanted to. "So, I'll meet you there. I'd better have my car anyway in case something comes up with the case."

"Sure. Sounds good."

Two minutes later, she'd pulled her hair up in a ponytail, noticing her arm felt only slightly sore. Her head didn't hurt until she scraped it with the brush. She paused. Should she go running? Maybe just a walk. She donned her running clothes and shoes. And then it occurred to her that she still hadn't asked Alena if she'd known Walter.

Making a fast decision, she stepped outside and knocked on the door to Alena's part of the duplex. The last two times she'd tried to get her, the girl had been out.

Roscoe gave three deep barks before Alena opened the door. Surprise flickered in her eyes.

Kit asked, "Hey, I noticed you don't go to church on Sunday mornings. You want to go for a run this morning?" She touched her head. "Or maybe just a walk?"

"Sure. Let me grab my shoes and Roscoe's leash."

A minute later, the pair made their way down the street at a clip that wasn't a jog but more of a fast walk, Roscoe trotting happily between them.

"I grew up going to church," Alena finally said.

"So why don't you go now?"

"No reason, really. I guess I just kind of got out of the habit." She laughed. "That was my mother you saw the other night. Sorry I didn't introduce you."

"That's all right. There really wasn't a good time."

"She was visiting."

"How did that go?"

"It went. She goes out of her way to come see me about once a month. And every time she does, she brings God into the conversation." Alena blew out a breath and pulled in a deep one in order to keep talking. Kit gave her a few beats. "She always says, 'Alena, God made you for a purpose. Are you messing that up?'"

Kit listened to the pounding of their tennis shoes. Then she asked, "What do you think about God?"

Alena breathed a small laugh. "I think he exists. I don't know that I believe he's all that interested in my day-to-day life. Seems like he'd have more important things to do. He sure wasn't around when my dad was beating on me. I survived that alone. Why would I need him now that I'm out of that situation?"

Kit thought about that. She didn't think she totally agreed with the statement that God wasn't interested. Not after watching Noah in action. But what could she say? The girl felt the way she did for a reason.

More pounding and they rounded the curve.

Alena asked, "Don't you have a killer to catch?"

"Yeah." Kit's ponytail slapped her back, keeping rhythm with her feet. "That's one thing I wanted to talk to you about. You're a law student at the same college these victims went to. You need to watch your back."

The girl frowned as her feet ate up the asphalt. "I know. I've been taking extra precautions." A few more yards and Alena asked, "Have you got any leads?"

"Not much. Which brings me to a question I've been wanting to ask you. Did you know Walter Davis or Bonnie Gray?"

"Walter? Yes, I think so. Kind of a cocky dude with bad hair. Bonnie? I don't remember her name. I might recognize her if I saw a picture of her."

"You don't watch the news?"

"No way. Too depressing." Alena shot her a brief smile, then frowned. "It's awful what's happening. Somebody killing law students off. Scary."

"I know. You really need to be careful."

"Trust me. I am." She paused as they rounded the next corner, then picked back up the conversation. Her words came in spurts, between pacing the run and her breathing. "I know Walter was going to graduate in a couple of weeks. This is my first year, so it's not like we had any classes together. I didn't know him very well, just recognize his name. I sat in on the jury of a mock trial as an alternate, so I met a lot of the graduating seniors. Not to mention someone really special." She gave Kit another little grin.

"Who?"

"Corey."

"Nice?"

Alena gave a breathless laugh. "Oh yeah. He was in Iraq. Now, he's thinking about going back to school to get his law degree. Anyway, the last mock trial is set for next week. It's part of the graduating seniors' final exam. I'll probably go watch that one too. You can learn so much from them because the judge actually takes the time to explain what each person is doing right or wrong. It's really cool."

Kit's feet kept the rhythm she'd started out with. Her nerves tingled and she couldn't help but watch the surrounding houses. Specifically their roofs. She watched for movement, for anything that seemed out of place. She hated that this guy who had taken two shots at her already had made her so on edge. More so than usual. Cops generally stayed hyperalert, but now . . .

Nothing caught her attention, nothing seemed out of place. Relaxing a little, she asked, "What about Susan Chalmers?"

"No, she was ahead of me, also. I think I met her once or twice, but . . ." She shrugged. They'd made it around the block once and were on their second lap, pacing themselves so they could talk.

"Walter was nice, though. Like I said, he was a little full of himself, but from what I understand, he would have been a brilliant lawyer. It's a real shame." Taking a water bottle from the fanny pack strapped to her side, Alena took a swig. She jammed it back and then they quit talking as they picked up the pace for the next thirty minutes.

Back at the house, Kit wiped the sweat from her cheek with her shirtsleeve and said, "Just watch yourself, Alena. Be careful who you hang around with, who you're alone with. This guy seems to be someone his victims know and trust." She placed a hand on Alena's arm. "All law students."

The girl shuddered and nodded. "I know. But I'll be careful." She patted the dog's head. "And I have Roscoe."

Kit smiled. "Talk to you soon. Maybe we can run again in the morning."

"Depending on your schedule." Alena grinned. "I know. You know where to find me."

Kit saluted. "Right."

Back in her side of the duplex, she showered and dressed in jeans and a green short-sleeved shirt. A glance at the clock told her it was time to get going to her biological parents' house.

Excitement thrummed through her. She'd moved here specifically to get to know her birth family better. And then this case had been dropped in her lap and she'd been so busy with it, she hadn't spent nearly as much time with her family as she'd planned.

She grabbed her keys and opened the door. Samantha would be there with little Andy, and of course, Jamie would be waiting. Her twin.

Unbelievable. She had a twin. She still couldn't wrap her mind around it.

27

The fifteen-minute drive to her parents' house went by fast. She had only a few minutes to ponder the case and was still coming up empty when she pulled into the drive.

Samantha showed up right behind her.

Kit got out of the car and smiled. "Hey there."

"Hey. Andy's asleep. Wonder how long he'll stay that way?"

Laughing, Kit peeked over her sister's shoulder and looked down at the peaceful tot. "He's so cute."

"Yeah, well, he wasn't so cute this morning at two o'clock."

"I thought he was sleeping through the night now."

"Most nights. Something woke him up last night and it took forever to get him back to sleep."

"Then maybe you need to take a little nap while you've got some babysitters around today."

Sam grinned. "I might just take you up on that." Reaching in, she grasped the baby carrier and, with a grunt, pulled it gently from the base. "I thought I had pretty strong arms until I had to lug one of these around on a regular basis."

"Hey," Jamie called from the porch, "you guys going to stand in the drive and talk all day or come eat some of Mom's famous chicken casserole and corn bread?"

Kit's stomach sent up its vote in a very vocal way. Sam raised a brow and they burst into laughter. "Coming!"

Inside the house, Kit breathed in the scent of roasting chicken, vegetables, and corn bread. Her stomach growled again and she couldn't wait to dig in.

A pang grabbed her heart and she thought about her mom. She really should call and check on her.

But not from here. That would be like rubbing her face in the fact that Kit was here—with her birth mother—while her adoptive mother was in the hospital with only her friend to rely on.

She felt her throat clog and cleared it with an effort.

Andy still snored gently in his carrier, so Sam set him in front of the fireplace.

Jamie walked over and stared down at him, then whispered a sigh. "He's beautiful, Sam."

An amused smile curled her sister's lips. "You say that every time you see him."

"I know. I guess I'm just amazed that you could produce something that adorable."

Kit laughed as Sam tossed a pillow at her younger sibling. Then her birth mother entered the room wiping her hands on a dish towel. "Hello, girls." Tears came to her eyes as they often did when she saw all three of them together. But she blinked them away and motioned them into the kitchen. "Let's eat before we're out of time and Sam has to eat while holding a baby." She took a deep breath. "Charles had a golf game set up so he left about thirty minutes ago." She hugged Kit as they walked inside. "Then I want to show you something, Kit."

Kit lifted a brow. "All right." Curiosity ate at her, but she sat at the table, dished up her food, and after waiting for someone to say the blessing, dug in.

"You're a wonderful cook . . ." She trailed off, still not able to call the woman "Mom" but unable to call her Mrs. Cash either. So she just didn't call her anything.

Sam and Jamie exchanged a look. "All right," Samantha spoke up. "We need to figure out how you're going to address Mom."

Kit felt the heat of embarrassment crawl up her neck. "I'm sorry." She bit her lip and studied the table. "I didn't mean for this to be awkward even though I knew it would. I just . . ." A sigh broke from her and she felt her throat clog with tears she hadn't realized were so close to the surface.

"Now don't you worry about a thing." Her mother bustled around the table to lay a comforting hand on Kit's shoulder. "I have to admit, I wasn't too sure about you when you first appeared on my doorstep, but Faith Kenyon has been my best friend for a long time." Tears flooded her eyes. "I knew she'd do a good job with you and she did. That's the only reason I let her have you. But I'm so glad you're back in our lives and we want you to be comfortable."

"That's right." Jamie reached over the table to grasp Kit's fingers and gave them a squeeze.

Taking a deep breath, Kit pushed aside her too-close-to-the-surface emotions and said, "Okay. So," she looked at the woman who'd birthed her, "what do I call you? I can't bring myself to call you 'Mom,' but 'Mother' seems so . . . not you."

Samantha laughed. "No, she's definitely not 'Mother.'"

"Well, the boys call me 'Ma.' Would that work for you?"

Kit tried it out. "Ma." She smiled. "Sure, that works."

"Great, I'm glad we got that settled. Now, if you girls are finished eating, I want to show Kit something."

They put their dishes in the sink and headed for the den. "Ma" pulled a key from her skirt pocket. Unlocking the side drawer of a trunk with the key, she lifted a book from it and held it to her chest. Next, she pulled another book from the shelf and carried both of them over to the couch.

Little Andy stirred at their entrance and opened his blue eyes. He blinked and hollered for attention. Kit went to him and un-buckled his carrier.

She lifted him out and held him to her shoulder, patting his small back. He quieted and reared back to look her in the eye. When he grinned, her heart sputtered and she placed a light kiss on his button nose.

Sam had the baby bottle ready by the time Kit sat on the couch. She took the bottle from her sister and laughed when his little hands snagged it and pulled it into his mouth.

Ma looked on with a smile and a few more tears before she sat in the chair next to the couch. She opened one of the books, and Kit saw that it was a picture album. Ma said, "Okay, this is an album of when Jamie was a child. From birth to around ten years or so. Sam has one too."

Eager to see, Kit shifted and Andy grunted his displeasure. Sam reached over and took her son, smoothly transferring him to her arms without Andy ever losing the bottle in his mouth.

Then Ma opened the book she'd taken from the locked drawer, and Kit gasped as she stared at the first picture. "That's me!"

The woman nodded. "Faith would send me pictures about every three months or so. They were the only reason I was able to leave you where you were and not come get you. I think she knew this. And as long as she never heard from me, she was secure that she wasn't going to lose you. So she kept the pictures coming."

"And you made me an album too."

"Yes." Ma smiled a sad, nostalgic smile and traced Kit's face on the picture. "It was hard. So very hard, but I knew you were loved. And it was obvious that Faith and your father doted on you. I couldn't interrupt your life at that point."

Kit looked at the other album, the one with pictures of Jamie and Samantha together. The one of each of them separate. She belonged in that album. The three of them.

Or did she?

That was the real question. Where exactly was her place? Where did she belong?

Her fingers traced her sisters' younger images, and she didn't know whether to feel grateful or hurt. Or guilty for feeling like she missed out on something growing up. Ma was right.

She *had* been a spoiled child.

Spoiled rotten.

Her parents had given her everything her heart had desired.

Except a sibling.

Except crazy large family gatherings with relatives stretching the house's seams.

But other people had grown up just like she had and never had a problem with it. Or felt like they were missing out on something. Or if they did, they didn't have trouble accepting it.

But other people didn't find out they had a whole other family out there, either.

"Kit? Are you all right?" Sam looked at her with concern.

She blinked and forced a smile. "Sure, I'm fine." Kit scooted closer for a better view of the album and breathed in the scent she'd come to associate with this woman who'd given birth to her. "This is incredible. You watched me grow up," she whispered.

"I did. If I hadn't been able to, I might not have had the strength to leave you like I did." She sighed. "When you were in high school, I drove up one weekend to watch you play soccer."

Dumbstruck, Kit just stared at the woman. "You did?"

"Yes. You scored the first goal of the game. I stood with the crowd, watching as you passed on your way off the field. I patted your back, told you what a great game you played. You just flashed that smile and thanked me politely." She gave a little chuckle. "Although I'm sure you were wondering who I was."

"I . . . I'm sorry. I don't remember."

Ma flashed her a sweet smile. "It's okay. I do."

A knock on the door, followed by, "Ma? Sam? Are you in here?"

Sam's face lit up. "Connor? We're in the den."

Heavy footsteps sounded on the wood floor and Connor stuck his head in. "Hey, is there anything left over?"

Ma set the album aside and got to her feet. "Of course. Is Dakota with you?"

"Yep, and Noah too."

"Noah?"

Kit felt her stomach swoop at the sound of his name. He was here?

He stepped into the room and immediately locked eyes with her.

Oh yeah, he was here. In the flesh.

She smiled.

He smiled back.

Then she caught Jamie's eyes bouncing back and forth between her and Noah. She cleared her throat and opened her mouth to speak when Noah's cell phone rang.

He looked at Ma and said, "Hi, Ma, they told me I could call you that. I'm Noah, Kit's partner. It's great to meet you, but I gotta take this call. Be back soon."

Kit blinked when he left the room. Jamie opened her mouth and Kit shot her a glare. "Not a word."

Jamie's mouth snapped shut, but her lips spread into a knowing grin. Sam's followed suit, and the guys just stared at them, brows raised in question.

Footsteps sounded again. Noah came back into the room, this time his face looking grim, his eyes dark. "Our serial killer has struck again. We'll have to eat later. We need to get over there."

From his position across the street, the Judge watched them race to their cars. He supposed they'd found Corey's body by now. Didn't take them as long as he'd thought it might. He frowned. He'd been hoping for a little more time to observe his future wife. To his surprise, Kit had a twin. It had shocked him to see the two of them together. At first he couldn't tell them apart, but after watching through the window, he'd been able to spot their subtle differences.

Kit's dimple was in her right cheek. Her twin's was in the left.

And then there was Kit holding the baby, feeding him the bottle.

The Judge settled back into his little hiding place and felt satisfaction well up in him. Oh yes, Kit was perfect. She would be the perfect wife and mother.

And the little baby she'd been holding might just make him the perfect son.

28

In the parking lot of the grocery store, Noah leaned into the car and studied the killer's fourth victim. Through the opposite open door, Serena worked over him, shaking her head. "Whoever is doing this is a real sicko." She bagged something, then gestured to the dead man. "He was a marine. Check out the tat."

"Semper Fi," Kit muttered under her breath.

Noah rubbed his chin. "Yep. I can't believe our killer got the drop on a marine."

"The only way I can think of is that our victim knew him. Possibly trusted him. Had no idea the guy wanted to kill him. But how did he take him by surprise?" Kit voiced her questions hoping someone would have an answer.

"It's possible he drugged him somehow," Serena said. "I'll have a tox screen done and get back to you on that."

Noah looked at the ME. "This is probably a dumb question, but what's the cause of death?"

"Single gunshot wound to the back of the head."

"Like I said, probably a dumb question."

Kit stepped up beside them. "Sicko is right. He cut off his lips. What the heck does that mean? What possible reason would someone have to cut off another person's lips?"

Olivia, the profiler with the FBI, narrowed her eyes. "I don't know, but I'm working on some thoughts."

"Care to share?"

"I believe the killer is exacting his revenge. In his eyes, all of his victims have done something to him. Either hurt him physically or mentally. The lips thing, though? He may have said something the killer didn't like."

"Seems like he would cut out his tongue instead of remove his lips."

The ME shrugged. Olivia nodded. "I would think so too."

Noah looked up. "So why is he coming after Kit?"

Olivia shrugged. "Could be she stumbled across him at some point and she caught his attention. From the things he said to Kit in the cemetery, I would say we're looking for a young man who's unmarried. He has this picture in his head of what a wife and mother should be. Most likely, his own mother ran off or died when he was a young boy. Now, he's looking for a replacement."

"Kit?"

Olivia shoved her hair behind her ear and nodded. "She's met him. Talked to him. It's possible she would recognize him if she saw him, in spite of the fact that he had a mask on. He knows this and thrills to the fact that he can secretly watch her while he plans his next move."

"I don't like it one bit."

"I'm sorry I can't give you something to like. But this guy is twisted. While he thinks Kit is perfect at this point, if she does anything to distort that image, she's toast."

"Great."

The camera flashed as the crime scene photographer recorded the end of Corey's life. Noah felt the rage at this person slide through him and took a deep breath. He couldn't let it get the best of him or he would lose his ability to focus, think, reason.

"Who is our dead guy anyway? Another law student?"

Serena shook her head. "I don't know. He had some ID on

him, but no school badge." She passed the wallet to Noah. "He's thirty-six years old. Military ID."

Noah opened it and looked through the contents. "Has about three hundred dollars cash in here."

"So we can rule out robbery as a motive," Kit murmured.

Dakota reached for the wallet and Noah handed it to him.

"I'll get Jazz to run this and we'll find out all about him in a matter of minutes." Dakota pulled out his phone and stepped away from the buzz of activity.

Footsteps crunched behind Noah and he turned to see Stephen Wells approaching. His sidekick, Edward Richmond, followed behind him.

Noah removed his latex gloves and held out a hand. "Stephen, Edward." He still hadn't gotten the word from the captain about whether or not he wanted to be in on the questioning, so he kept his council—and his cool. The thing was, Olivia had just said the guy was probably unmarried. That would rule out the DA.

Or maybe the killer just didn't consider himself married.

Or just didn't care.

The man shook Noah's outstretched hand. Edward spoke up. "Another one?"

"Looks like it."

"And we're not making any progress on catching this guy at all?" Stephen asked.

Noah blew out a breath. "You know the task force has just been developed. We're on this 24/7 now. It can't be that much longer before we'll have a suspect." *Maybe sooner than you think.* He felt his jaw clench, then relaxed it by sheer force of will.

Stephen blew out a ragged breath and shook his head. Noah frowned. The man looked like he'd aged in the week all of this had been going on. His hair sported more gray and his face was more wrinkled.

Stress stamped its mark in the corners of his eyes and mouth. Did it have to do with a dead girl named Bonnie Gray? He wanted to ask that question in the worst way.

"I need this person found yesterday." He looked Noah in the eye. "Bonnie Gray's mother died yesterday morning."

Noah flinched. "I'm so sorry."

"Bonnie's father is my best friend. He's beyond grief. His life has fallen apart and I can't put the man responsible in jail." Intensity shook him. "I need to put this person away, Noah, and I need to do it now."

"I know that, sir. We all feel the same way. I assure you nothing more could be done than what's being done." Irritation flashed.

Regret flickered in Stephen's eyes. "I know. I just . . ."

Noah sighed and he laid a hand on the DA's arm to lead him away from the scene. Edward followed on the other side. "Look," Noah said, "there's nothing you can do here. As soon as we have anything, I promise I'll let you know. I know this case is personal for you. It's become rather personal for us too." In more ways than one.

Brows creased in concern, Stephen nodded. "I heard about the attempts on Kit's life. I'm glad everyone is all right."

Are you really? "My point is, this guy has come after us on three separate occasions." No sense in mentioning two of those had probably been aimed at Noah. "It's personal. It's a priority. It's all we're eating, sleeping, drinking. We're going to get this guy."

"Make sure it's soon, Noah. Soon."

"That's the plan."

Noah watched the DA and Edward walk back to the dark SUV and climb in. He shook his head. As much as he wanted to lay into the man, if he wasn't the killer, just a secret lover, then he understood where the man was coming from, and could feel some compassion for what he was going through. However, if it turned out the man killed her, killed all of them—or simply killed Bonnie to make it look like the person who killed Walter killed her . . .

And then there was the angle with Kit. Confusion swamped his tired brain and he had to struggle to shrug it off.

The photographer would take some pictures of those gathered around. And while sometimes the bad guy liked to hang around to watch the excitement, he wondered if the killer had just driven off in his SUV.

"Got the DA taken care of?" Kit asked as she scanned the crowd.

"Yeah. I have to say, it looks like the guy is hurting and I feel for him if he didn't have anything to do with Bonnie's death. But in my opinion, he needs to stay away from the crime scenes until we prove things one way or another."

Dakota walked up. "Our dead guy throws a monkey wrench into things."

"How so?" Kit frowned.

"He's not a student at the college. He's been working part-time as a mechanic at the Greenville-Spartanburg International Airport since he got back from Iraq last year."

Noah blew out a sigh. "All right, now we need to find the connection between him and the other three victims." He narrowed his eyes. "Because there is one. It may not be the law school after all. But there's a connection because the same guy who killed the first three, killed this one."

"I don't go to the law school," Kit muttered.

"What?"

"Think about it. We've been looking at this all wrong. We're trying to connect them through the school and maybe that's part of it. But I don't go to the school and he came after me. Granted, it wasn't to kill me after all, but . . ."

She paced between the cars, thinking, her head down, ponytail bouncing against her neck. Noah forced himself to focus on her words.

"He was telling me how perfect I was. How I would make the perfect mother and wife for him. And then my good Samaritan yelled and distracted him."

Noah watched her, could almost see her brain turning. "Okay, hold on a second." He darted to the car, grabbed a notepad and a pen. He had his small pocket notebook, but he needed something larger.

Back with Dakota, Connor, and Kit, he drew a grid, then started labeling. "I know we have all this back at the office, but let's just take a look here." More lines, then he started filling in the blanks. "Okay, we've got our first victim. Time, place, method of death."

"Walter Davis, early morning, dorm room, gunshot to the back of his head. Eye removed."

"Right. Second victim. Bonnie Gray, her home, gunshot to the back of her head. Nose cut off."

Kit leaned in. "Third victim. Susan Chalmers, on the side of the road, gunshot. Toes cut off."

Connor looked over his shoulder. "Fourth victim, Corey Samples. Also a gunshot wound. Lips removed."

"But he's not a student." She bit her lip. "I wonder what he would have removed from me."

Noah shuddered at the thought and forced that image from his mind. He said, "Let's talk to each victim's family and friends again and see if they know Corey. Even though he's not a student, maybe he's associated with the college in some way."

Kit held up a hand. "Wait a minute. Wait a minute. What's the guy's name again? Corey? And he was in the military?"

"Yeah, why?"

"Could be nothing, but I just wonder . . . I think I need to talk to my neighbor. I mean, there are a lot of guys out there named Corey, but—"

Noah groaned. "Great. Here come the news cameras."

Alena's eyes went wide as she saw who was on the breaking news announcement. The next victim of the serial killer. Corey. "No," she whispered to the television. "Please, no."

She'd dated him only a few times, but had found herself really liking the guy. Had thought she might have finally met the one she was supposed to spend the rest of her life with—and now this.

Roscoe whined at her side and she absently reached down to stroke his soft ears.

"Oh Corey."

Was Kit investigating his murder? Probably. She'd asked about Walter and he had been the first victim. Bolting to her feet, she looked at the clock. 6:06. Should she go over? Desperate for someone to talk to, she decided to see if Kit was home.

She and Roscoe walked the six feet separating her entrance from Kit's. Raising a shaking hand, she rapped on Kit's door. The porch light was on, but there wasn't any sign of life coming from inside. Kit's car wasn't in the driveway, but that didn't mean anything. Sometimes her partner dropped her off, then picked her up the next morning.

"Kit? Are you home?" The heat seemed to press in on her and she shivered even though the humidity had caused a fine sheen of sweat to break across her forehead the minute she'd stepped outside.

Even though the news hadn't shown a picture of Corey dead, Alena couldn't stop her imagination from picturing the worst. Nearly sobbing now, she went back to her side of the duplex and collapsed onto the couch. Roscoe hopped up beside her and lay his head on her thigh. She leaned over and buried her face in his fur and let the tears flow.

29

Still no word from the captain. Kit sat at her desk, looking at the chart Noah had come up with. The graph lines seemed to shift and her eyes crossed. How long had she been staring at it anyway?

"Got anything?"

Kit looked up to see Noah behind her. She hadn't heard him come up, but he sure looked good now that he was here. Her eyes needed the reprieve.

The term *eye candy* came to mind and she nearly giggled out loud. That sobered her. She was so tired she was giddy.

"Kit?"

"Right. No. I don't have anything. The knife we found at Bonnie's crime scene still bothers me."

"I know. And word just in. We got zip on the Tyvek suit from Walter's scene. The bleach did its job. However, the crime scene unit found a lot of hairs and are trying to match them up with who they belong to. We're asking for volunteers to come in and give us a hair sample."

Kit tapped her mouth. "Well, the real killer's not going to do that. But at least we can rule out some people and we'll have something to compare it to when we do nab him."

"That's the plan."

"And all we know about Corey is that he was drugged."

"He was?"

"Oh yeah, sorry." Kit nodded. "While you were on the phone with Dakota, Serena called. He had Rohypnol in his system."

"Roofies? A date rape drug?"

"Yep."

Noah blew out a breath. "I wonder if he knew what hit him."

She shrugged. "There's no way to know. It takes twenty to thirty minutes to work and then lasts for hours."

"Which means our guy may not have even been awake for his 'trial and execution.'" Noah wiggled his fingers around the last three words.

"Honestly, I hope that's the case." She passed him another report. "Susan's gas line was cut."

"Well, you're just a fount of information this afternoon, aren't you?"

He took the paper from her hand. His fingers brushed hers and an electric shock made her yelp.

Noah jerked and then laughed, leaned next to her ear, and whispered, "Touching you always does that to me."

An instantaneous flush suffused her and she gasped, unsure whether to laugh or hit him. "Noah . . ."

He backed off and said, "Sorry. What else do you have?"

Blowing out a sigh and resisting the urge to grab a notepad off her desk to fan her hot cheeks with, she said, "Olivia noted that this guy is a planner, yet he sometimes acts impulsively."

"Such as when he followed us to North Carolina."

"Right."

"Got a package for you." The announcement made Kit jump, her heart pounding. She'd been so focused on Noah and their conversation she hadn't heard anyone approach.

One of the department's secretaries handed her a plain brown envelope. As she took it, she noted no return address. "Who brought this?"

"I don't know. I found it on my desk when I got back from lunch." Kit thanked her and the woman left.

"Open it and let's see what we've got."

"It's addressed to me." Taking a deep breath, she blew out a little laugh. "I might want to call the bomb squad the way things have been going for me lately."

He laughed, but his smile didn't reach his eyes. "It's flat, like a letter or a photo or something."

"Or anthrax," she muttered.

Noah held out a hand. "Want me to do it?"

"Nope." Kit opened her bottom desk drawer and pulled out a pair of latex gloves.

At his wide eyes and raised brow, she shrugged. "Never hurts to be prepared."

With a shake of his head, he covered a small grin, but not before she caught it. And her heart somersaulted into the pit of her stomach. Her mind flashed to that kiss that had singed the enamel from her teeth.

"What are you waiting for?"

She blinked. "Right."

The envelope had made it past security. There was nothing to worry about.

But like she said, being prepared never hurt anyone.

Slipping a gloved finger under the flap, she pulled it apart and opened the envelope. She tilted it and several pictures fell out.

She picked up the top one and gave a gasp. "That's Stephen Wells and Bonnie Gray."

"Having a pretty intimate dinner, if you ask me."

"Well, we definitely need to ask him about this." She looked at Noah. "Why don't you try the captain again?"

While he dialed, she looked at the next picture. "Hey, isn't this victim number four?"

"It sure is." He hung up and slipped his phone back into his pocket. "No answer." He leaned over her shoulder to get a look. "They're shaking hands. Where is this? Some kind of ceremony?"

Then he drew in a breath. "Hey, wait a minute. I recognize this," he said slowly. "It was on the news about two weeks ago. There was a big to-do downtown recognizing military personnel for their service in Iraq."

"So that puts the DA with two of our victims." She looked up at him. "Do you think we could place him in the company of the other two?"

"I'm almost afraid to ask him." Noah blew out a sigh and pulled out his cell phone again. It vibrated in his hand.

He looked at the number, then at Kit. "It's the captain."

Stephen Wells did not look happy. Kit didn't care. If the man was a killer, she wanted him behind bars. Out of respect for the man's position, they were all seated in the captain's office.

Stephen stared straight ahead. "What is it that can't wait until Monday morning?"

"The death of Bonnie Gray," Kit said bluntly.

The man blanched. "All right. What have you found?"

Did she dare be blunt? No doubt it would come back to haunt her but . . . "A reason to believe that you killed her."

His face paled. "What? I can't believe you would think I had something to do with Bonnie's death."

Noah handed him the envelope. "Open it."

"Why?"

"Just do it."

With one more disgruntled look at the three of them, he did as requested. When the pictures slid out, Kit wouldn't have thought the man could possibly lose any more color in his face, but she watched it happen. He looked up and swallowed. "Who took these?"

"We don't know. They were delivered to me about an hour ago." She paused, then asked softly, "You had an affair with her, didn't you?"

"What would make you come to that conclusion?"

"The picture. The fact that her father reported that she seemed to get over losing Justin Marlowe in record time. And," she ticked off the next finger, "her friend Chelsea said Bonnie had been very quiet and mysterious about her love life but told her that she would be able to tell her everything soon."

"And the jewelry," Noah added.

Kit nodded. "And the jewelry I found in her room. We went back to get some photos of it so we could trace it and it was gone. That's because when I mentioned doing that the day of Bonnie's murder, you freaked. Later, you went back to the house under the guise of friendship and snatched the items. Didn't you?"

The man didn't speak for a few minutes. When he looked up, his ragged features held guilt and self-condemnation. But he still protested. "I just don't understand how you've come to this horrid conclusion."

"We've got you on an ATM video camera walking to the jewelry store. You wore a hat and sunglasses. The lady who sold you the pieces remembered you because you paid cash."

"Did you copycat her murder, Stephen?" the captain asked. "Because I know you didn't kill Walter. I called your wife and asked her your whereabouts that day. You were on a plane coming home from Washington."

The man flinched. "No. No, I didn't copycat her murder." The DA's voice was so low she almost couldn't hear it. "But," he looked up, defeat taking the place of his earlier look of guilt, "I was having an affair with her. Yes."

Kit felt a roll of revulsion in the pit of her stomach. Not necessarily at the age difference, but at the betrayal of a man who trusted him. His best friend. And his poor wife . . .

Stephen must have read something in her look, because he looked away and muttered, "You're not thinking anything I haven't already told myself but I had absolutely no reason to kill Bonnie."

"You did if she was pressuring you to leave your wife. Or threatening to tell your wife about the affair."

Again Stephen flinched. He closed his eyes.

"Do you have an alibi for the night of her murder?" Noah interjected.

The man's eyes popped open. "I . . . I don't know. I'll have to check my schedule."

"Come on, Stephen. You know exactly where you were that night. If you didn't kill her, then you're beating yourself up for not being with her, protecting her." Kit had switched into her hostage negotiation voice almost automatically.

He looked at her. "I was home. In bed with my wife. Our grandchildren were spending the night."

"So, you feel guilty for being with your wife while your mistress was being killed."

He blew out a sigh and shook his head. "It's crazy, isn't it? I'd feel guilty for being with Bonnie, and when I was with my wife, I'd feel guilty for being with her." His throat convulsed and he looked out the window. "I really messed up." Then he took a deep breath and seemed to compose himself a bit. "Look, is there any way to keep this under wraps? I've done nothing wrong in the eyes of the law. In the eyes of all that's ethical and moral, that's another story. However, Bonnie was of legal age. No crime has been committed."

Noah, the captain, and Kit glanced at each other. Then the captain stood. "For now. But we're still investigating this and we need to search your home."

The man paled. "For what?"

"Because we have a motive for Bonnie's murder!" For the first time, the captain looked agitated. "Your wife is your alibi. Come on. If this were any other suspect, what would you say?"

Stephen hung his head. "I'd say get a warrant and then visit the judge."

"Right. So you're going to stay put until we're done with your house."

❖

"Do you think he killed her?" Kit leaned back in her chair and propped her feet on her desk.

"I don't know." Noah perched on the edge of the desk and crossed his arms. "Sounds like he's got a pretty solid alibi."

She lifted a brow at him. "His wife? A solid alibi?"

"Okay, so maybe not solid, but if she says he was with her all night . . ."

"I know."

"Let's get over to his house and see what we can find. I'm not sure I totally buy his story."

It was a twenty-minute drive to the outskirts of town, and Kit soon found herself looking at the houses along the way. "I guess I'm going to need to take vacation time if I'm ever going to do some serious house hunting."

"Oh, speaking of house hunting, I talked to Skip, my realtor buddy. Former buddy. Ex . . . whatever. He said he'd be glad to get some information from you and help you narrow down your search."

"That'd be great. How's he doing?"

"He's still grieving, but at least he's not casting blame so blatantly anymore. I managed to talk him into talking to the pastor of my church, so maybe that'll help too."

"You do that a lot, don't you?"

"What?"

He didn't even realize it, she thought. "Steer people toward church."

He paused a minute. "I look at it as steering people toward God, not necessarily church. I know the pastor of my church is a godly man and listens well. I feel good about referring people to him." He tossed her a smile. "And isn't that what it's all about? Making a difference in the lives of others? Even if it means reaching them one by one?"

This time it was her turn for a moment of silence. Then she said, "You're a good man, Noah Lambert, aren't you?"

A flush climbed into his cheeks and he shrugged. She decided to let him off the hook. "After we search the good DA's house, I want to find Justin Marlowe."

"Still hung up on that knife thing, are you?" He looked relieved at the change of topic.

"Yes, I am. He was lying about how he lost it. I want to talk to him without his father around."

"Sounds good to me." He made a turn and pulled into a circular driveway and parked at the top in view of the front door.

Climbing out of the vehicle, they made their way up the steps and Kit rang the bell.

For a moment there was only the echoing sound of the doorbell coming from within, then footsteps crossing the foyer. Kit saw the shadow right before she heard the deadbolt disengage. "That's probably his wife. She's in for a shock."

"Yes." His lips pressed together hard enough to form a white line around them.

Before she had a chance to ask him if he was all right, the door opened and a classy lady in her fifties stared up at them. A question formed in her eyes, then made it to her lips. "Can I help you?"

Kit held up her badge. "I'm Detective Kit Kenyon. This is my partner, Detective Noah Lambert."

"Oh, you must work with Stephen. I don't believe we've met. I'm Dee Wells. Please. Come in." She stepped back and Noah and Kit entered the well-kept home.

Dee Wells. When they'd first figured out that Stephen might be involved in the killings, Kit had done her homework. Mrs. Wells came from old money and high society. She worked with various charities and ate lunch at The Debutante's Caviar every Tuesday at 12:30 sharp.

She led them into the den area and motioned for them to have a seat on the brown leather sectional couch. Noah cleared his throat. "Ma'am, we're here on official business. We have a warrant to search the house."

Color receding as his words sank in, Mrs. Wells placed a hand at the base of her throat. "Excuse me?"

"Ah, we have reason to believe that District Attorney Wells is somehow involved in the killings of the Wofford Law College students."

She shook as though stranded in a blizzard. "Oh . . . oh my. But . . . but that's just not possible."

Kit stepped forward and took the lady's hand. "Please, sit down. This all may be for nothing, but it's a lead we've got to investigate. Try not to get upset yet. Is there someone I can call for you?"

"Stephen. You can call Stephen."

Glancing at Noah, she caught movement at the door. "The other officers are here. I'm going to let them in."

He nodded and said, "Mrs. Wells, who can I call for you besides your husband?"

"Oh dear. I just don't know. I suppose I should call my best friend, Rachel."

"What's her number?"

While Noah took care of the woman, Kit opened the door and waved the crew in. "Go easy on the place, okay? Treat this house with respect, but search every nook and cranny."

The lead officer nodded and waved his team in. They got busy and Kit walked back into the den. "Where's Mr. Wells's office?"

"Um, the second door on the left down the hall. But he's very particular. He doesn't want anyone in there."

"I'm sorry, Mrs. Wells. He doesn't have a choice today."

The woman followed Kit. "I don't understand. What has he done? He'd never do anything illegal. Never."

"I understand that you feel that way, but we have some evidence that simply needs corroborating. If we find that—" She broke off as she entered the office—and nearly swallowed her tongue.

Grabbing her radio, she called for Noah. "Get in here. You've got to see this."

30

Noah directed Mrs. Wells into the care of another officer, then stepped inside the office, looked around, and zeroed in on the opposite wall. "Whoa."

"Exactly."

The wall behind the man's desk was covered with photos from Walter's crime scene. Next to those were Bonnie's photos. And then the third one, Susan Chalmers.

"He's got a copy of each victim's file and the crime scene photos," Noah muttered. "Okay, this is a little odd, but not inconceivable. This is likely the biggest case of his career and he's going to be the one to prosecute it, right?"

"Maybe. He's definitely been working on this after-hours."

"Studying the case? Or trying to cover up what he's done?"

"Maybe he's trying to solve his lover's murder without anyone finding out why he's so obsessed with it," Kit muttered.

Noah walked closer, eyes narrowed, studying the photos. "Look. There."

Kit leaned in to see what he pointed at, and he inhaled, pulling in her fresh clean scent.

"Is that the knife?"

"Yeah." He cleared his throat. "The knife. And then look at this one."

"The jewelry."

"Our photographer went upstairs and snapped pictures before we got there."

"Wait a minute, I asked him about the jewelry and he said he didn't have any pictures of it. He never saw it."

"That's because I took the pictures."

Noah and Kit whirled as one as Stephen walked into his office, shoulders slumped. The captain followed close on his heels.

Frowning, Noah asked, "What are you doing here?"

"He told me what you would find," the captain sighed and shook his head. "Said he wanted to come explain some things himself." A shrug. "Figured I'd let him come explain."

"Like the pictures of Bonnie's room and of the jewelry." The DA shoved his hands into his pockets and faced them with as much enthusiasm as an inquisition victim.

"Why didn't the department photographer take them?"

"After Kit came downstairs and mentioned the jewelry, I told the photographer not to worry about her room, to keep his focus on the murder scene itself," Stephen admitted. "But . . ." He rubbed a hand over his eyes. "But I couldn't destroy evidence if it would help find her killer. Even though I knew the jewelry wasn't going to provide any sort of lead to find the killer, I felt like I should take the pictures anyway. Just . . . because. I figured if I took the pictures of her room and kept up with everything you were investigating, maybe I could piece it all together without . . ."

He looked at the floor.

"Without revealing your affair," Noah finished for him.

"Yes," he admitted.

Anger, swift and hot, shot through Noah. "Do you realize what you've done to this investigation?"

"I've done nothing except try to help," the man protested. "That jewelry had nothing to do with Bonnie's death. I," he jabbed himself in the chest with a thumb, "had nothing to do with her death. And yes, if I were standing in your shoes, I'd be questioning my sanity too, but I swear I didn't kill her."

"And how many times have you heard that one on the stand, sir?" Noah asked coldly.

"More times than I can count. Look," he paced to the wall and stared at it, "I was wrong. I cheated on my wife. I've betrayed a man who is—was—my best friend, and I've disgraced the God I claim to follow . . ." His throat bobbed at that admission and tears misted his eyes. Then he straightened his back and turned to look Noah, the captain, and Kit in the eye one by one. "But I did not kill Bonnie Gray."

Kit crossed her arms. "Well, you're either the best liar I've ever come across or you're telling the truth."

"At the very least, you're guilty of obstructing justice," Captain Caruthers muttered. "Tampering with a crime scene."

Stephen nodded his head. "I know and I'll face the consequences of that, but . . . I need you to keep the focus off of me. Because if you don't, then the killer is going to get away with what he's done." His jaw tightened and the lines around his mouth turned white. "And that just can't happen."

31

"Ring around the rosie, pocket full of posie, ashes, ashes, we all fall down."

The childhood chant echoed in his ears and the Judge cringed. He hated that little song. Hated it, hated it. "Shut up!" he called from his car window.

The children stopped their game and watched him, wide-eyed. Then one ran off toward the nearest house, screaming, "Mom! Mom! Stranger danger! Stranger danger!"

The Judge cursed, put his car in gear, and drove off. In the rearview mirror, he saw the child's mother rupture through the door and onto the porch. But he knew he was far enough down the street that she couldn't get a read on his car. She might get the color, but little else.

Stupid kids. Just like the ones who used to make fun of him. They called him Binky. "Ring around the Binky, so ugly and so stinky . . ."

"Stop it! Stop it!" he ordered himself. His voice echoed in the car and helped halt the humiliating memories. To bring his mind back into partial focus.

His jaw jutted as he thought about his son. The son Kit would have for him. The perfect woman, the perfect wife, the perfect mother.

The Judge sighed and pushed those thoughts away.

And smiled.

Because by the end of the week, those who had laughed, had mocked him, would be begging at his feet, their snide comments silenced, their sneering expression wiped off their faces to be replaced with the frozen mask of death.

Yes. Silenced forever.

Justice would be served.

MONDAY

32

Kit rolled over and looked at the clock. Stephen's alibi had checked out. His wife swore the man was in bed with her all night long. When asked why she knew that beyond a shadow of a doubt, she showed them her medication—a sleeping pill.

That she hadn't taken because the grandchildren were there. She'd been up most of the night with insomnia.

Stephen Wells had been at home that night. There was no way he could have killed Bonnie.

And he certainly hadn't been in North Carolina in the cemetery that day. No, if he'd killed Bonnie, he'd covered it up well. The other victims had been killed by someone else.

Much to her disgust, strings had been pulled and Wells had gotten off with a slap on the wrist for interfering in an investigation. At least that's the way it appeared. Who knew what went on behind the scenes when the upper-level authorities got involved? Maybe she would be surprised.

She needed a distraction. Alena's lights had been off when Kit had gotten home late last night. She really wanted to talk to the girl about Corey, but realized with chagrin she didn't even have a phone number for her.

Not that she couldn't find one pretty quick if she'd done a

little digging, but she'd been exhausted and had fallen asleep on the couch around two this morning.

Now, four hours later, she was wide awake and ready for a run. Maybe Alena would keep her company.

Kit got up and threw on her jogging clothes then went next door to knock on Alena's door. "Alena? You up?"

She pounded again. "Alena?"

Nothing. Except Roscoe's short, clipped barks. Kit waited a few more minutes to see if Alena would come to the door. She didn't.

Deciding the girl wanted to sleep in, Kit had just started down the steps when the door opened.

"Kit?"

Bleary eyes blinked out at her.

A pang of remorse shot through Kit. "I'm sorry, I shouldn't have knocked."

"Of course you should have. I told you if you ever got up to run to come get me." She pushed her dark hair from her face and shrugged. "I just don't feel like it today." Tears gathered in her eyes. "I guess you heard about Corey."

"I did," Kit whispered softly. "I'm so sorry."

Twin tears chased down Alena's olive-toned cheeks. "I don't know why he went after Corey. I just don't understand. Do you have any idea?"

"No, hon, I sure don't, but we're investigating every angle and we're going to get this guy."

"Before he kills again?"

"That's the plan." Kit switched gears. "Do you mind if I come inside and talk to you a few minutes about Corey?"

The girl sniffed, then shrugged. "Sure. Let me let Roscoe out. Have a seat in the den. My mother's on the way. I think I'm going to go home with her for a couple of days."

Kit stepped inside. The layout of the small duplex half was exactly opposite of what hers was. She made her way into the den and seated herself in the recliner. Alena opened the back door that led to the small fenced-in yard and Roscoe bounded out to take care of doggie business.

When she came back, Alena dropped onto the couch and leaned her head back to stare at the ceiling. "What do you need to know?"

"Did Corey ever mention any enemies? Anyone he'd made mad? Anything?"

One shoulder lifted in a halfhearted shrug. "Not that I can think of. He played pool a lot at the college and is always winning, so I guess he could have made some of the students there mad. But I wouldn't think that would be motive for murder."

"You'd be surprised what sets some people off."

Alena nodded. "Yeah, I know." She bit her lip. "I know when he sat in on the mock trial, there was another student who was pretty belligerent toward Corey. It had something to do with the war in Iraq."

"What about it?"

"Oh, something stupid. Just that Corey shouldn't be fighting a fight that wasn't his." She waved a hand. "I just admire the men and women who serve our country so much, and this guy's comments were completely uncalled for. It made me pretty mad too. Then Edward jumped in and there was almost a free-for-all."

"Edward?"

"Edward Richmond."

"The DA's intern?"

"Yes."

"So he was involved in this mock trial?"

"Uh-huh. He told the other guy to shut up and stay focused. That they weren't there to argue war politics. They were there to practice law."

"What happened after he said that?"

"The guy got in Edward's face and told him what a twit he was."

"How did Edward react?"

"He laughed and shrugged. He seemed to find the whole thing

kind of funny. And yet he seemed ticked that Corey and that guy were wasting class time arguing. He walked away and sat down. By that time, our professor had called security and we broke for the day."

"Who was the guy that Corey was arguing with?"

"Um . . . I'm not sure. I've only seen him around campus some. He never really says much and he's definitely not very social. I think I've only had one class with him, and it was in one of those big auditoriums with about a hundred people in it. Edward would know his name, though. They're both getting ready to graduate, so they've been together since day one of law school. I'm sorry, I just can't think of it."

"That's all right." Kit stared out the window. The sun was starting to put in an appearance on the horizon. "Can you think of anything else?"

"No," Alena whispered. "Please catch who did this. I know Corey was a lot older than I am, but I think I could have really loved him." More silent tears fell.

Kit put her arms around the girl's shoulders and let her cry while her mind clicked with things to do. She took inventory. Her shoulder was healing nicely and her head no longer throbbed. So, number one, she was going to take her run. Some part of her wondered if that was a smart thing to do since she possibly had a killer after her. Then again, she wasn't going to cower in fear and give this guy that much control over her life.

Number two, she was going to call Noah and they were going to track down the person Corey had gotten into an argument with.

And number three, she was going to confront Justin Marlowe and get the truth about how he lost that knife if it was the last thing she did before closing her eyes tonight.

But first, the run.

Maybe Jamie would go with her. She placed the text and gave her a few minutes to respond.

No answer.

Fine. She'd go by herself. She needed to think anyway. And on second thought, if she had a killer watching her, she certainly didn't need to place Jamie in danger. No, it was better she go alone. She sent another text to Jamie telling her to never mind.

Fifteen minutes later, Kit's feet pounded out the rhythm that she'd come to love. Running cleared her mind and pushed the stress out of her life for a brief while and she needed that.

Desperately.

At the entrance to the subdivision, she followed the sidewalk as it turned right and led to a small back road lined with trees. If she kept going, she would come to the main road, then circle around through the neighborhood that bordered hers. The entire route was four and a half miles. Sometimes, she cut it short and only did three miles. This morning she felt like doing the whole thing.

She especially loved the little stretch across the bridge where a river ran beneath. Often she stopped to look down, contemplating the purpose of the river. It gave life to the fish in it and offered a drink for some of the thirsty wildlife that still roamed in this area.

What was her purpose in life?

Noah came to mind.

His purpose was to make a difference in the life of everyone he came into contact with.

As for her purpose?

To catch the bad guys.

And to help those who couldn't help themselves.

She smiled as she approached the bridge, loving the sound of the rushing water that flowed beneath. She pounded onto the sidewalk made for joggers, leaving plenty of room for passing cars.

Noah had definitely made a difference in her life.

He'd gotten her thinking about—and sometimes talking to—God again.

A car passed and she lifted a hand in an absent greeting. The brake lights came on and it slowed. Then sped up and disappeared around the corner.

At this point, her cop instincts sharpened. Why had it slowed down so much? The road was flat and even—there wasn't a need for brakes at that spot.

She jogged off the bridge and kept going, her mind clicking.

What color was the car? A green one. What kind was it? She couldn't remember. Possibly a Mazda? Or a Honda?

Not many cars used this road, which is why she liked to run on it.

The deserted stretch mocked her. Stupid, it seemed to say. With a chill, she stared ahead. A sick feeling churned in her gut. She was so determined to have her own way, control everything around her, that she'd possibly put herself in danger.

She wondered if she would need the small pistol she had strapped around her right ankle.

Clouds hovered overhead adding to her suddenly dark mood.

Sweat dripped down her back.

Her feet slapped the pavement even as she pondered turning around and heading home.

And her pulse thundered in her ears.

As her adrenaline spiked, so did her breathing, coming faster and more labored.

With an effort, she managed to regulate it.

But couldn't get rid of the feeling she was in danger.

She did a one-eighty and decided to head home. So she'd only get in two miles today. Right now that was fine with her.

Tomorrow, she'd choose another route.

One that had some traffic on it.

Lesson learned. She couldn't control everything, no matter how much she wanted to. Especially the actions of a killer.

A car sounded behind her and her pulse spiked.

Already on edge, she glanced over her shoulder.

And saw the same green car that had passed her only moments before.

She picked up the pace.

If he had a gun, she was dead. Her little small-caliber pistol wouldn't be any kind of match for someone using a car as a shield. Her best hope was to just get away.

A quick glance around showed no place to hide.

The car came closer . . .

Kit pushed her legs faster.

. . . and closer . . .

Another glance over her shoulder got her nothing except a view of the front of the car.

A Dodge.

. . . closer still . . .

And she had nowhere to go, no place to hide . . . and a possible killer on her tail.

33

The car swerved in front of her. The door opened and the masked man stepped out, gun pointed in her direction. Kit knew she had less than a second to act. She flung herself over the side of the bridge and let herself fall. Keeping herself limp, she hit the water, held her breath, and went under.

The river was about seven feet deep in some areas. Fortunately, she hit a deep part and the current carried her downstream before she could even start to kick.

Lungs screamed for oxygen as she floated underwater, ordering herself to remain calm.

Kicking out, she searched for the surface, desperate for a breath of air.

Finally, when she thought she might pass out or suck in a lungful of river water, she broke through.

And gasped. She drew in another breath of sweet, life-giving oxygen even as her eyes went to the bridge that grew smaller by the moment. But she could see him watching.

A hand lifted as though to wave goodbye.

But she wasn't dead yet—and had no intention of dying anytime soon. She let herself go back under, holding her breath and going with the flow.

Under the water, she kicked and struggled toward the edge, fighting to reach a place where she could plant a solid foot.

Out of sight of the man on the bridge.

Two more strokes, then she was around the bend and up for air. She pushed her way through the water, felt her feet touch bottom. Shoved one more time and her foot came free of her shoe. Not caring, just wanting to get out of the river in case her assailant came looking to finish the job, she gave another push and made it to the bank. Grasping an overhanging branch, she pulled herself from the water with her good arm and collapsed against the ground. Her shoulder and head throbbed in time with her heartbeat.

Okay, so this had been a really bad idea.

Kit gave herself twenty seconds to catch her breath, then stumbled to her feet to start the trek home.

Ignoring her pounding headache, she patted her pocket. No cell phone. And her safety strap on her gun had unsnapped when she'd hit the water.

Chilled, she shivered, even though the temperature hovered in the mideighties already.

Keeping her eyes peeled for any movement, any indication that she needed to move fast, she tried to keep her steps even and quiet. However, her breath came in shallow pants, and she knew if the killer were looking for her, all he had to do was stop and listen for a minute.

Ten minutes into fighting her way through the wooded area, Kit wanted her shoe back. Not wanting to think about what her foot was going to look like by the time she made it home, she continued to keep alert for any unwanted company.

So far nothing had set off her internal alarms.

She didn't count on that to last long.

Finally, she limped to the edge of the woods and stopped. Her arm and her head hurt. So did her foot.

But she was alive. No thanks to anything like smart thinking on her part. More like dumb luck.

Or maybe God wasn't ready for her to stand before him yet. Whatever the reason, she vowed to start using her brain and keep her issues—like her stubbornness—under control.

At least until the killer was caught.

Before she ventured onto the sidewalk that would lead her home, she studied the area surrounding it.

No green car.

Nothing out of the ordinary.

Except the large German Shepherd bounding down the middle of the road.

Noah tried Kit's number one more time.

Nothing. Straight to voice mail.

Now that was odd.

He hung up and paced the office floor. Then he snatched his phone back out and dialed Connor's number.

The man answered on the first ring. "Wolfe."

"Connor, this is Noah. Have you seen or heard anything from Kit?"

"No, why?"

"She's not answering her cell. It's going straight to voice mail."

"I haven't talked to her since yesterday. I don't think Samantha has either. Did you try her home phone?"

"Yeah, voice mail too."

"That doesn't sound like Kit." Connor's concern came through loud and clear.

"True, but just Saturday she left her cell phone on silent and missed my calls. I tracked her down just as she was leaving to go to North Carolina. But I still don't like it. She knows we could get a break in this case any minute."

"I agree. Want to head over to her house and see what's going on?"

"Yeah, I was hoping you'd say that."

"Meet you there."

"Ah!" He couldn't believe she'd jumped off the bridge! But she'd lived. His intention hadn't been to try to kill her, he'd wanted to grab her. He'd thought she'd be trapped on the bridge, but his plan backfired. And she'd jumped. He almost laughed. What an incredible woman.

And soon she'd be his. She just didn't understand that.

But she would.

Kit stumbled after Roscoe, swiping away the water that dripped into her eyes. Her foot hurt, but she could walk on it without too much aggravation. Probably just some superficial scrapes and cuts. Still, she'd need to clean and bandage it as soon as she got home.

If she ever got there.

"Roscoe! Come here, boy."

The dog ignored her and went about his business.

Kit decided she didn't have time to mess with him. He'd find his way home like he always did.

Grunting, she covered the last half mile to her house and stopped short. Alena's door stood open.

Hurrying, ignoring the bite of pain with every step, she made her way up the steps. The brief thought that she should enter her side and grab her gun flitted through her mind, but if Alena needed help now, Kit needed to get in there and help her.

She paused at the door and looked in. Nothing seemed out of place. Except for the open door. And the wet spot on the floor from the overturned glass.

Very odd.

"Alena?"

No answer.

"Alena?" Kit stepped inside, her eyes darting, taking in the details.

Had Alena left and just not shut the door firmly? That would explain how Roscoe had gotten out.

But Alena was so careful with her pet, Kit couldn't see that happening.

A car approached and Kit moved back to the door, her eyes narrowed on the vehicle turning into her side of the drive.

Noah.

And Connor.

Slipping back out onto the porch, she caught Connor's eye and held a finger to her lips.

Immediately, they went into full-alert mode, guns drawn and pointed in front of them. Noah came up beside her, his eyes wide at her soggy, one-shoed appearance. "Later," she whispered. Connor slipped up next to her and she looked at them both. "I went for a run and nearly got creamed by a car. I found Roscoe in the road, and when I got back here, the door was open. I don't know if anyone's still inside."

"I've got the back," Connor said as he headed back down the steps and around the side of the house.

"You stay here. I've got a weapon," Noah ordered, voice low, lips tense.

Kit nodded.

He entered with caution, swinging his arms to the left and back to the right. She knew that part of the house was clear since she'd just come from it. He moved farther in and Kit followed behind him.

He headed toward the back of the house and she swept her gaze into the kitchen. Nothing out of place. Then the back bedroom. Again, everything seemed fine.

"Clear."

"Clear out here," Connor called.

Kit let out the breath she'd been holding. "Then where's Alena?"

"Maybe she forgot to shut the door good when she left."

"That's what I thought too, but I can't see her doing that. She's too careful about Roscoe." Biting her lip, she walked back into the den area. "Look, two glasses. One spilled on the floor, the other in the middle of the coffee table."

"That doesn't look good."

"She wouldn't just leave it like that. And especially the door . . ." Kit pulled in a deep breath. "I'm worried."

"Let's process this like a crime scene," Connor said. "I'll call Jake and get him out here. I want to know if there are any prints on the glasses and who they belong to. If we know who she was having a drink with, we might find out what happened here."

Connor walked off to make the call while Kit limped for the front door. "I'm going to change and bandage my foot." She grimaced. "I hope I didn't contaminate anything. If you find blood on the floor that belongs to me, you know why."

Noah followed her over to her side of the building. "What happened?"

Kit rolled her eyes as she unsnapped her keys from her belt loop and unlocked the door. Fortunately, those hadn't drowned along with her cell phone. "Long story short, I went for a run this morning."

"So you said. I couldn't explode at that point. I can now. Are you insane?!"

Kit gulped. "Yes, apparently." Her eyes slid from his, then she forced herself to look back at him. His outrage at her stupidity was clearly displayed. "Look. I'm sorry. I know it was dumb, but I just . . ." She stopped, gulped. That could wait. Pulling in a deep breath, she slowly let it out, donned her professionalism, and said, "When I got to the bridge, a car passed me, turned around, and came back. I had to jump off the bridge into the river to get away." She shuddered as she replayed the scene in her head.

"What?!" More outrage.

"I know. I lost my shoe, my cell, and my pistol. I still have my work phone on my dresser, so that's just going to have to be my backup until I can get another one."

Noah paced two steps away, then back. "Did you get a look at the car?"

"A dark green Dodge something. And no, I didn't get the plates."

The lines around his eyes tightened as he took in her information. He started to say something else and Kit held up a hand to silence him. "Hold that thought. I've got to get out of these clothes."

His eyes flared and narrowed as they gave her the once-over and she felt the flush start to rise from her neck. That might have been the wrong thing to say to a man who'd kissed her like he had the other day. "Don't say it, don't even think it," she blurted, then turned on her heel and headed for the bedroom.

"Hey Noah," she heard Connor's voice and paused in the hall.

Looking back, she felt her blood freeze at the object in Connor's hand. "We found this under her sofa."

A miniature gavel.

34

The task force met in the large conference room. Noah couldn't help thinking about Kit's comment. He'd wanted to offer to help her with the clothes thing, but thought better of it. When she'd left with her parting comment, he realized she'd read his thoughts like he'd had them stamped on his forehead.

How did she do that?

To survive the turmoil of his childhood, he'd learned at an early age how to keep his face expressionless, nothing about it revealing his innermost thoughts, and yet Kit seemed to do it without even thinking about it.

Unbidden, snapshots of his childhood flitted through his mind's eye. Years in an orphanage, refusing to give in to the fear of the older kids, hiding his emotions, then his heartbreaking despair as he was shuffled from one foster home to the next with no adoption in sight—now Kit.

She stumped him.

He looked across at her and his heart twisted inside itself. He was going to have to share his past with her if he wanted to pursue a relationship.

"Noah? You have something you want to add?"

The question jerked him from his rare inattention and he

flushed, his brain racing to catch up. What was the last thing he'd heard?

"Actually, Captain, I have something," Kit interrupted.

Noah breathed a sigh of grateful relief. He owed her.

She said, "We've had no more bodies show up, but I don't expect that to last long." She swallowed hard. "I think he's taken the girl who lives next to me, and if we don't act fast, she's going to die sometime soon. The crime scene unit found a miniature gavel under her sofa." Kit drew in a deep breath and Noah ached for her sorrow.

She continued. "I feel like that was a message for me. For some reason, he's zeroed in on me. He's attempted to kill me three times. And now with Alena's disappearance, I'd like to set myself up as bait and try to draw him in."

That got his attention. Noah's spine went rigid, his blood ran cold. Before he could protest, she went on. "I spoke with Alena this morning before my dip in the river, and she said that Corey had gotten into an argument with someone on the mock jury. She couldn't remember his name, but I think we need to get a list of those jurors and start asking questions."

"Sounds like an excellent idea, Kit," the captain nodded. "Anything else?"

"One more thing. I think we need to talk to Justin Marlowe one more time without his father present. And while I don't think he was lying about killing Bonnie, I do think he was lying about the knife that was used to cut off her nose, and I want to know why."

"Do it."

The meeting adjourned and Kit rose to leave. Noah followed her as she made her way back to her office.

He leaned against her desk. "Hey, thanks for saving my hide in there."

She gave a small smile. "You owe me."

"Yes, I do." He cocked his head to the side. "What would you say if I think my friend has found you a house?"

"I'd say great. Where?"

"When this case is over and we find your friend, I'll take you to see it."

❖

A knock on the side of her cubicle swiveled her attention to a man in his late forties. Salt-and-pepper hair cut in a fashionably shaggy style graced his head and black-rimmed glasses straddled his nose.

Kit lifted a brow. "Can I help you?"

"Are you the detectives investigating the law students' murders?"

Kit lowered her feet to the floor and Noah stood from his perch on the side of her desk to hold out a hand. The man shook it and Noah said, "We are."

"I've debated whether this had to do with anything or not but after Corey's death . . ." His eyes teared up and he coughed. "Sorry. Corey was my nephew."

"Oh, I'm so sorry." Kit laid a hand on the man's arm and directed him to a chair in the cramped quarters. He sat and Kit handed him a tissue. She said, "You must be Nelson Moseby. We have you on our list to question about Corey's murder. We had a bit of an emergency with . . . uh . . . another suspect so we hadn't gotten to calling you yet."

"I'll be glad to answer any questions you might have, but I think I may have found a connection between all of the murders."

Kit's gaze sharpened. "What do you mean? The only connection we really had was that the victims were law students." She refrained from saying anything about the body parts that had been removed. That hadn't been released for public knowledge. "And then your nephew is killed in exactly the same way as the other victims. The only thing is, he's not a law student."

"But he did sit in on the mock jury."

"You mean the trial that all of the law students participate in?"

"Yes. I teach law at the college. I arrange the mock trials and sit as the judge over them. I pick several very promising students to act as the defendant and the prosecutor, alternating them throughout the trial to give them a taste of what it's like. We do this throughout the semester, but only those with the highest grade-point average argue in the last one." He sighed. "It's sort of a tradition. Most law schools don't do this, pick the best of the best, so to speak, but we do—and it's the reason we get an incredible number of applications each year. Everyone wants to prove they're the best."

"Interesting."

"They're also responsible for picking the jury from the list of volunteers. Once they have twelve jurors and two alternates, the trial begins. Then right before the closing argument, the jury votes on whose closing argument they want to hear. All the students must prepare one, but only one gets to present it."

"Very competitive. And your nephew was on this jury?"

"Yes. As were all of the other victims."

Kit scrambled for a pen. "We need the names of all of the others who were involved in the trial." So, she'd been on the right track after all.

"Sure, I figured you would." He handed over a piece of paper he'd been holding for the duration of the conversation.

Kit took the paper and scanned through it. Her eyes screeched to a halt as she recognized a name. "And there's Alena's name," she whispered.

Noah leaned over her shoulder. "Your missing friend?"

"Yes. Alena Pappas. She's my neighbor. She was on the jury."

"And now she's missing. That's the link. The jury. We have to warn all these people and get some protection on them."

Kit's phone rang and she snatched it up. "Hello?"

"Kit, it's Connor, the captain and I need you and Noah in my office. Samantha just got a threat texted to her phone—with a picture of Andy attached."

Kit bolted to her feet. "Be right there."

She hung up and Noah raised a brow. With a thudding heart, she said, "Come with me, we've got a problem."

"Let me just give this list to the captain." Noah fingered the paper.

"He's with Connor."

Noah turned to the professor, who stood gaping at them. "Sir, I want you to stay here until someone comes to escort you home. Your life may be in danger and I don't want to take any chances on you walking out of here without an officer with you."

"What? Are—are you serious?" As the impact of Noah's words hit, he paled and his throat worked, but he nodded. "All right."

"You have any other family around here?"

The man shook his head. "No. My wife died last year and all my children are scattered around the globe."

Noah took three minutes to track down the right officer and explain the situation, then he and Kit headed to Connor's office. The assistant DA and Edward Richmond stood to the side, twin grim looks on their faces.

Edward shrugged at Kit's startled look. "I hurried over as soon as you left the DA's. Since he is no longer able to . . . um . . . supervise me, my professor arranged for me to shadow the ADA. He called and told me I needed to be in on this."

"Right." She really didn't care right now.

Captain Caruthers sat looking at something on a Blackberry phone. Samantha held Andy in her arms. He watched his surroundings with wide blue eyes. When he saw Kit, he grinned around his pacifier and her heart melted. She walked over and planted a kiss on his bald head.

The tension in the room caused her blood pressure to spike.

Connor looked ready to rupture something. A vein pulsed in his head; his left hand opened and closed, balling into a fist, then releasing. Granted, she'd known him for less than a year, but she'd never seen him this angry.

"What is it? What happened?"

Samantha's usually smiling face looked strained—and furious. "The creep you're after threatened my son."

"How did he get your cell number?"

"I have no idea. And don't even really care. I'm taking Andy and getting out of town for a while. I'm not taking any chances with his life. Not after—" She broke off and swallowed hard.

Kit had heard the story of how Jamie's stalker had come after Samantha, entering her home and nearly killing her while she was pregnant with Andy. "Let me see the picture." She held out a hand and the captain passed the phone over to her.

Andy, asleep in his crib. The picture had obviously been taken through the window. The blinds were cracked, but the photographer's intent was clear.

The next picture showed him awake and staring at the window.

Samantha paced and patted the baby's back. "He took that picture of him sleeping and then another when he was awake. Why didn't I know he was outside my house? Why didn't I know someone was watching my child?"

Connor crossed the room and pulled her into his arms. He looked at Kit and drilled her first, then Noah, with his gaze. "Whatever it takes, whatever we have to do, we have to find this guy."

"Absolutely. That goes without saying." Kit shoved her desire for revenge to the back of her mind and focused on what they needed to do first. "The photo is date stamped. Look."

Noah and Connor looked over her shoulder.

"That's Saturday." She looked at Sam. "Remember how you said he didn't sleep well the night before?"

"Yes." The light went on, then fury sparked her eyes. "He took those pictures Saturday evening."

Kit squinted. "It looks like he put the camera right up to the window. He may have hit it or made some noise that woke up Andy."

"He'd have had to have a pretty nice camera to do that. One that could shoot in the dark," Connor muttered.

Sam shook her head. "I don't care what kind of camera he had. I want him caught. Now. Did the victims' computers have anything on them?"

"Nothing related to the deaths," Noah said. "Nothing that would lead us to a suspect. No threatening emails, nothing."

"Well, I'm out of here. My bags are packed and I'm ready to go visit Brenda Allen, a friend from college. She lives in Florida. My flight leaves in three hours."

"I'll be with her until she takes off," Connor said, "then I'll be ready to find this guy."

Kit blew out a sigh. "All right. Be safe." She looked at Noah and Captain Caruthers, who'd been uncharacteristically quiet during the discussion. "I want to find Justin Marlowe. Now. Alena is missing and I would like to find her. Alive. Because that's the only way we're going to find who's threatened Andy." She felt a tension headache building. "That was a very big mistake."

35

Later, the Judge paced as he considered what to do. He looked at his latest victim. She slept. A peaceful sleep that would soon come to an end. The drug had worked so well with Corey that he'd decided to stick with it. He supposed the authorities would find the spilled glass and realize he'd drugged her drink.

Then they would say he'd developed another "signature." A serial killer, they called him. Well, he supposed that's what they had to say. After all, they didn't know that all this was predestined. Ordained, even.

Alena had let him right in, offered him a drink, and when she'd gone to get the cookies he'd asked for, he'd slipped the roofies in her Coke. Easy as pie.

He hadn't planned to make her his next victim.

He'd planned to make her his sister. She'd been the one. The kind of sister he'd dreamed about as a child.

Anger suffused him as he thought about her betrayal. Anger at her, anger at himself. How had he allowed himself to be so blind to her true nature? How had she managed to fool him for so long? He'd thought she was his friend, as close to a true sister as he could expect to find. Then for some reason, she turned to Corey.

"Corey, Alena?" he asked aloud to his unconscious victim.

"Corey?" Shaking his head in confused disgust, he walked to the other side of the room and sat at the desk. "How could you? You should have listened to your older brother. But you didn't and now I have to protect you this way."

She stirred, moaning softly.

The Judge frowned. He hadn't planned on her waking quite so soon. He looked around and his eyes landed on his father. The old man had just stared at him as he'd carried Alena through the door. Hadn't said a word since the Judge had arrived. Just stared. With those big wide eyes that watched his every move. And that stupid grin that often turned to mocking laughter. Fortunately, it didn't bother him anymore. He'd outgrown his tears and desperate need for his father's love.

The Judge ignored him and tested Alena's bonds to make sure she couldn't get loose until he was ready for her. He hadn't quite decided what he was going to do.

She'd have her chance to fill her role as his baby sister. If she shirked that role or didn't offer him the gratitude and respect he deserved as her older brother, she would die.

Right now, he had a plan to carry out.

Kit pulled up in front of Justin Marlowe's home. Noah sat in the passenger seat. "His car is here."

"And his father is in court." She breathed out a satisfied sigh. "I checked."

"I can't believe it took us this long to track this guy down."

"I don't understand parents who let their children just mooch off them. Does Justin's father really believe letting his son party with his friends all night and sleep all day is going to turn him into a productive citizen?"

Noah shook his head. "I have no idea."

"What about your parents?" Curiosity tinged her tone. "How do they feel about you being a cop?"

"They . . . don't really care one way or the other. Look." He pointed and she turned to see what had captured his attention. Justin. Dressed in a robe and slippers at four o'clock on a Monday afternoon. Checking the mail.

"Now's our chance."

They opened the doors to the car and stepped out. Kit called, "Justin, could we have a minute of your time?"

He spun from the mailbox and fear flashed in his eyes. "I didn't do anything, I swear."

Kit put on her negotiator's face. "Hey, it's okay. We know you didn't kill Bonnie. It's all right."

The young man's shoulders sagged in relief. "Oh. Okay. Well, good. What do you want?"

"We wanted to ask you about that knife that you admitted belonged to you."

Nervousness made him shudder. He licked his lips and his eyes darted as though seeking escape.

With a look at Noah, Kit stepped in again. "Okay, could we just go inside and sit down?"

"Inside?"

"Yes. Just to talk. You're not under arrest and you're not going to be under arrest unless you did something illegal with that knife. You say you didn't, that you lost it. We want to know more details about that."

Justin studied her face, then looked over at Noah. "All right. Come on in. Dad's not here right now. Is this conversation private? You know, confidential and all that?"

"Of course," Noah said. "You're a grown man. We're not obligated to talk to your father, if that's what you're concerned about."

Justin opened the door and led them into the den. "Just sit here and I'll go change."

Did they want to let him do that? Would he run?

She and Noah exchanged a glance. Kit shrugged. "Are you going to run?"

Justin lifted an eyebrow and let out a sad little laugh. "I thought about it. But no."

"Then go, but don't take too long, all right?"

"Yeah."

He turned and made his way up the curving steps to the second floor, disappeared through an open door, then shut it with a soft click.

Kit looked at Noah. "You think you might want to cover the back of the house?"

Her partner considered it. "No, I think he's all right. If I'm wrong, I'll do the chase on foot and you can have the car."

"Deal." She sat on the couch and looked around while Noah moved toward the stairs, betraying the fact he wasn't as confident about Justin as he'd sounded. She said, "You never answered my question."

"What question?"

He knew exactly what question, she thought. "Never mind."

Noah stood at the foot of the stairs, listening. "I can hear him up there."

"Good, at least that means he's still in the house." A door opened, then shut somewhere above.

Noah mused, "I wonder where all the help is?"

"They quit," Justin said from the landing.

"Quit?" Noah asked.

Kit looked up to see Justin had changed into a pair of jeans and a T-shirt advertising some heavy metal group she'd never heard of. "Why?"

"I think they were tired of my father's rather overbearing manner. In the end, it was just the housekeeper. Dad fussed at her about not cleaning something to his satisfaction, and she tossed a rag at him and told him he could clean it himself."

"And you delighted in that, didn't you?" Kit noted.

His eyes gleamed with the first smile she'd seen. "Oh yeah." Then he sobered. "Okay. The knife."

"You lied at the police station."

"I didn't want my father to know how I lost it."

He paused and Noah leaned in. "Gambling?"

Shock crossed Justin's face, then he laughed. "Well, that was easy. Yes, gambling. I like to play pool with the college kids."

"Why didn't you finish school? Why drop out?"

He shrugged and sniffed. "It's ironic. I got into the drugs so I could stay awake and study." He rolled his eyes. "School was never easy for me. Unlike my father, who apparently was able to breeze through undergrad and law school without cracking a book, I had to study. Constantly. I fell asleep studying for an exam. When I woke up, I had ten minutes to get to that class. I failed the exam."

"And decided drugs were the answer?"

"Yep. And easy enough to score." He shrugged. "At first, they helped. Then Bonnie found out about them and dumped me."

"And then she got involved with someone else."

Pain twisted his face. "I figured she'd moved on. I just never was able to figure out who it was with."

Kit and Noah exchanged a look. So, it couldn't have been Justin who'd sent the pictures to the DA. If he was telling the truth.

He continued. "Anyway, I took the drugs to do better in school and flunked school because I got hooked on the drugs. Dad sent me to rehab and now I'm clean."

"Right." Kit shot him a look of disbelief.

"Seriously. I drink and party a little too hard occasionally, but I don't touch drugs anymore. I can't afford to."

"But you can afford to sell them to other students?"

A flush crept up his throat, but he clamped his lips together, and Kit realized she needed to back off in order to get the information she needed. Clearing her throat, she asked, "Why don't you go back to school?"

He closed his eyes and leaned his head back against the sofa. "Because that's what my father wants me to do."

"And yet you live in his house and do what?"

"Nothing. Because I am nothing, as he's told me pretty often."

Kit winced and Noah's brows met at the bridge of his nose.

His hand reached up to his shirt pocket and he pulled something out. She knew it was a card with his pastor's number on there. That poor pastor. She hoped he had an associate or two to help him with all the people Noah sent his way!

She couldn't help the admiration that welled up. One by one. With effort, she focused back on Justin. "About the knife . . ."

"Yeah, I gambled it away in a pool game." He heaved a sigh. "Dad would have been furious. It belonged to my grandfather— who shares the same initials I do."

"Who won it from you?"

"A guy by the name of Edward Richmond."

"Edward? The intern?"

"Yes, well, they're all interns. But he's interning with the DA, Stephen Wells."

"Not anymore," Kit muttered under her breath. She looked at Noah. "I think we need to pay Edward a little visit right after we find the guy Corey was arguing with during the mock trial. Also, one more question."

Justin lifted a brow, and Kit asked, "Do you know anything about Alena Pappas and why someone would want to hurt her?" She left off the fact that they knew the killer had her, they just needed a name.

"No, but I think I know who she is."

Noah held out his iPhone and pulled her picture up. "That's her."

The young man studied the picture, then shook his head. "I've seen her around. But no, I don't know much about her. I think she's friends with Edward. Yeah, she would hang around with him while he played pool. Kind of like his personal cheerleader or something. Then again, it seems like some guy named Porter Haynes was hitting on her the other day."

"Is that it?"

A shrug. "It's all I can think of."

Noah handed Justin the card. "If you need anything, call me . . . or him. I'd be glad to get together with you and tell you how you can really turn your life around."

Justin looked down at the card and smirked. "Religion?"

Noah shook his head and gave a small smile. "No, no religion. Something way bigger."

Back inside the car, Noah placed a call to Professor Nelson Moseby while Kit navigated through the back streets to head toward the DA's office. The professor answered on the third ring. "Hello?"

"Professor Moseby, this is Detective Noah Lambert. We spoke with you earlier about the mock trial and the jury."

"Right, right. Have you found Corey's killer?"

"Not yet, but we're closing in. Could you tell me the name of the young man that Corey had an argument with the day of the mock trial?"

"Ah yes, I ended up calling campus security. I felt sure those two were going to come to blows. His name is Porter Haynes."

Nick shot a look at Kit. She mouthed, "Porter?"

He nodded and spoke back into the phone. "Any idea where we might be able to find him?"

"I know he lives on campus in one of the apartments, but aside from when he's in my class, I couldn't tell you his schedule."

"No problem, I'll get it from the registrar's office. Thanks so much."

"Let me know if there's anything else I can do for you."

Noah hung up and looked at Kit. "Porter Haynes."

"Interesting. So, Porter was hitting on Alena, and Edward and Alena are friends. Maybe Edward knows something about all this. You want to track Porter down first or Edward?"

Hesitating, he thought about it. "Let's go with Edward. I want to see what he has to say about the knife."

Her phone rang and she grabbed it. Noah listened as she said, "Thank you, I'll be by to pick it up."

"What?"

"I ordered a personal cell phone, since mine drowned when I jumped in the river. It's ready."

He nodded. "That's good. We can swing by the phone store, then catch up with Edward."

"Sounds like a plan."

She hesitated and he looked at her. "What is it? I can see your brain working."

"Just . . . thanks for being there, Noah. I appreciate it."

"Hey, that's what partners are for." He glanced at her.

"Just partners, huh?"

A small smile played around the corners of his lips, and he did his best not to break out into a full grin. Giving a nonchalant shrug, he said, "Depends on what kind of partner you're talking about."

She tilted an eyebrow at him. "What kind of partner are *you* talking about?"

He reached over and grasped her hand. Raising it to his lips, he grazed her knuckles, then chuckled as goose bumps became visible on her arm. Placing her hand back on the steering wheel, he said softly, "I think you know what I'm talking about."

Edward Richmond proved to be easy to find. He answered his cell phone on the first ring and said to meet at the library where he would be studying.

Kit could see the top of his head, his chin tucked almost into his chest. An open book lay in his lap. He looked relaxed and intent at the same time.

Focus, she ordered herself. Ignoring the fact that she still had goose bumps from hers and Noah's encounter in the car, she kept her gaze on Edward.

They approached him and he never moved.

"Edward?" Kit asked in a hushed voice, acutely aware of the other students working hard to ensure their future success.

He jerked, then looked up and blinked owlishly. When he saw who stood before him, he cleared his throat. "Yes? You're here already. I lost track of time, sorry."

"It's no problem. But is there some place we could talk privately?"

"Um . . . sure." He looked around as though unsure what to do next, then shrugged and stacked his books. Grabbing his backpack, he said, "We can go outside on the steps."

Kit flashed him a grateful smile. "That would work great."

They followed him outside and he led them over to the corner of the steps where he dropped his backpack and sat down, legs stretched out in front of him. "What kind of questions?"

Noah started while Kit watched the kid's expression. "We found a pocketknife at the crime scene of Bonnie Gray. One that was reported to have been won by you in a game of pool."

Derision crossed Edward's face. "Ah, you must have talked to Justin. I'm assuming you traced the knife back to him."

Kit narrowed her eyes. "Right."

Edward snorted. "What a loser. Yes, I won it off of him."

"Wait a minute. You were at the crime scene. Did you see the knife there?"

"No, I never saw the knife. When I saw the body, I got a little nauseous and walked outside to get some air." He looked at Kit. "Remember?"

"Yeah, I do. So, do you have any idea how the knife would have gotten to the crime scene? Why it would have the victim's blood on it?"

He frowned. "No. I ended up giving the stupid thing back to Justin. I told him it wasn't worth anything and I didn't have any need for a knife that had his initials on it." His frown tipped into a smile. "I just let him bet it because I knew I could win it and I wanted to see him squirm a little." Another careless shrug. "But I didn't keep the knife. You can ask anyone standing around watching the table that day. They all saw me give it back to him."

Kit wanted to grind her teeth in frustration. She felt like a dog chasing its tail. From the expression on Noah's face, she could tell he felt the same.

The question was: Was Edward telling the truth? If so, why hadn't Justin just said he'd gotten the knife back?

"Anything else?"

"Yeah, can you tell us anything about a Porter Haynes?"

Edward shook his head. "Another loser. And a real hothead. He and a guy named Corey got into it during the mock trial. The professor had to call security. It was pretty exciting."

"Exciting enough that he might want to kill Corey?"

"Who knows? I never met the guy except for that one time. Didn't like him much, either."

"Yeah, I got that feeling."

"Sorry, I just don't have time for that kind of juvenile behavior. I've got a career to plan for, and when that kind of stuff happens, it's just kind of irritating, you know?"

Kit nodded and Noah walked off, phone pressed to his ear. "All right," she said, "thanks for talking to us. If we have any more questions, we've got your cell number."

"Right."

"Thanks for your help. We'll be in touch."

Edward looked at his watch one more time. "I've got to get going. I have an appointment I can't miss. Call me if you need anything else." He lifted a hand to press it to his lips, then gave a sigh. "I sure hope you catch this person." His eyes darted from one side to the other. "It's kind of nerve-wracking being a law student these days."

"I'm sure. Thanks again."

"You're quite welcome. I'll see you soon."

"Sure, Edward. See you."

The young law student made his way back into the library and Kit watched Noah frown at the person on the other end of his conversation. When he hung up, he turned and said, "Stephen Wells has just been arrested for the murder of Bonnie Gray."

"What?" Kit nearly shrieked. "But he didn't do it!"

"That was Mark Holt. He's a DA from Greenville County. He's officially been put in charge of the investigation until further notice."

Kit shook her head. "This case just keeps getting weirder by the second."

36

The Judge absently listened to the loudspeaker as a female voice made announcements, then turned to watch the woman with the baby. This adventure had cost him a pretty penny. He'd had to purchase a ticket at the last minute, but as he observed the interaction between the mother and son, he decided it was well worth it. He just had to bide his time. Wait for the big man standing guard over them to leave—or get to a place where the Judge could take care of him without any danger of being caught. Of course, the way he was tossing back the coffee, he'd be needing the men's room before too long.

Samantha was on her guard too. Constantly looking over her shoulder. Pacing with Andy in his little umbrella stroller. Studying each and every person she passed.

The Judge made sure to look like he was absorbed in his laptop. In truth, he was watching every move she made with the webcam mounted on top of his screen. From her distance, she wouldn't be able to tell that the little camera pointed at her and not its owner. The roofies in his pocket had passed through security without incident. He shook his head. Idiots. Just put some pills in a bottle with a label on it and you could get anything past security.

The only problem was the bodyguard and the fact that Samantha wasn't drinking anything. He hadn't counted on that.

Think, he ordered himself, think.

Okay, Samantha wasn't drinking anything, but the bodyguard was. He'd simply change his focus, and instead of slipping one in Samantha's drink, he'd just have to figure out how to slip one in the bodyguard's drink. That might work better anyway.

A plan formed. The Judge smiled.

With efficient movements, he packed the laptop away and strode to the Starbucks counter positioned diagonally to the waiting area.

Samantha Wolfe and her son, Andy. But Andy wasn't really her son. Andy was his. The Judge's perfect son. He knew he was perfect because he'd overheard his perfect future wife say so. He recalled the day he'd followed Kit from her home to her twin's house. She'd stood on the porch and said what a perfect baby he was. And Andy settled into her arms like he belonged there.

That was all the Judge needed. It was the sign he'd been waiting for.

He'd found his perfect son.

Andy Wolfe would be his before the day was over.

As would Kit Kenyon.

37

Kit's phone rang and she grabbed it to glance at the caller ID.
Connor.

"Hey, Kit here."

"Andy's missing and Sam's hurt. I need you and Noah to meet me and Dakota at the airport." At first Kit couldn't process his words. She paused and his husky voice finally penetrated her shock. "Kit, it's my fault. I didn't go with her. I sent someone—" He broke off and she could hear the anguish eating him up.

"I got you, Connor. We're on the way. We'll find him. How's Sam? Is she all right?"

"She will be, just get here."

Frantic, she raced to the car. "Noah! Andy's missing. Let's go."

Matching her hurried lope, Noah grabbed for the passenger door as Kit cranked the vehicle. He slammed it and grabbed for the seat belt as he demanded, "What do you mean he's missing? I thought Sam was taking him to Florida."

Throat tight, she did her best to speak. "Someone attacked Samantha in the airport and grabbed Andy."

"I thought Connor was with her."

"He was supposed to be, but he sent a bodyguard instead because he didn't want to stop working the case."

Noah winced. "Ouch."

"He's blaming himself right now."

"Oh man."

Kit made it to the airport in record time. Pulling up in front, right behind two other emergency vehicles, she left her lights flashing. Displaying her badge, she pushed through the gawking crowd.

Kit raced for the escalator as she told Noah, "She's in Gate B."

He stayed right behind her. More badge flashing and she and Noah made it through security, up the next escalator, and into the area.

"What was the flight number?" Kit asked. Her mind had gone blank.

"We won't need it," Noah reassured her.

He was right.

Kit headed straight for the crowd. Once again, they pressed through. The airport had been placed on lockdown, no one coming into the airport and no one going out. Flights were still leaving; however, no one with an infant got on the plane without confirmation of ID.

Connor looked up as they approached. His pale face and tight lips told a story she didn't want to hear. Medical personnel surrounded Samantha, who looked like she'd gone a few rounds with Mike Tyson and lost. The bodyguard lay on a stretcher.

"Is he alive?" Noah asked the nearest paramedic.

"He's alive, just drugged."

Nostrils flaring, Connor didn't wait for Kit to speak as she hurried to his side. "He's got Andy."

Up until he said the words again, she'd managed to keep her fear under control. Now it blossomed into full-fledged terror. Taking a deep breath, she knelt beside her sister and placed a hand on her arm. The paramedic gave her some room even as he worked on Sam's head. "Sam?"

Sam blinked up at her with pain, shock . . . and unadulterated anger. Her eyes glittered with a rage Kit didn't think she'd ever seen in anyone before. "He took my baby. I'm getting him back." Samantha's words came out in a low, gutteral growl.

Kit nodded. Blinked back tears.

Noah spoke between tight lips. "We'll get him back. There's no other option. What happened?" He looked up at Connor. "Give us the details."

Although he'd spoken the words to Connor, Samantha stood with a grunt, pushing the professional hands away with a grimace of pain. "The detective wasn't feeling well, he said he was going to be sick. He went into the bathroom so I figured I'd do the same." Sam swallowed. "I pushed Andy into the restroom. The next thing I knew, I felt something hit the back of my head and . . ." Tears welled, her lips trembled, and Connor pulled her to his chest.

Gone were the hard-nosed cops, Kit noted with a pang. In their place were terrified parents of a kidnapped child. Then Samantha pulled away from her husband and raised a hand to her head. "All right, where do we start? I can't sit around crying and whining while this person has Andy. Let's get busy."

Connor nodded, lips tight, nostrils flaring with each breath. "I want to get my hands around this guy's throat."

The cops were back.

Alena turned her head and licked her lips. The throbbing in her temples made her wince. Where was she? What had happened? She blinked and focused on the light above her. A single bulb hung from the ceiling.

She tried to move and found herself stuck. Frowning, she tried again. Why couldn't she move her hands?

Or her feet?

The panic started in the pit of her belly and moved north. Frantic now, she let her eyes roam. When they landed on the chair opposite where she lay, she let out a scream.

❖

The Judge looked down at the woman at his feet. She'd been helpful in her role. Now that he didn't need her anymore, she was expendable.

He stuck the gun in the waistband of his jeans and walked over to the bed.

The baby lay on his stomach on the hotel's bedspread. He'd rolled over when the woman had placed him on his back, so the Judge had positioned pillows around him in case he rolled more. He couldn't have his new son taking a fall.

Satisfaction filled him. Yeah, he'd be a good dad. No, a great one.

Picking up the baby, he held him to his chest and breathed in his clean baby smell. A small hand reached out and grabbed his nose.

The Judge laughed.

And the baby smiled.

Which was good because if he cried too much, he wouldn't be the perfect son and he would have to die.

Now he just had to get the woman who would be the perfect mother for his perfect son and all would be right with his world.

38

"There." Kit pointed at the video. "That woman exchanged the cups. Right under the guard's nose."

Noah observed out loud, "Long brown hair, oversized glasses, and dark lipstick."

"She's tall. At least 5'10", 5'11". Maybe even six feet," Connor said.

"And she's smooth," Kit murmured. "Did you see how she switched the cups when Sam's back was turned and the bodyguard had his eyes on Sam? She knew exactly what she was doing."

"Wait a minute," Samantha interrupted. "A woman? So this person is working with someone else? Was that in the profile?"

Kit shook her head. "No, Olivia said he worked alone."

A minute later the guard's hand reached out to wrap his fingers around the cup and lift it for a sip.

"Okay, we've got him drinking the drug." She bit her lip as she watched Sam pace with Andy in front of the bodyguard. She checked her watch as an approaching plane pulled into the gate.

"Look," Noah pointed, "the woman sat across from the bodyguard—what's his name anyway?"

"Detective Martin," Connor said.

"The woman sat across from Detective Martin and pulled out a laptop," Noah finished.

Kit shifted. "She fixes the webcam—"

"—and is able to watch Sam's every move without letting on she's watching. The camera's backward."

Sam let out a small whimper. "I never noticed. I wasn't watching for a woman . . . I . . ." She swallowed. "From the profile Olivia gave us, I was looking for a man. Where did this woman come from?"

"And what did she hit you with?" Connor muttered. "No weapon was found. She couldn't have gotten through security with a gun, so what was it?"

A few minutes later, Detective Martin stood, stumbled a bit, then leaned over to tell Samantha something.

The woman watched, and Kit caught the small smile that crossed her lips before she looked back at the camera.

"What did he say?" Kit asked Samantha.

"He said he felt sick, dizzy," Sam said. "He needed to go to the bathroom." On the video, Sam nodded and followed the man to the restroom. "Then I told him I needed to go and would take Andy into the handicapped stall with me."

Sam and Andy disappeared into the bathroom, and the woman approached the detective, who slid down the wall and dropped his head against his chest.

The woman waved for help and soon he was surrounded by airport personnel.

Leaving Sam and Andy as perfect targets as she slipped into the women's bathroom.

Connor blew out a breath. "She pulled that off without a hitch."

"She knew they were going to be there," Kit breathed. "Who knew Sam was going to the airport?" She looked at her sister, who blinked and shook her head. "You, Mom and Dad, everyone in the meeting in the captain's office, my friend, of course." She rubbed her temples and frowned. Pain flashed across her face. "I think that's all. I mean I didn't make a public announcement."

"See if your mom and dad told anyone," Noah suggested.

Sam grabbed her cell phone and punched in the numbers.

Kit looked back at the video to see the woman exit the bathroom, pushing Andy in his stroller. No one paid the slightest bit of attention to her.

Sickness swirled in the pit of her stomach. *Oh God, if ever there was a time for you to listen to one of my prayers, please pick this one. Please bring that baby home safe.*

All of a sudden, the emotional turmoil she'd been living with seemed small, petty, and unimportant. Getting Andy back was all that mattered now.

But how?

"Play it again, will you?" Kit asked.

Was there something vaguely familiar about this woman or was that just a desperate wish on her part?

Noah spoke from behind her. "I've got the passenger manifests for the flights leaving from that gate. There were eight more flights left for today. We've got video of the woman coming into the airport about ten minutes after Samantha."

"Which counter did she go to?"

"She didn't. She went straight up to the gate and through security without a problem. She had her boarding pass already printed, so there's no telling which flight she bought the ticket for."

Sam paced behind Kit, hand held to her head, lips moving silently. No doubt she was praying.

Noah studied the video as it played out again. Tilting his head sideways, he absently listened as Dakota barked orders into his phone. Something about video from the parking garage.

That woman.

Something didn't ring true with her. What was it?

"Play the part where she switches the drinks again," he requested.

Kit shot him a questioning look and Noah shrugged. "I just want to see it again."

The video started.

He leaned in. "There, look at her hands. Do you notice anything weird about them?"

Beside him, Kit moved closer and Noah couldn't help but breathe in her subtle scent. It didn't distract him from the video, though.

She drew in a breath. "They're large."

"And rather masculine, don't you think? Look at the dusting of hair above the knuckles."

"And the fingernails. They definitely look like a man would keep his nails. Neat, but blunt and short."

Kit leaned back in her chair and looked at Noah. "You think that's a man disguised as a woman?"

"I don't know."

"I do." Dakota's voice came from behind them and Noah looked up to see the FBI agent's grim frown. "You're on the right track. The security camera in the garage got our woman climbing into a car. The passenger seat. We couldn't see her face, but we did get her pulling off her wig and tossing it in the backseat."

"So it is him," Sam breathed an agonized moan. "I was almost hoping it was some poor woman desperate for a baby. At least I could believe Andy was being cared for by someone—" She broke off and swallowed, cleared her throat. "But if it's the killer . . ." Her voice cracked. "Why would he want my baby? What possible reason could he have to steal my child?"

Noah heard the underlying hysteria. "We still don't know if it's him or not." He looked at Dakota. "Did you get a plate?"

"Yes."

"And?"

Dakota looked at Kit. "It's registered to an Olivia Pappas."

Kit gasped. "That's Alena's mother!"

39

Alena whimpered and stared at the sight before her. She'd long ago screamed herself voiceless. What was going on? Who had done this to her?

"Mom?"

Where was her mother? Panic fluttered inside her. She had to get loose. She had to get out of here before he came back. Squinting against her fear, she pulled at her bonds. Glanced at the recliner in the far corner and shuddered.

"Don't look at him," she whispered. "Don't look."

"Okay, here's the plan." Noah spoke abruptly. Dakota stopped his pacing and gave him his full attention, as did everyone else in the room. "I've got every possible person available questioning people at the airport. I've got someone on the way to Olivia Pappas's house. As soon as we find the car, we'll have forensics going over it with a fine-tooth comb. This guy has to have some DNA somewhere."

Dakota nodded. "I'm going to put in a visit at the crime lab. See if I can get some specialized attention on the evidence collected at our previous crime scenes. I know they've given this priority, but it's still not going fast enough."

Kit stood. "I'm going to grab the files and our list of suspects and start going back through them one by one. We've also got photos of all the people who gathered around the crime scenes. I'll study those and see if anyone stands out." Sometimes people like serial killers liked to be a part of the crowd as all of the excitement unfolded. She'd already looked at the photos, but this time she had even more of an incentive to push her brain to recognize something, someone, anything.

Samantha swiped a stray tear and sniffed. "Fine. What can I do?"

Connor pulled her back into his arms. "Pray."

Kit slapped the next picture over and rubbed her eyes. She'd looked through them all and nothing. Despair tightened its grip around her heart. *Please, God, please.*

Would he listen?

Her phone rang, jarring her from her thoughts. She checked the caller ID and didn't recognize the number. "Hello?"

"Detective Kenyon?"

"Yes?" The voice sounded familiar.

"This is Edward Richmond."

"Hello, Edward, what can I do for you?"

"I've been studying this case, following it, you know, and I think I may have something for you. Something the DA didn't tell you."

"Really? What's that?"

"I have a letter from Bonnie to Mr. Wells. I . . . um . . . well, I hate to spread tales, but I'm just . . . well, it wouldn't be ethical for me to sit on this." A sigh filtered over the phone. "I also have a box he asked me to keep for him in my cubicle they call an office."

"A box?"

"Yes, it had a lock on it and he said it was a surprise birthday gift for his wife, and he asked me to hide it because she drops in on him on a regular basis. Only . . . I just looked in it."

A definite feeling of unease flooded through her. "And what made you look in that box?"

Edward gave a small laugh. "Actually, I'd forgotten all about it until about ten minutes ago when I came in to do some catch-up work. When I saw it, I couldn't decide what to do with it. I thought I'd just drop it by the Wells home, then I decided I'd take a look inside. So, I picked the lock. When I found the letter, I looked through the rest of the stuff and I . . . um . . . thought you might want to know about it."

"I do. Tell me about the letter."

A pause, then the rustle of some paper. "I really hesitate to do this, but . . ." More hesitation.

Kit encouraged. "It's fine, Edward. If this is something I need to help catch a killer, please don't hold back on me." Had they been wrong about Stephen the whole time? After all, his wife as an alibi was pretty flimsy. And he had hidden the pictures. He'd also had newspaper clippings and police reports detailing all of the crime scenes.

A feeling of fury surged through her. Had he been playing them the whole time?

"Okay, I know. You're right. The letter is basically Bonnie saying that if Stephen didn't leave his wife, she was going to expose him and ruin his career."

The breath blew out of Kit. "Whoa." She made up her mind. "Never mind about reading the letter, Edward, I'll just come get it, but what else was in the box?"

"Um . . . some little miniature gavels and . . ."

Kit shot out of her seat. "Where are you? I'm on my way."

The Judge smiled at the baby in his arms as he approached the door to the house. "This is your new home, Andy." He frowned.

"We'll have to change your name. How about Ed? Eddie? Yeah," he breathed. "Eddie Junior. I like that. What do you think about that?"

Eddie yawned and scrubbed his eyes. A frown formed on his face and he stuck a fist into his mouth. The Judge was amused. How could his little boy fit that big fist into his mouth? Oh, this was going to be fun.

The Judge opened the door and stepped inside. He went up the stairs and into the room he'd share with Kit once they were married.

Alena had been working hard on the ropes that bound her wrists, he noticed. "Give it up, Alena. You can't get away."

"Why are you doing this?" she pleaded with him.

"Because you deserve a better life."

"I liked my life just the way it was!" she screamed.

The Judge flinched and tightened his hold on the baby.

Eddie let out a squall and the Judge felt his blood pressure rising. "Shut up, Alena. I don't like it when people yell at me."

Alena let out a choked laugh, then whatever she saw in the Judge's expression made her clamp her lips together and close her eyes. "Edward, will you please let me go?"

At her soft request, the Judge felt himself loosen a bit. "If I let you go, will you get Eddie something to eat? I think he's hungry."

Alena blinked at the request and the Judge realized she hadn't noticed the baby in his arms until just now. She gasped and her eyes went wide. "Andy?"

He smiled. "So you already know him?"

"Yes, that's Kit's nephew."

"Wrong!" The Judge felt the rage building. Had he chosen so stupidly? When she cringed, he told himself to calm down. He had to explain things to her. "Wrong," he said softly. Eddie Junior started to cry and the Judge felt the shift inside him once again.

❖

Be calm, Alena, be calm. Take control. Say what you need to say. She tried to remember everything Kit had ever told her about being a hostage negotiator. She could almost hear Kit encouraging her. "Say whatever it takes to get the situation under control." He'd told her to call him the Judge or Big Brother. All right, that's what she would do.

Alena pulled in a deep breath and looked into the eyes of the man she'd once considered a friend. "All right. I'm sorry. What do you want me to do . . . um . . . big brother?"

Almost like magic, her captor's eyes lost that mad gleam that sent shivers of terror through her. He left the room for a short time, then returned with a knife in his hands. "I'm going to cut the ropes on your wrists and then you're going to go into the kitchen and fix *your* nephew, my son, a bottle and then you're going to feed it to him, understand?"

Her nephew? His son?

"Okay."

"And if you try to run, I'll kill him, then I'll kill you. Am I clear?"

"Yes." Her eyes darted to the recliner in the corner. His harsh laugh jerked her attention back to him.

"I see you've met Father."

"That's your father?"

"Indeed. Did he say much while I was gone?"

Another glance to the recliner. Did he think the man in the chair could actually talk? "Um. No. He didn't say a word."

The Judge . . . er . . . Big Brother frowned. "Huh. He never shuts up when it's just the two of us."

Alena felt the panic grab at her throat and had to take several breaths to keep the screams at bay. Play along, she told herself, just play along. "Right."

He approached her and she shuddered as he drew close. A whimper escaped and she clamped her teeth down hard on her tongue.

After a few tugs, the ropes fell free. He did the same with

her feet. All one-handed, holding the now fussing baby Andy in his left arm.

"Here." He shoved the baby into her arms, and she grasped him close, doing her best not to drop him as the blood started flowing through her throbbing limbs again.

Then hope surged as she realized that if Andy was here, Kit and Andy's parents couldn't be too far behind. She just had to stay alert and be prepared to escape when the opportunity presented itself.

She pulled in a deep breath. "All right, show me where the formula is."

Kit looked at the clock. Fifty-seven minutes had passed since Andy had disappeared from the airport.

Her phone rang and she snatched it up. Dakota's voice filled her ear. "We found Olivia Pappas. Actually, a maid found her on the floor in one of the rooms at the Crescent Inn. She's alive but barely. She has a bullet in her head so there's not much hope. Ballistics will have to tell us if the bullet matches the ones found in our other victims, but I'm guessing we already know the answer to that."

Grief for Alena punched her. She knew how close she was to her mother. But she didn't have time to dwell on that right now. At least she was still alive. "All right. I'm going to pick something up from Edward Richmond. He says he has some evidence that points back to Stephen Wells as the killer."

"What? I thought he was cleared. Well, except for the obstruction of justice thing."

"He was. And probably won't face any time for those obstruction charges. But I'm going to check it out and will be in touch."

"Good deal. Talk to you soon."

Kit hung up and dialed Noah's number. No answer. Not bothering to leave a message, she climbed behind the wheel of her car and headed to the address Edward had given her.

Noah's phone rang as he pulled into the parking lot of the office. Connor and Samantha sat in the backseat. She'd refused to go home and Noah could understand her rabid need to help.

"Hello?" He held up a finger to halt Connor and Samantha's exit from the vehicle.

The voice on the other end said, "There's been something found in one of the apartments on campus that seems to be linked to your serial killer case. The captain wants you over there ASAP."

"Give me the location." Noah wrote down the information. "I'm on my way." He looked back at Connor and Samantha and relayed what he'd heard. "Are you two going with me or going inside?"

"We're with you," Connor growled. "If there's evidence, I want to know what it is."

"Me too," Sam agreed.

Noah restarted the car and headed for the law school campus.

Kit arrived at the address given to her by Edward and parked in front of the small house. It had been easy to find, only a few miles from the law school campus.

A two-story small brick, it sat on the back of the lot on about an acre and a half of land. The houses in the neighborhood looked run-down and weary, as did this one. Not poverty stricken or ready for the wrecking ball, but definitely in need of some repair.

She wondered why Edward lived in a campus apartment when he had this place so close.

Shrugging off her curiosity, realizing there could be a million reasons why he wouldn't want to live at home, she cut the engine and climbed out. Cramming the keys into her front pocket, she strode up the front walk.

The door opened and Edward smiled at her.

40

Noah climbed the stairs to the third floor of the apartment building. Connor and Samantha followed behind. He had a CSU team on standby in case this turned out to actually be related to the case.

"3B," Connor said.

"Got it." Noah stopped outside the door, raised his hand, and rapped on it.

The door opened so fast he realized the young man now facing him had been waiting just inside. "I'm Jeff. Come in. You gotta see this. I mean, this is just too weird, man."

Noah placed a hand on his shoulder. "Just calm down. Show me what you found."

Upon walking farther into the den area, Noah noticed another young man seated on the couch. "Gordon?"

"Hi, Detective Lambert."

"How are you mixed up in this?"

Gordon held up his hands as though in surrender. "I'm not, I promise. All I was doing was tossing a baseball back and forth, and it rolled into the bedroom at the end of the hall."

Jeff picked up the story. "And when it did, it went under the bed and knocked into this box."

"Show me."

Jeff led the way. Connor and Samantha brought up the rear. Entering the room, Noah noticed an opened box in the middle of the twin bed. "How'd the box get up here?"

A flush appeared on Jeff's already ruddy features. "Um . . . well, I got a little nosey and looked inside. I thought maybe it was, uh . . . you know."

"Dirty magazines?"

A shrug. Jeff looked at the floor, then back up. "But it wasn't." He swallowed hard. "It's newspaper clippings. I started going through them and realized they were of all of the murders. Then I noticed the school schedules for several different students and even their home addresses, family member names. Weird stuff. Why would he have this unless he was somehow involved in the killings?"

Noah called the CSU team, then looked at Jeff. "So who is your roommate?"

"Edward Richmond."

For some reason, a strange, uneasy twist to her stomach alerted Kit to be on her guard. Against what, she wasn't sure, but she never ignored that feeling.

All of a sudden, the gun on her hip felt reassuring. Edward beckoned her inside, and she stepped through the door into a small foyer.

The minute the door shut behind her, the odor hit her. Stale, musty, closed up—and lingering in the air, the unmistakable smell of death.

"Edward, what's going on?"

"Come inside, Kit, don't keep us waiting."

"Us?"

"Your family. We've been waiting on you."

Her family? Waiting on her?

"What are you talking about?"

He gave an odd little giggle and pressed his hand to his mouth. And with a blast of clarity it hit her. The video clip from the airport played in her mind. The switching of the cups, the hand pressed against his lips.

Edward Richmond.

The serial killer she'd been chasing.

And she'd just walked into his house without backup.

Drawing in a deep breath, she ordered herself to keep calm. "Oh, hey, I left something in my car. I'll be right back."

She turned to find herself staring down the business end of a gun.

"I don't think so."

Immediately, she went into negotiator mode. Using a soothing, quiet voice, she asked, "Why did you kill Alena's mother?" No sense in letting the man know she was still alive. She might very well be dead anyway.

"She'd lost her usefulness." He waved a hand as though to dismiss the topic. Unfortunately, the gun didn't waver.

Kit pushed her hands into her front pockets and leaned against the nearest wall. An attempt to show that she was comfortable and willing to listen to whatever Edward had to say. He seemed to be waiting on her, so she said, "That was very clever of you to disguise yourself as a woman in the airport."

Surprise flickered. "I thought so, but how did you figure it out?"

She wanted to blast him and yell at him that he wasn't as smart as he thought he was, but she clamped down the impulse. He had Andy and Alena somewhere. Probably in this house. She said softly, "Your hands gave you away."

A pause. "My hands?"

"When you switched the coffee cups. You just don't have very feminine hands."

He seemed to be thinking about that. "I should have shaved the hair on them, I suppose." Another moment of silence. "But you wouldn't have recognized my hands. It was something else, wasn't it? What did I do to give myself away?"

"You have the habit of pressing your lips with your fingers when you're amused. I saw you do it the day Brian shot the guy in the trailer. And again at Bonnie Gray's house. Then a couple more times. You did it at the airport in view of the security video—and just now."

"You're very observant, aren't you?"

"I try." No sense in reminding him that's what made her good at her job. Noticing the little things, registering the details. "Where are Andy and Alena?"

"They're where I want them for now. And it's not Andy, it's Eddie."

So he did have them. Kit studied the man before her. He had the gun pointed away from her at the moment. Could she get to hers before he could raise and fire his?

"Give me your gun."

She startled. Had something in her face given away her thoughts?

"Why would I want to do that?"

"Because if you don't, Alena and Eddie will die before you can blink." He let that sink in for about two seconds, then demanded again. "Now, I'm just going to ask you one more time. If you hesitate, they die. Actually, we all die. Very simple. Now . . . give me the gun."

Without hesitation, Kit reached down to her holster and grasped the butt of the gun.

"Slowly," he ordered. "If you shoot me and I die, so do they."

What did he have rigged?

A bomb?

How would they die if he died? Did he have something rigged to himself that would transfer to Andy and Alena?

She couldn't take a chance. "I don't want them to die. You can have the gun."

A triumphant smile lit his face. But it never reached his eyes. Why hadn't she ever noticed his cold, flat eyes before?

"I thought you'd feel that way." He grabbed the gun from her outstretched hand and shoved it into the waistband of his pants. "In fact, I knew you would."

Kit shuddered. What made him so confident? He knew something she didn't and was reveling in that fact. "Why is that, Edward? How would you know what I would or wouldn't do?" She kept her voice calm, in spite of the anxiety and fear shooting through her. *Please don't let him hurt Andy. Help me get Andy out of here.*

"That day of the shooting, I knew."

"The shooting?"

"When the sniper killed that man you tried so hard to save. It was that day that I knew."

"Knew what?" Her heart beat double time. She drew in a deep breath. In through her nose, out through her mouth. *Control. Focus. Use your skills.* She pushed away her desperate need to know about Andy and Alena and drilled Edward with her attention.

He continued, "That you were the one. You were so passionate, so furious with that SWAT guy. You were willing to do anything to save that man in the trailer. And I knew you were the one I wanted for the mother of my child. If you would do that for someone you knew for just a few hours, I could only imagine what you would do for someone you love. Tell me, Kit, would you do anything, sacrifice everything to protect your child?"

"Yes." One simple word. A world full of meaning.

"And you'd never leave that child, would you?" Edward's voice sent waves of fury pulsing through her. "Abandon your little boy who needed you? Needed a mother's love?"

"No, of course not. Is that what your mother did?" She kept her voice soft, sympathetic.

"That's why you're perfect," he whispered, like he hadn't heard the question, and she flinched.

How she wanted to wrap her hands around his throat and demand he hand over Andy and Alena. But she couldn't. He'd started this game and she wasn't clear on the rules yet. *Watch his body language. Keep his eyes and hands where you can see them. Visually monitor his respirations, be alert for any subtle twitchings . . .*

She knew what she needed to do on that end. "What do I have to do to keep Andy and Alena safe?"

A baby crying sounded from upstairs and Kit turned without thought toward the steps. A hand on her arm yanked her back.

"Not so fast." Toward the staircase, he yelled, "Keep him quiet!"

"Is Andy all right?" Kit blurted as she yanked her arm from his grip and backed away from him.

"That's Eddie. Eddie Junior. And he's fine for now. The perfect baby. I heard you say that about him."

Kit froze. When had she said that?

"The day you went over to your sister Jamie's house. You stood on the front porch holding him and said how perfect he is."

Sickness churned in her gut. "He's simply a baby, Edward. Because I love him, I think he's perfect, but he's still going to cry when he's hungry or tired or—"

"He better not cry too much. The perfect baby wouldn't do that to his father." He sounded a little tense.

Kit's fingers curled into a fist. How she wished she could wrap them around this guy's neck. *Breathe*, she ordered herself. *Breathe*. "I understand." Her voice came out smooth, with not a hint of her inner turmoil.

But her mind raced, seeking a way out, churning for an idea of how to get to Andy and Alena and escape. She still had her cell phone in her back pocket. Why hadn't he asked her for it? Had he been so focused on getting her gun that he hadn't thought about asking for her cell phone?

She could only hope, because somehow she had to get word to Noah.

Noah punched the end button for the fourth call he'd placed to Kit. Why wasn't she answering her phone? Where was she?

It didn't go straight to voice mail so her battery was still good. Her phone was on.

So why didn't she answer it?

With a sigh, he sent up a prayer for her safety.

The message he left on her voice mail as to the identity of the killer would have to do for now.

Noah didn't bother with a greeting when his phone rang. "What," he barked.

"Connor just called me and filled me in," Dakota bullet-spoke into his ear. "Kit's on her way over to see Edward Richmond."

"What?" Noah shouted at the man.

"She said Edward called her and said he had something, some kind of evidence that Stephen Wells was the killer. She decided to go pick it up."

Oh no, oh Lord, please . . . "Do we have an address?"

"Yeah, she wrote it down on a sticky note, googled the address on her computer, printed the directions. I got our computer guy to get the information off her computer. I'm on my way over there."

"Give me the address and I'll meet you there."

"Good deal. I've already called in everyone else. They're on the way."

Everyone else, including the SWAT team and a host of FBI agents and local police.

No doubt the media would catch wind of it soon and be there too. Not if he could help it.

"Try to keep it as quiet as possible. We don't want this guy knowing we're on to him yet."

"That's the way we're playing it."

"He's got her, doesn't he?" She was in the hands of a serial killer. A man who'd killed without regard to human life, without remorse for the killing. The paralyzing fear that hit him at the thought of losing her was the biggest shock. He loved her, he realized in a blinding moment of awareness.

He loved her.

"See you in ten."

41

Noah pulled up beside the SWAT van, feeling the sweat break out all over him. He'd gotten there just in time to see the front door open and Kit disappear inside. *God, keep her safe, please. I really need you to keep her safe. Protect her, Alena, and little Andy.*

Climbing into the van, he saw the same setup he'd walked into only a week ago when Kit had been in the trailer with Virgil Mann. Had it been only a week? He'd lost track.

Another thought occurred to him. Who was the SWAT shooter?

Chad and Charlie gave him only a brief glance as he entered. Commander Flynn, the SWAT team leader, raised a brow at his entrance but waved him on in.

"Do you have ears?" Noah asked. He pulled in a deep breath meant to calm his racing heart and pounding blood.

Too bad it didn't work.

"Not yet."

"All right," he said, "then we've got to get near the house to get a microphone into position on the window."

The man tossed him a look. "Working on it right now."

Of course they were. "Sorry. I don't mean to tell you how to do your job."

"I appreciate that."

From his vantage point, Noah could see the house, but couldn't see what was happening behind it. Then movement caught the corner of his eye. "Wait a minute. What's that?"

"What?" Charlie asked.

"Hand me a pair of binoculars, will you?"

A pair slapped into his hands and he lifted them to see the driver's door of Kit's vehicle open. Connor slid out and started moving toward the house.

"Oh no. Tell me he's not—"

"Aw man," Charlie muttered as he saw what Noah was talking about. "He is."

Commander Flynn cursed. "Is he insane? If that guy knows we're out here, there's no telling what he'll do."

"I'm going after him. I'm sure he believes that Andy is in that house somewhere."

"He won't do anything to put his kid in danger," Charlie protested.

Noah wasn't taking any chances. Right now, Connor was emotional. He didn't trust that at all. Certainly not with Kit's life riding on the line too.

"I'm still going. He might need some backup. Give me an earpiece so I can communicate with you, will you?"

The commander hesitated, then nodded, and Chad fitted him within seconds.

Before he could set foot outside the van, the door flew open and Samantha stepped in.

"I need a computer," Sam growled.

Chad nodded to the laptop on the desk behind him.

Samantha whirled and attacked the keyboard with a vengeance. "I want to know every detail about this sicko." Her hands flew over the keys, fingers tapping, jaw tight. As the information came available, she read aloud, "He's clean as far as stuff with the law, but his mother ran off when he was seven. And um . . . here. His DSS record. It says he was taken from his father when

314

he was thirteen and placed in foster care. He bounced around a couple of foster homes, was kicked out of the eighth grade, and then became a model student in the ninth grade. Graduated at the top of his class, then went to college where he graduated with honors."

"Then on to law school, right?" Noah asked. He kept an eye on Connor. Right now, the man stood at the corner of the house. He seemed to be trying to decide what to do.

"Right."

"Where's his father now?" Noah inched toward the door. He needed to get to Connor.

"It doesn't say."

Connor rounded the corner and Noah lost sight of him.

Without another word, Noah slipped out of the van and did his best to approach the house without being noticed. It was a quiet street and the houses were spread out, not all cramped together like in the newer neighborhoods. Tall oaks and a lot of pine trees dotted the area. The houses backed up to the woods. It wasn't the upper-class area of town, but it wasn't the projects either.

This house blended in nicely with the rest of the neighborhood.

You'd never know a killer resided within.

42

Kit did her best to keep her breathing even. How had this guy fooled everyone?

Her cell phone vibrated one more time and she wished with everything in her she could reach back there, snatch it out, and yell for help.

The only thing that gave her a small measure of hope was the fact that she'd told Dakota who she was going to see. The bad thing was, how long before someone would check her computer and see she'd looked up the address?

But he would figure it out. If he thought about it. And when she didn't call him or report in, he'd be doing a lot of thinking.

"Where are Andy and Alena?"

Edward tapped his lips with the barrel of the gun. Briefly she considered rushing him to pull the trigger.

But she still didn't know about Andy and Alena.

"Go upstairs," he suddenly ordered.

"Why?"

"Just go!" he yelled, snapping the gun to point it at her. "I'm getting worried I may have made a mistake in choosing you."

Don't question him. One more thing to remember. He wanted unquestioned obedience.

"You didn't make a mistake, Edward," she soothed, eye on his trigger finger, "just try to be a little patient with me, all right? I'm still learning your expectations."

Her words seemed to mollify him. Enough so that he pointed the gun to the right of her instead of straight at her heart. She headed for the stairs, her mind clicking on how to let someone know where she was before something triggered Edward and he decided to kill them all.

Noah rounded the corner of the house and came face-to-face with the barrel of Connor's Glock. He threw his hands up. "Whoa, partner, I'm here to help."

Connor grunted and lowered the gun. "You almost got helped into eternity."

The man looked a little pale. The pinched expression stated clearly his tense emotional state.

Noah tried to reason with him. "Look, you can't do this. We need to get back to the van and—"

"I'm not leaving. Somehow, we have to signal Kit that we're here. Otherwise, she might take a risk to get word to us. We need to eliminate that risk."

Noah thought about that. Connor was right. Kit would be brainstorming a way to get word of her situation out, because surely by now she knew Edward wasn't in his right mind.

Noah's earpiece came to life. "We've got eyes and ears on the lower floor, Noah."

"What do you see?"

"An empty den area. We're working on the top floor."

"Any sign of anyone?"

"Negative. But there's a baby stroller in the kitchen."

Noah glanced at Connor. "Keep me updated."

"Will do."

Stationed at the back of the house, Noah noticed the windows were nailed shut. The blinds were pulled and he had no way to see inside.

That meant he had to *get* inside.

He could see Connor scoping the house too. "Are you thinking what I'm thinking?"

"Probably." He lifted a brow. "We need to find a way in."

"Bottom floor is reported clear."

"Any security cameras that I can't see?"

"None reported."

Connor firmed his jaw. "Then let's find a way in."

Kit stopped at the top of the stairs. The long hallway branched to the right. Or she could go left. Before she could ask for direction, she heard Andy cry.

Left it was.

Without waiting for the psycho behind her to say a word, she headed toward the baby's cry, her heart pulled by Andy's distress while the relief of knowing he was alive flooded her again.

Her fingers wrapped around the doorknob and she twisted it. Slowly, it swung in and she held her breath, almost afraid of what she'd find. After all, she hadn't heard one word from Alena, just Andy crying.

And then she saw them. Alena sat on the bed holding Andy, an empty baby bottle on the floor at her feet. But that wasn't what made Kit's heart nearly stop in fear.

It was the necklace Alena wore.

Only it wasn't a pretty piece of jewelry, it was a bomb. And if it went off, so would Alena's head.

Noah slid the credit card into the crack near the doorknob and jiggled it. He could have picked the lock, but because the door was pretty old and had a loose seal, this way was faster and easier.

Connor kept watch at the window. He'd found a broken blind and had a partial view of the room. And then Noah had the door open.

Into his microphone, he whispered, "I'm in."

The SWAT team closed in behind him.

❖

The triple-banded metal collar looked like an ordinary bomb. Kit had had enough training to recognize the wires and know what they meant. But unless she managed to incapacitate Edward, she wouldn't have the opportunity to even try to disarm the bomb. Heart pounding, her first priority was to get the now wailing Andy away from Alena. She took one step toward them, then stopped and turned to Edward.

And nearly screamed.

Empty black orbs stared back at her.

Her gaze shot to Edward. "Who is that?"

A shrug. "That's my father."

"When did he die?"

"Die?" Edward looked confused—and irritated as Andy continued to cry out his unhappiness.

Did the man not realize the skeleton seated in the chair in the corner of the room was no longer breathing? "He's dead, Edward." Upon looking closer, she saw the skull was tied so that it would stay on the neck bones. She guessed underneath the dirty white T-shirt and a pair of ratty jeans, more rope and wire held together the rest of the major bones.

Edward blinked. "No, he's not. He talks to me all the time."

A fear like none other invaded her. Edward was certifiably insane. She wasn't a psychiatrist, but she didn't need one to make that diagnosis. "Right, okay." When they got out of this, her sister Jamie would be able to tell them when and how the man had died.

But first . . .

Taking a deep breath, she asked, "May I please take the baby?"

He looked surprised that she asked, then frowned at Andy, whose cries had reached a near-fever pitch. Alena's arms shook. She'd obviously been holding him a while. The more Andy cried, the more Edward tensed. Waving the gun, he shouted, "Shut him up! Shut him up!" Then he bit his lip and pulled in a deep breath. "No, I won't be like him. I won't be like him. I won't . . ."

"Be like who, Edward?"

"Him!" He shoved the gun in the direction of the skeleton, and Alena gave a choked cry.

Ignoring her impulse to cross the room and snatch the baby from Alena, Kit forced herself to wait on Edward's instruction. "Please? I can get him to stop crying."

"Shut up!" he yelled at the baby. And lifted the gun to aim it at him.

Fear choked her and she moved, almost without thinking, to place herself in front of the gun. She held up a hand. "Edward, look at me. Please."

"What? What?" He paced to the door, then back, the barrel of the gun now pointed toward the ceiling while the back of his hand pressed against the side of his head. His agitation grew by the minute. "Make him stop crying!"

Kit stepped backward, keeping herself between Andy and Alena and the gun. "I'm going to take him from Alena, all right?"

Edward blinked, his eyes focused. In a voice of calm that held no hint of the former impatience, he said, "Of course, dear. I think that Eddie Junior would want his mama holding him."

Kit turned and took the squalling baby from the scared college girl. She mouthed, "Stay calm."

Alena gave a fraction of a nod even as tears streamed down her cheeks.

Pulling Andy to her, she held him securely and whispered reassurances in his ear. Immediately he quieted, hiccupped, and sniffled.

The sudden quiet sounded loud. She looked at Edward and he flashed her a brilliant smile. "See? I told you that you were the perfect mother."

"Thank you, Edward." She bounced the baby on her shoulder while she played his game. It would be best if she could get Andy to sleep. Then she'd have to find a place to lay him down. Somewhere that offered shelter in case that bomb went off. Of course she didn't know the strength of the bomb, but it looked like C-4.

Only where was the detonator? Cold chills ruptured through her. She couldn't use her cell phone. Because a cell phone could set off the bomb, there was no way she could try to contact someone, even if she found a way to get Edward to leave her alone somewhere.

Now seemed like a good time to start praying.

Noah slipped inside the foyer, gun ready. "Kitchen's clear," he whispered.

Connor aimed his gun toward the stairs. Noah exited the kitchen and nodded toward the stairs. The SWAT team headed that way, rifles held to their shoulders.

Noah placed a foot on the steps and crept up behind them. Connor followed and Noah could feel the man's tension. In his ear, he heard, "I've got audio. I'm patching you through."

He tapped one time on the piece to let the man know he got the message. Then Kit's voice sounded, sending his heartbeat skyrocketing. "Is there someplace I can put Andy down for a nap?"

"It's Eddie!" Edward screamed. "Eddie Junior, understand?"

"Absolutely." Andy shifted and wrinkled his little forehead like he might start wailing again. Kit jiggled him and whispered reassurances in his ear. He opened his eyes and looked at her, yawned, and fell back to sleep. Kit let out a relieved sigh and looked at Edward. "Please, is there someplace I can put *Eddie* down?"

A brilliant smile crossed Edward's face. "Yes. I have the perfect place for him. You can put him in the nursery."

Footsteps sounded and Noah motioned for the lead SWAT team member to do his thing.

"If he passes this way, put a bullet in him," Noah whispered.

Kit carried Andy out of the bedroom. She cast a look over her shoulder in Alena's direction. One that she hoped conveyed her promise to get the terrified girl out of this.

She walked down the hall toward the bedroom Edward indicated.

"Stop here."

When he reached around her to open the door, she wished she had a way to attack him, but with the baby in her arms, she just couldn't do anything.

The door swung open without a sound. Her eyes widened as she took in the sight. And she swallowed hard. "Oh my," she breathed. "This nursery looks just like the one . . ." Trailing off, she did a one-eighty.

Edward stepped in after her.

"Yes, his nursery's like the one at Connor and Samantha's house. I spent quite a bit of time outside his window, watching, waiting for her to open the blinds. I thought it might help him adjust to his new home if he had familiar surroundings."

Kit's eyes caught movement in the mirror above the dressing table and she frowned. The crib lay to her left and she moved over to place Andy in it, faceup. He scrubbed his eyes and yawned, but didn't cry.

Again, she saw movement, but couldn't make out anything more than a shadow.

And the barrel of a rifle.

Hope blossomed. They'd figured it out.

Thank you, God, she prayed. And didn't feel the slightest bit surprised when she did it. Somehow Dakota had figured it out and sent in reinforcements.

And just as fast she realized the guys in the hallway didn't know about Alena and the bomb around her neck. Thinking fast, she took a deep breath and said, "You did a good job with the nursery, Edward."

He looked pleased. "Thank you."

"Why don't we go back to Alena and you can tell me how to get that bomb off her neck." She'd let the SWAT team know there was a bomb to diffuse. Hopefully, someone with bomb training was on the team. Brian, the sniper she'd been so mad at on their last call out, would be able to disable it. Her gut tightened as Edward's frown returned along with a ferocious scowl. She hurried to say, "I know you don't want to hurt her. You wouldn't have taken her if you did. Or me. You want us to be a family, right?"

His eyes narrowed as though he didn't quite believe her, yet desperately wanted to.

She made herself walk toward him. "Let's leave Andy here to take his nap so he'll be happy when he wakes up, all right?"

Edward hesitated, then nodded.

Kit reached out a hand and placed it on his arm, then pulled back as though hesitant. She never broke eye contact with him— she wanted his eyes on her, not the mirror. His eyes flared and he watched her carefully.

Just what she wanted.

The men in the stairwell had gotten her message. They'd backed off. If Alena hadn't had the bomb around her neck, Kit would have shoved Edward down the stairs as they passed the dark opening. Instead, she placed herself on the right of Edward to keep his eyes and attention on her, not giving him the opportunity to look left into the stairwell. "I'm amazed at what you've managed to put together here while working and going to school."

"It wasn't easy, but I was determined. I had to show my father that I wasn't a loser, that he was wrong about me." A satisfied glint sparked in his eyes. "And I'm almost finished. I'll graduate and get a good job and we'll be a family. The perfect family."

Just a few more steps and they'd be back in the room where they'd left Alena. She just prayed the SWAT team would do their job and get Andy out while they could.

Then Edward directed her past the room. "Come this way. While you're up here, I want to show you where we'll sleep once we're married."

Nausea churned in her gut, but she ignored it and told herself to treat him like she would any other hostage situation. This wasn't personal.

But it sure felt like it.

"All right. Show it to me." It was at the opposite end of the long hallway. Far enough away from Andy that someone would be able to get in, get the baby, and get out. Hopefully, another would head for Alena and diffuse the bomb.

When he reached the room at the end of the hallway and opened the door, she slipped inside. How long could she keep him in here?

Slowly, as though taking in every detail, she wandered over to the dresser. "You have good taste in furniture, Edward."

"It was my grandmother's."

Kit ran her fingers over the oak top and found it free of dust. "What was your grandmother like?"

At first he didn't answer. She turned to look at him to make sure she still had his attention. The frown on his face didn't encourage her. "I'm sorry. I shouldn't have asked." Two more steps toward the door that appeared to lead to a bathroom. "Although, if we're supposed to be married, I believe I would like to know a few more things about my future husband." She looked him in the eye. "That's only fair, isn't it?"

Edward shifted and licked his lips. Then he gave a small smile. "I suppose." He wandered over, gun still in his hand, although Kit felt like he wasn't even aware he still held it. But she couldn't rush him because she didn't know where the detonator for the bomb was.

Then from down the hall, she heard Andy cry.

43

Noah watched Connor head out of the room, Andy in his arms. Unfortunately, the baby hadn't liked being rousted from his nap and let up a wail like Noah had never heard before.

Keeping his eye on the door to the room where Kit and the killer had disappeared, he checked in on Alena and the SWAT member, Brian Sands, who worked feverishly to disarm the bomb around her neck.

Another glance back at the room where Kit was revealed a shadow on the door. Noah slipped inside with Alena and gave the man the hurry-up motion. Brian sat back and swiped an arm across his brow. "More time," he whispered.

Noah shook his head.

Footsteps sounded in the hall.

"Edward, he's stopped crying. Come back!"

Noah spoke into his microphone. "Don't shoot. Repeat. Don't shoot. Bomb is still active."

Alena's eyes went wide and he slipped behind the door just as Brian slid behind the bed. Edward stepped into the room, followed by a breathless Kit.

"I saw something," Edward muttered. He held the gun in front of him.

"What? What did you see?"

"I saw something move. A shadow. Someone's here." His eyes squinted.

"Edward, there's no one here," Kit insisted, drawing his attention back to her. "Now will you show me the rest of the house?"

Alena choked out a scream and her hands went to the device around her neck. "Get me out of this! Take it off! Take it off!"

Kit gasped and rushed to the girl's side as her fingers felt for something, anything.

Noah sucked in a deep breath at the crazed look in Alena's eyes. Muscles bunched, he prepared to launch himself at Edward when he saw that Kit had her arms around Alena, holding her, steadying her, soothing her. He couldn't take a chance on detonating the bomb if he attacked Edward.

Kit whispered, "Don't do this, Alena. It's going to be okay." She kept her eyes on Edward. "As soon as Edward realizes he can trust you, he'll take it off, won't you, Edward?"

The killer licked his lips. "I . . . I don't know. Can I trust you, Alena?"

"Yes!" she sobbed into Kit's shoulder. "I'll do anything. Anything."

"Then tell me who was in the room, Alena," Edward said, his voice turning silky, cunning, low—and menacing. "I know someone was in here. If you want me to take the bomb off, show me I can trust you."

Alena's eyes darted to the door where Noah hid. Then swiveled to look behind her.

"Alena?" Edward insisted.

Noah saw Kit grip the girl's hand in warning.

"He's behind the—"

Before she could finish the sentence, Brian bolted to his feet and aimed his rifle right at Edward. "Drop the weapon, sir."

Alena screamed, "There! See? You can trust me! Now, get it off, please take it off of me." Her last word ended on a sob as she dropped her chin and wept.

Edward now had his gun pointed at the man behind the bed. The two were in a standoff.

Edward gave a low hiss. "I knew someone was in here. How did you get in?"

Brian kept his weapon steady on Edward. "We're all in here, sir. All eight of us plus a couple of police detectives. Now if you'll just put your weapon down, we can end this peacefully."

Noah waited. Kit still didn't know he was the one behind the door. He almost didn't dare to breathe as she moved out of his line of vision, then back in when she slid closer to Edward.

Kit heard the SWAT team member speak and forced herself not to react.

Brian.

Breathing her second prayer of the day, she let go of Alena and moved toward Edward, who was now beginning to look frantic, frustrated, and decidedly angry. She saw Noah behind the door and watched him go rigid, drew in a deep breath. He frowned a warning at her, but she ignored it. She had to get the detonator from Edward. With unswerving certainty, Kit knew if his plan didn't go according to the way he thought it should go, he would kill everyone in the room.

By detonating the bomb around Alena's neck.

And his plan was definitely not going the way he wanted it to.

She moved closer. Two more SWAT members moved into the room.

"Get out," Edward ordered Brian, his voice low, angry—and determined. "All of you, get out of this house."

Brian spoke again. "Can't do that. Now keep your hands where I can see them."

"'Can't do that,'" Edward mocked. "If you don't get out of my house, we all die. Your choice."

❖

His finger caressed the trigger on his gun and Kit suddenly knew where the detonator was. If he fired the gun, the bomb would go off.

Noah circled behind Edward, his eyes locked on Kit. She bit her lip and said softly, "Send them out."

Edward shifted his narrowed gaze to her. "You brought them here, didn't you?"

"How would I have done that, Edward? You called me. I came straight to your house. I haven't called anyone or talked to anyone since I got here."

Confusion flickered across his face. "Then how did they know to come here?"

"I don't know, but it doesn't really matter, does it? All that matters is finding a way to get through this, right?"

Little-boy longing appeared in his eyes. "So we can all be together as a family."

"That's right. So we can all be together." She was repeating him, telling him what he wanted to hear. Anything to keep him from pulling that trigger.

Then fury appeared. "You're a liar!"

Fear ruptured inside her. This guy was so out of touch with reality that talking to him might not work. She might be more successful walking on eggshells than talking him down. But she couldn't stop now. "Why would I lie?"

"Because that's what you do." He waved the gun. "I'm not stupid, you know. I know how hostage negotiation works. And I know you're in love with that cop. Aren't you? Aren't you!"

Kit couldn't stop the shudder that wracked through her, but kept her face neutral as she signaled to Brian to stand down. If he put a bullet in Edward, his finger could twitch and set the bomb off. Or he could drop the gun. "I had feelings for him. Yes." The fury on his face ratcheted up a notch. She held up a hand. "But that was before I knew about you and how you felt about family."

He blinked, cocked his head, and glared. "What do you mean?"

"You want a real family. So do I." When he just stared, she went on, "I just found out I was adopted. I spent all those years with people who lied to me about who I was. How do you think that felt when I discovered that?"

She'd thrown him off, distracted him. Then his face went red once more, and he pointed the gun at her, only this time he didn't have his finger wrapped around the trigger, he had it straight out. "Liar!"

And she knew it was time to act. The plan unfolded in her mind even as she launched herself at him. Gripping his wrist, the gun pointing over her right shoulder, she slipped her hand between the trigger and his extended finger. She slammed her weight against that finger and felt the bones snap even as he screamed and dropped to the floor.

The element of surprise had worked for a brief moment. Now he fought her. Vaguely, she was aware of men yelling, Brian jockeying for a position to shoot, and Noah coming at Edward's back.

"The detonator's in the gun!" she yelled.

Noah snatched it and passed it to a waiting SWAT member, who immediately left the room. Then he grabbed the man by the arm to pull him off of her. Edward elbowed back and caught Noah in the solar plexus. Noah went down with a grunt, and Kit gasped as Edward wrapped a leg over hers, then got in a punch that glanced off her shoulder. She winced, but didn't let go of the hand that had held the gun, putting pressure on the broken finger. He yelled in pain once more.

"You broke my finger, you—" He screamed a few choice words in her ear.

Kit yanked a leg free of his and kicked her foot out in a sweeping motion. Catching him in the stomach with her knee, she saw Noah hand his gun off to Brian and look for an opening.

Noah finally leapt forward to tackle Edward, freeing Kit. She rolled, only to see Noah catch a kick to the gut. Edward went for Noah's gun and Kit threw herself onto Edward. The wiry man gave a twist of his waist and she stumbled off balance, gasping when his left hand twisted into her ponytail and jerked her back against him.

Panting, chest heaving with the effort to pull in much needed air, Kit gritted her teeth and winced at the sudden stab of pain just over her right kidney. With frustrated fury, she realized he'd had a knife on him. One she hadn't noticed. The pain intensified and she cried out as she felt warm wetness trickle down.

"You're ruining it!" His enraged scream pierced her eardrum. Spittle flew from his mouth, catching her on the cheek. She grimaced as he screeched, "Why are you ruining it? I thought you wanted this!"

A gun fired and a bullet slammed into the wall behind her. Edward gave another pained yell and the knife dug deeper into her back.

"Don't shoot! He's got a knife in my back!" She bit her lip against the fire arcing from her lower right side and did her best to ignore it.

Edward yanked her back until they were up against the wall opposite the bed where Alena huddled. The door stood open to her left. Noah stood next to it, eyes intense, fingers wrapped around his weapon.

Her eyes caught Brian's intense stare even as she said through gritted teeth, "Edward, it's over. Give them the knife."

Brian's gaze never left hers.

She stared back. Could he get off a shot? His eyes said yes. She raised a hand to signal him to take the shot.

Noah's chest raised at the signal and his eyes flared. Kit almost didn't care if Edward pushed the knife in. She wanted this man caught. She was willing to risk a life-threatening injury to accomplish that.

Then Edward shoved her to the right to cover him better. Keeping her head between his and Brian's, he'd just messed up the sniper's shot.

Edward hissed in her ear. "Tell them to back off."

Alena cowered on the bed, arms wrapped around her knees, rocking back and forth.

"And where will you go if they back off, Edward?"

"I don't know. I don't know. I don't know." The knife pressed harder and she winced.

Noah watched the scene play out before him with an almost uncontrollable desire to plant every bullet in the gun he'd retrieved from Brian into the man holding a knife to Kit.

Then reload and do it again.

Fighting the instinct to act now, he watched and waited.

Brian and Kit had it under control for now.

His weapon felt heavy, ready.

He just needed an opening.

Of course that's what Brian was waiting for too.

At Kit's wince, Noah's finger gave an involuntary twitch. But he couldn't put it on the trigger just yet.

Brian shifted. Alena whimpered, but never raised her head from where she rested it on her knees. Kit breathed hard, her eyes jumping between Noah and Brian. Noah knew she'd given Brian the signal to shoot.

What was taking the man so long?

"Get Alena out of the room," Kit said softly.

"No," Edward said. "She stays put."

"I'll go with you wherever you want, Edward," Kit promised. "Just let them get Alena out."

"No!"

Noah didn't know why she continued to try to reason with the man. He was too far gone, too out of touch with what was going to happen. He still thought he had a chance to walk out of here alive.

Or at least thought he could escape.

Over Noah's dead body.

His earpiece had been quiet the last few minutes, but he knew those in the van outside were listening to everything going on in the room. Because Kit was a trained negotiator, they were letting her handle it. She hadn't yet given the signal she wanted someone to come in and take over the negotiations with Edward.

He spoke. "Edward." The man turned frantic eyes in his direction. Recognition flared and hatred glared at him.

"It's because of him, isn't it?" he hissed at Kit. "He's the one you really want, isn't he?"

At Edward's scalding words, Kit knew her time had just run out. Time to act. Catching Brian's dead calm gaze, she blinked, then winked her right eye.

He winked his left.

Kit let her knees collapse, felt the knife dig as she twisted to the right.

Brian's gun snapped as did two more from the SWAT members inside the door. Something clinked—a bullet hitting the knife. The knife went flying, and Edward dropped to the floor behind her. Breathless, Kit turned to look at his still form. Sightless eyes stared back at her.

Warm hands on her arm jerked her attention to see Noah's concerned—and relieved—gaze silently questioning her.

"I'm okay." At least she thought she was. Her back felt like she'd been singed by fire, but nothing hurt deep inside. Maybe she'd managed to avoid a full stab.

Brian immediately went to Alena and got the girl to look at him. "Now, we're going to take our time and get this thing off of you, all right?" He looked at Kit and his unspoken message was clear. Time to get out.

Alena's eyes darted between the remaining people in the room. Kit saw the tears had stopped, but the fear hadn't faded one bit.

Noah helped Kit to her feet and she swayed, then got her legs to work. His pale features worried her, but she had to check on Alena. She walked over to the girl and took her hand. "Brian is the best. He was on the bomb squad once upon a time and is still here to talk about his experiences, all right?" Alena's fingers felt ice cold and they wrapped around Kit's in a grip she didn't think she'd be able to break even if she wanted to. She looked at Noah. "Get everyone else out."

Noah spoke into the microphone connected to his earpiece and faint sounds of the house being vacated filtered up from below. The SWAT members all saluted and left with one last look at Brian.

Kit interpreted the looks to mean, Don't mess up.

"All right, guys," Brian ordered. "You two are next. Go on. Get out."

Alena's fingers spasmed and Kit squeezed. "No way. I'm going to stay right here with you, Alena, all right?"

"Kit . . ." Noah's soft voice tinged with warning reached her, and she shot him a look that said she meant business. "I'm staying with her." Turning her attention to Brian, she said, "Let's get this done."

Taking a deep breath, Brian exchanged a look with Noah, then using the wire cutter he had on a belt loop, he got to work on the bomb around Alena's neck.

Alena let go of Kit's hand. "Wait."

Brian paused.

Alena bit her lip, then said, "I don't want anything to happen to you. Please. Go."

Kit shook her head. "Not a chance."

"Then wait where I can't see you, okay?"

Confused, Kit looked at the girl, but didn't want to waste time questioning her. "Sure."

Noah's grip tightened as he pulled her across the room, wrapped his arms around her, and buried his face in her hair. "You scared me," he whispered.

"I was pretty scared myself," she muttered into his chest. A chest that felt good to lean into. He smelled of aftershave and sweat. She breathed in the scent, glad she was alive to experience the wonderful sensation of being in his arms once more.

"Please don't ever do that again."

"What? Walk blithely into a serial killer's house?"

"Yeah. That."

"Okay. Sounds good to me."

She pulled out of his arms and turned to find Brian watching them. He'd freed Alena from the bomb. He offered a half smile. "From the brief look I got before Edward discovered us, I was already 99 percent sure which wires to cut. Didn't take long."

His voice was light, but hurt and resignation mingled in his gaze. She walked over and offered him a sad smile. "Thanks. You did good."

"You too."

"Um, Kit?" Noah's voice made her turn. She cocked a brow at him.

He held up a hand covered in blood, and she gasped and stepped toward him. "Noah, are you hurt?"

"No, darlin', you are."

"Um . . . Noah?" She placed a hand against the side of his neck that disappeared into the collar of his shirt and pulled back a matching blood-covered hand. "You are too."

His eyes rolled back and he dropped to the floor.

44

At the hospital, Kit paced the floor in the surgery waiting room. When Noah had passed out on her, she'd nearly gone into shock. Thankfully the paramedics had been right there and had gotten to him quickly.

No one knew how he'd been wounded yet, but CSU was on the job and Kit hoped they'd have an answer soon. She looked around the waiting room. At least thirty people had gathered in one corner. All concerned and waiting to hear about Noah.

Kit shoved her hands into her pockets and winced as she pulled the stitches in her back. She'd had a nice cut, but stitches and yet another antibiotic would fix her right up.

But Noah . . .

Please, God, she prayed, *please let him be okay. I know I haven't been a big fan of yours for a while, but I want that to change. And not just because of Noah,* she hastened to assure the Almighty, *but because of his example. He's shown me who you really are and I want the kind of relationship with you that he has. So, please . . .*

She broke off her plea when she felt a hand on her shoulder. Swinging around, she saw an older man with the face of a bulldog. A very tall, intimidating man who reminded her of someone associated with the Mafia.

But he had the kindest eyes she'd ever looked into.

"You must be Kit."

Kit smiled. "I am. And you are?"

"I'm Myles Cleary."

"From the boys' home."

Myles raised a brow. "He told you about me?"

"A little." She looked around. "Where are his parents? Family?" Her own had stopped by to reassure themselves she was okay and now waited in a huddle in the opposite corner from all of Noah's friends. All except Dakota, who'd been called out to another case. Jamie went back to work in the morgue and Samantha held a sleeping Andy against her while Connor couldn't seem to keep his hands off either of them. Tucking Andy's blanket around him, running a hand through Samantha's hair, or just holding her hand. He'd had his world well and truly rocked.

But all was well now except for Noah.

Please, God . . .

The man frowned down at her. "He hasn't told you?"

A little wary now, Kit cut her eyes at him. "Told me what?"

Looking decidedly uncomfortable, Myles shifted, then shrugged. "Well, if he hasn't said anything about his childhood, then I guess he has good reason."

"It's all right. You don't have to tell me."

He seemed to make up his mind. "No. I don't think Noah would care. At least he never has in the past. Noah doesn't know who his blood relatives are. He grew up in foster homes and orphanages. For some reason he was never adopted even as an infant."

Kit gasped and felt the blood drain from her face. "What?"

"He's an orphan in the truest sense of the word."

She could feel herself gaping at the man but couldn't seem to stop.

He raised a hand to tap her chin. "Don't look so shocked. It happens to some children."

"But . . . but . . ."

Myles swept his hand over the people who'd come to wait for Noah to get out of surgery. "These are his family. Family's not just made up of people who share the same blood, it's made up of people who love you."

If he'd punched her in the gut, she would have had the same trouble breathing. She had to sit down. Her fingers groped behind her for the arm of the chair and she plopped into it without taking her eyes from the man in front of her. "Noah? An orphan?"

He nodded. "When he landed in my home, he was an angry sixteen-year-old. He'd been bounced around so much, all he was living for was his eighteenth birthday so he could finally just be on his own."

"And then what did he plan on doing?"

Myles gave a small chuckle. "He wasn't thinking that far ahead. He just wanted out of his current circumstances."

"Of course." Kit took in his words, but her mind swirled. Why hadn't Noah ever said anything?

Because she'd already whined to him about what she was going through because she had *two* families that she felt torn between! *Two* families who loved her and wanted her.

No wonder he dodged her questions about his personal life.

Suddenly she felt incredibly selfish. And petty.

And the tears surged. She jumped up. "Excuse me. I'll be in the chapel. Please come get me when he's out of surgery."

And without another word, she fled the room.

Bypassing the elevator, she hit the stairs at a run. It was only one flight. And then she was in the chapel. Silence hit her as she stepped inside.

Two others sat in the pew to her left. She walked on quiet feet to the front row and slid in.

Bowing her head, she prayed. *Oh Lord, I've been so selfish, so consumed with myself I haven't been able to see anyone else's pain but my own. I've let anger blind me. I've let self-righteousness stop me in my tracks and keep me from having the kind of relationship with you that I want. I need to let it go. I need to make things right with my mother, and I really, really need for you to let Noah live because I love him so much. I want to be there for him. I want to share his life. I want him to feel like he can open up and tell me about that life. And I want so much to be able to tell him this. So please . . .*

Tears fell as she sobbed out everything in her heart to the Lord she'd shoved aside. *I want to make a difference like Noah. One by one, helping others find you like Noah helped me. I'm sorry for allowing my anger to cause a rift between us. Thank you for not giving up on me. Thank you for forgiving me. And thank you for who you've allowed me to be. Even though I don't like myself very much right now.*

Another sob gripped her.

The hand on her shoulder made her jerk, and she swung around to see her adoptive mother standing there. The woman looked at her with such compassion and love that the only thing Kit could think to do was to throw her arms around her mom and cling.

Her mother let her, as Kit let more tears fall.

"I'm sorry, darling."

"It's okay, Mom. It's all really okay. Or at least it will be."

"Noah's out of surgery."

Kit pulled back and swiped at her eyes with her palms. Relief hit her. "So he's okay?"

"He's fine. The doctor's got the bleeding stopped."

"What about you? What are you doing here? How are you feeling? I was going to come back and see you when the case was over."

The spurt of questions flooded from her, and her mother just smiled. "I'm recovering. But there was no way I was staying home while you were going through all this trauma. Brig drove me down, and I figured I'd be sitting with you in a hospital so if something happened, help was close by."

Kit breathed a laugh and then sobered. "Thank you. I needed you to be here."

It was her mother's turn to tear up. "Oh my. I love you so much, Kit."

"I know, Mom. And I love you too. I'm sorry I've been such a pain."

"Well, you've certainly been that. But you had your reasons." She looked away and bit her lip. "Ones that I can't necessarily fault you on."

"It's in the past. Let's look to the future, okay?"

Surprise and hope flared on her mother's face. "That sounds wonderful."

"Now, I want to go check on Noah."

Together, they made their way to the elevator and Kit felt like an enormous weight had been lifted from her shoulders. Peace like nothing she ever remembered feeling before flooded her soul. And while she was still worried about Noah, she now knew who to turn her worries over to.

Now to go convince a very good man that she loved him and wanted to spend the rest of her life with him.

Noah blinked against the light. Had he fallen asleep in the kitchen again?

And why was he so thirsty?

He tried to move and groaned. Pain. All right, where had that come from?

"Noah, wake up, Noah."

The light got brighter. Had he died and gone to heaven?

"Noah. I need you to wake up."

Kit. His senses became sharper. The memories flooded him. He remembered the hostage situation. Edward. Smells assaulted him. The room came into focus. A hospital.

But why was he in the hospital? Kit had been the one hurt.

He turned his head. And winced at the tug on his neck.

"Wha—?"

The door opened, but he kept his attention on Kit. She rubbed his hand and he squeezed his fingers around hers. A tear leaked out and he tried to brush it away. He wound up knocking a knuckle against her lip. She breathed a little laugh, then frowned. "A fragment from a bullet bounced off the knife Edward held and caught you in the neck. Amazingly enough, it lodged in your carotid artery. When it moved, you started bleeding profusely and passed out."

"Good thing you had some excellent paramedics right outside," the doctor said from the foot of the bed. "Otherwise, we wouldn't be having this conversation."

"And that would make me very sad," Kit whispered.

Noah looked at her and said the words he'd been wanting to say for a while. "I love you, Kit."

He watched her blink furiously against more tears. "I love you too."

"Um . . . I'm just going to be outside," the physician muttered. "Buzz me if you need me."

Noah vaguely registered the doctor's departure. It took all of his energy to focus on her words. Had she really said she loved him? "Oh, I need to tell you about my family."

"You can tell me later. You need to rest and regain your strength and then we'll talk. Because I've got a lot to tell you too."

"Okay." His eyes fluttered shut against his will. He forced them back open. "What do you need to tell me?"

"I want to go to church with you when you feel better."

"Really?" Joy flooded through him.

"Yeah, God and I had a pretty intense conversation and I believe he's who you kept telling me he is. I want to be like you, Noah, and love God with my whole heart."

He'd been waiting to hear those words. He hadn't realized they'd make him cry.

She squeezed his hand and wiped a stray tear from his temple. Then he felt her lips on his, very soft, very sweet.

He felt himself slipping back into sleep. Struggled against it one more time. "Oh, I bought you a house."

Then the blackness covered him and he gave in to it.

45

Kit stood at the edge of the property and gaped. Two weeks ago she'd been afraid the man at her side might die. She'd taken medical leave from the department and except for filling out paperwork and talking to Internal Affairs, she'd not left Noah's side.

He'd told her about his childhood, his raging insecurities up until he'd moved in with Myles Cleary and how the man had made an amazing difference in his life in a two-year period. Through Myles's patience with the angry teen, Noah had finally come to understand that Myles wasn't going to give up on him and send him away.

Just like the God he served.

And Noah watched Myles make a difference in the lives of the kids who came through his door.

One by one.

Kit shifted and slid her hand into Noah's. "It's absolutely gorgeous."

A sigh of relief slipped from his lips. "So you like it?"

"I love it."

"Good. I signed the papers yesterday."

She squealed. "I thought that was the drugs talking when you said you bought me a house!"

He laughed. "No, I didn't realize I said that out loud."

"And then when you didn't say another word about it, I just forgot about it." The two-story brick house sat at the top of a small hill surrounded by green grass and a white fence. A horse pasture lay behind it. And yet it was close enough to be at the office within fifteen minutes. "Are you serious?"

Noah turned and pulled her against him. He placed his lips against hers for a long, lingering kiss. When he lifted his head, he said, "I've never been more serious about anything in my life. I can't believe everything that's happened in the last few months, but I knew the moment I met you that you were special. That hasn't changed."

"Ah Noah. I don't know what to say." Tears clogged her vision. "You're too good to be true."

He gave a choked laugh. "Not hardly. I just know what I want, and that's a lifetime with you."

"When did you have time to do this? How? Who helped?"

"The iPhone is a great tool. Skip found it and emailed me about a hundred pictures. Then I drove out here before work one morning. I prayed about it a lot too."

She blinked and felt emotion well up inside her. "You got me to get over my spiritual temper tantrum and showed me how to get close to God again."

A brow raised. "I did that?"

She gave him a light punch in the side. "You know you did. How did you manage to put up with me?"

He planted a kiss on the top of her head. "It wasn't that hard, I promise."

She gave a laugh and wrapped her arms around his waist to give him a squeeze. "I can't believe this. This whole day has been unreal."

"How so?"

"Jamie called me this morning. She's pregnant. I'm going to be an aunt again. And then this . . . it's enough to take a girl's breath away."

"Jamie and Dakota are going to have a baby, huh? That's great."

"I know. I'm so excited for her. After all she's been through . . ."

"So what do you say we get married so little Andy and Baby Richards have a cousin who's not too much younger?"

Joy and love ruptured through her. "I say that sounds like the best offer I've ever had."

His lips met hers again and she sent up a silent prayer of thanks to the God who didn't give up on her and loved her enough to bless her in spite of herself.

"Want to go ring shopping?"

She grinned. "Are you thinking what I'm thinking?"

"Yeah, let's go tell Ms. Michelle at the jewelry store she knew what she was talking about when she said she'd see us again."

Hand in hand they headed for his car.

Acknowledgments

Thank you to my family. You are my strength, my reason for getting up in the morning, and the reason I write. I love you so much!

Thank you to my incredible editor, Andrea Doering, for believing in me and this series. I can't believe this is the last book!

Thank you to Michele Misiak, who always seems to know what to do, when to do it, and how to do it exactly right.

Thank you to the cover art staff. You guys are so talented! Thanks for doing such an awesome job!

Thank you, Barb, for your wonderful editing suggestions.

Thank you to those who read the story and offered their feedback, especially my police officer buddy, Jim Hall, who fixes all of my police procedural stuff and then says, "But I know it's fiction, so you might want to do it this way . . ." Needless to say, if there's something inaccurate, it's totally my fault!

Lynette Eason grew up in Greenville, South Carolina. She graduated from the University of South Carolina, Columbia, and then obtained her master's in education at Converse College. She is also a member of American Christian Fiction Writers (ACFW) and Romance Writers of America (RWA). In 1996, Lynette married "the boy next door," and now she and her husband and two children make their home in Spartanburg, South Carolina.

Visit Lynette at www.lynetteeason.com.

"I enjoyed every minute."
—DEE HENDERSON

"*Too Close to Home* by Lynette Eason is a fast-moving tale filled with nonstop action. No chance to catch your breath with this one!"

—**Irene Hannon**, bestselling author, the Heroes of Quantico series

"Nonstop action. No chance to catch your breath!"

—**IRENE HANNON,** bestselling author, the Heroes of Quantico series

Filled with heart-stopping suspense, gritty realism, and a touch of romance, *Don't Look Back* hooks you from the beginning. Once you are in Lynette Eason's world, you're trapped until you turn the very last page.